ABOUT THE AUTHOR

GILLIAN HAWSER is an internationally renowned casting director who has worked for over thirty years across film, television and theatre in the UK, Europe and the US. From Bill Kenwright to Warner Bros, Sony, HBO and Universal, she has developed close working relationships with leading producers on both sides of the Atlantic to deliver casts of exceptional talent, imagination and diversity. For more than the past decade Gillian has been a prominent presence at the heart of BAFTA, sitting on the BAFTA film committee, as well as being instrumental in obtaining the first ever BAFTA award for casting in both television and film.

THE RAKE

GILLIAN HAWSER

Matador
9 Priory Business Park,
Wistow Road, Kibworth Beauchamp,
Leicestershire. LE8 0RX
Tel: 0116 279 2299
Email: books@troubador.co.uk
Web: www.troubador.co.uk/matador
Twitter: @matadorbooks

ISBN 978 1800463 004

This book is dedicated to my children;
Peregrine, Elliot and Clemency
and to my grandchildren;
Elodie, Carys, Jagger, Hunter, Noah, Tom and Joe.
They bring unmitigated joy into my life.

CHAPTER ONE

M y Lord Heddington was an extraordinarily good-looking man. Perhaps the most handsome to grace the drawing rooms of the *ton* this many a year. He was dark, with curling black hair which he wore carelessly swept into the latest style emulated by his good friend Mr Brummell. There was nothing dandified about his appearance however; his figure was that of an athlete. Broad shoulders which showed off his well-cut coats to perfection, and were the envy of those mortals less well-endowed. A leg which when attired in breeches or tight pantaloons would not have shamed the most exacting of men. He carried himself proudly, the last of a long line of illustrious barons who had owned estates in Sussex since the fourteenth century. He was possessed of an enormous fortune, said to be in the region of fifty thousand a year. His face was generally accredited as near to perfect as was deemed possible. If there was a fault, perhaps, it lay in his eyes; these were hard and inclined to be cold.

All these attributes should have made him the object of every mama with a beautiful daughter to dispose of, but these same mamas gave my Lord Heddington a very wide berth, scooping their vulnerable offspring out of his path as soon as they saw him enter a room. Not that he was not received everywhere. Men of his distinction and fortune are rarely not welcome, and the doors of all the best houses were flung open to him on every opportunity, hostesses vying with each other to make sure that, were they privileged enough to secure his presence at their entertainments, he should not lack for pleasure. However, the fact, unpalatable as it might be, remained: my Lord Heddington was a rake.

He was the despair of all his family. His favourite sister, Petronilla, had tried everything she knew to restrain his predilection for seducing, without compunction, any damsel pretty enough to take his fancy. To be fair, he did not cast his conquests to the world unrewarded. He was generous to a point to these young persons.

For the most part, his many amatory adventures signified little. The *haut ton* was tolerant to a point with his many affairs. They lasted little time and were regarded by many as insignificant. Whether the numerous poor damsels who suffered at his hands felt the same was a different matter. They were discarded with a coolness and a speed that was as cruel as it was unexpected. Flattered by the attentions of a man whose address was famed, few noticed that the smile which charmed them so much never reached his eyes, and that the mouth which uttered such pulchritudinous platitudes never ceased to lose its mocking slant. He showered them with expensive presents, and whilst the chase was on was assiduous in his attentions; however, once capitulation took place, as it inevitably did, he lost interest and they found themselves cast back upon the world, richer perhaps, but damaged by the complete and sudden reversal in his feelings.

Some of the older members of society, who had briefly been his mistresses, survived the experience. They were for the most part married ladies with complaisant husbands, who had no choice but to hold their heads up high, and hide their broken hearts. With the younger and more trusting girls on the fringes, their lives and reputations ruined, this was not such an easy thing to do. The hurt went deeper. They had not the married status to protect them; they often found themselves cast out by their families, with little choice in many cases but to turn to prostitution to keep themselves. The *ton*, on the whole, turned a blind eye to most of Jaspar's peccadilloes, but the present scandal was different.

Whilst riding in the park one day, Jaspar had stopped to pay his respects to Marjery, Lady Ambrose, who had at one time been his mistress. It had lasted three months, a surprisingly long time. During their time together she had never shown the slightest inclination to vapours. Blessed with a pleasing sense of humour, she had never, indeed, seemed to be particularly in love with him. A passionate creature, they had enjoyed each other for the time that their mutual ardour lasted and had parted with no recriminations.

As he reined in to greet her, he became aware that she was not alone. The delectable creature with her was unknown to him. Wiser and less indolent women would most certainly not have exposed any young female to Lord Heddington's attention, but this thought had never occurred to Lady Ambrose, who, blessed with little imagination, was inclined to think that everyone resembled her. She, therefore, lazily presented her goddaughter.

Laura Ludgrove was the most beautiful girl Jasper had ever seen. She had a quantity of apricot blonde curls, which, when the sunlight caught them seemed as if her small heart-shaped face was tinged with gold. Her enormous eyes were a bright blue and fringed with dark lashes which swept her face as she lowered them following Lady Ambrose's introduction. Her generous lips were a delicate red. Her complexion was a perfect pink. She was breathtaking. She was dressed in a simple muslin gown that was not the height of fashion and, although respectable, was certainly not expensive. Jasper had never encountered such beauty and he knew he must have her.

He caught her small hand up in his and kissed her little fingers. "Enchanted, Miss Ludgrove. Will you permit me to walk with you a little?"

Tossing the reins of his horse to the elderly groom who accompanied him, he offered her his arm. As luck would have it, at that moment Lady Ambrose's eye was caught by my Lady Cowper, who summoned her to her side. Laura raised her eyes to his face. She nodded shyly, glancing at her chaperone who was by this time engaged in an important discourse with Lady Cowper.

"Have you been in London long? I know that I have not had the pleasure of meeting you before. Such beauty as yours would never be forgotten."

She shook her head. "I only arrived yesterday," she said in a little voice. "I am from the country. I am to stay with Lady Ambrose for two weeks."

"Do you like London? It is thin of company at this time of year." He smiled at her, a smile of great charm, gazing into the blueness of her eyes.

"I do not know whether I like it yet. I have only seen the park." She looked around. "It is so very big and noisy."

"I imagine that for a girl from the country it must appear so." He smiled again.

"Indeed," she responded shyly to his smile.

He took her arm. As far as he was concerned, beautiful country bumpkins were to be his for the asking. Having sauntered along the paths with her, he was more than convinced that she was a nobody with no connections. How she came to be staying with Lady Ambrose he did not bother to enquire. She was extremely beautiful, but of limited intelligence, and he knew he would tire of her very soon, but in the meantime a flirtation and conquest of a girl as beautiful as she was would occupy him pleasurably for the next couple of weeks.

He called the next day at Lady Ambrose's house in Curzon Street. The young butler who admitted him informed him that Her Ladyship was not at home. She had been unavoidably called away, her sister in Kent having been taken unexpectedly ill.

Jaspar was sorry; he had brought a bouquet for Miss

Ludgrove, perhaps he could leave it? The butler informed him that Miss had not gone with my lady, but had been left to see the sights of London chaperoned by Miss Clarges, Lady Ambrose's old governess, who lived with them.

Lord Heddington asked if he might leave his bouquet himself and was presently shown to the morning room where Miss Ludgrove, in the presence of Miss Clarges, was engaged in tapestry.

She jumped to her feet as he was announced and held out her hands.

"How delightful to see you." She smiled shyly up into his eyes, her own huge orbs glowing with pleasure. "I have so few acquaintances in London, and with Lady Ambrose gone out of town, I was quite sure that I would not see anything of London."

"Please, my dear Miss Ludgrove, consider that I am yours to command. Let me show you London. What are you most desirous of seeing?"

"I do not know, my lord, I have heard of Vauxhall Gardens and Astley's Amphitheatre," she answered wistfully.

"Done! I shall arrange for you to see the sights of London immediately." Having requested of Miss Clarges, who was too flustered to deny it, permission he then sent for his carriage.

Laura, meanwhile, ran upstairs. She was terribly excited. She had not, as yet, met many men, and those she had were young gauche boys from the village where she lived on Lord Farleigh's estate, her father being his man of business. Men of my Lord Heddington's address and breeding were quite without her sphere of experience, and she found that the brooding look in his dark eyes made her feel somewhat weak inside. No one had ever looked at her before with quite that degree of quizzical warmth; it made her tremble with a kind of swift joy.

When she reached her bedchamber, she rang the bell to summon the young abigail who had been detailed to wait on her whilst she stayed with Lady Ambrose.

"Polly! Polly, quick I am to go out driving with my Lord Heddington. What shall I wear?"

Polly was a stout damsel, much given to romantic fiction, and she entered into Laura's sense of flustered excitement heartily .

"I think, miss, the blue muslin with the flowers, that my lady had made up for you. She would want you to look your best for such a one as His Lordship."

Laura nodded and the dress was duly brought. It was a present from my lady, who had discovered that her goddaughter's wardrobe was woefully inadequate for a girl spending two weeks in London, even if the season were nearly finished and the *ton* had mostly put up their shutters and removed their knockers.

Polly helped Laura put the dress on and arranged the curls in a becoming cluster over the delicate head. Then she stood back to admire her handiwork. She nodded her plump face enthusiastically.

"Well, miss, if there is a prettier girl in the 'ole world I'm sure I've not seem 'em."

"Do you think so, truly?"

Polly nodded again, her bouncy curls bobbing up and down in her eagerness. "Yes, miss, you is really so beautiful."

"He is so good looking and so rich. Do you think he likes me?"

Polly laughed at the naive question. She was hardly very experienced herself, but she felt most worldly wise in comparison with her ingenuous charge.

"Of course he likes you! Men like him do not a'come a'vissting when my lady is away if theys a'do not like you," she said scornfully. "I would not be surprised if he likes you so much, he does not want to marry you."

"Do you really think so?" The prospect seemed so overwhelmingly wonderful to the innocent Laura, that it quite took her breath away.

"Oh, I'm as sure as the nose on me face, that that is his intention, after all," remarked Polly, from the great years of seventeen, "he is quite old! He must be a'wishing to settle down, and he'll never find anything so pretty as you, miss."

Buoyed up by her kindly words, Laura floated downstairs to His Lordship standing in the hall. He was seen to gasp at her beauty, and truly she was very lovely.

"You are magnificent." He held out his hand to her. She smiled her shy smile.

"Do you really think so?" She peeped at him underneath the long dark lashes. He nodded without pretence.

"The most beautiful girl to grace the *ton* this many a year," he replied, amused by her sweet artlessness. "Do you not realise, my dear, how many admirers you will have once Lady Ambrose takes you about more? In the meantime I must make the best of you before anyone else sees you," he responded, smiling at her, and tucking the tiny hand into his arm. He led her to his curricle and handed her up, as if she were a precious piece of porcelain, and sprang up beside her. Laura could hardly breathe with the thrill of it all. For a man like my Lord Heddington to admire her so much, for him to sound so put out that perhaps other men of fashion would cherish her as well, it was all so enrapturing.

She could not believe it. Only a week ago she had been in the breakfast room of the square solid red brick house on Lord Farleigh's estate that her papa occupied, when her godmother's letter had been brought to her papa, as he partook of his morning repast.

"What is this, then?" He had turned over the letter on its smart velum paper. Then, tantalisingly, he had put it by his plate and continued with his fare.

Mr Ludgrove was a solid, serious man. It had not always been so, and when he had run off with Laura's mother, he had altogether been more dashing. Laura found this hard to believe now, as she watched him anxiously, ploughing his way through a substantial meal. Eventually he finished, then he opened the intriguing missive and perused it thoroughly.

 7

"Well, here is a to-do," he pronounced finally. "It seems that this high-and-mighty godmama of yours wishes that you go and spend a couple of weeks with her in London."

"Oh, Papa, may I go, please? Please?"

Laura waited in agony and perused it thoroughly. Her father smiled at her. He, like most men, was not totally exempt to the wiles of his beguiling daughter.

He smiled again. "Well, puss, you are a good girl, I think we might let you go for just the two weeks." It seemed to him that such beauty as his daughter possessed should not be wasted on the local clodhopping lads of Vernham Dean. It must be seen by a wider audience.

So now here she was, bowling along with a pink of the *ton*, in the smartest of vehicles. Laura could not believe her luck. She just had to grin.

"At what are you smiling?" enquired Jaspar, somewhat amused. Really this country bumpkin had an ingenuous quality that was quite charming.

"Just at how lucky I am to be driving with someone like you. I have never enjoyed anything in my life like this," she answered directly.

Jaspar laughed. "I am not so very special, you know."

"Oh yes you are," came the candid reply. "You are quite the most illustrious man I have ever met and you are driving me!"

Lord Heddington laughed again. "I thought today we would drive in the park, and tomorrow perhaps I can get up a party and take you to Vauxhall."

By now, they were in Hyde Park. It was the hour of five, and various members of the *ton* who had not yet left London could be seen driving, riding or walking. Laura had never seen so many fashionable people, and she was naive enough to be delighted by the rural picture presented by the sheep and cows which grazed benignly under the trees.

The Hon. August Arbuthnot and my Lord Alvanley were

strolling agreeably along the side of Rotten Row. "Who is that, that Jaspar has with him?" Alvanley lisped in his good-natured way. One of the greatest dandies in society, he was also one of the most popular. His wit and kindness made him excellent company, and whereas his predilection for apricot tarts might, in a lesser man, have made him an object of ridicule, in Alvanley it was smiled upon as a charming foible.

"What a pearl of beauty!" August replied, quite the seasoned flirt himself. "What a pity that Jaspar should have seen her first. I confess, I would like to try my way with such a beauty."

"But, August, my dear chap," responded Alvanley, "surely you do not want to take on Heddington?"

August laughed. "No, most definitely not an outcome to be wished. I've no desire to be out on Wimbledon Common, facing the dear Jaspar's ire!"

"It is not an agreeable prospect, I admit to you, not that Jaspar would harm you. He would hardly consider it worthwhile injuring a hair of a friend's head for any woman, and certainly not a juvenile piece like that, but fighting duels is not an enviable pastime!" Alvanley rejoindered reflectively, thinking of his own experiences on the common.

By now, my Lord Heddington's curricle was parallel to the two men. Alvanley hailed Jaspar, who reined in and waved a greeting to his friends. "Jaspar, my dear fellow, you still in town?"

"William." His Lordship leant down from the curricle and shook his friend's hand warmly. "It can hardly be described as unfashionable when such a one as you, Alvanley, remains in Park Street."

Alvanley laughed. He raised an eyebrow in the direction of Laura, whose large eyes were staring in wonderment at the elegant visions before her. Jaspar jumped down, throwing the reins to his groom. He tenderly handed Laura onto the path.

"Miss Laura Ludgrove, may I present Lord Alvanley and Mr Arbuthnot."

Laura clasped her hands together excitedly, then she politely extended a small hand in the direction of both men, who, in turn, kissed the gloved fingers.

"Charming, Jaspar. How do you find them?" murmured August under his breath as Lord Alvanley walked ahead, conversing in his good-natured way with Laura.

His friend grinned back at him. "I seem to have no trouble finding delectable morsels on which to feed."

Mr Arbuthnot laughed again. "That much, my dear Jaspar, I know. Your intrigues are notorious. Please do not forget that we were friends at Eton. I remember that pretty little chambermaid. How old were you? Fourteen? Fifteen?"

"My goodness, I must take the greatest care to remain friends with you, you have such an intimate knowledge of my past adventures that you could, if you wished, produce a comprehensive biography of my scandals," Jaspar teased.

"No, for the most part I will not admit to scandals. Dalliances, yes, Heddington, but you seem to have skilfully avoided any truly outrageous intrigues!"

Jaspar laughed again; he watched Alvanley and Laura as they wandered ahead, my lord waving at such members of the *ton* who had not flown to Brighton or Worthing. August followed his glance.

"Very pretty but very young. Where did you find her?"

Jaspar was saved from responding to this question by hearing his name and Alvanley's called by an elegant gentleman.

"Jaspar, William. How glad I am that there still seem to be some members of society who have not flown to the salty seizures of the sea!"

"George, my excellent fellow." Alvanley clasped his hand.

"Allow me to present Miss Laura Ludgrove. Miss Ludgrove, Mr Brummell."

Laura felt her knees go quite weak. Her heart beat fast with excitement. Mr Brummell. The great Beau Brummell. Here, clasping her hands and smiling into her eyes with his steady grey ones.

Beau Brummell was of medium height. He was dressed with an understated elegance that Laura, even in her inexperience, recognised as all the thing. His muslin neckcloth was starched and creased to perfection. His tasselled hessians gleamed, and his pantaloons were without a wrinkle.

He was a graceful man with a pleasant personality. The indubitable leader of fashion, he was neither vulgar nor excessive in his dress or habits. His slavish followers might starch their neckcloths so high that they cut their chins or were unable to move their heads, or wear coats that were so embroidered with silk and gold lace they resembled an over-decorated flower bed, but this was not for the Beau. He discouraged the excessive use of silk and satin, preferring the subtlety of superfine or Bath coating for his coats, although he still permitted the wearing of embroidered waistcoats.

"Delighted, Miss Ludgrove. May I compliment you on your beauty."

Mr Brummell smiled at her. Laura blushed a delicate pink, she found herself shyly returning his smile. "Thank you, sir."

Brummell raised an eyebrow at Jaspar. "Exquisite as usual, my friend." Then he kissed Laura's fingers and waved. "*Adieu*, Heddington. Do you two dine at the Dandy Club?"

"You go to Watier's?" enquired Lord Alvanley of Mr Brummell, who nodded.

"Then we shall accompany you," pronounced His Lordship, raising an eyebrow to August, who nodded agreement, and tucked his arm in that of his friend.

Jaspar turned to Laura; her eyes were aglow. He laughed as he handed her back into the curricle.

"You look much pleased," he remarked.

"Mr Brummell," Laura returned in accents of awe. "Is Beau Brummell truly a friend of yours?"

He laughed. "Indeed, we were at Eton together. Then I went to Oxford, while the Prince gave him a cornetcy in the 10th Light Dragoons, but we remained the closest of companions. He is the greatest of good friends."

Jaspar returned his delicate charge to Curzon Street in time for her to dine with the old governess, but before he departed he promised to let them know the arrangements for the promised treat to Vauxhall.

Chapter Two

Laura having been successfully set down in Curzon Street, Jaspar, on a sudden impulse, turned his horses towards Berkeley Square and the mansion where his favourite sister, Petronilla, lived with her husband, the fifth Earl of Morntarny. Petronilla was a mere fourteen months older than he, and so nearly resembled him, that as children they were often mistaken for twins.

A young footman, who was quite unknown to him, informed him proudly that my lady was dressing for dinner but the butler, who swiftly followed his inferior into the hall, had been a footman on the Bardfield estates. He had known the brother and sister all their lives. He waved away the footman and welcomed Jaspar warmly.

"My lord. Lady Morntarny is in her dressing room. Please be so good as to follow me."

Jaspar's mouth twitched with amusement. "Parker, what an excellent fellow you are."

Parker nodded grandly but the twinkle in his eyes showed his appreciation of my lord's compliment.

He led the way up the huge central stairway, decorated some thirty years earlier by Robert Adam, and turned left along the corridor to my lady's rooms. Opening the door he announced: "My Lord Heddington, my lady." Petronilla, who was sitting restlessly at the table having her hair dressed in the latest mode, turned with real pleasure.

"Jaspar dearest! How perfectly lovely to see you." She grinned broadly at her beloved brother. She was indeed as handsome as he, except that her eyes were kinder and her face softer. Tall, often described as statuesque, she had been in her day considered as something of a termagant. Nevertheless, she had made in her first season what was generally agreed to be a brilliant match, catching the charming and very wealthy earl. He was an unruffled man who dealt placidly with all of his beloved wife's exploits, and under his beneficent influence she had calmed down. The truth was that Petronilla adored him and he her; she would never have done anything anymore that would have seriously displeased him, whilst he, on the other hand, would not have been happy with a wife who did not have a lively and spirited nature. They suited each other admirably and were generally known as a most loving and successful couple.

The countess jumped up, scattering hairpins and ornaments all over the floor, and impetuously threw her arms around her brother's neck. He kissed her warmly and, holding her slightly away from him, regarded her with frank admiration.

"How beautiful you are, Nillie, I have never seen anyone with your looks."

"What perfect rubbish you do talk, Jaspar, you with all your *amours*."

Jaspar raised an eyebrow questioningly. "My whats?"

"Oh, do not be silly. I am not a child. Why, I am over thirty now." She shuddered in mock horror and went on, "And I was never an innocent, you know."

"Then I am amazed that Greville wished to marry you. I did not think that he was keen on others' leftovers," he teased.

His sister picked up a bowl of hairpins and playfully emptied them all over his head. He grabbed her.

"For two pins," she giggled.

"Or rather one I have never known anyone who hundred pins," he went on, extracting a hairpin from his head, "I would put you over my knee and spank you." A faint note of protest from the dresser made Petronilla look up.

"Oh, Quarmby, leave us a minute. I wish to converse with my brother."

"Very good, my lady," muttered Quarmby, somewhat disapprovingly. She too had come from the Bardfield estate and had known the two as children, when they were never out of scrapes. Utterly devoted to Petronilla, she was secretly convinced that Jaspar was to blame for all the japes. This, however, was very far from the truth. Petronilla was the naughtiest of children, always thinking up new impish tricks.

"My 'amours', as you call them, mean nothing. You know that my heart belongs to you."

His sister giggled again. "Jaspar, be serious. I have never known anyone who has had so many…" She stopped and looked at him, for his face had become stern. She kissed his cheek.

"But it is true," he said harshly. "They all bore me… except you."

"Oh, Jaspar, I am sorry, I wish you could find someone like Greville." She moved away from him, sitting down on the chair in front of the mirror again. Propping her chin in her hands, and without really seeing herself, she went on: "I cannot describe to you how wonderful it is to love someone like that."

Jaspar crossed to the window, fiddling with the cord as he looked out over the square.

"You know, we have been married eleven years, have three children, and I still long to see him, miss him terribly when he is away, and when I see him across a room my heart still goes bump." She grinned. "Does that sound very silly?"

Jaspar shook his head. "No… it sounds… Oh, Nillie, I wish you were not my sister. You are so perfect."

"No I am not," replied his sister wisely. "I would drive you mad. All those wild scrapes. Anyway I would hate to be married to someone as impatient as you!"

He grinned at her. "Vixen," he remarked friendlily.

"But it is true, you know, Grandmama is right. You ought to be thinking of getting married. You need an heir."

Jaspar sighed again. "I know, but really, they are so dull."

"How about Lady Sophia Bannock? She is very beautiful."

"But fair… I prefer dark, tempestuous beauties," he responded, putting his hand around her neck and gazing over her shoulder at their reflections in the mirror.

"Well… how about… Netta?"

"Netta?" Jaspar sounded surprised. Netta was the daughter of the local squire. She was a childhood friend of theirs. A sensible homely girl who had never married. "Nillie, have you gone mad?"

"It is just that she is such a rational person. She would make an admirable wife and would be so reasonable about your affairs."

"But… l do not want that kind of marriage, Nillie. I want to love someone. I do not want a marriage of convenience," her brother answered vehemently.

Petronilla was slightly surprised. Jaspar without affairs? It was inconceivable. She was about to continue when the earl's head appeared around the door. Jaspar watched as his sister's eyes lit up. She jumped out of the chair and ran to her husband, throwing her arms around his neck. As he hugged her he commented gently: "Petronilla, here is Jaspar not wanting to see all this, I am sure." He released his wife and crossed to his brother-in-law, warmly clasping his hand. He was a very tall, very handsome man, with a peaceable quality. His brown hair was fashionably brushed à la Brutus. He wore buckskins and riding boots.

"Jaspar, what brings you to us? Not that you are not welcome at all times." He smiled, his brown eyes warm.

"Greville, in truth I do have a task. Nillie, I would like to take a party to Vauxhall tomorrow. It is a masquerade night, and I wish you to dine with us and join me."

Greville was not particularly fond of the gardens and was about to refuse, when he met his wife's eyes. She shook her head slightly.

"Of course. We will be delighted to accept. Who else will be of the party?"

"I am not sure, but it is primarily for the amusement of a chit called Laura Ludgrove, who is staying with Marjery, and who has an inordinate desire to visit the gardens."

"Why do you not dine here beforehand instead?" Nillie asked. "Ask Miss Ludgrove to join us and then we can go to Vauxhall afterwards. Oh, and you can do something for me."

"Anything! Your wish is my command."

"Ask Mrs Darcy and her niece to come to Vauxhall with us."

"No! That I will not do even for you. She is the most horrible harridan."

"Agreed, but her poor niece, who is Lucy Darcy's daughter..." He raised an eyebrow in question.

"John Darcy was killed last year?" Greville added.

"Yes... yes. I do remember now you remind me... but Mrs Darcy is still appalling and that bat-faced daughter? No, not even for you." He shuddered.

"I had a letter from old Mrs Darcy today. She told me that poor Clarissa has been sent to her aunt for the season and is treated as nothing more than a servant. I promised to help."

"Alright, as long as I do not have to exchange two words with that harridan." He kissed his sister farewell and left.

Petronilla sat down at the dressing table again. Greville bent over her; he kissed her firmly. Delighted, she put her arms around his neck and he pulled her gently to her feet so that her fine body was next to him. He regarded her steadily. "What is it, Petronilla?"

"I do not know, but Jaspar is strange… talking about marriage and love and, oh, do you think he could be in love with the chit?"

Her husband shook his head slightly. "Unlikely, I would have thought."

"Nevertheless, he was odd…" she mused.

Greville kissed her again and then suggested that she best get ready; they were due to dine with the Cavendishes and if they did not make haste they would be late.

The message with the arrangements for the following day arrived as Laura left the dining room to follow the elderly governess into the drawing room, after they had dined. The note from Lord Heddington was brief and to the point. They were bidden to dine with his sister and he would send the carriage for them. Laura read and reread the few lines; her head was a whirl. She had had quite the most exciting day of her life. She sat down, her embroidery on her knee, but not a stitch did she set. She had much to think upon, much to look forward to; the prospect of the projected treat tomorrow occupied her mind greatly.

"Laura, my love, you seem much distracted," observed Miss Clarges. She was a skinny, nondescript, fluttery lady of indeterminate age, who had been governess to Lady Ambrose's two sons and had remained long after the boys had gone to Eton. Her servile nature suited Lady Ambrose, who was far too indolent to fetch and carry for herself and was in need of a willing slave to pick up or retrieve her stray belongings.

Laura sighed. "Do you not think that my Lord Heddington is not the most handsome of men?"

Miss Clarges, far too stupid not to indulge such dangerous romantic fantasies, remarked: "Indeed, and he seems to be very taken with you, my love. Imagine. We are asked to dine in

Berkeley Square with Lady Morntarny. He would not take you to his sister unless his intentions were… oh…" She was suddenly caught by the most momentous thought. "Would it not be a most wonderful thing if he were to offer for you?"

As this was the most wonderful thing that Laura could conceive, she found herself forced to agree in glowing terms.

"Oh, dear Miss Clarges, do you think so? It would be of all things the most acceptable, my papa would be so delighted. He wishes for me to make a great match and Lord Heddington must be considered that."

Miss Clarges tittered. "Oh, Miss Ludgrove, oh, sweetest child. You would be the greatest lady in the land! You would have houses and carriages and oh… everything you could wish for." She clasped her bony hands together in glee. "Oh, my dear, let us hope that that is what he intends!"

The next day dawned fair and mild. The night had seemed interminable to Laura, so excited was she by the prospect of the evening. Her papa had given her twenty pounds to spend in London and she prevailed upon Miss Clarges to take her shopping. She possessed one evening dress, high-waisted with puff sleeves. It was made of pale silk with tiny bundles of lace around the top and hem. Having carefully perused the volumes of *La Belle Assemblée* and *The Lady's Magazine* that were liberally scattered around Lady Ambrose's, she could see that it was not of the first stare, however, she thought that if she were to purchase new gloves and a shawl, it would not disgrace her.

Miss Clarges agreed readily; she ordered the carriage and took her charge to Bond Street. She was enjoying herself with the little country bumpkin. With Lady Ambrose she had to be careful not to advance her ideas, as Her Ladyship had no opinion of her notions. Miss Ludgrove, however, hung on her every word, and Miss Clarges was not modest enough not to get a great deal of pleasure from her devotion. She rapidly explained that it was not done to visit Bond Street in the afternoon and that therefore their purchases must be completed by the end of the morning, but Laura was so entranced by her visit to this exclusive enclave; by the drapers and hatmakers; dressmakers; bootmakers and the shops that sold delicate accessories; that she had considerable difficulty dragging her away.

The afternoon was spent with Laura counting the hours until it was time for the carriage to collect her. She was dressed and ready a good hour before the coachman arrived at the door. The short journey to Berkeley Square was soon accomplished, and Laura had her first vision of the mansion that was the town house of the Earls of Morntarny. She sat quite silent in the corner of the carriage, and gazed at it. Her papa being the manager of the estates of Lord Farleigh, she was used to country mansions, but she had never before seen such elegant squares and houses as abounded in London.

They were shown into the saloon on the first floor. It was a vast room that stretched across the front of the house. It had been decorated by Adam and bore the distinguishing characteristics of that gentleman. The ceiling was embossed plasterwork with shell patterns which entirely complemented the ones woven into the carpet. Six long windows with French doors opened onto a balcony. The decoration scheme was pink and pale green, and the dark mahogany embossed doors with their gilt overlay looked magnificent against the pale walls. The chairs were rosewood, their seats embroidered with delicate flowers and cupids. Laura followed Parker into the room. She felt absurdly nervous but as the countess rose to greet them, she found herself staring. Lady Morntarny was so exactly like her brother it was uncanny. Her Ladyship laughed at Laura's amazed expression.

"I do look exactly like Jaspar," she remarked, "but we are not twins, you know."

Laura blushed rosily. "I… b… beg your pardon… my lady, I did not mean to be rude."

"I know you did not, my dear. Come sit beside me and tell me about yourself." She patted the sofa invitingly, taking the opportunity of Jaspar's absence to discover what she could about this girl.

Shyly Laura told her of her good fortune in being invited to stay with Lady Ambrose, and the better fortune in being introduced to Lord Heddington. Petronilla found herself a little uneasy; the girl was so clearly besotted with Jaspar. This, on its own, was nothing new; many a young lady had formed an attachment for her brother. However, this girl was obviously so very young, so very innocent.

"My sincere apologies for not being ready when you arrived." The earl came in, welcoming Laura with his charming smile. He kissed her hand.

"Delighted." Then he turned to his wife. "How exquisite you look, my love, but where is Jaspar?"

"Late, I am afraid," his devoted spouse replied. "I have been getting to know Miss Ludgrove."

The butler threw open the door. "My Lord Heddington," he announced; Petronilla watched Laura's small face. Her eyes opened with joy; she regarded Jaspar adoringly. Petronilla met her husband's eyes for a second. Then Jaspar was across the room apologising for his lateness and kissing her fondly.

As soon as dinner was over, they left for Vauxhall. Jaspar had taken a box, and in the party he had included Lord Alvanley, Lord Slaughan, the terrible Mrs Darcy, who brought her daughter Henrietta, a plain girl with large teeth, and her niece Clarissa, a very pretty but rather shy girl, whose modesty was very becoming.

The drive to Vauxhall took place in the most luxurious carriage in which Laura had ever travelled and was completed all too quickly, for she was much enjoying the opulence. However, her disappointment at leaving the sumptuous carriage was mitigated by her first sight of the gardens. The glory of these reduced her to silence. She gazed in wonder at the multitudinous tiny coloured lights that garlanded the trees and the triumphal arches. Pavilions which resembled decorated cakes glittered in the dark, and above them cascades of water wound around sylvan grottoes. Music drifted from the orchestra pavilion and there was the promise of fireworks, tumblers, rope dancers, Indian jugglers and sword swallowers to entertain the unworldly.

Eventually, her eyes wide in wonderment, she managed, "Oh! Lord Heddington, it is… is… unbelievable!" She clapped her hands together and ingenuously turned her luminous eyes up to his, a glance that did not escape the watchful gaze of his sister, who viewed it with some disquiet, or the silly woman in charge of Laura, who viewed it with unavailing hope.

Jaspar laughed; the expression on Laura's exquisite face was enchanting, so unpretentious and unspoilt. He found it endearing to have someone exclaim with genuine pleasure rather than affect a bored complacency.

"I am delighted that it meets with your approval," he answered, a gleam of amusement in his eyes.

"Oh truly, my lord, I have never seen anything so pleasing, it is beyond anything!" she replied, her bright blue eyes sparkling.

Jaspar held out his hand to her and led the way to the box, half hidden in a leafy arbour. At the door they were accosted by a tall dark man. He was remarkably good looking with broad shoulders, an excellent leg, and the brightest blue eyes that ever Laura had seen.

"Gideon! On time for once! Come, allow me to present Miss Ludgrove… Miss Ludgrove, Lord Slaughan."

"Delectable. How do you do it, Jaspar?" the marquis murmured under his breath, bending over her hand. "Miss Ludgrove, your servant." He smiled engagingly at Laura, who was by now completely overwhelmed by the world into whose company she had suddenly been thrust.

 22

"Your first visit to Vauxhall! You must allow me to show you around," Lord Slaughan continued.

"Ahem, just a moment, Gidi," Jaspar, amused, started. "I think before you run off with her, she should make the acquaintance of the rest of my guests."

Lord Slaughan laughed, bowed slightly and moved away to greet Petronilla. By this time Mrs Darcy, Miss Darcy and Miss Clarissa had joined them in the box, and Jaspar lost no time in presenting Laura. She curtsied prettily and Nillie, still watching carefully, was pleased to notice that her manners, at least, were unexceptional.

Mrs Darcy turned her beaky nose in the air. She looked Laura over piercingly, found her wanting and promptly determined to find out who was this girl who was engaging the eligibles that she considered so particularly her own property. That was, until she had snared one for her beloved Henrietta. She commenced battle in her outspoken way.

"So, Miss Ludgrove, tell us about yourself. Where do you come from? Who is your papa? I do not remember seeing you earlier in the season."

Before Laura was forced to provide an answer to this impertinence, Lord Alvanley was by her side, kissing her hand tenderly.

"My dear Miss Ludgrove, how delightful to see you again and in such looks." He took her arm. "Let me show you the rope dancers and jugglers."

Mrs Darcy suddenly thought better of continuing her interrogation. If this hatefully beautiful girl was known to Alvanley, then perhaps she was not the nobody that Mrs Darcy suspected, although the question of her parentage still remained. Mrs Darcy, to whom the peerage was night-time reading, had never heard of a Laura Ludgrove. She was certainly not prepared to let Henrietta mix with just anyone, but if she was accepted by Alvanley then it was quite another story.

She watched Laura leave with His Lordship and then went to pay her respects to Petronilla. Perhaps she would know something. "My dear Lady Morntarny, my dearest Henrietta you know of course. Henrietta come and sit here next to Her Ladyship."

The ungainly Henrietta started to obey her mama but before she reached Nillie, the countess impetuously interrupted. "I am not acquainted with your niece, I believe?"

Mrs Darcy was left with no alternative but to present Clarissa with as good grace as she could muster. "My niece, Clarissa Darcy," she muttered. The girl curtsied shyly to Nillie.

"Clarissa Darcy. Oh yes, I knew your poor papa. Do come and sit by me." She patted the sofa and Clarissa gladly sat beside this friendly stranger.

"How is your mama?" Her Ladyship enquired.

Clarissa's papa had been killed the previous winter in a hunting accident. Her mama being too distraught to present her, she had been sent to her father's brother's wife for the season. Mrs Darcy, who resented anyone who was prettier that Henrietta; which meant most young women under the age of forty; made her life a misery. She had to fetch and carry, and although she was included in some of the parties, if Mrs Darcy could think of an excuse to leave her at home she would do so. The countess had quite decided that this cavalier treatment must not be continued.

Laura explored Vauxhall with Lord Alvanley. He was an engaging guide, prepared to laugh with her at the antics of the tumblers, prepared to marvel at the daring of the sword swallowers.

"How brave they are!" commented Laura. "I am sure that I could never do what they do."

"It seems highly unlikely that you will be called upon to resort to swallowing swords, Miss Ludgrove. A girl with such beauty as yours must surely be hoping for a marriage with an eligible *parti*," Lord Alvanley, teasing, replied.

Laura blushed prettily, dropping her long lashes over her beautiful eyes.

"Ah, have you a lucky gentleman in mind?" His Lordship continued. "How privileged he will be to receive such beauty as yours."

Laura, totally inexperienced in the ways of the world, did not recognise this light banter for what it was. The effect it had on her was to make her happiness unqualified. It must be true. If Lord Alvanley, Lord Heddington's great friend, clearly thought, as did Miss Clarges, that Jaspar meant to declare himself and whisk her off to never-ending love, it must happen. She was almost breathless with joy. Alvanley, not the most perceptive of men, entertained none of these thoughts, he merely, as was his wont, flirted outrageously with such an enchanting girl.

If Laura had had a sensible mama, or even had Mrs Darcy been so minded, she might have warned Laura firmly about such absurd notions, but as she was not interested in anything that did not pertain to her own daughter she did nothing. Petronilla, too, was concerned and might have issued a gentle caution, but she had no further chance of speech with Laura alone, the rest of the girl's evening being occupied with dalliances with Jaspar, the Marquis of Slaughan and Lord Alvanley, all notable flirts, and Lady Morntarny's indignation found another target. Having been ingenuously and simply informed by Clarissa of the treatment she received from Mrs Darcy made Nillie resolve to do something about that situation forthwith.

CHAPTER THREE

The next week passed in a haze of glory for Laura. She was continually forced to pinch herself to remember that this was real and not a dream. My Lord Heddington was all attention. Each day huge bunches of flowers arrived for her, until Lady Ambrose's house resembled a florist's. The bouquets were accompanied by exquisite presents. Not so elaborate and expensive that Laura would have felt obliged to refuse them but small charming objects, such that no mama, even the most exacting, could have felt constrained to have returned. Laura's heart was completely lost. Her hours passed in a daze, she thought of nothing but Jaspar; from the moment she awoke until she eventually fell asleep her recollections were only of him. She was utterly and completely in love.

Laura's mama had brought her daughters up carefully. If she had a fault, it was that she overprotected them, afeared, perhaps, they might be tempted to repeat the mistakes that she herself had made, in marrying unsuitably. So Laura had been deliberately kept in ignorance of the world. Even after her mama's death, she had continued to be shielded from any experience that might have made her a little more worldly. Her papa discussed nothing. All that she understood was that a girl should love her husband and that if she were lucky, he would revere and care for her. Laura had no notion that all-consuming and overwhelming passion could exist, and was, therefore, totally bewildered and unprepared for the wave of desire that overwhelmed her. Had there been a discerning lady to confide in, perhaps sense might have prevailed but her only confidant was Miss Clarges, who, romantic to the last, abetted the girl in everything she believed and encouraged her to suppose that Lord Heddington felt the same way. As girls in love before her, Laura talked of little else and, lacking any sensible friend who might have pointed her thoughts in a proper direction, was merely encouraged to persist in her fancy.

"Do you truly believe he loves me?" Laura would ask for the hundredth time.

"La! Of course he does! Dotes on you, clear as the nose on my face. I declare," repeated Miss Clarges also for the hundredth time, "I declare," she tittered, "or rather, he declares... Oh, my dear, when do you think it will be?"

"I do not know. Oh, Miss Clarges, I do hope that it will be soon! I have only three more days in London. Do you think he will declare himself before then?"

Whilst they were at home, the vexed and very interesting question of Jaspar's proposal occupied their thoughts and conversation for most of the time.

"Of course he will, why, I have no doubts in the matter. Oh, my dear Laura, it is so romantic. Do you think he will carry you away on a charger like young Lochinvar? How idyllic it would be to be swept up in someone's arms and carried to the altar in some remote and wild spot."

Miss Clarges was quite overcome by her own imagery and was forced to wipe away a tear.

"A charger? Oh, but I am not at all a good rider, you know."

"Silly girl. All you have to do is cling to his firm and handsome chest... Oh... ah..." she sighed deeply, "he will hold you so tight, like the precious thing that you are to him. He will love and honour you. He will adore and worship you."

Laura had no complaint to make about these plans. As Miss Clarges continued with her fantasies, the doorbell pealed.

"La, who do you think it is?" she demanded, hardly able to contain her excitement.

"Him!" exhaled Miss Clarges. "Your beloved! Your lord, your future husband, he has come to whisk you away from this place."

She clasped her hands together and standing, declaiming, her eyes half closed, her face ecstatic, "Your future is here, my dear. Your bridegroom, the man who reveres and worships you is come, come to you... come to take you from this plebeian world. To remove you to a new and wonderful place where you will be happy for ever more... where cupids dance and nymphs sing, where love triumphs and waterfalls herald and announce love's glory. Oh, my dearest girl, are you not the luckiest of creatures?"

There was a faint knock at the door. The footman coughed deprecatingly. "Well?" Miss Clarges returned from her transported state.

"A note, miss. Requires an answer." Laura blushed. "From my Lord Heddington."

Laura jumped across the room and grabbed the paper from him. She tore it open. The lines were slightly disappointing.

"Lord Heddington begs the pleasure of the company of Miss Ludgrove and Miss Clarges to join his party to a visit to Astley's Amphitheatre tonight," she read.

"Oooh, you see," Miss Clarges started again.

Laura, of a more practical turn of mind, stopped her. "Thank you. Please tell Lord Heddington that we would be pleased to accept." He bowed and left.

"This is it. This is the night. I just know inside my heart he will declare himself. He will! He will! He will." Miss Clarges returned to her ecstatic warblings.

"Oh, do you think so? If only it were to be... but when? We will be in a party, no time for private conversation."

"He will bring you home."

"But you are with me," Laura pointed out. The continual presence of her chaperone was at times irksome.

"Wait, I have an idea… a gem, it comes… Like Lord Byron, the muse attends."

"But what is it? What will you do?"

"Have no fear, it will work, by tonight you will be betrothed to him… I know it! I know it! I know it!" The last phrase increased in a crescendo. Miss Clarges leapt onto a chair; she threw her arms out wide. "You will be a bride!" she declaimed.

Laura laughed. This middle-aged spinster, with her wispy hair and frumpy clothes, her raddled face and saggy neck, which wobbled slightly as she declared herself in a frenzy of passion, made her giggle.

Miss Clarges jumped down. "No time to waste… we have no time to waste. We must make sure that today it happens!"

The evening was warm and balmy. Laura dressed in much excitement in a sprigged yellow dress with tiny puffed sleeves and a low neck that showed off her fine shoulders. Miss Clarges dressed her golden hair in a simple but most becoming style. Around her neck she clasped a fine row of pearls, which had been her mama's. She took the shawl that they had purchased in Bond Street and announced herself ready. Miss Clarges, red spots of colour ornamenting her usually grey face, looked mysterious and most pleased with herself. She, however, did not impart any information on what she intended to do to Laura, who merely waited with longing until she saw Jaspar.

The carriage which was to transport them to Heddington House arrived in excellent time and they stepped into it. As they drew up outside the mansion that was Jaspar's London home, Laura peered avidly from the window, taking in every detail of what she hoped would be her future abode.

The house seemed very large. It was six storeys high and was built of brick, with each window carefully detailed with red.

The imposing front door was flanked by four windows. It was surmounted by an ornate portico supported by marble columns. Six long windows spanned the first story and each window opened onto a small balcony heavily decorated with summer flowers. Laura thought she had never seen such an impressive residence.

Liveried footmen let down the steps of the carriage and helped her. A stern-faced butler stood at the top of the steps. He led the way through into the entrance. Laura looked around her. The hall was vast. Marble columns stood at each corner and an enormous staircase of marble and iron wound its way upwards. The stately butler preceded Laura and Miss Clarges up the stairs and announced their arrival to the company in the saloon; Lord Heddington rose to greet her. Laura found herself breathless as she gazed into his dark eyes. He smiled at her and she felt as if her heart would burst. He took her hand and led her into the room, introducing her to Lady Jersey, Sir Hugo Nugent and Lady Nugent, who were the only members of the party with whom she was not acquainted.

The evening was truly marvellous, the dinner most excellent, the company entertaining; Laura was confounded by her first sight of Astley's. The exterior was unimposing, as most of Astley's building material consisted of ships' masts and spars with canvas stretched over them. The interior, however, was splendid. A huge chandelier of fifty lamps hung over an enormous ring of sawdust, and behind it reposed the largest stage in London. Three rows of boxes and a gallery housed the numerous spectators, who roared and applauded at the daring feats of horsemanship which provided Astley's entertainment. Laura had never seen such tricks or such fantastical equestrian melodramas and wanted the show to go on for ever.

The end of the evening, however, had to come and it was then that Laura discovered that Miss Clarges was no longer with them. She looked around for her enquiringly; Lord Heddington, observing her, reassured her.

"Miss Clarges, it appears, felt unwell. She charges me particularly with returning you safely."

Laura nodded; she was far too happy to worry about the old governess. Her whole body trembled with an unaccustomed feeling, half joy and half excitement. Throughout the evening she had been heedful of Jaspar the entire time. Wherever he went, taking care of his guests, ordering food, observing the acts, she was with him, her mind and body his. He seemed unaware of her preoccupation, although whenever her eyes met his, he smiled encouragingly.

Finally, he bade farewell to the last of his guests and summoned his carriage. Laura stood beside him. As they waited for it to draw up, her arm just touched his sleeve; his closeness made her feel she could hardly breathe. The groom let down the steps and Jaspar took Laura's hand to help her in; he held it in his, so firm and so warm. Laura trembled slightly. She sat in the corner of the luxurious coach, and Jaspar climbed in, in a leisurely fashion, and sat down close beside her. The groom put up the steps and closed the door; the horses sprang forward.

The scent of apple blossom wafted sweetly into the interior of the carriage. It was far too warm to wear a shawl, and Laura's shoulders and arms were bare, smooth and white. Jaspar looked at her. She was so exquisite. He was overcome with a strong desire for her. He ran the tips of his fingers very gently down the slim arm next to him, running his hand over the top of hers and cradling it in his. She quivered and turned her head towards him; her beautiful blue eyes sparkled; she smiled bewitchingly at him. This was it. She just knew it. It was just as Miss Clarges had predicted. Her eyes locked with his.

"Oh, my beauty," he murmured. "Be mine…"

"Oh yes, yes!" she cried, flinging her arms around his neck. He caught her to him, rocking her gently to and fro, holding her tightly, then, releasing her slightly, he looked into her flushed face again.

"You are sure, my sweet girl?"

"Yes! Oh yes… l am sure. I have been sure since the first moment I saw you."

He bent his lips to hers. Very gently he ran them along her mouth. She sighed with pleasure. He ran one finger down her neck towards her breast. She felt a deep quivering inside her. He stopped and pulled down the window, giving quick instructions to the coachman. Then he turned back to Laura pulling her gently into his arms, her golden head nestling on his chest. He caressed her bare arm, and murmured into her soft curls. Laura felt his hand slide over her cheeks; she breathed in deeply. It was true, he was eloping with her just as Miss Clarges had said, just as they had planned. It was all too perfect. She sighed again, in deep contentment. They stayed thus until Laura became aware that the carriage was stopping. The coachman let down the steps and Jaspar lifted her out. They were at some kind of an inn. They did not seem to have travelled very far but perhaps an early change of horses was necessary. She was too exhilarated to question anything. His Lordship issued some quick instructions and Laura tripped happily in behind him. The landlord, who clearly knew him well, bowed low and led the way upstairs to a huge bedchamber. It was most luxuriously furnished with a vast four-poster bed. They were obviously going to spend the night here. Laura wondered if this was her room or Jaspar's but did not like to enquire while the landlord stood there. He bowed and left, closing the door behind him. Jaspar came to Laura; he pulled her into his arms; running his hands over her bare back, slowly he slid the sleeves from her shoulders while his lips sought hers. She put her arms around his neck as he kissed her, his lips becoming more demanding.

Jaspar woke early, the sun was streaming in through the window. He slid out of bed. He did not like to be without his valet. Dressing himself was fine but he did not at all relish having to take care of his own clothes, and the idea of wearing his evening dress was abhorrent to him. He had only slept a few hours and he did not feel refreshed. He glanced at Laura. She slept like a small child curled up, one hand tucked under her flushed cheek. She looked very young and very vulnerable. In the cold light of dawn Jaspar felt a slight, surprising pang. He must leave her enough to return to town in comfort. He finished dressing and reached inside his coat and took out a bag of coins. He dropped them on the table, but as he did so Laura jerked awake. She stared at him uncomprehending.

"My lord… where are you going? Wait, I will dress." She jumped out of bed.

"I am returning home, of course," Jaspar replied somewhat impatiently. "I suggest you go back to sleep."

She blinked and ran a hand over her head. "What do you mean? I do not understand."

"Get back into bed, Laura…"

"But, my lord…" Suddenly she understood; she smiled. "Oh, I see, you will return home to collect what you need for our journey."

"Our journey?" Now it was Jaspar's turn to look perplexed. "What journey?"

"To Gretna… We are eloping, are we not?"

"What!" Jaspar exclaimed. "What did you say?" He regarded her angrily.

She backed away from him. "Eloping. We are eloping. Are we not?" she repeated desperately.

"We are most certainly not doing anything of the sort. What gave you such an absurd idea?"

"But you are going to marry me?"

"Marry you! Did I ask you to marry me? If I wanted to marry you, which I do not, I would have no need to elope with you. I would have asked your father's permission."

An icy fear started in the pit of her stomach. In the cold dawn, the implications of what she had entered into so headily the previous night crept over her. Jaspar did not resemble the loving passionate gentleman of before. His eyes were no longer warm and caring; they were dark and forbidding, and looked angry... She shivered.

"Laura, I have no Intention or desire to marry you and I cannot think what gave you such an idiotic notion."

"But... bu... but... I thought..." Tears filled her eyes. Laura was very beautiful; she was smooth and elegant and most things she did, she did with grace and refinement. However, crying was one of the few things she did unattractively.

"You thought! And tell me, just what did you think?" Jaspar replied unpleasantly. He hated scenes and was very much regretting his involvement. All he wanted was to get away from here as fast as possible.

Tears started to flow down her cheeks as she returned to reality with a bump, and as she realised just what it was that she had done, Laura started to howl.

"No! No!" she wailed. "You cannot leave me!"

He picked up the bag of coins and threw it to her. "Here is more than enough to get you back to London in the morning."

Laura bawled loudly; she clung to him. "No! No, you cannot! Please, you... said... you would marry me."

"I did not." He disentangled his arm from her grip. "Let me go. Believe me it will be better without a scene." He pushed her away.

She grabbed him again, begging noisily, "Please do not leave me... you cannot, I will not let you... you have ruined me... My papa..."

It was the worst thing she could have said. Jaspar, who was suffering from slight feelings of guilt, was not a man to be threatened.

"You, my dear child, ruined yourself. Throwing yourself at me in a most unattractively forward manner." He removed her hand, in the way of a man removing a dirty piece of matter.

"What shall I do? What will become of me?"

"You will survive. Creatures like you always do." And with that parting shot he was gone.

Miss Clarges arrived back at Curzon Street in a state of high excitement. She had done it! She congratulated herself. She had been the instrument that had meant Laura would make a brilliant match and she, Miss Clarges, had brought it about. She hoped that Laura and her family would be grateful. In truth, she was heartily tired of being Lady Ambrose's slave; it would be refreshing to be able to leave and set herself up in a small house. During the short ride home she mused on her excellent future. As the hackney drew up outside the house she realised that it was ablaze with lights. She peered at the windows, then climbed down, paid the jarvey and knocked on the front door. The butler opened it.

"Ah, Miss Clarges, my lady has returned. She awaits you in the library."

Miss Clarges swept by him. Not much longer to endure the patronising stares of butlers; soon she would be her own boss. Emboldened by this thought, she entered the library. Lady Ambrose was sitting in the wing chair; she did not look her best, but wait until Euphemia Clarges imparted her news, that would cheer her up. She would be grateful to the governess, so grateful that she had arranged things so well for her goddaughter.

"We did not expect you so soon, my lady," Miss Clarges started.

"Well, I am back. Lady Jersey wrote to me to say that she was concerned that Laura was too much in the company of Lord Heddington. Is this true?" Without giving Euphemia a chance to reply she went on, "I hope not! You are such a silly creature, it would be just like you to encourage her to no good end!"

Miss Clarges felt angry, when she had achieved so much for Laura. "I hope, my lady, that I would not be such a foolish person," she responded indignantly. "In fact, I have arranged things wonderfully for Laura. She is to marry His Lordship!"

"Marry! Jaspar?" Lady Ambrose felt a slight pang. However easygoing she seemed, Jaspar had pierced her heart, although it would have cost her dear to admit so to anyone. "Is this true?"

The governess enjoyed a smirk. She was well aware of how her mistress felt about His Lordship and she was not so noble that she did not feel a small thrill of pleasure to see her nose put out of joint.

"Of course I am sure! La! Lady Ambrose, do you think I would tell an untruth about such a matter?"

"No, I suppose you would not," Her Ladyship replied slowly. "But why did Laura not come and tell me her good news herself?"

"Oh, she is not with me, His Lordship took her to… to… his mama," she said airily.

"His mama has been dead for twenty-nine years. Do you mean his grandmother?"

"Oh yes, that is what I mean," fabricated Miss Clarges. "Wonderful, isn't it?"

"Ye…s, ye…s, it is very good for Laura." Lady Ambrose digested the news.

It seemed such an unlikely eventuality that Jaspar had been so bowled over by a pretty face as to offer marriage. He would be bored in six weeks. The girl was sweet but clearly not very bright. She dismissed the governess and made her way to bed. Miss Clarges bounced out; she was elated with the success of her scheme. No more slights. No more running after lazy old women. She grinned with pleasure as she climbed into bed and fell asleep, dreaming pleasant dreams. Her mistress's slumbers were not so pleasant. She did not know whether she hoped that the chit had made such a momentous match or whether she hoped that it was all a hum, invented by Euphemia.

As the door closed behind Jaspar, Laura collapsed on the floor. She cried and cried. She was totally inexperienced in the ways of the world but was wise enough to know that she was now ruined. She was in utter despair; then a thought crossed her mind. Maybe Jaspar would be forced to marry her. Perhaps it would be such a disgrace to the family, that he would be forced to do the honourable thing. She paused in the wailing, sitting up and sniffing. She would go to his sister. Lady Morntarny would make him realise that he must wed her. She scrambled to her feet, and ran to the glass; she looked at herself, horrified. Her hair was rumpled and her eyes looked as if they had shrunk to the size of glove buttons. Her normally smooth complexion was mottled and blotchy. She dipped a towel in the jug of water and tried to see what amends could be made to her beauty. When she had finished, she went down and shyly asked for transport.

The landlord looked her over disparagingly. "My lord left instructions that a coach should convey you back to town, miss," he sneered at her knowingly, "when you was a'ready to go."

"Where are we?" Laura vouched quietly.

"Why, in Wimbledon, miss, the Dog and Hounds," he sniggered. "Fancy you not knowing where you spent the night!"

The smirk on his round face made Laura hate him. She blushed bright red and, biting her lips to prevent the tears, just said, "As soon as my coach is ready…"

"Very well, miss…"

CHAPTER FOUR

Nillie stretched luxuriously in her comfortable bed. As usual, her first thought on rousing was of Greville. In those first delicious moments between sleep and waking, she was always sensible of her husband's love encircling her. She opened her eyes sleepily and glanced at the clock. It was still very early. The sun pouring through the blinds had given her the impression that it was far later than it was. She turned over, prepared to go back to sleep. As she drifted off, she heard a loud knocking on the front door. It was so unexpected that she sat up, curious and at the same time irritated that anyone should be disturbing the slumbers of her house at this unconscionable hour. The knocking continued. She heard the bolts being drawn back as someone opened the door. She could just discern two voices; one she recognised as that of her irate butler but the other? It sounded young, female and it was obviously upset. Wide awake now, she wondered what was transpiring. Slowly she rang the bell. She hated to disturb Quarmby this early, but she had to discover who needed her so urgently that she would dare to disturb the sleeping peace of Berkeley Square at this hour. The grumbling dresser, still attired in her nightdress and nightcap entered. "My lady?" she said sleepily.

"Who is at the door?"

"I do not know, my lady. Shall I go to find out?"

"Yes, Quarmby, would I have woken you otherwise?"

Quarmby sniffed. "Very good, my lady."

Nillie, thoroughly awake by this time, listened hard but all she could hear was the faint buzz of voices. Her dresser returned.

"It is just some girl… weeping… wants to see you urgently. Parker is sending her away."

"Who is she? Tell Parker not to send her anywhere until I know who it is and please ascertain this information for me instantly."

The dresser grunted but she did as she was bidden. She had heard that tone in her mistress's voice before, and she knew better than to question it. Nillie pulled back her covers. She slipped out of bed and put on the silk dressing gown that Quarmby had laid out for her. Who could it be?

She sat at the dressing table and, picking up a hairbrush, started to pull it through the dark curls.

"It's Miss Ludgrove, my lady, in a fair state she is." The dresser sniffed again. "Little madam!"

"That will do, Quarmby. Where is she?"

"Parker put her in the breakfast room."

"Good, I will be down directly." She stood up.

Laura sat huddled in the corner of the breakfast parlour. The confidence that she had felt at the inn had dissipated. She was scared and totally wretched. She did not quite see why she had come to Lady Morntarny. She now fully expected the countess to turn her away, as had her brother. How could she have been so silly?

The door opened, and as Petronilla entered her eye caught sight of the dishevelled bundle, crouched in the corner. It was crying noisily, tears sliding down its face and onto the crumpled dress.

Nillie smiled at her gently. "Come, Laura, what is it? You look distraught."

The kindness in her tone made Laura collapse into agitated sobs again. She put her head on the table and cried and cried. Nillie went round and sat next to her. She put an arm around the heaving shoulders and waited for the tears to abate; eventually they did.

"Come, Laura," Nillie repeated, "I cannot help you unless you tell me what is wrong."

"Oh, Lady M... M... M... Morntarny." She shuddered convulsively. "I... I... have been so very... wrong... I... th... th... thought he loved m... me." She sniffed. Silently Her Ladyship handed her a handkerchief. "Miss Clarges... was sure of it."

Petronilla stiffened when she heard the governess's name. "She is not very sensible, you know."

Laura nodded between sobs. "I... She told m... me I would b... be h... his wife... that it was on...ly t... time before he declared himself... I believed her... She a... arranged for Lord H... Heddington to take me home. She I... left an... an... and he... I thought."

She burst into floods of tears. Nillie's spirits sank. She was not angry with the girl. She was extremely stupid and unwise but she was little more than a child. But for the first time Nillie was cross with her beloved brother and furious with the idiotic governess, who must have known better.

"You had better tell me exactly what happened, Laura," Nillie asked seriously.

"I... went with him... Miss Clarges said it would be romantic to elope... she talked of chargers and knights and..."

"But, Laura, you do know that to elope is terribly wrong."

Laura nodded. "I lost my mind... I... I love h... him... I thought... I thought." She started to sob again, her golden head hanging down.

Nillie was much perturbed. She did not need to be told any more. She knew just what had occurred. How could Jaspar be so irresponsible? Now what to do? She got up and paced the room, thinking hard. Eventually she sat down again by Laura; she took the girl's wan face in her hands.

"Look at me, Laura, and please try not to cry." The girl did as she was bid. "I have thought about this predicament and I think I should take you back to your father."

"No! No! He must not know what has occurred... he will be s... so angry, so disappointed in me. How could I have done such a thing? How could I?"

"We all do silly things. Unfortunately this has... has awful consequences," she sighed, "for everyone... I too wish that it had not happened but... I am afraid it has." She stopped. "How can I explain to you?" She peered at Laura. "The most important thing is that no one knows what occurred. I can promise you that my brother will not spread it around," she continued fiercely. "If he did, he would have me to deal with, but, in any case, he is no blabbermouth. So you are safe from that."

"My papa will try to force him to marry me." She brightened. "Do you think he could?"

"No. It would not serve. For a start you would not be happy with Jaspar. Believe me."

"Oh, I would I love him so much! I cannot tell you how wonderful he is."

Nillie looked at her amazed. "W... wonderful, Laura? How can you say such an idiotic thing? Have you no conception of what he has done to you?"

Laura looked at her coquettishly. "Oh, but he is so marvellous."

"Stop it! Do not think so. He will not marry you, that I promise."

"But will not the world look askance on him if he abandons me?"

Privately Nillie thought there was some truth in this remark. However, it was a notion that must swiftly be put out of Laura's head. "No, I am afraid the reality is that the world will think very badly of you, for what you have allowed."

"But that is hardly fair."

Petronilla was by now getting slightly exasperated with this girl, who seemed to have little idea of the disgrace which would amount from her actions.

"Laura, you seem to… Oh, never mind. Where do you live? I shall take you to your father."

"I expect if Lord Heddington does not marry me, my papa will call him out," Laura went on with some relish. "Miss Clarges says it is very exciting to have a duel fought over you!"

"Laura!" Her Ladyship exclaimed crossly. "That at all costs must be prevented. What happened last night must not be known to anyone. Now ring the bell and I shall order the coach. I am hopeful that we can keep the matter concealed. We must prevent a scandal!"

That wish, however, was not to be granted. For by the time Nillie reached town again after one of the worst days of her life, Lady Ambrose had been busy with her tongue. She meant no real harm to Laura, she had merely spread the tidings confided to her by Miss Clarges.

Petronilla had a perfectly horrible time with Mr Ludgrove. As they neared the square red brick house where she lived, Laura, who had been steadily growing paler and quieter as they got closer and closer to her home, was trembling with fear and quite unable to help. Lady Morntarny had been shown into the undistinguished library where she had had to confront an anguished papa. As Laura had predicted, Mr Ludgrove was determined that Jaspar would marry his daughter, or if he refused that, then he would be forced to call him out. Nillie had had a hard time dissuading him from either of these two courses. The first, she had pointed out, would mean misery for Laura, even had they persuaded Jaspar to agree, which she insisted would be an impossible task. The second would result in a most undesirable scandal, and in any case Jaspar was a notable shot and fenced as a master. It took all her persuasive powers but eventually she managed to convince Mr Ludgrove not to pursue her brother. By this time, she was exhausted and thoroughly fed up with His Lordship. She bade farewell to Laura, promised to do everything to help the girl and clambered back into her coach for the return drive to town. It was only as she lay back on the squabs that she realised that she had been gone for twelve hours and she had not even left a note for Greville. She prayed that he would not worry too much.

This hope was not to be satisfied either. When she finally reached Berkeley Square, pale with fatigue and with her forehead throbbing, she discovered an irate and anxious husband pacing the floor. One look, however, at her ashen face was enough to make him forget his anger, to put his arms around her and to gently convey her to her bedroom. Once she was tucked up safely, he sat on the end of the bed and demanded, "Now, my love, tell me where have you been and why? Parker merely said that you left with Laura Ludgrove."

"Greville, it is so terrible, I am afraid. Jaspar… Jaspar seduced the girl."

"What? It cannot be true. He is not normally so imprudent."

"It is true. Mind you, the girl was foolish beyond permission. She went off with him quite willingly. Apparently that stupid woman, Miss Clarges, had put it into the girl's head that to elope was romantic! Laura thought she was on her way to Gretna. Jaspar, of course, had no such intention. He spent the night with her, then left and told her to find her way home."

Greville's normal urbane equanimity was outraged. "Nillie! I do think that this time Jaspar has gone too far."

She nodded agreement. "I have had the most horrible time trying to persuade Mr Ludgrove not to attempt to force Jaspar to marry Laura, which most certainly would not do, my love, or alternatively to call him out. Jaspar might kill him and then think of the scandal!"

"No, he would balk at that, surely."

"I suppose so, although today, I must admit to a distinct lack of faith in that reprobate, I can tell you. My ambition is to keep the matter a secret, there is nothing to be served from anyone knowing. It would not look good for Jaspar or for Laura. I do hope that now that I have persuaded Mr Ludgrove to do nothing, concealment may be achieved."

He nodded. "It would be best, but now, my love, I think you should rest." He kissed her tenderly and went back to his library.

As he sat over his favourite Milton, he found his thoughts straying. They were not sanguine. He was not as hopeful as his wife that scandal could be averted. Eventually, to throw off his unaccustomed restlessness, he left the house and sauntered down to Brooks'. He trod the portals, making his way upstairs, intending to sit in the library. At the top of the stairs he changed his mind and turned left, to peer into the Great Subscription Room, with its glittering chandelier and round tables, where men in green shades gambled away their fortunes. The room was full and hot and stuffy. He sighed and was about to retrace his steps to the comfort of the library, when he was hailed. It was Brummell and Lord Yarmouth, seated on a long sofa next to the fireplace. He sauntered across to them, a smile on his handsome face.

"Greville! The best of evenings." The Beau clasped his hand warmly.

"Yarmouth! George! Your devoted." Greville smiled, seating himself beside them. A footman brought him wine.

"A pony on the Padre to win next week," Yarmouth challenged. "You will be one of our party, Greville?"

"Oh, you must know our dear Morntarny is not one for a mill, Yarmouth. He is, most surprisingly, a peaceful creature. Not for him the sight of a man knocked out, his nose streaming with a river of red." George Brummell shuddered slightly. "I have to admit to a growing fastidiousness myself. Perhaps I should make fighting out of fashion," he considered.

Greville laughed. "My dear George. You are arrogant! Do you really suppose that your distaste with a sport could make it no longer in vogue?"

"Why, yes," Beau Brummell answered simply. "I know it to be the case." Then he grinned at Greville, his grey eyes dancing. "Ridiculous, is it not?"

Colonel James Staunton bowed to them and made to come and join them. He was a portly, self-important man who considered himself all the go. Brummell was known to despise him. "La, Lord Morntarny well met. Your brother up to his old tricks or has she caught him this time, the Ludgrove? They are laying bets, you know!"

Greville glanced quickly at George, his face reflecting his misgivings. His friend assessed the situation and in response raised his glass and scrutinised the colonel through it.

"Why, may I ask, do you distress the eye with such a waistcoat? Do you call that thing a coat, Staunton?" He turned away.

The colonel flushed a dull red; such a public setdown from the acknowledged leader of the *ton* was not something that could be passed off without mortification. He looked with repugnance at Beau Brummell but was too nervous of his reputation to risk any more reprimands, so he contented himself with a closing barb.

"My lord, you may think to divert from the scandal by using Mr Brummell but you will not escape that easily. Lady Ambrose has boasted all over town of her goddaughter's triumph in catching Heddington. Think of the infamy if it should all be a hum. Breach of promise, perhaps?"

Greville was by now seriously concerned. He was sure from what Nillie had said that Jaspar had no intention of marrying Laura, but how could her seduction have become an *on dit* in such a short time and why was Marjery glorying in such a story that could only do harm to poor Laura? He was most perturbed. Staunton flounced off.

"Really! George," laughed Yarmouth, "you should not give such a crushing retort to such as Staunton."

"Oh, he is such a pompous dolt. I have no time for such pretension."

"Yes, fool he may be, but he is, I am afraid, a malevolent one and I suspect will spread dangerous gossip."

He inclined his head in the direction of Lord Morntarny. "What is it, Greville?"

His Lordship thought for a moment. He knew that he could trust these men, and they were both much attached to Jaspar, so he decided they must know the truth.

"Better you should know what has happened from me, but please, I speak in confidence."

Both men nodded.

"It would seem that my idiotic brother-in-law has seduced this Ludgrove chit."

"Nothing new in that," remarked Yarmouth sagely, "always seducing people, Jaspar."

"Yes, but it would appear that the girl is an innocent."

"It does not look well, and if Staunton is spreading the story it will not look good for Jaspar, he is always trying to discredit him," considered Brummell.

"George, I must agree with you. The girl arrived on our doorstep early this morning. She was, understandably, very agitated. Nillie managed to persuade Laura to let her convey her to Mr Ludgrove. Bless my dearest wife, she even managed to prevail upon the papa to take no action, and we thought a scandal could be averted, but it now seems that Lady Ambrose cannot keep her mouth shut, although why she should tell such a tale, I must say, I am at a loss to understand. It does her no credit."

"Perhaps she believes it to be true," asserted George.

"Oh no!" gasped Greville. "That will be it! That asinine governess, Miss Clarges, filled the girl's head with nonsensical notions about Jaspar wanting to marry her."

"Lady Ambrose hardly renowned for her sense either," declared Yarmouth. "That will be it. Allowed herself to be persuaded by the Clarges woman."

"Oh! It grows more horrible by the minute and I cannot wash my hands of it because he's Nillie's brother."

"Tell you what I think," mentioned Yarmouth sagely, "should go out of town, Jaspar. Should leave. It will all die down. Worst infamies get forgotten in a week, if the central figure's not around."

"Yes, you are right. I must return to Nillie. Better she hears this from me than some other well-meaning meddler."

He bade his friends *adieu* and walked thoughtfully home. He had too much respect for his wife to think of keeping the exact truth from her. When he reached Berkeley Square, he found her sitting up in bed drinking tea, her headache quite gone. He dismissed Quarmby and sat on her bed and explained what he had heard. Petronilla was aghast.

"Oh, Greville, I am appalled. What is to be done? My day's work is for nothing it would seem. Do you think Jaspar might marry her? No, that is a silly question. It would not serve. Laura would be crushed to pieces."

"I think Yarmouth has a point. Jaspar must leave town. It is thin of company; you must persuade him, Nillie."

Petronilla sighed. "Will he listen to me, do you think?"

"I think you have the fairest chance." He ruffled her curls. "It is imperative that you convince him, my love."

"I know, but I do not think it will be easy. I will have to see

Lady Ambrose as well tomorrow. I confess I am not looking forward to it."

Greville leant forward and kissed her. "I do understand and I will do what I can to help."

CHAPTER FIVE

Nillie did not pass a peaceful night. Greville was wont to tease her for her ability to tumble deeply asleep in the wink of an eye and remain undisturbed until she awoke the next day refreshed and bright as a linnet. After the perturbing disclosures of this evening, however, Petronilla tossed and turned, unable to sink into her customary repose. Eventually, at about six o'clock, she gave up and climbed out of bed. Sitting at her dressing table, her head cupped in her hands, she pondered how best to deal with the events of yesterday. Indubitably, she adored her brother. He had been her preceptor, her dearest friend, her ally, her companion in scrapes. Whenever she had devised some particularly daring escapade, she had always known that Jaspar would enter into it with impish willingness. They were inseparable. This morning, for the first time, she found herself, sadly, antagonistic to him. It was not an agreeable feeling.

Her mama had died giving birth to Jaspar, the longed-for son, after four daughters, and Nillie had been brought to see her baby brother. He was pink and crumpled and Petronilla, little more than a baby herself, had fallen in love with him. She had worshipped Jaspar since then, and it was hard to reconcile her present exasperation with all the closeness and kindness that she had received from him. She sighed. It was a regular pickle.

However sorry she felt for Laura, her loyalties remained with Jaspar and it was he whom she wanted to protect. Sitting there reflecting, she suddenly realised that she was very hungry. She had been far too tired the night before to do more than swallow a cool draught of lemonade, and too fraught during that long day to eat anything. She had awoken staving.

Nillie was a considerate employer. Quarmby had been with the family for years and was now quite aged. It did not occur to Petronilla to get her up two days in succession, any earlier than was strictly necessary. Having decided, therefore, that she would not wait until the dresser arose, she pulled on her gown and tiptoed down the main stairs across the hall and through the green door which led onto the servants' quarters, down the stone passages and into the kitchens, which, because Lord Morntarny insisted on the most modern equipment in his houses, were provided with the latest range: a new cupboard fed by warm pipes which kept the food hot; and various other devices, all enabling the staff to save time and work. The main kitchen was very large. Various sculleries led off it, and up a few steps to the left was the commodious butler's pantry. This was very much Parker's domain. It had floor-to-ceiling cupboards lined with green baize, containing silver and priceless porcelain. In earlier days the youngest footman slept on the floor to protect the silver but the tradition had recently been abolished.

A thin kitchen maid was scrubbing the floor. She was the only servant up yet. She gasped as she saw Nillie and leapt to her feet, curtseying deeply. Her thin face, underneath the streaks of dirt, flushed red. She was about fourteen, with blue eyes and dark hair which was pulled back over a high forehead.

Nillie smiled at her. "Good morning. What is your name?"

The girl looked terrified but managed to answer. "G… good morning, Your Ladyship. If you please, Nib."

"Well, Nib, I find that I cannot sleep and I am very hungry. Do you think you can help me find some breakfast?" she asked.

The girl nodded vigorously. "Yes, my lady. What would you be requiring?" She bobbed another curtsey.

"How about some chocolate and perhaps an egg and toast?" Nillie crossed to the larder, pulling open the door.

"Oh, please, Your Ladyship, I do not think yous should be doing that," Nib's worried voice stopped her.

She laughed. "I do not expect that I know where to find things. I had better leave it to you." The countess smiled encouragingly at the girl, who put down her scrubbing brush and went to the larder cupboard where she pulled out a jug of milk, which she put to heat, some eggs which she whisked in a large basin.

Nillie sat at the huge oak table. "Thank you, Nib. Will you join me?"

The girl gasped again; her face flushed a darker shade of red. "Oh, my lady, I… I… What would Mr Parker say?"

"Nothing, I imagine. He cannot discipline you for something I have asked you to do."

Nib swallowed hard. "Yes, my lady." She poured out a cup of chocolate for Petronilla and sat nervously opposite her.

Nillie smiled reassuringly. "How old are you, Nib?"

"Thirteen. Well, near fourteen, my lady."

"How long have you worked for us?"

"Two year. My mother works at Morntarny. She's head laundry." The girl's confidence grew under the beneficent gaze of Nillie. "We all work for you, my lady. My dad was a groom." She stopped; a tear sparkled in her eye, running down the streaks on her face.

Nillie put her hand over the girl's. She noticed for the first time how red and rough it was, the skin red from scrubbing. "What happened?" she enquired gently. Nib rubbed the back of her hand across her face; the water from her tears glinted on the coarse-coloured skin. She sniffed.

"Died, my lady, just a month ago. I wanted to go to the funeral."

"Would not Parker let you?" Nillie was incensed.

"Dunno. I did not dare ask." She raised her eyes to Nillie's and explained cautiously, "I'm the bottom, my lady, the scullery."

"Mmm." Nillie knew that it would not do to interfere with the butler's control of his staff, but the girl appealed to her. She changed the subject. "What do you want to do?" she enquired. "What is your ambition? That means…"

"I know what it means, my lady," Nillie looked faintly surprised, "and I know what I want. What I's always wanted. More than anything in the world." Her eyes sparkled. "I want to read. I want to learn to read and write."

"Read and write?" Nillie was amazed. She deliberated for a moment. Then made a decision. "Well, why not? I will arrange it, Nib. For you and any other servants who also desire it. It is scandalous that you should not be taught to read." She stood up. "I think I will take my breakfast up in my room. Please bring it up to me."

When she was dressed Nillie ordered her carriage and went first to Curzon Street. She was shown into Lady Ambrose's morning room and after a few moments Her Ladyship joined her.

"Nillie, my dear, how perfectly lovely to see you." She examined her keenly. "You look a little tired, my sweet."

"Not surprising! It has not been an agreeable two days." Nillie peeled off her gloves and sat on the chair indicated by her hostess. Taking a breath she plunged straight in. "I am afraid that what I am about to say is both humiliating and unpleasant." She looked directly at Marjery. "It concerns your goddaughter."

"Laura? But Miss Clarges led me to believe that everything was remarkable where she was concerned. She is to marry your brother. Oh, I understand you consider that it is something of a misalliance, Petronilla, but Laura's mama was a Merchant. Jane Merchant, Merchant's eldest daughter. We were at school together. Of course, she made a shocking match but the girl has some breeding."

"Stop! Stop, Marjery. You mistake the matter. Jaspar has no more intention of marrying Laura than of marrying... Miss Clarges."

"What? What do you say? Euphemia told me that Jaspar had taken her to Lady Heddington."

"I do not know where she fabricated that fantasy. Jaspar took Laura to a hotel in Wimbledon, she went quite willingly. He... he..." she felt ashamed for her brother, "... left the next morning... Laura came to me. I took her back to her papa. I had the greatest difficulty persuading him not to call Jaspar out. My one concern was to prevent a scandal but now it seems, Marjery, that you have been busy. It would seem you have told the world."

Lady Ambrose went white; she stood up and swallowed, turning away from Nillie. "Jaspar seduced the girl. Oh my God."

"Yes, Marjery, and you introduced her to Jaspar and then left her here with that idiot of a woman." In her exasperation she lashed out. "How could you do something so silly? So... oh..." Nillie shook her clenched fists in the air, as she tried to control her anger.

"Now, Nillie, be reasonable, I am not to blame. How was I to know Jaspar would make a play for Laura?"

"Marjery!" Nillie started furiously, desirous of shaking Her Ladyship, but realising that this would not help the situation, she took a breath. "Margery, you know Jaspar! All too well. A girl as pretty as that but... but... what made Miss Clarges abet the girl in that irresponsible manner? That I cannot understand."

"She shall answer for this." Lady Ambrose moved swiftly to ring the bell and when the butler appeared she demanded that Miss Clarges be sent for immediately.

Euphemia Clarges received the peremptory summons from her employer with annoyance. Not long now before she was rid of all this. Inwardly she quivered in excitement, but until that desired moment, she had better obey. She put down her stitching and went to the morning room. She knocked on the door.

"Come in."

Euphemia went in, her face surly. Lady Ambrose was seated at the table. She was white as a sheet. Lady Morntarny was standing by the window; she looked enraged and tired.

"Yes, my lady." Miss Clarges spoke somewhat off-handedly.

"Euphemia Clarges, you... you... you will leave my employ this moment!"

"Oh, I was going to leave anyway. Now that Laura has made such a brilliant match I am sure she will take care of me," the governess replied insolently.

Both Lady Ambrose and Lady Morntarny stared at her in disbelief.

"Made a brilliant match? I suppose you encouraged her in this," said Nillie, her voice deceptively smooth.

Miss Clarges nodded vehemently. "Indeed I did. I made it possible for them to run off together." She giggled archly. "I made sure that Lord Heddington took her home alone so he could propose." She finished proudly, "It was all my doing!"

Lady Ambrose crossed to her, she slapped her hard across the cheek. "You idiot, you fool, you utter imbecile. You have made it possible for Jaspar to seduce Laura and abandon her."

Miss Clarges's face paled.

"Oh yes, you may look like that. What can have possessed you to invite her to run off with him, quite willingly? He did not abduct her. Oh no," she continued bitterly, "she jumped into his coach and into his arms, into her ruin, encouraged by you, nay, engineered by you."

Euphemia went white. "S... seduce her... ruin... abandon her... What do you mean?"

"You told me, Euphemia Clarges, that Lord Heddington had taken her to his mama. Where did you get that idea? Who told you that? Did Laura?" Euphemia started to cry. "Oh, I see it. You made it up. So not content with allowing the girl to go to her ruin, you exacerbate the issue by allowing me to tell the *ton* the tissue of rubbish that you have fabricated. That Jaspar is to marry my goddaughter." Her voice grew louder and louder until she was screaming at the governess. "You! You ignoramus! You blockhead! You booby! You…" She collapsed down into her chair again, crying herself, with anger and frustration.

Nillie crossed to Miss Clarges who was indulging in a fit of hysterics; she slapped her again. "Stop it. You have done enough damage without indulging in a fit of the vapours."

She turned to Marjery. "We shall have to put it out that you were mistaken. That Laura returned to her papa, as he was not well." Lady Ambrose nodded speechlessly. "And if we discover that you breathe a word of this to anyone, Euphemia Clarges, we will make sure you are thrown on the streets with no character. I am going to see Jaspar now. I will insist he leaves town. Better that no one sees him at all."

She kissed Lady Ambrose goodbye and, climbing into her carriage, gave orders to be driven to Grosvenor Square.

As he closed the door, Jaspar could hear Laura sobbing noisily, He shuddered, gratified to be away from such an unnecessary display of emotion. He went down, demanding his carriage to be brought round immediately. And with some relief, left the Dog and Hounds.

As he drove back to town he found himself unpredictably disconcerted with his behaviour. He felt soiled somehow. Grubby and dishonourable. These were entirely unexpected feelings; he could not ever remember entertaining such a reaction in previous circumstances, and he could not quite understand why these feelings of disquiet kept obtruding into his thoughts. It was not like him. Perhaps he was getting old? He was glad when he reached home. He stripped off his clothes, partook of a bath and fell into his own bed. He was not able to spend long asleep, however, for that very day he was pledged to Sir John Wade. He had engaged to race the whip to Hemel Hempstead, and was due at the appointed meeting place at eight o'clock. The exigencies of the contest kept his mind clear of all obtrusive thoughts of Laura, and it was very late before he returned exhausted but triumphant to his house.

The next morning he got up late and was still finishing breakfast when his sister was announced. He rose to his feet and kissed her tenderly.

"Good morning, Nillie, can I offer you some breakfast?" His sister shook her head. "To what do I owe the honour of a visit at this early hour?"

"Jaspar! It is not that early! At least not for me. I have been awake since six." Her brother looked shocked. "And I have visited Lady Ambrose already."

She watched his face intently to see what reaction he made to her pronouncement, but her infuriating brother merely sat there finishing his ham.

"I see that you do not know. Where were you yesterday, Jaspar?"

"Yesterday. Let me see. Ah I remember. Raced Johnny Lake to Hemel Hempstead. I won, in case you were interested."

Nillie, aggravated beyond what was possible, stood up and slapped his face hard. It was the first time she had ever hit him. His eyes glimmered with hurt. He was suddenly sober.

"Nillie, what is it? What have I done?"

"What have you done? Oooh... I could hit you again." Wringing her hands together she sat down at the table. "What have you done? Jaspar... you... you seduce a girl... then leave her." She dropped her head into her hands.

Now it was His Lordship's turn to be angry. "Really, my dear Petronilla, it is little, nay nothing, to do with you how I... what I do."

"Nothing to do with me! That is a fine one! When I have weeping girls on my doorstep at seven o'clock in the morning and spend all my day chasing over the countryside soothing aggrieved papas who are going to call you out."

"Let them. I can fight any papa."

"Oh, you callous wretch. I know you can kill an old man. It was not you of whom I was thinking. It was Mr Ludgove; that and of preventing a hideous scandal. Not that that was effective. Lady Ambrose and her stupid tongue," she said furiously.

Light was beginning to dawn. "Laura?"

"Yes. Laura!"

"How dare she involve you. Nillie, I apologise. It is unpardonable of her."

"Jaspar! The poor girl was desperate. She came to me because she had nowhere else to go. That idiotic governess filled her head with notions that… that you… you intended to carry her off and marry her. She is very silly, but also very young. Why, Jaspar? Why? Why an innocent like that?"

He shrugged. "I guess she was there. She was willing. I do not know, Nillie." He flopped back into his chair. "My love, I am truly sorry that you should have been embroiled in my troubles." He picked up her hand and kissed it. "Friends, Nillie?"

She grinned at him. "Yes but you must promise me one thing."

"What?"

"No, promise first."

He shrugged again. "Not if it is never to seduce a girl again! I will never keep such a promise, Nillie."

"No," she laughed again, "it is not that. I want you to go out of town just for a few weeks. We will put it about that you were never with Laura, that you merely took her to her papa. Please, Jaspar."

He looked at her. He could refuse her nothing. "Alright. I should go and see Grandmama but only a few weeks, mind you."

Nillie sighed with relief; it had been easier than she anticipated. She got up and hugged him. "Go today, please."

He nodded. "Anything for you."

"No clubs! No people! Just go!"

"Yes… yes!"

It was early afternoon before Jaspar left town. There had been various arrangements to make. He decided to ride. He had spent the previous day cooped up in a carriage and his horse, Valiant, really did need exercise. In any case, if he were to go into enforced seclusion in Sussex he wanted his horse with him and he was loath to let anyone, even his groom, Harper, ride him. Harper and his valet, Pickering, he sent ahead in the small travelling coach loaded with all that he would need. He would not require them, for he certainly did not anticipate an overnight stay, even if he took the journey in easy stages, resting Valiant when necessary. He liked to be alone with the horse and his thoughts; Jaspar had bred the animal himself. His father had left him an extensive stud and an obsession with horse breeding. Valiant had been one of the first foals to be born after his father's death. One of the first that had been Jaspar's alone. He had been present at the birth, had broken the animal personally; their bond was as strong as most humans'.

He made good progress, stopping at various inns on the route. He was well known at all the best coaching inns on the Brighton road. He made his last stop at Minchinham, about ten miles from home. Valiant cantered comfortably to the Angel and Harp, where Jaspar jumped off, throwing the reins to the ostler.

"Doug, make sure that you rub him down carefully. I will give him a couple of hours' rest and then I will want him again."

He strode into the inn, which was fairly large for such a small village. A group of men were in the taproom, from whence came raucous laughter. A girl and someone whom he took to be a maid were seated beside the fireplace, which on such a hot day merely contained unlit logs.

Mine host bustled out. He bowed low. "My Lord Heddington." The girl raised her head slightly in surprise.

"How honoured we are to have you with us again." The innkeeper rubbed his hands together at the thought of the largesse that would result from Jaspar's visit.

Jaspar smiled. "Good day, Melow. I trust I find you and Mrs Melow in the best of health?"

"Indeed, my lord."

Unseen, the girl watched Jaspar carefully from under her lashes.

"I would like a private parlour, and I think I will dine. Valiant needs a couple of hours' rest and I might as well fill them sampling Mrs Melow's excellent fare."

"Immediately, my lord. Will you not come this way, please?" The landlord led the way to the end of a narrow panelled corridor, which ran off to the right of the stairs. He flung open the door of the back parlour. All the time the girl watched intently. Lord Heddington paused in the doorway.

"Thank you, Melow. Please send me in a bottle of wine," he asked, his voice reverberating clearly down into the hall, where the girl sat, unmoving.

"Very good, my lord, and may I say, my lord, what a pleasure it is to have you with us again?" The landlord bustled away.

As soon as he reached the main part of the house and hastened out to the kitchen to order My Lordship's dinner, the girl rose. She looked around quickly to make sure that no one was watching her. Then she made her way down the passage to the parlour. She stopped outside the door and adjusted her cloak. Then she knocked gently. On being bidden to come in, she opened the door and entered.

CHAPTER SIX

Jaspar turned as the door opened. Surprise flickered across his face as he beheld, not the expected rotund figure of Mrs Melow, but a slim girl. He gazed at her with frank astonishment. She was about twenty, with bright red hair and the palest blue eyes he had ever seen. They were so pale that they looked almost like diamonds as they glinted at him. Her cheeks were covered in a multitude of tiny freckles which appeared to have been thrown onto her face by a malevolent fairy. Her shoulders and arms, however, were free of these brown specks and were smooth and very white. She was quite tall, her small head held high on a graceful neck. Her nose was straight and very pretty, and her lips were full and a delicate pink. If it had not been for the awful red hair, which was a colour that Jaspar particularly loathed, and the appalling freckles, she would have been quite beautiful.

She looked at him and smiled; her smile was absolutely enchanting; it lit up the huge crystal eyes, which he noticed were fringed with almost black lashes. The red hair, which was not a carrot colour, but rather a multitude of differing shades from spun gold to nearly blonde, was, he reflected, most remarkable. It was thick, naturally wavy and she wore it unfashionably long, with curls caught up on either side of her face and cascading down her back. She was dressed in a round gown of the palest blue which almost matched her eyes and her cloak was deep blue velvet. She was most unusual. She looked at him with an unembarrassed and straightforward gaze.

"Are you Lord Heddington?" she enquired. Her voice was low and very husky. "Jaspar, Lord Heddington?"

"Yes," he replied, slightly amused. "But you have the edge on me. Who are you?"

She laughed, coming closer towards him. "I am Hestia, I am Polymnia, I am Aphrodite, I am who you will," she giggled. It was a very pretty sound.

He was intrigued. "How do you know who I am?"

"I heard the landlord," she replied in her direct way.

She came closer to him. She smelt sweet, of musk or lilies. She lifted her dark lashes; the translucent eyes looked into his. He caught his breath. He did not like red hair, it was a colour that he had always found abhorrent. He hated freckles; they were anathema to him. Hers was not the kind of beauty that appealed at all, and yet here she was in his private parlour, obviously his for the asking. He had a couple of hours to waste, a couple of hours that could be most agreeably spent with this Venus creature. He touched her cheek very gently; she closed her eyes slightly. He ran one finger over the pink lips and down her neck. She raised her chin. Opening her eyes she looked deep into his dark orbs. He bent down and kissed her. Her lips were soft and yielding. He felt a tremor of excitement inside him. He loosed her cloak; it slid silently to the floor. He ran his hand along her bare arms; her skin was like silk and quite the softest he had ever touched. He pulled her towards him and, feeling her slim shoulders, he ran his hand down until he cupped the delicate breast in his hand. She put her arms around his neck. He could feel her trembling slightly. Then suddenly, simultaneously, he heard a gigantic retort and felt a searing pain. He reeled, the force of the shot hurling him backwards onto the floor. Blood spurted from the hole in his shoulder; the pain was acute. The girl stood. She looked at him without moving. He clutched his shoulder, blood running through his fingers and into pools on the floor.

"Please help me," he whispered, breathing heavily. "I… I… n… need your assistance." She remained motionless. He tried to crawl across to the door. "Please c… call some h… help."

She regarded him. The icy eyes hard as diamonds. "You will survive. Creatures like you always do," she remarked. She threw a bag of coins at him, picked up her cloak, turned heel and left. As she did so Jaspar felt himself slipping into unconsciousness.

When he came round Melow was leaning over him anxiously. "My lord! My lord!" His anguished voice permeated the mists of Jaspar's consciousness. He groaned. Then another voice, which he recognised as that of mine host's devoted spouse.

"Mind, Melow! Come now, out of the way." She pushed her husband unceremoniously away from Jaspar's side.

Then she put a cushion under his head. Jaspar had by now completely regained consciousness. He was bleeding copiously but within minutes Mrs Melow had torn some linen into strips and had bound a pad of cotton onto the wound.

Once content with her handiwork, she ordered her inferiors to lift Jaspar and convey him to a bedchamber. This was dutifully done. The pain from the ball was agony and Jaspar was hard pushed not to cry out as they lifted him. He felt considerably more comfortable once he was installed in Mrs Melow's best bed. The pain meant that he drifted in and out of a swoon. Then he heard Mrs Melow come back.

"Here you is, me lord, I have brot the doctor." Jaspar managed to open his eyes weakly. He quite expected to see Mr Watpell, who had cared for the dowager and the entire Heddington family all their lives; the man who stood next to the bed was quite unknown to him. He was a stocky young man dressed very simply, in breeches made of everlasting, long boots and yellow frieze waistcoat.

"Mr Watpell?" enquired Jaspar faintly.

"Don't you worry, me lord," continued Mrs Melow. "This 'ere is Dr Sugden, he is new in the neighbourhood, but he's a fair miracle."

"I can fetch Mr Watpell if you prefer it." The young man spoke with a distinct northern burr to his voice. "But I do not think we should wait long to treat that injury, my lord," he observed.

Jaspar found himself slipping away again; he nodded. The young man set to work; he had quite the gentlest, although firmest hands that Jaspar had ever experienced. He clearly knew what he was doing for he removed the ball in a trice. He then sprinkled some white powder on the wound and bound up the shoulder most efficiently.

"Now, my lord, I think you will find that much more comfortable," he pronounced. "Please keep putting this powder on the hole, it will prevent infection." Then he nodded to Mr Melow, told Mrs Melow to look after his patient and, giving him a draught to take against pain, he promised to return the next day.

Mrs Melow wasted no time. She immediately prepared the draught and gave it to Jaspar. It had a soothing effect and he found himself drifting into a deep sleep. His slumber was interrupted by his dreams, which involved a maiden carved in ice, who melted into flames of reddish gold hair. He must have slept for several hours, for when he awoke it was very dark. His shoulder pained him less and he wondered what time it was. The inn was very quiet so he deduced that it was in all probability the middle of the night. He was very thirsty. He raised himself into a sitting position and put his hand out. Mrs Melow, in her considerate way, had placed a large glass of water by his bed. He drank it all, feeling much better. He knew it would be stupid to attempt to leave before morning, so he lay back on the pillows. However, he found himself quite unable to sleep. Memories of the previous evening flooded over him. Now he recollected what had occurred. He remembered the red-haired girl. He recalled the feel of her lips, the touch of her skin. Why had she shot him? He was sure that he had never seen her before. He could never have forgotten that hair, those glacial blue eyes, that calm expression, that wonderful smile. Who was she? Where did she come from? Why did she shoot him? There was something else. He strained to remember but it would not come. He lay in the dark going over it and over it in his mind. What had he done to this fiery ice maiden to make her want to kill him? There seemed no reason.

When he next awoke it was light. A chorus of dawn birds was singing its heart out. He pulled himself up and, sliding his legs over the side of the bed, he slowly stood up. His head spun and he felt almost light-headed. He found he had to flop back onto the bed until he was used to the upright position. *I must leave*, he thought, *I do not want to face questions on what happened. I should not have stayed last night.* He was grateful that, apart from his shirt arm which had been torn to enable the doctor to treat him, he was still in the clothes he had worn yesterday. For he knew that to try to dress himself with the pain from his shoulder would have been well nigh impossible. It proved a hard enough task to pull on his boots with one hand, and he was sweating profusely and ashen with pain by the time he had accomplished this simple chore. He sat for a moment to regain his breath, suddenly doubtful whether he could complete the journey to his home, but it was only a matter of ten miles, and he had ridden it many times. A short rest, and he felt recovered enough to stand again. He left some money for Melow on the table and crept downstairs, letting himself out through the back. It was a beautiful day; the sky was very blue and the fresh morning air revived him somewhat. Breathing deeply, he became more hopeful that the trip could be accomplished easily. He went round to the stable; a sleepy boy was mucking out the stalls. Jaspar called to him.

"Please saddle my horse." He indicated Valiant, who tossed his head as he saw his beloved master. The boy gave him a scared glance but he did as he was bidden and received a sovereign for his trouble.

"Thankee, sir," he responded delightedly.

"Give me a leg up." Jaspar found it infuriating to have to ask for help in such a task but the boy did not seem to notice. He hoisted him into the saddle and, clutching his coin, wide-eyed, returned to his mucking-out.

Jaspar picked up the reins. "Come, Valiant." A gentle pressure to the horse's sides spurred the animal forward. They moved slowly out of the yard. Jasper found that he had underestimated the restriction the damage to his shoulder would occasion to his speed. The bumping from trotting caused intense agony, and although cantering was slightly better, it was simply not possible to travel at anything even remotely resembling his customary speed. The horse seemed to understand his master's injuries; he needed little to no guidance on which way to go and instinctively seem to prevent jolting as much as possible. However, in spite of this, Jaspar was beginning to regret his foolishness in not remaining at the inn for another day. He could have sent word to Bardfield Hall; they could have brought his well-sprung travelling chaise for him. The idea of lying back on soft cushions seemed infinitely attractive. In addition to the problems from his wound, it was also, by now, very hot and he was not sure that he could travel much further. Jaspar had done this journey hundreds of times before but he had not anticipated how difficult it would be, and it was with considerable relief that he approached the small forest which bordered onto his own land. As they turned into the shady woods, the welcome coolness and the proximity to home revived him a little. Valiant picked his way carefully down the familiar paths. He and his master had ridden every inch of the forest and the animal had little problem finding his way. They were about halfway through the trees when Jaspar heard a sound of horses. His spirits lifted; perhaps they came from his estate? He could ask for help.

The three men who approached him were unknown to him. The leader was a man of about forty. He was roughly dressed and his horse, although obviously strong, was ill-kempt. The other two were equally disreputable looking, unshaven and dirty.

"What have we 'ere?" pronounced the leader. He laughed. It was not a pleasant sound, menacing and rather threatening. Jaspar wondered whether the sense of foreboding that came over him was imagination due, in part, to his vulnerable condition. The leader grabbed Valiant's bridle; the horse threw up his head in distaste; the leader jerked it down. Valiant whinnied in pain.

"Stop that!" Jaspar found his ordinarily strong voice was weak and not very effective. The man laughed again and the others joined in, a raucous, coarse sound. One of them dismounted. He pulled Jaspar from the horse and threw him on the ground; Jaspar winced with pain.

"Give us your money!"

"I have no money," Jaspar managed to reply.

The man tore off Jaspar's coat and started to search the pockets. He found the bag of gold that the girl had flung at Jaspar and that Melow, or someone, had replaced in his pocket. He poured the coins out into his hand and threw the bag onto the leaves. He held the money out to the leader in triumph.

"Ah ha, you lie to us," said the leader. He hit Jaspar hard across the face with his crop. The mark started to seep with blood.

"I forgot I had that," Jaspar muttered.

"A likely tale." The man on the ground kicked Jaspar in the back. He flinched. The man pulled off Jaspar's signet ring and removed his watch and fob, which he put in his filthy coat pocket.

The leader who had been holding Valiant remarked, "Nothing more."

Jem shook his head. "Well, this is a good animal. I could do wif a 'orse like this. I think I will have him."

"Please," Jaspar begged. "No, do not steal Valiant, please." He had never in his life begged any person for anything but to lose his beloved friend was too much.

"Ha ha, I will 'ave him," the leader laughed viciously at Jaspar's discomfort. "Don't want to lose 'im, eh? Lucky you don't lose your life."

Never had Jaspar felt so powerless, never in his life had he been dominated by anyone. It was not, he discovered, at all agreeable to be in another's power.

"Leave the horse, I beg you," he tried one last time.

The leader sniggered in exultation. "He begs us! 'ear that, Jem, he begs us. Well, we…" He paused. "We will… take the 'orse."

He wheeled his horse around, jerking at Valiant's bridle. Valiant reared, his front hooves hitting the leader in the face. The man dropped the bridle and Valiant galloped off. The leader, blood pouring from an eye, screamed in fury. "Follow 'im, damn the animal. We'll get you, you damned 'horse."

The two men, Jaspar forgotten, tore off after Valiant. The leader, brushing blood from his eyes, followed.

Jaspar heaved a sigh of relief. He knew they would never catch Valiant; the horse knew every inch of the forest and was far faster than the ill-bred animals that they were riding. He hoped they would not come back to finish him off. He raised his head and looked around; he realised with some satisfaction that he was very near 'The Hidden House'. This had been christened thus by Netta and Nillie, when as children they had played in the woods. It was hardly a house, merely a hollowed-out space under the roots of an enormous oak tree, but as children it had been their favourite place. Jaspar crawled towards it. His shoulder was bleeding copiously again and the gash on his face meant blood dripped into his eyes. However, he was strong and determined, and it was a comfort when he saw the gap that led to their childish hiding place. He slid his body into the hole. He was quite hidden from view.

He heard the sound of the men returning. The leader's voice called, "Find 'im, Jem. lf we can't have the 'orse we'll have him."

He heard Jem's surprised voice reply, " 'e's gorn."

"What! He can't 'ave gorn."

" e 'as, I tells you."

" 'e must be 'ere. Look for 'im."

Jaspar heard them search the undergrowth, without success. Then with relief he heard Jem say, "Ah, come on, he ain't 'ere. Let's go before someone comes."

Then he caught the sound of the horses' hooves retreating into the distance. He breathed more easily. Eventually he pulled himself out of the hollow tree. He would have to get home somehow. He started to crawl along the forest paths.

Chapter Seven

Throwing back his head wildly, Valiant careered away from the men. Without pausing he galloped out of the woods, skillfully avoiding the branches and trees in his path, until he came to the gates of Bardfield Hall.

The hall had been substantially rebuilt at the end of the eighteenth century. The master had conceived a mansion that was, at the same time, both simple and impressive. Built of warm golden brick, it stood poised in solitary splendour at the end of a long straight drive. The front facade was over 400 feet; in the middle, a resplendent porticoed main entrance stood proud to the world; to each side were wings, so positioned to effect a sense of balance and symmetry. The parks surrounding the drive were open in aspect, lawns and lakes duly placed to create an impression of space and serenity, and visitors, seeing the mansion for the first time, were known to gasp at the beauty of this long, continuous road, with its uninterrupted view of the house.

Valiant paused at the gates and then started down the drive, as he had done so many times before with Jaspar spurring him on. Eventually, he reached the front door. He stopped as if unsure of what to do next. Then he neighed loudly. No one came. He picked up his hoof and pawed at the panels, beating and beating on them. Suddenly, the horse pricked up his ears. Sounds of the bolts being drawn back. The door swung open. Savage, the butler, stared in speechless astonishment at the riderless animal, who was flecked with foam and sweating profusely.

Harper and Pickering, His Lordship's valet, had arrived the previous evening and informed Her Ladyship and Savage that His Lordship was following immediately. When Lord Heddington had not arrived that night, none of His Lordship's servants had been too concerned, they were used to his ways. His grandmother, Lady Heddington, was faintly surprised; Jaspar may have been extremely unmindful of the feelings of the female sex generally, but he adored her, and she was sure would never do anything to deliberately hurt or disconcert her.

Hence the abrupt arrival of Valiant, and in such condition, cast His Lordship's household into utter disarray. Savage, normally much on his dignity, called frantically to Harper and Pickering. The groom arrived first. He took one look at the horse and his wrinkled brown face collapsed with apprehension. He snatched the bridle from Savage and stroked Valiant's neck.

"Where's 'is Lordship?" It was hard to know whether he addressed the horse or the butler. Then he issued orders to the undergroom who had followed him.

"Quick, rub him down. Get his blanket. What would His Lordship say to 'im in this state?"

Savage answered his question in a worried voice. "Mr Harper, we do not know." He paused. "Do you think that something has happened?"

Harper regarded him in horror. "Oh no, Mr Savage."

At that moment Pickering arrived. He was the youngest of the trio. A small man, not above five foot four inches in height, with a slender frame. He had joined His Lordship's household only three years previously. Despite his slight build, he was a prince of valets and although he had originally been regarded with suspicion by the older members of His Lordship's staff, the sheer virtuosity of his way with His Lordship's apparel had earned him a grudging respect and eventually a liking from the other important members of the household.

"No, what?" he demanded. "What has occurred?"

Wordlessly Harper pointed to the horse. "Came back like this." Savage's voice broke. "His Lordship. His Lordship. Where is His Lordship?"

Pickering looked from the worried face of the butler to the miserable face of the groom. "I think we must look for him." He spoke decisively. "It would seem to me that something untoward has happened to 'is Lordship and we must search for him."

The other two men nodded. At that moment Valiant threw back his head; he whinnied again, pulling at his bridle. The trio exchanged glances.

"Maybe he knows where he is." Harper spoke the thoughts of the other two. Then he turned to the undergroom. "Fetch horses and His Lordship's travelling carriage," he commanded. "Mr Pickering, I think you must go and inform Her Ladyship what has happened." The valet nodded.

The dowager Lady Heddington occupied rooms in the west wing of the house, their decoration reflecting the quiet elegance of the dowager herself. She was a small, indomitable woman, who remained, in old age, very beautiful. She had lost her husband and two sons but through the sheer strength of her character had managed to overcome these losses, which would have rendered many lesser women prostrate. Jaspar's eldest sister, Margaret, lived with her, acting as companion and whipping girl when the dowager lost her temper, which was not often, although she was not one to tolerate fools easily. Margaret had never married. She was a plain, nervous girl, who had been utterly terrified of all men. Now that she was older and no longer expected to contract an alliance she had lost some of her fear, but it was never likely to be completely relinquished. She doted on her grandmama and her numerous nephews and nieces, and was confidant and friend to Netta Egremount, who lived in the next village. Netta was the daughter of the local squire and had had the run of the Bardfield estate ever since she could walk. A little younger than Jaspar and Nillie, she had been an adoring shadow, entering into all their schemes in her wide-eyed way. Naturally of a more serious mien than the other two, she had, however, joined in with whatever project they were engaged. Although she hid it from him, it was common knowledge to members of the family that she was hopelessly in love with Jaspar.

Pickering knocked at the dowager's door. It was opened by Margaret. Both she and Netta were sitting with Her Ladyship. She looked askance as she saw Pickering's troubled face, but enquired in her calm way, "What is it, Pickering?"

"May I have a word with Her Ladyship, please, Miss Margaret?"

"Of course, won't you come in?" She opened the door and the little valet hurried to bow to Lady Heddington.

"Beg pardon for disturbing you, my lady, but Harper thought I had better inform you."

"Inform me?" Her ladyship's voice was sharp and firm.

"It seems... well... we are not sure... but... we think..."

"Come on. You think what Pickering?"

"My lord. Valiant came back, all puffed he was. His Lordship nowhere to be seen."

Netta turned pale. "I thought Jaspar was riding?" she asked.

"He was, Miss Netta. He said he would be here last night. We did not worry. Well, you know His Lordship," he continued in an anxious voice. "But now, with Valiant..."

"You mean that you think something may have happened to my grandson?"

"Yes, that's the long and the short of it, Your Ladyship."

"Then we must send out search parties immediately."

"That's what I have come to tell you. Mr Harper thinks Valiant might be able to lead us to His Lordship, so we are setting off with the horse."

Her Ladyship nodded brusquely. "Very wise. He's an excellent animal. Very intelligent too." She dismissed the valet. "Hurry now, no time to waste."

Lady Heddington turned to Netta. "Will you bear us company while we wait?"

Netta gasped. She nodded. "D... do you think he has met with an accident?"

"We shall have to wait and see, my dear," reflected Her Ladyship in composed tones.

Jaspar could move no more. He had only travelled a few hundred yards. He lay on the mossy ground. Blood seeped from his shoulder. In spite of the heat of the day, he was starting to shiver and he could not seem to stop. He was much regretting his stupidity in not staying at the Angel and Harp; anything was better than meeting his end in the forest. The trees above him looked no longer green but black and menacing against the blue sky. They kept going round and round. He tried to keep alert but to no avail. Slowly he found himself drifting into unconsciousness.

Valiant led the way. He knew exactly where he was going. It was only a few miles. Harper held his bridle whilst Pickering followed in the coach, which had some difficulty negotiating the branches, slowing their progress. As they grew closer to where Valiant had left Jaspar, the horse increased his pace, leaving the carriage behind them.

Suddenly Valiant stopped. There lying under the tree was Jaspar. Harper threw himself off his horse. He ran to him. His first thought was that his master was dead, so ashen and cold he was, but leaning over him he could feel his heart beating. He stripped off his own coat and wrapped His Lordship in it. Then he tore his shirt into strips and bound up the shoulder. Peering anxiously for Pickering, his eye alighted on Jaspar's coat and the small coin bag which lay where they had been discarded by the thieves. He picked them up. The coach seemed to be taking an age. It was with joy that he heard it, crashing through the undergrowth. He jumped up and waved at the under-groom who was driving.

"Over here! Over here!" he yelled.

Pickering sprang out of the carriage, his eyes bright with tears as he beheld his master lying there. "Is he…?" he ventured.

"No! Quickly, help me lift him."

Netta paced the floor. Margaret went to the window every two minutes and stared out. The dowager sat stiff and still in her chair. No one spoke.

Then Margaret saw the carriage. "I see it. I see it. It is right at the top of the drive."

Netta rushed to the window. "Do you think they have found him?"

The dowager nodded. "They would not be back if they had not, you can rest assured of that," she said simply.

Netta and Margaret ran downstairs. They stood at the front door and watched the coach as it made its laborious progress down the drive. Netta clutched Margaret's hand. "Oh, please let him be alive," she prayed to herself.

Gradually, the carriage got closer and closer. Netta found her heart beating so fast she thought she might explode. Eventually it was outside the front door. Harper followed, leading Valiant.

"Led us straight there 'e did," he commented.

"Is Lord Heddington… all… right?" Netta hardly dared ask the question.

"Well, he is in a very bad way, Miss Netta, but yes he is alive."

Netta felt the most overpowering sense of relief. He was still alive. She was much shocked, however, to see how ill he looked as they bore him from the coach. She turned quickly and ran upstairs to prepare his room, while Margaret conveyed the tidings to the dowager. Savage, immediately in control, sent the underfootman scurrying for Dr Watpell.

Jaspar was laid tenderly in his bed. The head of the house of Heddington occupied an enormous bedchamber, in the south wing of the house. The most impressive feature was a vast eight-poster bed, which was surrounded by embroidered silk hangings. These curtains had been a present from Queen Caroline to her namesake and goddaughter, Lady Caroline Varn, when she married the sixth Lord Heddington. They were decorated with flowers and Chinese animals and figures. Jaspar had been first moved in here, on the death of his father, when he was only twelve, and how scared he had been at leaving the comfort of the nursery for this huge place.

He opened his eyes. Waves of icy shivers flooded over him. He shook uncontrollably. He screwed up his eyes, trying to bring into focus the cupids which adorned the pedestals above him. They were strangely familiar. He had gazed at them throughout his childhood, their joyous round faces comforting him in the vast darkness of the nights. Could he be dreaming? He was surely in the woods but no, he seemed to be in his bedchamber. It could not be possible. He peered at the hangings. Yes, the exquisite embroidery. He knew every figure, every flower, every bird and deer. His wandering eyes caught the face above him. It was Netta. She was washing his shoulder tenderly.

"Netta?" he asked weakly. "Am I…"

"Do not talk, Jaspar. Yes, you are rescued. Valiant led them to you!"

Jaspar gave a ghost of a smile. "What an animal." Then his eyes closed again.

When he next came round Watpell was bending over him. The elderly doctor was shaking his head. "I… l do not like this fever, I must bleed him," he told Netta and Margaret, firmly. When the bleeding did not work, he suggested leeches. Still Jaspar deteriorated. He was delirious for most of the time now, the periods of lucidity becoming less and less. Restlessly his eyes flickered; now he was outside his body; peace engulfed him, a sense of comfort; then images of floating over flower-filled forests; suddenly he was conscious of an intense glowing light ahead; he knew he had somehow to reach it. Beyond him, framed by the silver rays of light there stood a beautiful woman dressed in white; she stretched out her hand but he couldn't touch her. She was utterly familiar, part of him, but he didn't know her. "Come, come, my love." Her voice comforted him. As it faded he felt a sense of tumultuous loss, then the red-haired girl covered in ice caressed his shoulder, leading him away from the familiar woman; he didn't want to leave. Pain, pain. He groaned, mumbling, "Angel, angel, come back, please."

Netta was now frantic; he was hardly alive. One morning, in desperation, she wrote the truth to Nillie. The countess, on receiving this hateful missive with news of Jaspar's lack of improvement, immediately summoned her travelling carriage, arriving within the day in a whirl of anxiety. Netta, who had been staring disconsolately out of the window, saw her carriage pull up and ran down the stairs to greet her. Nillie strode into the enormous hall and threw down her cloak.

"How is he?" she demanded.

Netta wrung her hands and swallowed. "Not very good, I am afraid," she said in a flat voice.

Netta was having to face an awful truth; it seemed that Jaspar would die. The thought was so appalling that Netta found she wanted to die herself.

"I think he may…" In spite of herself the tears started. Nillie looked at her in horror; this was far worse than she had anticipated if the calm and sensible Netta were in such a state. She put her arm around the girl.

"Let us go and see him," she suggested, her thoughts racing.

Netta sniffed. She followed the countess up to the huge bedchamber. Nillie pulled back the curtains around the bed and stared in alarm at her beloved brother. Jaspar seemed to have shrunk. He was so thin and so white. His lips were a blue colour and the gash on his face was livid.

He was delirious and was muttering, "Fiery, icy angels, please, fire do not melt… fire no… no, do not melt the ice. Who are you? Come back."

Margaret was by his bed, her face pale with exhaustion. She was holding his hand and a small tear trickled slowly down her face.

She rose when she saw Petronilla, and smiled weakly. Nillie beckoned to her and together they went to the other end of the room, where Netta had seated herself next to Her Ladyship. Nillie kissed her grandmother, then looked from face to face.

"What can we do?" she demanded. "There must be something?"

"Dr Watpell has tried everything, bleeding, leeches, he has nothing more to suggest," Margaret answered despairingly.

"There must be. He cannot die," Nillie responded uncomprehendingly. "Send for him again."

Netta coughed deprecatingly, then she bit her lip. "I do not want to seem to criticise but I think Jaspar is not receiving quite the best treatment." She vouchsafed slowly, "I believe that there is a new young doctor in Fittleworth. I hear that he works miracles."

"Then we must send for him, without hesitation. Why have you not done so before?" Nillie flared up in anxiety.

She crossed to Jaspar's writing desk and scribbled a quick note, requesting the presence of Dr Sugdon as a matter of urgency.

He equally promptly sent back his regrets. He did not attend this kind of patient. Please send for Watpell. Nillie, to whom the entire situation was her worst nightmare, stared at it in dismay.

"Why will he not come to us? How dare he? Does he not know who we are? I shall order him to come."

Netta bit her lip again. "I do not think that that would be wise. Dr Sugdon believes that he should be caring for the poor and the needy. The only way for you to get him here is to go to him and plead with him."

Nillie ordered the carriage. If pleading must be done, then she would beg. Jaspar was going to die. She must save him.

The journey to the village of Fittleworth seemed to take an age, although, in truth it was only just over half an hour. Dr Sugdon's house was a small cottage on the edge of the common. It overlooked the village pond where a few fat ducks swam lazily in the sunshine. Nillie jumped down. A small urchin stared open-mouthed at her and the grand equipage that was drawn up outside the doctor's door. Nillie knocked loudly on this door. It was opened by a plump-cheeked housekeeper.

"Is Dr Sugdon in? I need to see him urgently." The housekeeper gazed at her in admiration. "I am Lady Morntarny. Please, is he in?"

The housekeeper dropped a curtsey. "Oh yes, my lady, please to follow me." She led the way into a front parlour. "The doctor will not be long, he is just seeing to a patient."

Nillie, left alone, paced the floor. When the door opened and the doctor came in she was nearly past herself with frustration. Closing the door behind him, he regarded his fair visitor. She was, he observed, a very beautiful dark woman, elegantly gowned, her lovely face tight with worry.

Nillie stared at him. Dr Horace Sugdon was far younger than she had imagined and was dressed in the simple style of a villager. She noticed that he was not very tall, with sandy hair, freckles and the ruddy complexion that generally attends these attributes. He had broad hands with stubby fingers, but as he greeted her, he smiled, and his smile was intelligent and kindly.

"Good day, Lady Morntarny. How can I help you?" he enquired politely. "Please, won't you sit down?"

"Oh, I could not sit. I just come to ask you to see my brother."

"I wrote to you, my lady. I do not treat people from his class, my work is solely confined to the poor. They have no one to look after them. My medicines are for them," he repeated gently.

"I will pay you whatever you desire, if you will only come. Please!"

He stiffened slightly. "It is not a question of money. I cannot be bribed, my lady."

"Oh, please, I did not mean to offend you. Is there nothing that you want? Anything? I will give you anything." Nillie looked at him, her eyes filling with tears, in spite of herself. They slid down her face, dropping onto her fine muslin dress. "Please, please."

"My lady, you have your own doctors. Call Dr Watpell, he will attend your brother."

"He has come with his leeches and blooding, but Jaspar is worse, much worse. I… I…" she wrung her hands together, "… have a dread!"

"Leeches, blooding?" The doctor's voice sounded disgusted. "What is wrong with your brother?"

"He was set upon by footpads. He was shot and his wound festers. He has now a high fever and each day…" she gave a small sob, "… each day he gets worse. I am afraid he is going to die."

The tears flowed unchecked; she brushed her hand across her nose and sniffed loudly. Dr Sugdon was touched by her affliction. Silently, he handed her his handkerchief; she blew her nose loudly.

"Please come. You see, Jaspar is everything to me. My mama died when he was born. I was only an infant myself but I can just remember him as a baby. He was like my twin, we were

always together. I love him so…" she gave a convulsive sob, "…
s… so much." She raised her eyes to the doctor. "What will I do
if he dies?" She clutched her hands together over her mouth,
her body shaking with sobs. "I wish he were poor. If he were
poor, you would save him. Nothing else matters, you know." She
sniffed again and swallowed hard.

Dr Sugdon was moved. He had not previously understood
the severity of the case, and he was not a man who could turn
his back on any person in pain and Nillie's distress was so real,
so heartfelt.

"I will come."

Petronilla clasped his hands. "Thank you. Thank you. I do
not know how to thank you."

"Save your thanks. I may still not be able to help your
brother. Now, I do not think we can waste any time."

He crossed to a white-painted cupboard where he took out
strips of bandage which he wrapped in a large towel. He took
from the shelf various powders and ointments. Then he declared
himself ready and he followed Nillie into her carriage, which
was waiting to convey them to the hall.

During the journey Nillie hardly spoke; she sat tense on the
edge of her seat, twisting his handkerchief in her hands, silently
willing the horses to move faster. The doctor watched her.

"Relax, Your Ladyship. Your anxiety will not help your
brother."

She turned her huge dark eyes to him; they were wide with
trepidation. "Oh, do you think you can help?"

"I do not know but I have studied with Dr Hickman in Ludlow.
He has some new ideas which I consider very important."

She sat back in her seat. "Do you think they will help my
brother?"

He smiled slightly. "I think they have great potential for
relieving suffering, but I do not know if they will aid your
brother."

Eventually they reached the top of the drive. The sun, beginning to set, was casting its pink light over the house. Dr Sugdon caught his breath. It was so beautiful. The coach bowled smoothly down the straight drive, sweeping up to the huge porticoed front door. This was swung open as soon as they turned the corner and the doctor's startled gaze encountered three ladies on the doorstep. One was about sixty-five; she was small, very erect and dressed in the wide skirts of a previous generation. Her grey hair was arranged carefully on the top of her head; her eyes were dark blue and very piercing. The next lady was of indeterminate age; greying hair escaped from her cap and her stooped shoulders made her plain frock hang from her. The third was younger than the other two and he recognised her. She was Miss Egremont, the squire's daughter; her warm face carried an anxious expression.

As the carriage stopped, and before the footman could let down the steps, Nillie sprang out.

"He has come! I have brought him!" she called in triumph. Dr Sugdon followed her in a more sedate fashion.

"My grandmama, my sister and Miss Egremont." Casually, she waved her hand in the direction of the three anxious figures. "Please, follow me to my brother."

The doctor bowed to Her Ladyship, who extended her hand to him. "Doctor, we are most grateful to you." She inclined her head and smiled her charming smile. In spite of himself, Dr Sugdon found himself responding to the warmth in her expression.

"I am delighted to help."

Nillie was halfway up the wide staircase by this time. "Please do not waste time, Grandmama, please let the doctor see Jaspar."

Her Ladyship smiled again. "My granddaughter exhibits an impatience that I think we all feel, Doctor."

"Then I will attend my patient." He bowed and followed her up the stairs. Netta wrung her hands. "Oh! I do pray that he can do something."

Petronilla led the way into Jaspar's room and brought the doctor across to the bed. She pulled back the curtains. Dr Sugdon's eyes opened in astonishment.

"But I have treated this gentleman, at the Angel and Harp. He suffered a shot, in the left shoulder. I gave instructions. I said I would return but when I did, he had gone."

Now it was Nillie's turn to look surprised. "But we thought… He was found in the forest. He had been robbed and set upon. We thought… How could you have treated him?"

"He was shot in the Angel and Harp," he explained gently. "But let us examine him."

He took Jaspar's burning hand in his cool one; the pulse was racing. He pulled back the covers and exposed the shoulder; the wound was red and festering.

"I gave him some ointment to put on this. What happened to it?" he demanded angrily.

Nillie shook her head. "I do not know." She turned to Margaret and Netta, who had followed them into the room.

"There was some ointment. Dr Watpell refused to let us put it on him," Netta replied, her voice anguished. "Oh, I am so sorry, if only we had done so." Her voice suspended with tears she was unable to continue.

Dr Sugdon smiled at her. "It is not your fault but now you must obey my instructions absolutely." She nodded.

"Please go to the kitchens and boil some water. It must be boiled for fifteen minutes. You must supervise this, for I find that servants do not understand the importance. This water, and only this water, must be used to wash His Lordship's injury. All the dressings that are put on the wound must also be boiled for fifteen minutes and before you touch my lord, you must all wash your hands with this soap." He pulled a tablet of soap from his bag and handed it to Netta. "He must only drink water that has been boiled and he must take this powder immediately and one later tonight."

Netta hurried away to boil the water; Dr Sugdon covered Jaspar. When she returned he washed his own hands with soap and removed the soiled dressings. He washed the wound carefully and instructed the devoted Netta on how to spread it with the ointment and dress it with the boiled bandages. Margaret, Petronilla and Lady Heddington all observed scrupulously so that they too could play their part in the nursing, but it was clear to them all that Netta was to be in charge. Dr Sugdon obviously placed great reliance on her abilities, and she responded with her customary good sense. When he had finished with Jaspar, His Lordship already appeared more comfortable, although his fever still raged and he was very delirious. Lady Heddington requested that Dr Sugdon join her for some refreshments in the book room; somewhat to his surprise he found that he wished to do so.

Jaspar's grandfather had had an obsession with his houses and a particular fondness for Grosvenor Square and Bardfield Hall. He had commissioned Adam to extensively remodel these two and had spared no expense to make them the most esteemed residences in the county. The library had been his favourite room and no expense had been spared for its glory. It stretched the full 400 feet of the rear of the mansion, with a breathtaking view over the gardens; these formed a consummate contrast to the simplicity which characterised the front of the house, being Italian in design, very elaborate and decorative. There was an enchanting maze, dozens of strategically placed statues, rose gardens and endless tiers of flowerbeds all carefully planted with seasonal blooms. The family were able to admire the superlative view through fifteen windows; seven of which with cushioned window seats, so that in inclement weather they were still able tostill gaze at the beauty of the vista; reposed on either side of the central bays, which were full length and opened out onto a gravel terrace. This terrace gave way to a double pair of stairs, which wound down onto a lower terrace, in the middle of which a vast fountain, decorated in an Italianate way with angels, cupids, baskets of fruit and flowers, tossed its crystal drops onto the white marble.

The library was curved at each end. Its ceiling was exquisitely painted, and the chairs and tables had been designed by Adam to complement the pink and green décor. The walls were lined with an extensive collection of books.

The doctor's natural appreciation of beauty was roused by the room and sight of Lady Heddington, who sat straight-backed in a chair by the open window, gazing out at the gardens. Her face had the slight lost look of someone who is suffering great anguish but she turned as he came in and greeted him warmly. He found himself responding afresh to her immense charm.

"Please, Dr Sugdon, come and sit with me." She indicated the chair opposite her. It was a beautiful evening and the smell from the flowers of the orange blossom wafted their scent into the room, filling the library with its fragrance. Lady Heddington nodded to a footman, who poured a glass of wine which he handed to the doctor.

"Can I offer you anything else?" she asked. He shook his head. She nodded dismissal to the footman and he withdrew. Then she turned to Dr Sugdon. "I do not think that I have had the pleasure of making your acquaintance before?" she went on. "How long have you been established at Fittleworth?"

He smiled. "About two years. I come from Yorkshire. My father was a village apothecary, in fact my grandfather, my great-grandfather and even, I believe, my great-great-grandfather were all apothecaries. I have grown up with an interest in medicine. When I was a small boy I was determined to be the best doctor in the world!" His eyes glowed and she smiled, picturing the small boy's eagerness. "To that end I went to St Bartholomew's medical school where I was privileged enough to work under David Pitcairn. I have also studied all over England and in Paris," he went on proudly.

She nodded and he noticed the real interest in her dark eyes. "Please tell me more," she demanded.

He smiled. "If you are sure I am not boring you, my lady." She shook her head vigorously. "Medicine is at the crossroads. Great changes will take place in the next twenty years, I am sure of it." He started to enlarge on the topic that obsessed him and found in Her Ladyship a ready listener.

Many of the concepts that he expounded were quite new to her, but she had a sharp intelligence and was extremely inquisitive about new ideas. She settled back to listen intently as he talked. It was dark when he finished describing all that he believed in.

CHAPTER EIGHT

Netta sat by Jaspar's bed. The sun was sinking and it was beginning to get dark. She was alone in the room but she did not mind, for she relished the moments by herself with Jaspar. They were quite precious. Before she rang for candles she allowed herself the indulgence of holding his hand. Jaspar's hands were beautiful, with long, elegant, strong fingers. As Netta picked it up she remarked its thinness. Caressing it gently, she watched him. He was very restive but she thought she detected a slight diminution in the heat, for although his hand was very dry and hot, it did not seem to be burning as it had before. Or perhaps it was just her hopeless imaginings. She stared intently at his face; even with its drawn appearance and the closed eyes, it was still extraordinarily handsome. She glanced over her shoulder; the room was hushed and silent. Then she bent over him and kissed his lips. They were rather dry, but still felt soft and smooth to hers. She sighed deeply, replaced his hand gently on the bed and, clasping her own together over her lips, she closed her eyes, dropping her head into her hands and running her fingers through her mousy curls. She loved him so desperately. If he died… She shivered. He groaned and turned restlessly, tossing his head slightly. She leant over him and, raising him carefully, she placed a glass of boiled water to his lips. Whereas, in previous days it had been almost impossible to get him to drink, now he gulped thirstily at the water, quickly finishing the glass. She poured another and this he also speedily dispatched. She did not want to allow herself to hope but her depressed spirits rose a little. The jug of boiled water was empty. She gently deposited Jaspar back on the pillows and moved across to ring for Pickering. The valet was with her almost before the bell had finished ringing.

"My lord has finished the water." Netta held the jug out to him. "Please go to the kitchen and prepare some more."

Pickering grinned as he took the empty jug from her outstretched hands. "Oh, Miss Netta, do you think…?" He paused, peering at his master in the gloom. "He looks a little less disturbed, don't you think?"

"I thought it might just be my imagination," Netta added, "but it is hard to see."

"Oh, miss, I will bring lights immediately!"

That was not quite what Netta had meant but she nodded agreement, and the valet hurried away to fulfil her orders. She sat back down on the chair, in which she had spent so many anxious hours over the last few weeks of Jaspar's illness. She picked up his hand again. No, it was not imagination, it did feel cooler. She put her hand on his brow; that too was not burning as it had through the last few weeks. Tears gushed unheeded from her eyes, plopping onto the smooth white linen sheets. She heard the door open behind her and, expecting the return of Pickering, she did not move.

"How is he?" came the dowager's firm voice. "Netta, why are you crying?"

Netta jumped up guiltily. She sniffed and, reaching for her handkerchief, she blew her nose noisily. "Oh, my lady," she swallowed. "I… I do not want to say it… but… but I think he feels a little cooler. The fever has not broken but he is less restless… and feel his head."

The dowager moved extremely fast for one of her years and

was beside the bed in a moment. She put her own hand on her grandson's head and she nodded satisfactorily.

"Yes, Netta, I agree." She opened her arms and hugged the girl. "Let us hope it does not change."

By this time Pickering had returned and they had the satisfaction of seeing Jaspar consume another whole jug of water. He then lay back on the covers and slept.

The night was long. Netta refused to leave her post. If it were true and Jaspar were improving, she wanted to be there, by his side. Lord Heddington was tossing and the earlier coolness seemed to have disappeared, or at least the drop in his temperature had not been maintained. However, he continued to consume large quantities of water. Somewhere just before dawn, Netta stood up stiffly. She stretched her cramped limbs and wandered over to the window.

The sky was streaked with bands of light, bright against the grey. The sun was rising and Netta watched the tiny arch of gold creeping up over the horizon. She breathed out quietly; it was going to be another beautiful day. She watched as it rapidly became light, then she turned back to Jaspar. Her hand flew to her mouth. Drops of sweat were running down his face. She moved quickly to his side and wiped them gently from his head, but within half an hour his bed was drenched. Joyously, she leapt to her feet and tugged the bell pull for Pickering. The valet, obeying her peremptory summons, hurried in, shaking the sleep from his eyes.

"It has broken! The fever has broken!" Netta, sobbing, grabbed Pickering, whirling him around. "Look! Look!" She pointed at his perspiring master.

The valet could hardly speak but eventually he stuttered, "Oh, Miss Netta, Miss Netta." He sniffed, then his practicality reasserted itself. "Come, we must change his sheets."

By the time that eight o'clock struck on the grandfather clock in the hall, the pile of soaking sheets had grown inordinately, but

His Lordship was without fever and sleeping peacefully. Netta and Pickering had worked without ceasing for three hours and Netta did not think she had ever been so exhausted or so happy.

"Miss Netta, enough now," Pickering reprimanded. "You must go and have some rest."

Netta, who by now was quite light-headed by lack of sleep, found herself giggling slightly hysterically. "Yes, yes, I will go but first I must convey the best of tidings to the family."

So she ran to Lady Heddington's suite, bursting in on Her Ladyship, shaking her awake, glowing with her excellent news.

"Lady Heddington! Lady Heddington! He is saved. He is without fever."

The dowager sat bolt upright. She looked at Netta wordlessly then she sprang out of bed and ran down the corridors to her grandson's room, clad only in her nightdress and her bedcap. Netta then hurried to wake up Margaret and Nillie and by eight-fifteen all four doting ladies were gathered around His Lordship's bed giggling happily at the sight of him, serenely asleep.

Later that morning Dr Sugdon arrived to see his patient. He was, not unnaturally, delighted by news of the improvement. Jaspar was awake when the doctor was shown in. He was very white and his eyes were still dull but he was making sense and all traces of the fever had abated. The doctor crossed to the bed.

"Good morning, my lord, I am pleased to see such progress, it is most gratifying." He smiled his pleasant smile.

Jaspar responded weakly. "I believe I have you to thank, Doctor, for my recovery," he said with some difficulty. "I remember it was…"

"Yes, the Angel and Harp… but do not exhaust yourself by trying to now."

Jaspar gestured by shaking his head and glancing at Nillie, who stood at the end of his room with Margaret.

"That is alright, my lord, I won't say anything more, but I should warn you that I did inform Lady Morntarny that I had treated you in the Angel. I really had no choice."

Jaspar inclined his head, indicating that he understood. Dr Sugdon patted him on the arm. "Now, as your doctor, I must insist that you rest."

Jaspar regained his strength remarkably quickly for one who had been so ill. Horace Sugdon was delighted with the progress made by his illustrious patient. It had not taken him long to find out that Lord Heddington, although partaking in many of the pursuits of the *ton*, did not subscribe to the worst excesses of society. He did not drink immoderately, nor did he overindulge himself with food. A natural athlete, he fenced with Signor Fancini; sparred with gentleman John Jackson at his salon in Bond Street. An inveterate hunter, his winter months were spent at Belvoir Castle or Cheveley, where he remained unaffected by the cold and dirt that so discomforted his best friend, Brummell. It was this natural vigour that, Horace decided, had contributed in such a large part to what, by any means, must be regarded as a miraculous recovery.

To start with, Jaspar was so weak that he did not oppose his enforced confinement. He lay in the immense eight-poster and watched the light on the faces of the carved cupids as it changed during the course of the day. His thoughts floated unrestrained, as if in space, returning again and again to the red-haired girl. He could remember with exactitude all the events that led up to his being shot. He remembered her eyes, her enchanting smile, the feel of her skin, his lips on hers. Who was she? Why had she shot him? He remembered Dr Sugdon treating him and the men in the woods, but there was something else. He forced his mind to try to bring his thoughts into focus. There was something. Something he had forgotten. Something he was sure that would help him find out who she was. As he became stronger, his inability to move became more irksome. One morning about two weeks later, he awoke feeling much recovered. He heaved himself into a sitting position and with some difficulty pulled back the bed curtains.

It was a fine October morning and the autumn sun was slanting through the windows, falling in pools on the Aubusson carpets. The birds were singing. It felt wonderful. He swung his legs over the side of the bed and stood up slowly. His limbs felt like jelly, and his head spun. He grasped the carved bedpost, took a deep breath and waited for the faintness to dissipate. When it did, he moved gingerly towards the windows and peered out. It was, he realised, very early and the sun was still coming up. It caught the copper tips of the beech trees in the home park, making them seem aflame. He watched as a half-grown fawn detached itself from the group of deer running between the trees. Its head held high, it sniffed the breeze as it slowly sauntered up across the lawns, under the spreading cedar trees, towards the house. Jaspar felt overcome with a great and unexpected love for his house and his gardens. He had never, before the accident, questioned his land, his mansions, his wealth; he had accepted all that he possessed without thought. Now he knew that he would never be the same. The brush with mortality had sharpened his senses, had made him deeply aware of despair, of the fragility of life. Of how precious it was. He stood at the window watching the fawn and the sun, and the copper trees waving in the wind. Then he sighed. He glanced around his room, the Aubusson tapestry hangings, the ornate carved furniture. His eyes lit on his Chippendale desk. It looked out of place in the room, which had not been redesigned by Adam but was as it had been in the previous centuries. He sat at the desk; its delicate sweeping lines pleased his eye. Idly he wondered whether to rid himself of the seventeenth-century carved oak and replace the furniture with the more modern Chippendale.

The desk was laden with neat piles of papers awaiting his attention. Next to these, his eye caught sight of the coin bag, carefully placed there by Harper. He picked it up and while examining it he remembered the ice maiden. She had thrown a bag of coins at him. But why? Inadvertently, he suspected that as she had tried to destroy his life by shooting him; no that was not true, the injury he had sustained at her hands was minor; she had, in fact, saved his life, as he was sure that the gold coins which the bag contained had certainly prevented the footpads from killing him outright. But why had she given him money? He pondered. Then as the world started to revolve again he thought he had better retreat to the protection of the eight-poster. Ensconced back on his pillows, the relief was intense, the disappointment severe. He had hoped that his return to health would be faster. However, it was not all discouraging for, for the first time, this morning he discovered that he was very hungry.

Jaspar was, on the whole, a considerate employer. He had been taught by his father that more was to be obtained from servants if they were well handled. Jaspar's father was not an altruistic man, but he saw clearly the efficacy of treating servants with regard. They worked harder and caused less problem. It would not, however, have occurred to Jaspar not to ring for Pickering at this hour. He was generous to a point to his staff, but expected them to be ready at any time for him. He tugged the bell hard. Within minutes Pickering, still clad in night attire, arrived, his thin face worried.

"Yes, my lord, are you quite well?"

"Quite well," smiled Jaspar, "but ravenously hungry. Please send to the kitchen for breakfast."

"Immediately, my lord. It is a pleasure to see Your Lordship so ready to partake of his food. It will be of great happiness, my lord, to us all, to see you."

"Yes, Pickering," interrupted Jaspar. "Enough. Breakfast."

The little valet scurried away down to the kitchens. He was sure that Jaspar's expensive French chef, Baptiste, would not yet be at his post, but hoped that the under-chef would be up and stirring. His hopes were realised. George was a young man with great ambitions. He liked to be at his post early, that way he could imagine himself in charge of the entire edifice.

Pickering hurried in, his face relaxed when he saw George, who was as tall as Pickering was short.

"Oh, good. His Lordship, hungry he is, wants his breakfast right now." He beamed.

George needed no further bidding as Pickering rushed away to dress. He whisked eggs, prepared coffee, made fresh slices of toast.

Jaspar lay in bed waiting for his breakfast. He considered the small leather bag of coins. What was it that he could not recollect? It was irritating him. Pickering returned; he drew back the curtains and fussed over the bedclothes.

"Pickering…"

"Yes, my lord. I did not hurt you, my lord, did I?"

"No," Jaspar, amused, replied. "I want you to ask Dr Sugdon to dine with me tonight."

"But, my lord, will you be well enough?"

"Pickering…" The familiar tone in His Lordship's voice made the valet realise with some pleasure that His Lordship was on the mend.

"Yes, my lord, of course. Dr Sugdon, I will send to him immediately." He scurried away to dispatch the invitation and procure the breakfast.

Jaspar rested for most of the day, consequently when his guest was shown into the room that evening, he felt robust enough to stand to greet him. He shook the doctor's hand.

"My lord, I am pleased to see you looking so well," Sugdon said simply.

Jaspar grinned. "Not half as pleased as I am to feel so very much better." Then he sat back onto the chaise and motioned to the doctor to sit on the chair which had been carefully placed by Pickering. Horace sat down. The footman brought him a drink on a silver tray, and once he had seen that his guest had refreshment, Jaspar dismissed the servants.

"I want to thank you," Jaspar started.

"No. No thanks necessary." The doctor made to demur.

Jaspar gestured to him to stop. "But they are… you saved my life and I am inordinately grateful."

"It was nothing."

Jaspar grinned again. The doctor thought his smile so particularly attractive it would be hard not to respond to it. "Perhaps nothing to you but as it is my life, it cannot be thought of as nothing by me."

Horace laughed. "Once the right treatment was administered it was your own strength, my lord, that effected the improvement. If you had not seen fit to ignore my original advice at the Angel and Harp, I profess that you would not have needed to be so ill."

Jaspar sighed. He nodded. "I see that now and as I lay in the woods, I much regretted my folly." He paused, looked shrewdly at the doctor's steady face. "I know that I can trust you."

Horace nodded. "Unnecessary, my lord."

"Yes." He hesitated again. "Th… well, as you know, I was shot in the Angel…" Horace watched his mobile face but said nothing. "I was shot by a…" Jaspar looked slightly embarrassed, "… a girl… a red-haired girl. Did you, perhaps, see her?" The doctor shook his head slightly as Jaspar continued. "No? Ah, I had hoped that someone would know who she was. I… I… do not know why she shot me nor indeed who shot me. I think when I was at my worst she was part of my dreams, she was there, and another woman was summoning me, warm and loving, whom strangely seemed part of me. She heartened me but yet I don't know who she was."

Horace regarded him sagely. "I have heard of others, patients, who near death are solaced by these things, lights, angels? We don't know what it means." He stopped, remaining silent for a moment. "You could, however, try asking Mr Melow." Jaspar looked doubtful and Horace well understood why he might feel reserved about making such enquiries. "I saw no one. I was summoned by Melow to treat you and when I reached the inn you were the only person in the room."

"I did not tell my family about the incident at the Angel. I did not understand it myself and as I was, indubitably, set upon by footpads in the woods, it seemed easier to allow them to believe that this was the sole cause of my injuries."

"Yes, I can see that," the doctor agreed wisely. "But do you have any idea who hated you so much that she would have wanted to kill you?"

"I do not think she wanted to kill me," Jaspar went on pensively. "If she had wanted to do that, she had every opportunity but I received only the merest scratch. That is what makes it even more inexplicable. I have enemies, what man in my position does not? Oddly, she saved my life."

Horace raised an eyebrow.

"Yes, strange, isn't it? She threw a bag of coins at me which, I imagine, Melow must have returned to my coat thinking them mine."

"No! That was me. I found them on the floor next to you and I placed them in your pocket."

"Oh, well those coins were, I believe, instrumental in saving my life. I told the thieves that I had nothing but one of the men went through my pockets and discovered them; they were quite pleased." Horace laughed. "I think if I had had nothing they would have put an end to me, just out of spite."

Savage knocked discreetly at the door. On being bidden to enter, he grandly announced dinner. Jaspar motioned agreement, so Savage gestured to the two footmen who stood in the doorway bearing trays, laden with delicacies painstakingly prepared by Baptiste for a master who needed, no doubt, to be tempted to eat and for a guest who had become, in the eyes of His Lordship's household, something of a god.

Jaspar and Horace sat down at opposite ends of the table to eat. Jaspar was still not recovered enough to do more than pick at the food but Horace made an excellent meal. Whilst they ate, Jaspar kept the subjects of conversation general, but once the servants had withdrawn, he announced that he had something of import to discuss with the doctor. At this point, however, Horace's professional expertise asserted itself. He stood up, came round to Jaspar, and took his pulse, which had increased somewhat, and noted that his patient was becoming very pale and his mouth was tinged with grey.

"I will stay and talk to you, my lord, but only if you return to your bed."

And it was only once Jaspar was safely restored to this sanctuary that Horace allowed him to continue.

"First, I want you to tell me a little about yourself," Jaspar demanded. "It is obvious to me that you possess the most superior healing skills, but from whence do they come? With whom have you studied?"

"It's quite a long story, my lord, but to summarise, as I told Lady Heddington, my father was an apothecary and his father before him and his father before that. We have all treated the sick, grew up with it, just as you grew up with the conception of caring for your estates." Jaspar inclined his head. He understood completely.

"My father was an exceptional man. True, he possessed no learning but I have never known a man so wise. He had an extraordinary, intuitive understanding of how people worked and a…" He paused. "I do not quite know how to describe it. A magic way of healing. He taught me all that he knew. Although the inherent, innate, instinct is something that one cannot learn. It is simply just there. In addition, he was obsessed by the learning he had not had. Hence him christening me Horace."

The brown eyes twinkled. "He was determined that I should be instructed in mathematics, Latin, the science of astronomy. Our village was lucky enough to possess a school. It had been started by the vicar and it was fortunate in its quite exceptional teacher."

To his surprise, he found himself confiding in Jaspar. He had come prepared to be indifferent to his host, whose notoriety was all too familiar to him and whose lifestyle he quite openly deplored, but he was finding it impossible to dislike Jaspar. Lord Heddington was one of those rare beings who possess an unconscious magnetic charm to which everyone responds. Men were drawn to him, women adored him. He, himself, was supremely unaware of this attraction, which only succeeded in making him all the more appealing. Jaspar, for his part, was unversed in the ways of men of Horace's persuasion, but he, too, found himself liking and respecting the man in front of him.

The Heddington family was part of the Whig aristocracy that had governed England throughout the eighteenth century. Unlike their foreign counterparts, the Whig aristocrats were a governing class and to them, this meant an obligation to govern. By the beginning of the nineteenth century their supremacy was in decline; it could only have lasted whilst they maintained the economic predominance, and the start of the Industrial Revolution changed the bias of the influences. The authority began to move to other ranks.

Jaspar had been educated in the great tradition of the Whigs. A confident knowledge of the world that was neither pedantic nor uncouth. Despite the huge houses and vast estates there was an appealing informality about the vitality with which they tolerated the individuals who peppered their society. Jaspar had this openness, this forbearance, this ability to appreciate and enjoy.

Both men's upbringing was alien to the other but both found themselves responding identically. The handsome, long-limbed, ironical, spirited aristocrat and the stocky, down-to-earth doctor discovered a mutual understanding that was as gratifying as it was unexpected.

After some little more discussion, Horace rose to go. It was clear to him that Jaspar was, by this time, very tired, although nothing would have compelled him to admit it. However, it was hard to escape the discerning eye of his doctor and new friend.

"My lord, I have talked quite enough for one night. I must take my leave of you now. You must rest."

"Dr Sugdon, one thing before you go. I have a request for you." The doctor looked slightly puzzled, but Jaspar continued. "I would like you to be the doctor to my tenants. To be the doctor on my estates."

Horace looked amazed. He had not expected this at all. "My lord, I am most flattered but I have already many patients. I must decline."

"No! Do not decline before you have heard my full proposition." Jaspar went on wearily, "I want to build you a hospital, here on my land. You may treat all your old patients and my tenants; we will make it the most…" He drew in his breath with exhaustion.

"No, my lord, you must not say any more. I order you to rest."

Jaspar smiled a half smile. "If… if you promise to agree."

Horace laughed. "I promise to return tomorrow and discuss it further."

"No, agree!"

Horace shook his head, smiling again. "Let me think tonight."

He rang for Pickering, who hurried in, clucking like a worried hen when he perceived how exhausted his master looked.

"Oh, sir, you have fair tired him out," he reprimanded.

"He will come to no harm, I assure you, but now he must rest." He took Jaspar's elegant hand in his own broad brown one. "Goodnight, my lord, and thank you."

 98

CHAPTER NINE

Horace rode home slowly. As he deliberated Jaspar's proposal its obvious advantages become clearer and clearer. He had always yearned for his own hospital. It had been his boyhood dream and now, through my Lord Heddington's generosity, that dream could become a reality. Horace had always had very precise ideas of what he wanted; indeed, it had been planned in his mind ever since he understood the function of hospitals. His ideas would, he knew, cost a great deal. For his hospital must be the best and that, of necessity, would be expensive; however, he had a feeling that Jaspar would be munificent. He rapidly decided that not only would it be churlish to refuse, it would also be idiotic. His only prerequisite must be that the control of it must be his. Then he laughed; it was hard to imagine Lord Heddington interfering in the care of the sick.

Having decided to accept, his thoughts turned to Jaspar. His experience of the aristocracy was very limited, indeed almost non-existent, but whatever opinions he might have had, had quite been reversed through his talk with Jaspar tonight. He wondered why he had never married. Even men with his predilection for licentiousness usually married, and then he corrected his thoughts; Jaspar was not dissolute. He had thought from his reputation that he would have been, but he had shown tonight that if an unprincipled part existed, it was only one facet of his personality. Horace liked him hugely. He felt drawn to the man. Jaspar was, he had to admit, very attractive. He laughed out loud; he could understand how those girls fell for him; he felt rather sorry for them. As he came to the outskirts of Fittleworth, he suddenly felt pleased. His own hospital, he could do so much good. He went to bed delighted with what had occurred.

Jaspar, too, as he lay in the vast bed, was pleased. He prided himself on his management of the estates. He enjoyed obtaining the latest and newest implements for his farms and to provide the latest and best in medical care. That was satisfying. He fell asleep.

Jaspar's progress from thence was very rapid. A month later he was almost completely recovered, his convalescence complete. Only the stiffness in the shoulder and the edict from Dr Sugdon that he must not as yet hunt remained. Another injury to the shoulder now might, the good doctor pointed out, mean permanent disability. So with some poor grace, Jaspar obeyed. It was now late November, as wet a November as he could ever remember. The rain lashed down relentlessly every day, making the ground so sodden that it became almost impossible to ride.

Certainly, riding as he liked, fast and hard over the countryside, was quite out of the question. Jaspar was bored. Once he had established the principle of building Horace's hospital, and had helped him to find the appropriate site and the doctor had gone off to finalise the plans, there was little more that Jaspar could do for the project at this time. He felt restless and irritable; his household fussed over him and it was as much as he could do not to snap at their solicitous enquiries.

One afternoon, he stood at the window in the library watching the sheets of rain that fell from an unremittingly grey sky. A few remaining leaves hung despairingly from the branches of the trees as if waiting to be washed away to nothingness. He sighed deeply; this lowness of spirits would not do. It was so unlike him. He had never before been afflicted with the regular bouts of unhappiness that affected other mortals. He sighed again. A gentle tap on the door and Netta came in. She took a look at him and concern flooded over her homely face. He looked so bleak, so drawn; she hated to see him like this.

"Oh, Jaspar, are you quite alright? You look a little pale. You are not in a draught, are you? Is your shoulder paining you? Please do sit down, it cannot be good for you to stand thus by the window."

"Oh, Netta! For God's sake stop it! Leave me alone! Do not fuss!" he snapped. "I am a grown man and not a child!"

Netta jumped as if he had slapped her; tears sprung to her eyes; she bit her lip, trying not to cry. Jaspar looked at her; he was too testy to notice the stricken look on her face. She sniffed, awkward, wanting to leave but unsure of how to get out of the room. She felt as if she had been stung. Jaspar had never spoken to her like that. At that moment she was saved; Margaret came into the library.

"Oh, Jaspar," she fluttered, "Grandmama wants you. Will you go to her, please?"

Jaspar flung out of the room. He knew he was unjustified in raking down Netta, the girl meant well but, truly, it was insufferable to be twitted over by a parcel of women. How he missed London; Brummell, Yarmouth, Brooks. *I am mad*, he thought, *I do not have to remain here any longer. To London I go. Now. Today.* He felt immediately much relieved; his bad temper melted away like snow in the sun. He felt cheerful and energetic and altogether more like his old self. How could he have been so idiotic to have remained here so long? He strode up the stairs to his grandmother's suite with a new purposeful stride, calling to Savage on the way to tell Pickering that they left for London immediately and to tell the butler to inform Harper to have the travelling coach brought around in an hour.

Lady Heddington was seated on a chaise by the window gazing at the rain. He kissed her cheek. As he did so, she noticed a change in him; the fractious, tense look that had been concerning her for the last few weeks had quite disappeared.

"How beautiful you are," Jaspar commented, kissing her hands. "If I were not a relative, I declare I would lose my heart to you. You wonderfully wicked old lady," he teased. She laughed, secretly delighted that he seemed to be returning to his old self. "I am going to London," he announced.

Her face changed. She looked shocked. "London! Do you think, dear, that you are?"

His face clouded. "Grandmama! If you start fussing over me I will return to my previous ill-humour. It is quite bad enough with Netta and Margaret like a pair of mother ducks."

Lady Heddington was a very astute woman. She was suddenly aware of how their natural concern over his misadventure had irked him. She stopped her next comment, and merely asked, "Good. When do you leave?"

"As soon as I have bade farewell to you!"

She patted the chaise. "Jaspar, dearest, come sit by me a second. I have something I want to say to you."

He sat down next to her. She paused. "I do not quite know you will receive what I say, but please hear me out… I say these things for two reasons: one, you are the head of the family and you have no heir. No brothers. No male cousins." She raised her eyes to his to see how he was receiving her words. "You owe it to the family…"

" I know. I understand." He stood up and walked towards the window. The rain was ceasing and the horizon seemed to be brightening. "I know I need to marry. I am not insensitive to what I owe to my name and to my estates. I have no heir and, as you point out, no brother with a quiverful of hopeful children." He turned back to her. "I, too, have been made aware of what would have occurred if I had died. Even before I was ill,

I was becoming conscious that I must wed but now it becomes imperative." He sighed, saying with wry humour, "But to whom?" He knelt down beside her and looked straight into her eyes. "Whom shall I make my bride?"

She looked perplexed, weighed up his benign mood and made her suggestion. "Netta?" she said quietly. "How about Netta?"

Jaspar's head went up in surprise. "Netta!" he exclaimed. "Netta!"

"She will make an excellent wife. She may not be quite to your choice, for I know you favour beauties."

He laughed. "Now, who told you that?"

"I may be an old woman but you need not think that I do not know what is going on in town."

"Indeed, I would never be so presumptuous," he went on, amused.

His mood being so receptive, she continued gently. "She is an admirable girl, Jaspar, and she is so eminently sensible that she will never interfere with you. You may do exactly as you please."

She watched him carefully to see how he greeted her words.

His mouth twisted and he replied wryly, "I am not sure that I want a wife who does not care what I do."

"Oh, do not mistake me, Netta cares greatly, it is just that she will not expect…" She stopped. "She will not be upset."

"It does not sound very agreeable," he rejoindered flatly. Then he smiled. "But if it will please you, my dearest…" He kissed her hand.

"Please me! No, Jaspar, that is not what I meant. You must want to marry her."

He turned away. "It is a matter of supreme indifference to me whom I marry, so I might as well please you."

Lady Heddington watched him unhappily. It was her dearest wish to see him settled comfortably and she was terribly fond of Netta and knew how much the girl loved Jaspar. She was intelligent, she knew how the estates worked. It seemed so sensible. They were both silent and the silence sat between them uneasily. Eventually Jaspar smiled.

"I will think on it. Now, I must go if I am to be in London by nightfall. Farewell." He kissed her cheek and whirled out of the room. On the stairway he encountered Netta. She blushed an unattractive pink as she saw him.

"I am sorry if I…" she mumbled.

He dismissed her stuttered apology with the wave of an arm. "Netta, I leave within the hour for London. I just want to bid you *adieu*."

Her face paled; she did not want him to go. She knew that. She swallowed and replied in an unnaturally bright voice, "I see, Jaspar. Is there anything you need?"

He found himself irrationally annoyed by her innocent enquiry, but biting back the retort that sprung to his lips he merely answered, "No," and passed by her, down the main corridor of the house towards his bedchamber.

Here he found Pickering surrounded by portmanteaux, and a huge pile of Jasper's clothes. He was somewhat desperately trying to pack with all speed, assisted by a young footman, who did not appear to be accomplishing his tasks to the high standards that Pickering set himself.

"Oh, my lord, if only you had given us just a little more notice," he said despairingly.

Jaspar laughed. "Pickering, you know I expect you to be ready at any moment. That is why I pay you those immoderate wages," he teased. "Simply stick them all in. And let's be off."

"My lord! My lord!" Pickering's shocked face made Jaspar laugh even more. "Our clothes! Our reputation! Suppose Mr Robinson were to hear of it." The valet swallowed in pain.

"But I will not tell anyone, least of all Brummell, and if George does not know, then how could his valet?"

Pickering gave a shudder. He drew himself up to his full height. "I cannot bear it, my lord. I shall be forced to hand in my notice." The valet beamed.

Within the hour they were on the road. As a concession to his wound, Jaspar let Harper drive. He felt inordinately happy. He loved Bardfield but for the first time in his life he was pleased to be leaving it. He had felt trapped over the last few weeks and it was an immense relief to be away from all that fretting about his welfare. Jaspar prided himself on his cattle, and the team that Harper had chosen were the best in Lord Heddington's stable. His coach was of the latest design. It was light and very well sprung. Jaspar threw off the travelling rug that Netta had solicitously placed on his knee, and watched the countryside speed by. It was an extraordinary evening. The sky was still grey with rain, but long rays from the setting sun shone through the banks of dark clouds, shedding a golden light on the bare fields and dripping trees, which stood black and spiky against the translucent horizon. He watched fascinated as the light dipped and fell over the fields and smiled as a huge rainbow flung itself across the sky, its colours brighter than he had ever seen them before. Slowly it grew dark and as they grew closer to London the sky cleared and it became much colder. Jaspar grinned. He picked up the rug and replaced it on his knees. He thought about Netta and his grandmother's proposition. He knew that he had altered since being shot but just how great those changes were, he did not yet know. Could he make the compromises necessary to marry someone of whom he was very fond but undoubtedly did not love, then love? He was sure that in ten years on the town he had never loved anyone. Not as Nillie loved Greville. As he pondered these matters, the coach swept into the city, and, at last, drew up outside the mansion in Grosvenor Square.

Jaspar sprang down without waiting for the groom to let down the steps. Harper threw the reins to the under-groom and banged on the door. It was swung open by a footman, who gasped as he saw Jaspar strolling up the steps. As he crossed his threshold, the household seemed to be in disarray. The butler, scrambling into his coat, half ran into the hall.

"Oh, my lord. Oh, my lord. You are recovered. You are here!"

"Yes, York. I am here. It seems that my presence has deprived my entire household of their wits." He waved a hand casually at the assembled servants, who were staring at him.

York, who by this time had regained his senses, gestured to the servants to be about their duties. He bowed low to Lord Heddington and, much on his dignity, led him into the book room.

Here a housemaid was swiftly lighting a fire.

"We did not expect Your Lordship," York continued reproachfully.

Jaspar laughed. "Nevertheless, I am here. I pay you to have this house at readiness at any time." He lifted a quizzical eyebrow, in some amusement, as his devoted butler flushed slightly. "But I appreciate that I have been unwell and I did not decide to come to London until this afternoon myself. I hope that I can dine?"

"Certainly, my lord. I will inform Mrs York of your arrival, and dinner and beds will be prepared immediately." He bustled out of the room. The little housemaid, having accomplished her task, hung her head in fear as she saw Jaspar. He smiled at her. She was hardly more than a child.

"I have not seen you before. What is your name?"

"Nan, my lord," she said in a small terrified voice. "I 'ave only bin here two weeks."

"Well, Nan, thank you for my fire. I think that I shall need it, the night has become very cold. I hope you will be happy here. That will be all."

"I will, my lord." She smiled shyly and ran out.

Jaspar warmed his hand on the fire, which was rapidly becoming hot. It was good to be here. He thought of sauntering down to Brooks' but decided to enjoy the solitary splendour of an evening without company.

The next morning he went to Berkeley Square to pay a visit to his sister. When Parker opened the door to him, it seemed to Jaspar that the man would be overcome with tears.

"Oh, my lord, my lord."

Jaspar, who, by now, was becoming inured to this reaction from his devoted retainers, merely smiled.

"Oh, my lord," he sniffed, "it is so good to see you so well. My lady will be so pleased…"

"Quite. Where is she, Parker?"

"Oh, in the morning room, my lord."

"Thank you, Parker." Jaspar moved swiftly away from the butler. He had returned to London to escape all the fretting but it appeared that he was to receive it here as well. He hoped that Nillie would be more sensible. He opened the morning room door. Nillie was seated at the oval table; she seemed to be writing on a slate. A girl in housemaid's uniform sat next to her.

"Now, Nib, I want you to look at what I have written. What does it say?"

The girl peered at it. She bit her lip with concentration. "Th…i…s is a h…ou…se. This is a house." She looked at Nillie with delighted eyes. "I read it, my lady, I did."

Nillie grinned back. "Yes, Nib, I am very pleased with you."

Nib caught sight of Jaspar leaning against the doorpost watching them, amusement in his eyes. Nillie turned in the direction of Nib's look.

"Jaspar!" She jumped up with joy and flung her arms around his neck. "Oh, Jaspar, I am so pleased to see you so well at last!"

"Nillie! Not you as well. I am heartily fed up with all this anxiety. If you fuss any more I shall disappear," he teased. "But please, you appear to be giving a lesson. I do not want to disturb you."

Nillie turned back to Nib who was carefully writing on the slate herself. "Yes, I am teaching Nib to read. That will be all for today. You must take the slate and chalk and practise yourself."

The girl scrambled to her feet; she curtsied to Jaspar and Nillie. "Thank you! Thank you, Lady Morntarny." She picked up the slate and ran out.

Jaspar hugged his sister. "I see you have become a teacher, my lady."

Nillie laughed. "Odd, isn't it! I went down to the kitchen very early one morning and there she was, all red hands and scrubbing knees. I asked her what her ambitions were, and she told me she wanted to learn to read. It seemed so wrong, Jaspar, that she did not have the chance. I borrowed some of Charles's books." Lord Steeple was Nillie's eldest son. A stocky boy of ten summers, who, apart from an obvious flare for his work, promised to be a bruising rider and a not inconsiderable sportsman. He was adored by his mama and respected by his father. He was Jaspar's godson.

"How is Charles? I have a plan to take him to the pull-me push-me."

"He is wonderful. Down at Morntarny at the moment with his sisters. You shall see him when we all descend on Bardfield for Christmas." Christmas at Bardfield was a tradition. The entire family came. Jaspar liked having everyone under his roof. Even his more eccentric relatives.

"But what brings you to town? I was sure that they would not let you out of their sight until at least the New Year."

Jaspar pulled a wry face. "Exactly! The concern was driving me mad, Nillie, all that agitation and chafing. It was just like prison."

Nillie regarded him shrewdly. She had discussed with Lady Heddington the prospect of Jaspar's marriage. They were both of a mind that Netta would suit, but she was wise enough to know that in this present frame of mind a suggestion such as that would only serve to annoy. She started to tell him the latest *on dits*, but before she could launch into a description of the Duke of Clarence's latest flame, a discreet knock on the door brought Parker, who informed her that Mrs Darcy, Miss Darcy and Miss Clarissa were in the drawing room. Nillie pulled a face.

"I'd better go to them." Her eyes lit up enchantingly. She grabbed her brother's arm. "And you, dearest brother, shall come with me."

Mrs Darcy and Henrietta were standing next to the fire, examining the extensive collection of miniatures that were arranged around it. Clarissa was sitting quietly on a chaise at the other end of the room.

"Oh, my dear Lady Morntarny," gushed Mrs Darcy, "so delightful to see you." Her beady eye then caught the man who followed Her Ladyship. The hard face broke into a wreath of smiles. Her luck was certainly in. To find Lord Heddington with his sister and so newly returned to town! Mrs Darcy, who prided herself on knowing everyone's movements, was well aware of his unfortunate accident at the hands of footpads. It had been much talked about among those ladies of fashion who have little else to do but gossip. She had not, however, heard that he had returned to the metropolis.

She beamed, she glowed, she grovelled. "My dear Lord Heddington, and so well. So completely recovered, I see." She curtsied ingratiatingly. "It must be a source of such delight to all that are privileged enough to call you a friend, that God should have seen fit to save your life."

Jaspar's eyes met those of his sister; they were brimming with amusement and mischief.

"Oh, dear Mrs Darcy. Is it not truly wonderful to see my brother so well? I am sure that we all feel as you do."

"Wretch," said Jaspar under his breath as he followed his sister into the room.

"You do remember my daughter, Henrietta, do you not?" continued Mrs Darcy, pushing the girl forward. "Come, my love, curtsey to Lord Heddington."

Henrietta curtsied. She was such a large girl that it was hard for her to do anything gracefully. She flushed dark red and looked sullenly at His Lordship. Jaspar smiled. "How do you do, Miss Darcy?" he said quite charmingly, shooting a challenging look at his sister who threatened to collapse under a flood of giggles.

He turned, and crossed to Clarissa who had risen at their entrance and was standing shyly at the other end of the room.

"Miss Clarissa, how well you look. Such a very pretty dress, the colour becomes you so well. Please, come tell me how your mama does."

He handed her to a seat and with a quick look at his sister, who gestured to Mrs Darcy and Henrietta to sit, sat down beside her. Clarissa was a delicate creature, not at first sight very pretty but as he looked at her closer, he realised that she had fine blue eyes that twinkled attractively. Her hair was pale brown and very straight, but she wore it scooped up on the top of her head and he realised, with some surprise, how much it suited her long elegant neck and tiny nose and mouth.

"She is much better, thank you," she answered in a direct way. "But one does not overcome these things very quickly, I think. She was devoted to my papa."

He found himself sympathetic to her, in a way that he would not have been before. "And you, have you enjoyed your stay in London?"

She shot him a look of faint surprise and then glanced at her aunt. "Mrs Darcy has been all that is cordial. I have been to a few parties."

He smiled again. "My apologies for my stupidity. My sister told me that you have not been entertained with all…"

She silenced him with a slight movement of her hand. "I do not believe that it would behove upon me to complain," she responded firmly.

He looked at her with growing respect and would have gone on, but that Mrs Darcy, seeing what was happening, stood up to take her leave.

"Come, Clarissa!" she commanded. "I am sure that His Lordship does not want to hear any more of this inconsequential chatter." She smiled one of her hateful grimaces.

"Will we see you at Almack's tomorrow, my lord? London is so thin of company in the little season, that your presence will be most doubly welcome."

Jaspar bowed over her hand. "Will Clarissa be there?" he asked provokingly.

"Oh, well, I do not think that I shall be able to obtain vouchers for her at this late time," finished Mrs Darcy triumphantly.

"Oh, that will be no problem, I am sure. I shall undertake to get them. Lady Jersey is my closest friend. Have you been to Almack's, my dear?" he enquired of Clarissa, who shook her head doubtfully. "Then you shall come tomorrow. If you cannot arrange it, please make sure she is here for dinner and Nillie and I will take her."

He looked defiantly at Mrs Darcy, who knew that she had been truly out-manoeuvred. But she was too wise to quibble with one such as Lord Heddington. She merely smiled and said flatly, "How kind. Come, girls." She swept them out.

Nillie collapsed with giggles. "Jaspar, you are incorrigible! Her face, I have not enjoyed anything so much for years."

"Hateful old witch. Clarissa seems an unexceptional girl who certainly deserves better."

"I believe that she has been with Mrs Darcy for a whole season and has not attended above a dozen routs. I intended to try to help her myself but with you being ill, I am afraid I did far less than I had wanted."

"Well, now is the time to make up for it. Do you wish that I obtain vouchers? I am sure Sally will give them to me."

"No, I can do it. I will bid her dine here beforehand. You will come, of course?" He nodded and the plans were set.

Chapter Ten

That evening Jaspar left Grosvenor Square for a stroll down St James's Street. He had decided that it would be most agreeable, after all this time away, to visit Brooks'. The endless rain of the last few weeks had ceased and it was a cold bright night. As he walked, he watched the new gas lamps flicker and dance in the breeze. It felt good to be back in London. When he reached the club he stopped, casting his eyes over its yellow stone, its flat Corinthian pillars and perfect lines, as if seeing them for the first time. Then he smiled slightly and strode up the low steps and into the hallway. As he crossed the portals, Toby, the fat, jovial porter, caught sight of him. His round face almost crumpled with affection.

"My lord! My lord. So good, so good… We heard… Lord Morntarny said… I was that afeared… I never thought…"

"Nevertheless, I am here and quite recovered," said Jaspar with a smile, handing him his caped greatcoat.

"Yes, Lord Heddington." Toby ran his hands over the coat reverently. "Cold tonight, my lord."

Jaspar nodded to him, then sauntered into the main body of the club. He paused, glancing around him, savouring anew Henry Holland's inspired design. A fire burned invitingly in the grate. The three arches on the left complemented exactly the fine staircase which stood opposite them. As members mounted the stairs, they viewed with appreciation the solid squareness of a hall which excellently endorsed Holland's expressed intent of building an elegant country house, but in London. Jaspar crossed the hall and went up. At the top, he turned right, wandering into the library, where he was greeted on all sides by men delighted by his improvement. He inclined his head in response to their salutations but did not stop to talk to anyone in particular. Then he retraced his steps, peering down over the banisters at the hall. He smiled, relishing his renewed presence in the club. Then he crossed into the Great Subscription Room. Its pale green walls and deep rose curtains were comfortingly familiar. At the round tables men were gambling seriously. He passed down the centre, turning right into the annexed room; as he did so he was hailed by Alvanley who was dining with Brummell and a third man who was hidden from Jaspar's view by William and George. These two leapt to their feet when His Lordship came into view.

"Zounds, if it isn't Jaspar," lisped Alvanley with pleasure, shaking his hand warmly. "Have you dined?" On receiving an answer in the negative, he waved at a waiting footman to draw up another chair.

"When did you come back and how are you?" demanded Brummell. "Are you quite restored to health?"

"Quite," replied Jaspar. "Just a little stiffness." He moved his arm to exhibit the remaining damage. "And an edict from the doctor not to hunt yet."

"What a bore!" remarked the third man.

"Roderick! You would feel so. Personally, I am grateful not to be tearing about the countryside getting filthy on smelly brutes," rejoindered Brummell, moving slightly to the left to reveal the man who was seated at the table with them.

Roderick laughed. He pulled himself to his feet with some difficulty. He was a mountain of a man, standing six foot four in his stockinged feet. He had the kindest face imaginable, with soft brown eyes and a quantity of curly brown hair. His face was tanned a dark brown and when he laughed his eyes crinkled at the corners. He was the younger son of the Earl of Farquar, who had entered the army at eighteen, and had swiftly reached the rank of colonel. He had served as one of Wellington's staff officers and was highly prized by that gentleman. He was renowned for his bravery, his good humour, the wonderful care he took of the men under him. Jaspar and he had been at Eton together; they were the closest of friends. On seeing that it was he, Jaspar's face lit up; he took Roderick's hand in his and held it forcefully.

"Roderick! My dear chap, more important, how are you?" Roderick had been badly injured at Salamanca and was now invalided out of the army.

"As you see, short of an arm, knee cap, a couple of toes, and no more fighting!" the man replied ruefully. "Can you believe it, Jaspar, I am to be found at my desk."

"Oh, but it is good that you are alive. I am so glad to see you. When have you returned?"

"Last month, with orders to take things gently. I am staffing with Moyle and am just permitted to go out a little. But tell me, Jaspar, what happened to you?"

As they ate Jaspar regaled them with the story of his attack in the woods. He did not mention the red-haired girl, but they were much interested in his tale of the estimable doctor, and the projected hospital. Before they parted for the evening Jaspar bade them all dine tomorrow to accompany him to Almack's. Roderick and Alvanley agreed but Brummell was forced to decline. He was promised to Lady Harriet Villiers, but he hoped to join them later.

The next evening found Jaspar, accompanied by Roderick, both dressed in the regulation black knee breeches, white cravat and three-cornered hat, without which they could not be admitted to Almack's, present themselves for dinner at his sister's.

Nillie was alone when they were shown into the elegant drawing room. She jumped to her feet and flung her arms around Roderick's neck, enchanted to see him again. They were old friends. In fact, it was a joke between them all that Roderick had lost his heart to her aged fifteen and that was the reason he had subsequently never married.

"Roderick! Roderick! I am so glad you are safe, my dear, I heard from Lady Cowper that you were back and well now."

He hugged her with his one arm. "Petronilla, and as beautiful as ever. Yes, you see I am recovered."

"I am so sorry for your arm," remarked Her Ladyship, leading him to a chaise and sitting next to him. "It is a deuced shame."

"So many did not come back that I should not complain."

"You would never complain," said Petronilla smiling at him mistily. "I never heard you ever utter a word against anything in your whole life."

He laughed, pinching her under her chin. "You should have heard my vociferous protestations when they cut off my arm. I complained then!"

"The pain. It must have been so great. How did you bear it?"

"Not well, I fear." He grinned ruefully. "But a famous victory, oh, such a famous victory, 40,000 men defeated in forty minutes. I am just proud to have been there."

Nillie leaned over and kissed him. He put his good arm around her shoulder, as Parker announced the arrival of the Darcys. They both rose again as Mrs Darcy, clad in a dark silk evening gown that rendered her even more formidable, if that were possible, than the beak nose, cold eyes and thin lips would have done, swept across the room. Henrietta, dressed in an unbecoming shade of pink which merely succeeded in accentuating her mottled skin, followed her, and Clarissa crept in after them. She was modestly attired in a pale muslin dress which, although it had clearly not been made by a fashionable modiste, suited her, its simplicity enhancing her lack of pretentiousness.

Nillie moved away from Roderick to greet her guests. "I believe you know my brother, Mrs Darcy, but I do not think you have had the pleasure of Mr Talkarne's acquaintance?"

"Indeed! I do count your brother as one of my dearest friends," Mrs Darcy crowed ingratiatingly. "But I have not yet met Mr Talkarne," she continued dismissively.

Jaspar caught Roderick's eyes which were brimming with amusement. "I see I have been away too long, if this is the kind of dearest friend you replace me with," he muttered under his breath. Jaspar grinned back, his smile being replaced with a look of polite resignation as Mrs Darcy bore down on them, Henrietta in her wake.

"My lord, how delightful!" He bowed unencouragingly but Mrs Darcy, in scent of her prey, was perfectly insensitive to atmosphere.

"So wonderful to be in your party for Almack's," she went on obsequiously, her plain face alight with the triumph of her position. Jaspar sighed resignedly; he could not understand why he had allowed himself to be subjected to such toadying, then Petronilla brought Clarissa across and he remembered.

"You know Lord Heddington, of course." Jaspar bowed and smiled kindly. "But I do not think you have met Mr Talkarne. Roderick, this is Miss Clarissa Darcy."

Clarissa curtsied gracefully and looked up to find herself regarding a pair of the most laughing eyes she had ever encountered. They were so attractive that she simply found herself grinning back into them. Roderick put out his hand, helping her to her feet, gazing down into the sweetest, prettiest face in the world. She must be quite the gentlest creature that he had ever beheld, and an overwhelming desire to protect and care for her swept over him.

"I most certainly have not had the pleasure," he remarked, holding the delicate hand carefully. "But I shall speedily make up for it."

Clarissa found herself smiling again. She was tiny beside this giant of a man but she immediately felt at home and happy. He led her to the sofa and sat next to her. Within seconds they were lost in conversation. Jaspar had never seen anyone fall in love, but as he watched his friend and Clarissa he knew that love at first sight did exist and that he was witnessing it. He could not have been happier. It was an arrangement made in heaven. She would care for him and he for her. It would take her away from her hateful aunt; it would give Roderick something to replace the loss of the army. Jaspar felt well pleased with the outcome of his actions. Even a night spent with the dreadful Mrs Darcy could be endured just to witness the happiness of his dear friend. He turned from observing them, to find Nillie at his shoulder. Her eyes followed his glance, then they met his. They were too close to need to say more.

"My apologies for my lateness." Greville strode into room. "I have been up at Morntarny, and this devilish rain has made the roads all but impassable." He picked up his wife's hand and kissed it. "Charles and his sisters send all their love, my dear, they are extremely well and up to their customary mischief."

Nillie laughed but was clearly pleased to hear such good tidings of her children. At the sight of her husband her eyes twinkled with pleasure. Jaspar was used to their subtle displays of affection but tonight he felt an unaccustomed pang as he watched, first his friend and then his sister.

"Of course we forgive you, my dear Lord Morntarny," fawned Mrs Darcy. "Such a charming room." Greville bowed politely, too well bred to show his distaste for her impudent remarks. "You know my beloved daughter?" she continued.

Greville glanced at Nillie as if to say, "why do I have to entertain such a creature?" but as he did so, Roderick stood up and grasped both of Greville's hands in his one hand.

"Greville, my dear chap."

He found his hand clasped equally warmly. "Roderick! I did

not know that I was to have the great pleasure of entertaining you. When did you return to town?"

"Last month but it is only this week that my doctor permits me to dine out," he grinned. "Apart from last night, when I met this reprobate," he indicated Jaspar by a mild wave of his hand, "I have been at my desk and have not visited anywhere."

"Then it is doubly my pleasure to welcome you here," said Greville, his eyes alight with affection for his dear friend. "I look forward to hearing of the battle."

"My Lord Alvanley, Sir Charles and Lady Carlton," announced Parker. Her guests complete, Petronilla indicated that dinner could now be served.

They reached Almack's by ten o'clock. The doors of the exclusive establishment were closed at eleven and no one was admitted after that. On one famous occasion even the Prince of Wales had been banned from the doors because he turned up past eleven. The rules of the club were absolute, its exclusivity resting on these decrees, which were laid down by seven patronesses. Tonight was Wednesday, and the Wednesday soirees were both select and the most fashionable. They may have only served orangeat and biscuits, but the company was of the most high and the mortification for those refused vouchers the most complete. Nillie was friendly with most of the patronesses and it had not been hard for her to obtain vouchers tor Clarissa, particularly when she explained to Sally Jersey about Mrs Darcy. Lady Jersey went further. Having heard of the cavalier treatment meted out to Clarissa, she decided that Mrs Darcy and her vulgarity were not to be permitted to enter the hallowed portals of King Street. She would be refused admission after tonight.

At dinner, Mrs Darcy had been exultant in her current success and it had been hard for Nillie to keep her tongue. As Mrs Darcy boasted and flaunted her vouchers, Nillie was tempted beyond even her ability for discretion. She opened her mouth to depress the pretension, but as she did so, she caught

Jaspar's eye. He shook his head slightly and Nillie realised that to do so would hurt Clarissa and as the object of enduring the company of her aunt was to help the girl, it would be stupid to endanger her by a chance put-down.

Although it was the little season, London was, indeed, short of company and Almack's rooms were not crowded. The abominable Mrs Darcy pranced in, a self-satisfied smirk on her face. She loudly told all her acquaintances that she was here with "My Lord Heddington". Jaspar was becoming gradually less and less patient with her arrogant behaviour and Nillie watched as the line of his mouth became even more fixed. In another minute, she gauged, he would give Mrs Darcy a blistering rake-down. This would do little to aid Clarissa's position, although the recipient of these concerns was blissfully unaware of her aunt's behaviour. She had never met anyone she liked as much as Roderick. His obvious kindness and the affability that emanated from his eyes touched her heart. Soon after they arrived, he asked her to dance and led her to the floor where a set for the cotillion was forming. So caught up by his presence had she been, that she had hardly noticed his missing arm, and when he apologised ruefully for the lack of it, she raised her eyes in surprise.

After the cotillion the musician struck up a waltz and regretfully Clarissa allowed herself to be led from the floor; she would have liked to dance with Mr Talkarne all night. It was not permitted for girls to dance the waltz unless previously granted permission by one of the patronesses. Clarissa had been carefully schooled in this by her aunt. It had been impressed upon her that to do so would be a solecism. It was alright for her cousin; Henrietta had been granted this privilege, but most definitely not for her. However, Mr Talkarne showed no desire to be free of her company so she settled happily in an alcove with a drink of orangeat. For the waltz, Nillie found herself in the arms of her brother. He was a naturally good dancer and she much enjoyed the sensation of being whirled around by him.

"We seem to have solved the problem of Roderick and Clarissa," Jaspar commented, his eyes following their progress across the room.

Nillie sighed. "Oh, I do hope so. It would be so wonderful for them both."

Jaspar smiled. "I do not think you need have any more worries in that direction."

"But suppose Mrs Darcy puts a spoke in, she is perfectly capable, I fear. Particularly as no one looks as if they will make an offer for the awful Henrietta in the near future." Nillie bit her lip as she considered the problem. "Although, I do not think that Roderick will be deterred by such a one as Mrs Darcy," she mused.

"No, but I do not trust her."

"Shall I ask Clarissa to stay with me?"

"Would not serve, I am afraid," he remarked thoughtfully. "Except if you ask Henrietta as well."

"What! Oh no! Jaspar, I could not possibly!"

"Nevertheless, it would be the answer. She could not interfere and she would be so pleased she would leave you alone."

Nillie considered the proposition, and was still considering it as the dance came to an end. It was now quarter to eleven and a slight commotion at the door indicated the arrival of Brummell. Both Nillie and Jaspar went to greet him.

"Petronilla, and more beautiful than ever." George kissed her hand, his grey eyes dancing.

"Flatterer," teased Nillle. "Trying to bring me into fashion."

"A girl such as you does not need my approbation. Good evening, Greville." He shook hands with the earl. "I was just telling Nillie how well she looks."

Greville laughed. "So enchanting that I claim a dance."

"Oh, Greville, how unfashionable I shall look dancing with my own husband!" laughed Nillie sliding into his arms. As he bore her off, Jaspar watched them, his eyes following them onto the dance floor. Suddenly he froze, unable to move. His heart missed a beat. At the end of the room, dressed in a pale blue floating evening dress, her golden-red hair tumbling down her back, was the red-haired girl. Jaspar stared; his limbs felt quite weak. Brummell followed his look.

"Who is that?" Jaspar demanded of his friend.

"That. Oh yes! Extraordinary, isn't she?"

"Yes, but who is she, George?" He turned to his friend. "Do you know who she is?"

Something in the intensity of Jaspar's voice made George frown slightly. "Steady, Jaspar. Yes I know who she is. Why, Grizelda Ludgrove of course." Then George remembered. "Sister of that chit you…" He stopped.

Jaspar exhaled slowly. Of course. That was the explanation. Why had he not thought of it before? The bag of money; her enmity; her words. It all fell into place. He grasped Brummell's arm. "I want to meet her," he demanded with fervour, "I have some…" He stopped. Brummell was a good friend but the less anyone knew the better. "Please introduce us."

George shrugged his shoulders. It was up to Jaspar. He nodded, leading him across the room to Grizelda.

She stood slightly apart from a group of people. She was quite still and Jaspar noticed she was neither embarrassed nor shy. She seemed quite at home with her own company. She watched the dancers twirling around the floor. The pale blue dress suited her. The low bodice showed off her smooth white skin and her wonderful hair hung in myriads of curls to her waist. As they approached, Jaspar realised that she had seen him. Her pale blue eyes narrowed in a look of abhorrence. She would have turned from them but Jaspar was too quick for her. He grabbed her arm, none too gently.

"Miss Ludgrove, do not go." She stopped, raised her chin defiantly and looked him straight in the eye. She was neither intimidated by Jaspar nor Mr Brummell, who stood next to him. George spoke.

"Miss Ludgrove, may I introduce Lord Heddington?"

Grizelda seemed as though she would refute the necessity of an introduction but Jaspar said firmly, "Delighted to make your acquaintance, Miss Ludgrove."

A slight change flitted across her intelligent face as she realised that to claim a previous knowledge of each other, would merely serve to invite comment. She inclined her head slightly.

"Would you do me the pleasure of dancing with me?" Jaspar asked. Again she made to refuse, her bright eyes flashing sparks of dislike at him. He smiled slightly, holding out his arms. She thought quickly; distaste for him and the inadvisability of quarrelling in front of Brummell and in such a public place flashed across her face. Sense won. She inclined her head coldly in acceptance, and stepped into his arms. They were playing a waltz. As they danced, he was conscious of the previous occasion when he had held her. He remembered her lips, the touch of her skin. Now she stayed, unyielding and stiff, but he could not forget the Angel and Harp.

"I am glad you consented to dance with me. I owe you an apology," he started. She looked surprised. "I did not behave well to your sister."

"Indeed," she said coldly, her face frozen. He remembered her voice, low and husky. "You behaved like a monster. I hate you. I will never forgive you for what you did. I am glad that I shot you," she pronounced in a matter-of-fact way.

"Then you will also be glad to know that I nearly died." He observed the slight look of consternation on her face, which was quickly replaced with indifference. He continued wryly, "Do you feel no remorse for almost killing me?"

She shook her head. "Do you feel remorse for what you did to Laura?" she retorted audaciously. Jaspar was amused. Girls did not look at him in that bold way, they were far more wont to agree with him, to simper, to hang onto his every phrase, but Grizelda stared at him with antagonism.

"Actually, I do. You may not accept it when I say that I feel very badly about what occurred, but it is the truth."

She looked at him with disfavour. "No. I do not accept it. Nor do I know why I am dancing with you," she hissed at him, starting to break away.

"You are dancing with me because it is imperative that we try to minimise the damage that was done."

"That you did."

"Alright, that I did, to your sister." He paused and sighed. "Trust me. I am truly sorry for what happened. I will do everything in my power to try to save what I can of your sister's reputation. Now, if you look daggers at me everyone will believe that what the gossips told them was true, but if you look as if you were my dearest friend people will doubt what they have been told. I will deny it. I will merely say that I took Laura down to your father who was ill. No use pretending that she did not go off with me. Too many people know that she did. What I suggest is sensible. Believe me, I know the way of this world." He glanced around. Several of the worst gossips were watching them closely. "Even now we are being watched."

Grizelda looked angry, but as her eyes swept the room she realised that what he said was true. She was determined to do what she could for Laura and if that meant being pleasant, in company, to this hateful man, then so be it. She was far too intelligent not to realise that the best way to squash the rumours, was for her to seem happy with him.

"l agree," she said simply.

He smiled. "If you agree, you had better start playing your part. Stop looking as if you loathe me and start smiling."

She laughed; her laugh was sweet and pure. Then she smiled at him. His heart missed another beat. Even if her smile was a pretence, it was utterly bewitching. He remembered it. It made it seem as if the sun had come out. He responded and for a moment they danced in silence. Grizelda was confused.

 123

She had not expected him to be contrite. His apology had been completely unexpected. It had taken her utterly by surprise. His desire to remedy the damage done to Laura was also quite bewildering. She thought he would be unrepentant and that she would be forced to deny what had happened alone, but she had found a most unexpected ally. She smiled again.

"Where are you staying in London?" he enquired.

"At my godmother's," she answered, and giggled as she saw the look of dismay that passed across his countenance. "No, not Lady Ambrose. Lady Melbourne is my god-mama."

He sighed with relief. "Elizabeth! Then may I call on you there?" he asked. "Will you drive in the park with me?"

"I do not think," she demurred.

"Come, you must help your sister, you must be seen to be my friend, what better place than Hyde Park," he remonstrated, his eyes dancing.

He led her back to Lady Melbourne, who had been observing them with some interest. "Good evening, Elizabeth," he remarked politely, kissing her on the cheek. "May I pay a call on you tomorrow?"

"Jaspar, of course you may. You know that you are always most welcome."

Jaspar bowed to Grizelda and returned to his party. Nillie grinned at him. "Dance with me!" she commanded.

He laughed and held out his arms.

His sister regarded him with a quizzical look. "And who is the red-haired damsel?" she enquired.

His mouth twisted slightly. "She is Laura Ludgrove's sister."

"Oh, Jaspar! No! You must have nothing to do with her."

"That would hardly be sensible. You did much to prevent damage to Laura's reputation. I must do the same. I told Miss Ludgrove that whatever she feels in private she must present an impassive face to the world." He looked suddenly very serious. "I did not act fairly to Laura. I must make reparation if I can."

Nillie was surprised. It was most unlike Jaspar. He was notoriously obdurate where women were concerned, yet here he was behaving for all the world as if he had a guilty conscience. It was most perplexing.

CHAPTER ELEVEN

Grizelda did not see Jaspar again that evening. She danced with a great many attentive men, and her conversation, although a trifle abstracted, was all her admirers could require. Eventually, even the indefatigable Lady Melbourne admitted to tiredness and Grizelda was pleased when she suggested that they depart. On the journey home Grizelda was uncommonly quiet, her thoughts in a jumble. Lady Melbourne watched her sagely; her normally composed goddaughter had been distracted by something that had occurred this evening. She devoutly hoped that it was not Lord Heddington. It would never serve. She thought about it. Should she caution Grizelda against that gentleman? However kind and interested he appeared, nothing had been known to last with him and she did not wish her goddaughter to be added to his list of broken hearts, but then Grizelda was sensible, and she had the example of her sister's infatuation, which had come to nothing, before her. No, she decided she would postpone her warning and see what transpired.

Grizelda was confused. She had come to hate Jaspar for his actions towards Laura and yet, tonight she had discovered that he was not as easy to abominate as she had imagined. She was also forced to acknowledge that much as she loved her sister, the girl could be very silly sometimes. It was only when she reached the sanctuary of her bed that she could truly examine the evening's events. Lord Heddington's smile was wonderful and when his eyes danced, it must be owned that he was very appealing. She could see why Laura had been so much in love with him. She determined to herself that she must not be affected by twinkling eyes and an open smile. It made good sense, however, that she should be pleasant to him. It would be silly to refuse to do that. He was right; the best way to prove that the *ton*'s beliefs were unfounded was for them to appear on the best of terms. No, for the moment, she must go along with his scheme; she fell asleep on that thought.

Jaspar drove home with his own thoughts in turmoil. He had found his red-haired ice maiden, but she had turned out to be the sister of the girl to whom, he now admitted, he had done a terrible wrong. He smiled ruefully to himself. He had never suffered any pangs of guilt in his previous amatory adventures. Was he perhaps getting old? No, that was not why he felt so bad. Was it because she was so young? No, he had had many younger. Was it because her birth, if not impeccable, was certainly respectable? No, he had had girls of higher birth than her before. Why did he feel that he had wronged Laura? It was not only since his illness; if he were honest, he knew that he had felt it when he left her in the inn in Wimbledon. Suddenly, it just did not feel right. He sighed. Shook himself.

When he reached Grosvenor Square the house felt very empty and quiet. He thought how much he appreciated its peace after the flutter of Bardfield. Silently servants slid about their duties. He threw his coat to a footman and retired to his library, summoning York to bring him a bottle of wine. He picked his favourite book and sat in front of the large fire which burnt in the grate. Even then he found his thoughts racing. He had promised his grandmother that he would contemplate her suggestion that he marry Netta and he knew that out of respect for them he must give it all his consideration. Away from Netta he found he remembered the girl with pleasure. He enumerated her qualities: she was intelligent, calm, an excellent organiser; his households would run effortlessly but then they ran extremely smoothly without Netta. He liked the girl; she would never cause him a moment's trouble. Then, he thought, with a pang, that he would enjoy something more spirited than Netta. Eventually he went to bed. For the first time for several months the dream that had haunted his illness returned. He dreamt of the flames of the red hair melting the ice maiden.

The next morning, as promised, he went to Westminster to pay a visit on Lady Melbourne. The Duke of York had taken a fancy to Lord Melbourne's mansion on Piccadilly and, ever keen to please influential people, especially Royal ones, Lady Melbourne had agreed to swap her house for the Duke's. The Lambs moved into York House on Whitehall.

Melbourne House, as it now became, stood behind a high brick wall. It had originally been built around an E shape, with the principal rooms overlooking St James's Park and the entrance courtyard facing Whitehall. The Duke of York had hired Holland to enlarge his house and add to its splendour. The admirable architect had built the famous Ionic entrance in Whitehall and had filled in the courtyard with a domed and pillared rotunda, which led the visitor up steps and into the main reception rooms. These had been delicately decorated by Lady Melbourne in pale green. The three rooms of the first floor opened out onto a small wrought iron balcony which ran the length of the house and which overlooked the park. It was supported on pillars which were covered with winding branches, and in the summer redolent with the smell of hundreds of flowers.

The day was cool but the sky was bright blue as Jaspar drove up to the Ionic portico. He ordered Harper to walk the team and he went to pay his visit to Lady Melbourne. Jaspar knew the house well; he had passed many agreeable and pleasant hours in dalliance and political discussion here. He climbed the stairs, passing the eight huge orange marble pillars. As he crossed the vestibule he could see sun streaming into the windows, lighting up the remarkable embossed plaster ceilings. Lady Melbourne was in the middle and smaller of the three rooms. She was seated reading, in front of a huge fire.

Elizabeth Milbanke, in her youth a great beauty, had married Sir Peniston Lamb. Through his money, and her maneuvering, he had attained a peerage and a seat in the House of Commons. This was really all he managed to do for he was, unfortunately, a man who did little else in his life except gamble away the money accumulated by his father. His wife, far cleverer than her lord, had quickly set herself up socially. She was really a man's woman, although she understood well the importance of friendship with the fair sex and became the confidant of Georgiana, the Duchess of Devonshire. They were, perhaps, an ill-assorted couple. Lady Melbourne, rather pedestrian and hard; the fair Georgiana, romantic and sensitive. It was, though, a friendship that prospered. Lady Melbourne was adept at listening and giving wise advice when necessary.

She had also had a brief affair with the Prince of Wales. Indeed it was thought that her son Frederic was probably sired by that gentleman. However, once the affair was over, she had managed to remain on the best of terms with the Regent. Men liked her, and many young men became her lovers. She was interesting, discreet and never known to create unfortunate scenes. She rose to greet Jaspar. They were old friends. Indeed, at some earlier time, she had been his mistress.

"Good morning, Elizabeth. I find you in the peak of good looks."

She smiled at him. "My dear Jaspar, you know that you are always most welcome at Melbourne House. Please sit down."

He sat opposite her, regarding her with pleasure. She was quite unique.

"I suppose that during your illness you had little time to observe the Liverpool victory in September. Sixty more seats. It appears that Grey and Granville are now in opposition. I must confess I cannot like or approve of Liverpool, he is such a dull man."

"I am not sure that I agree with you, Elizabeth. I have my suspicions that he will make an admirable first minister."

"Jaspar! And you, who hail from the finest Whig traditions."

"Yes, I know. I do not want to betray my origins but I think there are changes coming. We must accommodate them. Why, even Prinny has not sided with his old friends; I think they must have expected it."

"Possibly. But they were, I think, disappointed. Are you of the opinion that the Whigs will not be returned to government?"

"In truth, I am not at all sure that they will. Although much will depend on the war. Indubitably, the world is changing, Elizabeth. I am sure of it. I met this remarkable doctor when I was ill; actually he saved my life. He was the face of the future. I am building him a hospital."

She grinned. "He must have made an impression on you."

"He is an outstanding doctor, of that there is no doubt. I want the best for my tenants." There was a slight silence while Lady Melbourne waited for him to say something about Grizelda, but he remained quiet. So Her Ladyship was forced to bring up the subject. In her direct way she enquired: "It is good of you to come to visit Grizelda. After the scandal created by my Lady Ambrose and her indiscreet tongue, I thought perhaps you might want to stand clear of the family."

"Why should I care about a tissue of lies that were invented by a malicious nobody of a governess?" he remarked dispassionately.

"Oh, Jaspar, if it were untrue, why did you then leave London so quickly?"

"I went to see my grandmama, Elizabeth. There was nothing special about that. I am devoted to her as you know. I was set upon, I was ill, I was forced to remain. There is nothing more to it than that," he replied calmly.

"Oh, come, Jaspar. Everyone knew that Laura was your mistress."

"Then everyone was wrong. I did nothing to Laura," Jaspar lied, his face inscrutable.

She looked at him keenly. "Come, Jaspar, the truth," she repeated. "I am discreet, you know."

Jaspar hooted with laughter; he stood up and kissed her cheek affectionately. "I think that there are many of us who have much to appreciate in your discretion. Nevertheless, I did not have an affair with Laura. Oh, I admit the chit was attractive but young, very young, but I merely aided her, by driving her to her father's house. She begged my help. I could hardly refuse. Indiscreet perhaps, but hardly the scandal that everyone seems to believe." Jaspar regarded her steadily; he did not flinch from her intent scrutiny.

"Well, I suppose I believe you," she said doubtfully. "You took her to her father. I assume you saw Mr Ludgrove. Where was that?"

The direct question disconcerted him. How foolish not to have found out the name of the village, where the Ludgroves lived. "Mr Ludgrove was not well, Elizabeth."

"Jaspar, do not prevaricate." There was a slight laugh in her eyes as she interrogated him. "Where is Mr Ludgrove's abode?"

"I took Laura to…" He paused. Had Nillie mentioned where she had taken Laura?

"Why, straight home to Vernham Dean, to Papa of course." Grizelda's husky voice came from the doorway clear and firm. Jaspar met her eyes; they were dancing; he smiled, a smile of gratitude. Lady Melbourne, far too astute not to have missed this silent interchange, said nothing. Jaspar watched Grizelda appreciatively; she was dressed for riding in a green velvet habit. Her hair was caught firmly up at the back of her head, under a fetching hat. She carried a whip and gloves.

 131

"Good morning, Lord Heddington." She curtsied to him, her pale eyes meeting his dark ones steadily. "Aunt Elizabeth, I am to ride with Emily. How pleasant to see you again, my lord." She smiled, and turned as if to leave the room. Jaspar was conscious of a pang of disappointment. He wanted her to stay.

"Miss Ludgrove, I had hoped that I would have the pleasure of driving you in the park."

"I am sorry but I am pledged to Emily. I cannot let her down."

"May I accompany you, to see you mounted?" he enquired.

She nodded, without particular enthusiasm. "If you wish."

Then she kissed Lady Melbourne, and Jaspar bade Her Ladyship farewell.

"I hope you will both drive with me soon, Elizabeth." Her Ladyship nodded acquiescence, and Jaspar followed Grizelda down the wide staircase and out to the stables.

"Thank you for rescuing me. How stupid of me to embark on a tissue of lies without first obtaining the correct information." He smiled.

"Do you think she believed you?"

Jaspar shook his head. "But she has no proof and that is what is important. I do not want to be caught like that again, I think had better come and meet your father. She looked doubtful. "Yes, I realise that after what occurred, he may well not want to see me, but I do want to apologise and see what expiation I can make."

She was pensive for a moment and then she nodded. "I think that what you say is wise, but you realise he may not greet you with approbation."

"I know. Do you return for Christmas?"

"Yes, most certainly."

"Then perhaps I can visit you?"

She thought for a moment, then nodded. By this time they had reached the stables. Emily Cowper had not yet arrived as a groom brought out Grizelda's mare. It was not a particularly impressive animal, Jaspar noted.

He held her to help her mount, and as he did so he was acutely aware of her. Her faint musky scent and the delicacy of her bones. Once on the horse he observed that she had an excellent seat and obviously light hands.

He patted the horse's neck. "Is this your animal?" he enquired.

She laughed. "You do not have much faith in me. Do I look as if I would choose a nag like this?"

"Well, I hoped not, but I did not want to pass comment on its attributes if it were your own."

"Attributes! It has none. It is the slowest, most sluggish animal. I believe it was bought for Lady Caroline and they did not want anything too excitable. Not that this creature possesses the smallest amount of life. A plodder of the worst kind."

"Then why are you riding her?" he asked.

"Because I have no choice," she replied acerbically. "I do not have a horse of my own and if I want to ride I am forced to rely on the generosity of my godmama."

"I apologise." His eyes laughed at her. "No need to get cross."

"You would be cross if you had to ride this thing."

"Jaspar, how delightful." Emily Cowper rode up; she was bewitchingly pretty with soft dark curls, and a great deal of warm-hearted kindness. She held out her hand to him; he picked it up obediently and kissed the delicate fingers. She was riding a beautiful mare that Jaspar noticed Grizelda regarded with resignation. "Have you been visiting Mama?"

"Yes, but I came to see Miss Ludgrove mounted."

"An awful nag that, I cannot understand why William bought it. Still, I suppose it is better than nothing, is it not, Grizelda?"

Grizelda grinned ruefully. "Of course, I am grateful to be able to ride at all. Now we had better be off. Goodbye, my lord." She pushed the mare into a trot and was off with Emily following. Jaspar watched her go; she was clearly a bruising rider. Her seat was far superior to Emily's and she rode with a naturalness that cannot be learnt.

Jaspar did not go straight home. He drove first to the Hyde Park turnpike where he visited Tattersalls'. Here he bought a delightful little mare. Jaspar was an excellent judge of horseflesh and this particular mare had been previously owned by Lady Oakley, the wife of Sir Barney Oakley. This gentleman had been drawing the bustle rather considerably over the last few months and he had lost a fortune at faro. His creditors were selling off his possessions. Jaspar was fortunate in that he walked into Tattersalls' just before the mare was put under the hammer. She was much coveted and he paid 1,000 guineas for her.

He returned home well pleased with his purchase. He sent the mare around to the stables and then he sat down and wrote a short note to Grizelda.

Grosvenor Square

Dear Miss Ludgrove,

I find this mare, Launcie, in my stables. She will become very unfit if she has no one to ride her, so I beg your indulgence and ask if you would be good enough to exercise her for me.

Yours

Then he sent for the under-groom and dispatched the mare and his note to Whitehall.

Grizelda was sitting with her godmother and Lady Cowper when Jaspar's note was brought to her. She opened it, staring at it with a great deal of astonishment. Silently she passed it to Lady Melbourne.

"Of course, I cannot accept such an offer," she remarked.

"Nonsense," replied her godmama. "It would be churlish to refuse to help."

"Oh, I had not thought of it quite that way."

"Well, all he has asked is that you exercise the horse for him. Let us go and look at it before we decide, after all it may be no better than the nag that William bought for Caroline."

Privately Grizelda thought that this would be well nigh impossible but she kept her opinions to herself, merely following her godmother outside into the dark and cold evening.

When they reached the stables, however, it was Lady Melbourne's turn to took astonished. For she recognised the mare, she had frequently seen Lady Oakley riding it; indeed it had been coveted by half the *ton*.

"Why, it's Lady Oa…" Emily started, but a fierce look from her mama shut her up quickly.

"What?" Grizelda asked.

"I… oh, nothing," answered Emily vaguely. "It's such a pretty ladies' mare."

"Oh, it is." Grizelda had taken one look at the horse and she knew she could not refuse it. She had never had the chance to ride anything so beautiful and she knew she could not give her up. Anyway, Lady Melbourne was right, it would be churlish to refuse to help. She went into the stable and put her arms around the mare's neck, feeling her smooth soft coat and inhaling the pure smell of her.

"You beauty, you beauty, Launcie," she whispered to the mare, who blew gently as if she understood.

"Well, I think that is settled," Lady Melbourne pronounced. "I think you had better write Lord Heddington a nice note to say that you will be delighted to accept and to thank him. Come, we are pledged to the Morrisons tonight and we shall be late if we do not change now."

Grizelda nodded, leaving the stable regretfully; she would have liked to jump straight onto the horse's back and ride and ride. However, she obediently wrote a note to say she was much obliged to Lord Heddington.

As it turned out, she had a chance to thank him personally, for he was also to be found at the Morrison's rout. Lady Morrison was a very large matron. She had been the scion of a minor baron, whose only claim to move in the best circles was that he was a second cousin to Lord Alvanley. His daughter, although not blessed with any great beauty, was possessed of the kindest heart imaginable, and it was this genial good nature that had made her popular enough to catch a very rich banker. Sir John Morrison was also not of the highest *ton*, but he was fabulously rich, and this, coupled with his lady's engaging nature had made them a popular couple. Lady Morrison had never been known to lose her temper. If her character had been less endearing and her fortune not so vast, she would not have moved in the first circles. However, she had managed in a jolly and unassuming way to be accepted by all.

The Morrisons lived in a huge mansion in Park Street. It was furnished very fashionably in a plethora of chinoiserie. Lady Morrison had been much impressed by the Pavilion when they had taken a house in Brighton for the summer and had redecorated her house accordingly. They had two daughters who possessed the rather unprepossessing looks of their mama but luckily also her temperament. The eldest was to make her debut next season and their mama had brought them both to town for the little season to acquire some town polish.

"Nothing so unamiable, Sir John," his lady announced, "than girls who have not a word to say for themselves and who are gauche and tongue-tied. So we must entertain."

Privately, Sir John thought it was most improbable that his high-spirited and loquacious daughters would ever deserve that epithet. However, he was quite ready to indulge them in any way, and if their mama thought parties were necessary, then parties they would have. The present one was quite small: some fifty couples for dancing.

It was late by the time Jaspar walked in accompanied by Lord Alvanley, Lord Slaughan and Roderick. They had dined at

Boodle's, and as Lady Morrison was Alvanley's cousin and he had promised faithfully to attend her evening party, they made their way dutifully to her house in Park Street.

Grizelda was dancing with Lord Mannock when Jaspar arrived; he was a portly, self-important man; utterly puffed up in his conceit, he was busy telling her how to run her life. Too vain to think that anyone might tire of having his advice thrust at them, he continued relentlessly. The dowager Lady Mannock watched sulkily from the other side of the room. She had ambitions for her son, ambitions which did not include him dancing for at least twenty minutes with a nobody. Jaspar caught sight of Grizelda. She was wearing a resigned expression and certainly did not appear to be bothering to hide her boredom. He was amused, for she did little to placate Lord Mannock. She neither courted him for his fortune, nor went after him for his title. Jaspar liked her the better for it. Lord Mannock, for all his pomposity, must be considered a catch, and most young girls wanted both his wealth and his title, but it appeared to Jaspar that his red-haired ice maiden was indifferent to such aspirations and resorted to none of the fallacious wiles employed by other girls to obtain their ends.

Eventually the dance came to an end. Jaspar could not hear a word of what His Lordship was saying but he observed that he had obviously asked for another dance, which Grizelda steadfastly refused. He crossed the room and from behind her he said, "Miss Ludgrove, our dance, I think." She whirled around and met his laughing eyes. He watched as pleasure at seeing him flashed across her face. This reflection was so short, that he was not quite sure whether he had been mistaken.

"Lord Heddington." Her husky voice was detached. "Yes, I believe that we are engaged for this dance. Thank you, Lord Mannock." She curtsied to him and put her arm out to Jaspar. He led her to the set that was just forming. There was little time for conversation as they moved in and out of the changing patterns of the dance, but as it finished, Grizelda put her hand on Jaspar's arm.

"I believe I must thank you."

"Can I get you a drink?" Jaspar asked, leading her to a seat in the side room.

"My lord, I want to thank you."

"Why? I have not yet obtained a drink," he teased.

"For a far greater service than providing a mere lemonade," she replied in mock indignation. "I certainly would not be attempting, with such resolve, to thank you for such a petty service." She grinned at him. "I am referring, as you well know, to Launcie. Such an excellent animal. Although, I suppose, perhaps a glass of lemonade might be considered by some to be preferable. I am not of their number."

He burst out laughing. "I am grateful that you ride Launcie. I am loath to let an animal like that sit in the stables eating her heart off."

"I am beholden to you," she said suddenly serious. "She is wonderful. How do I thank you?"

"Just let me ride with you. I admired your seat this morning and would like to see you put her through her paces."

"Why is she in your stables? Who was supposed to ride her?" she asked curiously.

Jaspar thought quickly. "Oh, my sisters."

"Your sisters? But surely they are all married with establishments of their own?"

"All except Margaret. I thought she would be in town more and would need a mount but she has remained in Sussex to care for my grandmama."

She looked as if she might question him further but at that moment Roderick appeared at their sides. "Jaspar, I think I shall go home and rest. The party is a trifle flat."

"Clarissa not here?"

Roderick had the grace to blush slightly as he protested,

"No, no… just my wound, you know, makes me tired."

"Oh yes, that is why you stayed so late last night dancing and not seeming a whit exhausted," Jaspar teased.

"Ah, but I cannot do that for two days running," his friend countered.

Jaspar hooted with laughter. "Touché, but I forget my manners, my dear chap. Miss Grizelda Ludgrove, Mr Roderick Talkarne."

Grizelda looked up in the calm twinkling eyes of a veritable mountain. She extended her hand. "Mr Talkarne, I am delighted to make your acquaintance but how were you wounded, pray?"

"Salamanca, I am afraid."

"Oh, please tell me about it." She patted the seat next to her.

"No, it is hardly the subject for a delicately brought-up girl. Battles and guns and wounds."

Jaspar raised an eyebrow and met Grizelda's eyes. "Oh, I do not think that Miss Ludgrove possesses any squeamish sensibilities, she will not faint away by hearing of a gun."

"No, indeed, I will not. I am not so fainthearted and I am very interested in the political implications of the war with Napoleon. He must at all cost be removed from Portugal."

Jaspar was only slightly surprised. It was clear that his ice maiden was a very unusual girl, with a keen intelligence. "Then I leave you. I am convinced that you are all Roderick needs to convince him that the party is not at all flat." He kissed her hand. "I look forward to our ride."

Chapter Twelve

The projected ride, however, did not take place until several days later. The weather, which had been cold and bright, became wet, windy and very icy, not the climate that Jaspar preferred for his horses in town. The days passed agreeably enough; he fenced lightly with one hand, played cards and visited his friends. One afternoon he paid a call on his current mistress. Mrs Susan Devereaux was the spoilt and indolent wife of a cit. Her husband, when not making money, spent most of his days incarcerated in their estate in the country, while his wife dallied away her time and his fortune in London. She was an amply built lady who, in spite of her penchant for good food and judicious afternoons gambling with her friends, remained, nevertheless, very ambitious socially. Being the mistress to one such as Jaspar could, she knew, do her much good, but the matter was more complicated than the mere enhancement of her position. Susan was much in love with His Lordship, although far too wise to show him how much he meant to her and far too sensible to chase after him in any way. She had heard of his illness and had worried much about him, and since his return to town she had been longing to see him, but had prudently made no move to contact him, until such time as he saw fit to visit her.

He found her snoozing gently, with a well-built-up fire burning in the grate next to her. As the butler announced him, she lifted her head. She had a lovely face, with dark luminous eyes and a generous and welcoming mouth. He bent over her and kissed her, and as he did so she tossed her head back with pleasure, the dark curls escaping from her cap and cascading down her back.

"Jaspar, how perfectly lovely to see you. I hope you have…"

"Please do not ask me if I have recovered, I have been driven quite mad with solicitous enquiries."

She laughed, a throaty chuckle. "Then I will not follow the pattern of the mob, but come sit next to me."

He willingly obeyed her. She ran her hand through his curls and examined his face minutely. To her sensitive eyes he seemed slightly different; the outward appearance, of course, was as handsome as ever, but a look in his eyes… She wondered. A slight feeling of unease crept over her. She knew she suited him well; she was a sensual creature and far too clever to try to entrap him in any way. She pushed away the unwelcome thought and waited. Jaspar gazed at her. He was fond of her, he had enjoyed her; she made no demands on him and her luxurious body had brought him great pleasure. But now, as he thought, it all seemed wrong. He stood up and went to the window.

"Jaspar?" she asked gently. "What is it?"

He did not answer her. She pulled herself to her feet. She was dressed in an elegant, dull pink, silk gown which suited her generous form. She moved next to him; he could smell her warm, sweet smell. She put one hand on his arm.

"Have you come to tell me that it is over between us?"

This had not been his intention at all. He had come for an afternoon of voluptuous pleasure but he nodded.

She bit her lip, trying to keep back the tears. She wanted him to remember her with satisfaction. She said nothing. She did not plead or rail; one did not with men of Lord Heddington's stamp. She knew that if she made a fuss he would never return to her, but if she accepted bravely, without complaint, then maybe, maybe, he would come back.

"I am sorry." She smiled wryly. "I had hoped that our friendship would continue as before," she went on passively. "You know that I am always here for you if you want to come and see me." Her heart was in turmoil, although she betrayed nothing of the disorder in her spirits, seeming all calmness and resignation.

"Oh, Susan, you are a good creature." He bent over and kissed her. Feeling the softness of her lips, and the open yielding sensation of her body, he was almost tempted but somehow he could not.

"Is it someone else?" The question she had been determined not to ask just popped out.

"No, no one else. You are lovely, Susan. It is me. Since my illness I... I know that I must change my way of life. No, that is not the correct interpretation. I just feel I have altered." He crossed and sat down again. "I thought I would die." He found himself confiding in her. "I thought I would cease to exist and leave nothing of me behind. It is strange, we know we are mortal but when the reality strikes it is both terrifying and salutary." She watched him carefully. She understood what he was saying, although he, himself, did not quite comprehend it. He would marry, she thought, but maybe after he did they could resume their friendship. She picked up his hand and brought it to her lips.

"I understand." Her voice choked. However hard she tried to stay unperturbed, her voice would tremble. He did not seem to hear it, and by swallowing hard and forcing her face into a smile, she managed to say goodbye to him with an equanimity of demeanour that did not betray the despair that hovered inside her.

When he had left she sat on the chaise and indulged in a long fit of weeping. She knew she would miss him dreadfully; it was as if a bright light had gone from her life. She knew he would be impossible to replace.

Jaspar left her regretfully. She was a delightful creature. He did not understand why he had felt it necessary to break with her. But he knew he had to do it. There was suddenly no choice. He drove to Madden and Rice, his favourite jewellers, where, as a most favoured client, he was shown into the inner sanctum of Mr Madden. The old man got to his feet. "My lord, how delightful to see you so recovered." Jaspar accepted his good wishes. He was heartily tired of them but it would be ungracious to dismiss the wishes of a man who had been jeweller to the Heddington family for some forty years.

"Thank you, Madden. Now, I require some presents."

"Immediately, my lord." He hurried away to re-emerge some few minutes later with a tray of jewellery. Jaspar picked up various pieces and examined them. There was an exquisite diamond and sapphire necklace which he instantly wanted to purchase for Grizelda, except that he knew that she would never accept it. He smiled wryly at himself. The object of his presence in the shop was to buy a farewell present for Susan. Eventually he chose a diamond necklet, which he asked Madden to dispatch. He sat down and wrote a note, which he enclosed with his gift. He still found that he wanted to buy jewels for Grizelda, although he thought she might refuse them. But then he remembered, fortuitously, the season. Surely she would not refuse a Christmas present? It must be acceptable. He chose a row of creamy pearls and then added a small brooch made of gold and amethysts for Laura. It was less likely that Grizelda would decline a Christmas gift if Laura had one too. He also made some other small purchases for Christmas for Nillie and his grandmother, however, it did not occur to him to buy anything for Netta, an oversight which he was forced to remedy later.

It was not until the following Friday that the weather permitted riding in the park. He sent a footman to Whitehall to ask if Grizelda would ride with him, and he received a note in her bold hand thanking him and pledging that she would be ready at whatever time he required. He found that he was looking forward to seeing her inordinately. It was slightly surprising to him. He was used to forgetting the objects of his flirtations as soon as they were not in his immediate sights. He recognised in himself a desire to be with her and to do things for her, which he had certainly never felt before for anyone who was not a member of his family. He had little expectation of this feeling lasting.

The day was bright and sunny but very cold and the ground was hard; it was an excellent day for hunting. He sighed. His shoulder was making good progress and he could feel that very soon it would be completely recovered. It would be silly to jeopardise its full recovery by hunting too soon, still he longed for more and regular exercise. He was unused to not being able to use his athletic prowess.

He rode Valiant through St James's Park to Melbourne House. There was a thin film of frost on the grass, which crunched as Valiant's hooves trotted over it. The bare branches of the trees were spiky against the blue of the sky. It was not yet so cold that the lake had iced over, and the sun made the water sparkle. It was most agreeable to be out again after the previous few days.

Grizelda was ready for him when he arrived. She was wearing the very becoming green velvet riding habit, and the tumultuous curls were once again firmly fastened under her hat. He was rather impressed by her punctuality. He always secretly expected women to keep him waiting, which sometimes rendered him impatient and sometimes did not, depending not only on the quality of his temper but also on the strength of his feelings for the tardy person. He would have waited for Grizelda, but he did not have to. Together they went down to the stables. Mounted on Launcie she was, as he had anticipated, truly splendid.

"You look wonderful," he commented as they left the confines of St James's for the wider acres of Hyde Park. The sun had melted the frost and the ground no longer seemed too hard for a canter.

"Shall we shake the fidgets out of the horses?"

She grinned provocatively. "Oh yes, I cannot tell you how long I have longed for a decent gallop."

She kicked Launcie and the horse sprang forward willingly. Laughing, Jaspar followed her, Valiant easily catching the little mare. They raced down Rotten Row and out onto the wide spaces. Grizelda rode effortlessly, Launcie's smaller strides keeping up well with the longer ones of Valiant.

"You ride remarkably," he complimented, as they slowed down to a brisk trot.

She smiled again, tossing her head. "It would be impossible not to ride well on such a creature." She laid her head down onto Launcie's neck. "You amazing animal," she whispered into the softness.

"She is very special," Jaspar remarked.

"Thank you once more for letting me ride her." She smiled at him. When she smiled like that, it made Jaspar feel weak; she was so beautiful. On impulse he caught her hand and kissed it. She stiffened slightly and he felt her withdraw. He knew that whatever her demeanour, she had not forgiven him and she did not trust him. The knowledge made him feel surprisingly dejected.

By now they were back on the regular paths and Jaspar found himself hailed by Lady Morrison, who was riding in a carriage with her two daughters, and Lady Hamel, a woman whom Jaspar disliked excessively.

"Oh dear, Lady Morrison, we can hardly ignore her." He pulled a face.

"Indeed not," reproved Grizelda. "We are both beholden to her for her excellent hospitality. Anyway I like her."

"So do I, but I see you do not yet know Lady Hamel."

By now the carriage had drawn up next to them. "Lord Heddington, how delightful," beamed Lady Morrison in her good-natured way. "And Miss Ludgrove, but I do not believe you know Lady Hamel, and her daughter, Miss Hamel."

Lady Hamel was a hatchet-faced dame with a beak nose and crossed eyes. Her daughter looked disdainful. Grizelda greeted them politely.

"Have you been for a fast ride?" asked Lady Morrison. "How brave of you in this weather." She shivered slightly.

"Oh, Mama, how silly, it would be wonderful to ride today, especially on an animal like that," Miss Eliza Morrison remarked enviously. "It is a marvellous horse."

"Oh yes, she is," asserted Grizelda enthusiastically.

"Did you buy her from Lady Oakley, Miss Ludgrove?" enquired Lady Hamel in her presumptuous fashion. "She must have cost you a pretty packet. I gather that when she was sold last week there were several disappointed customers. I know the duchess would have liked her."

Grizelda froze as the implications of this deliberately spiteful remark bore in on her. Could it be true, had the mare only been sold a week ago? Jaspar had lied to her. She felt her temper rising, her mouth set in a firm line and her eyes flashed fire. Jaspar was furious. He had always disliked Lady Hamel and he vowed that after this malicious piece of meddling, she would find herself cut firmly. He watched Grizelda's face. She looked fiercely angry. He remembered well that look from before.

They made their farewells and hardly were they out of earshot before Grizelda turned on him in fury. "For your sisters! In your stables! You lied to me; you bought this horse only last week. How dare you. I will never ride her again. I will not be treated like this!"

She slid defiantly off Launcie's back. Jaspar grabbed the mare's rein. He nearly laughed. She was magnificent in her anger, and he found it most refreshing not to be subjected to the customary sycophantic toadying which was usually his lot.

"Calm down, just a minute, let me explain."

"Explain! There can be no adequate explanation! You are a dissembler and... and a... a..."

Grizelda's problem was that by dismounting she had put herself at a disadvantage. She was having to half run after Jaspar and her insults were rapidly running out of steam as she herself ran out of breath. He, infuriating man, slowed down not a whit.

"Slow down! How can I argue with you when you go so fast!" She stopped breathless as he cantered away. Grizelda threw her crop on the ground in fury and then she giggled. Well aware that she possessed a singular and vehement temper, she also possessed a strong sense of the ridiculous, and the thought of herself running irately after a cantering Jaspar made her laugh so much she could hardly catch her breath. He peeped back over his shoulder and watched her sitting on the ground, shaking with gales of laughter. He wheeled the horses around and came back to her.

"Better?" he commented encouragingly.

She nodded, unable to speak through laughter.

He dismounted. "I apologise for lying. I thought you would not consent to ride the horse if you thought that I had bought it for you."

"You were correct in your assumption. I cannot ride her if that is the case."

"It's not quite that. I was looking for a new hunter when I saw the mare, and horses like that come up so rarely that I had to have her. I thought I would keep her for my sisters or my wife."

Grizelda felt a pang. She stopped laughing. His wife? Surely he was not intending to get married. Suddenly, she felt inexplicably sad. However, she left the remark unanswered and listened as he went on.

"So please, will you ride her for me?" This was said with such beguiling charm that Grizelda knew she would never be able to resist. Really this man had a dangerous appeal.

"Yes and I apologise. My awful temper. It goes with my red hair I am afraid."

"Well, at least you did not feel moved to shoot me this time!" He grinned.

They rode back in companionable silence, and Launcie remained in the stables at Melbourne House.

It was nearly Christmas and a time for the commencement of the customary festivities. The next week found the Duchess of Staplefield's annual party, which Jaspar always attended. The Staplefield Christmas party was a traditional event. The duchess issued cards to all her particular friends and their various children, the range of ages only adding to the charm.

When Jaspar arrived at Staplefield House in Berkeley Square, the house was ablaze with welcoming lights. He came in and handed his greatcoat to a footman, noticing with amusement that the enormous marble hall was overrun with excited children, liberated from the schoolroom for this important night. Jaspar grinned. As he did so he found himself enveloped in a bear-like hug by his godson and niece. The young viscount was a particular favourite, as was his sister, who so exactly resembled her mother as to make Jaspar nostalgic for his childhood. Lucy hung onto his arm while Charles led him solemnly up the wide staircase to his hosts.

"Oh, Uncle Jaspar, it is too exciting!" Lucy jumped up and down, her thin limbs and dark eyes vibrating with the thrills. "And you know that Abigail is allowed to come this year, although she has to stay with Nurse in the saloon. I truly like this time of the year best of all," she giggled.

"Better than your summer holidays, or your birthday?"

She nodded again. "Umm, perhaps I like my birthday as well."

By this time they had reached the top of the stairs and Jaspar put out his hand to greet his hosts. The duke and duchess stood outside the door of the huge saloon to welcome their guests. They made a handsome couple, his grace very dark while the duchess was fair and fragile. Jaspar liked the duke but had never been particularly fond of his wife, whom he regarded as a self-centred woman who thought little of anyone but herself. It was curious to him how she seemed always to manage to get her own way in all things. It had been Jaspar's observation that this was often the case with these spoilt manipulative people, but just how they achieved it he could never fathom. She held out her hand, smiling warmly; she was certainly not averse to flattery from handsome young men, although the polite scrutiny that she generally received from Jaspar somewhat disconcerted her.

"Jaspar! How well you look. I am glad you are still in town." The duke's bright blue eyes lit up.

"Augustus." Jaspar wrung his hand. "I would not miss the Mordaunts' Christmas party for anything."

The duke smiled. "You will find that we are all here, except for my little grandson George. He, at nine months, is too young to attend."

The duke had six children, of whom five had inherited the extraordinary looks of their parents. Their eldest son and heir, Gideon, Lord Slaughan, was a particular friend of Jaspar's. In the past he had paid scant attention to Gidi's sister Perpetua. She was quite different from the rest, being a small, mousy, insignificant girl, possessed of no conversation and who, to Jaspar's eyes, had always looked like a scared rabbit. She had, however, recently married Lord Milton and as she welcomed Jaspar, he discerned a change in her.

"My Lord Heddington." Petty smiled; her smile was sweet and direct.

"Lady Milton. It is a pleasure to see you again."

She looked him straight in the eye, her blue eyes holding a slight challenge. "Again?" she murmured.

He understood and laughed. She was not stupid at any event. "You look so happy and very…" He stopped, searching for a word that could not be seen as offensive.

She grinned. "I am. You know it is wonderful not to be scared the whole time. When I was in London, I used to be afraid to speak. Do you remember?"

He did and appreciated her honesty. "I do. How brave you are to admit it." His respect for her grew and he thought he had rather underestimated this plain girl in the past. She was not plain now, he realised. She glowed with life.

"Thank you. It is so much easier to speak out, I find, than I had thought possible. Still you are very polite, it cannot have been much of a pleasure to meet me before," she continued.

Jaspar hooted with laughter. "No, perhaps not but I think it will in the future."

"It is being married, you know. It is wonderful and my baby is a miracle." At that moment her husband joined them. He glanced at this wife and the wordless interchange that passed between Lord and Lady Milton made Jaspar feel quite dispirited. It was only momentary but it spoke volumes, and this exchange, between two people who clearly loved and understood each other, was, Jaspar discovered, something that he wanted very much.

"Do you know Edward?" Petty enquired.

"I do not think I have had the pleasure."

"Edward, this is Lord Heddington. Jaspar, this is Lord Milton."

The two men shook hands. Jaspar liked what he saw. Lord Milton was a tall dark man with an intelligent face. He put his hand lightly around his wife's shoulders as he spoke. It was a gentle, caring gesture that again aroused in Jaspar a slight feeling of envy.

"I am delighted to make your acquaintance but we neglect you, it would appear that you have not yet had a drink." He waved to the butler but as he did so Gideon erupted up the stairs.

"Jas, my best friend, and Petty!" He hugged his sister, grasped Jaspar's hand and went on impetuously, "Edward, I intend to take Jaspar and introduce him to Aurelia. She is Edward's sister," he explained, "and you will find is quite the most beautiful creature in the world. At least she is the most beautiful girl I have ever seen."

"If she is so exceptional, I wonder you are introducing her to me," Jaspar teased. "I am not known to ignore great beauty, you know, you will find your nose quite put out of joint by me!"

Edward laughed. "I think Aurelia regards Gidi as a naughty brother."

The marquis looked indignant. "You make me seem as if I come straight from the schoolroom. However, I have no designs on Aurelia, but one must admire her, you know."

"A good thing! For if you had 'designs' as you call them, I would be forced to come the heavy brother, and whisk her out of your unsuitable way!"

"Then you better whisk Jaspar away, he is far more dangerous than I am," said Gideon enticingly.

"Possibly!" Lord Milton continued. He met Jaspar's eyes. Then surmised, "I think Aurelia will be safe with you, my lord."

"What! Jaspar!" laughed Gideon, unable to stop himself. "Why, he is the worst rake in town."

There was a sudden silence. Jaspar pulled himself up stiffly and Petty, intrigued, noticed a faint look of regret flit over his face. Gideon looked like a naughty schoolboy who has allowed a secret to slip out. Petty glanced quickly from one to the other. She tucked her arm in Jaspar's.

"Come, my lord, I shall take you to meet Aurelia."

"Oh, Jas, I apologise," Gideon said ruefully, "I did not mean…"

"You did, Gidi, and it was deserved." Jaspar's mouth twisted. "I have a reputation. A rightful reputation. You should not expose your beautiful sister to me, Lady Milton," he continued somewhat bitterly. He found it strange in himself that he should suddenly care. It had never bothered him a whit that he was considered a rascal and a rake, but suddenly it mattered a great deal.

"Fiddle!" exclaimed Petty, who understood. "Aurelia will come to no harm with you, my lord." She smiled at him and led him away.

Aurelia was at the end of the ballroom which was decorated with Christmas greens, tall candles wound with holly and ivy. She was dancing with two children, who swirled about her. Jaspar realised that Gidi had not exaggerated. She was the most exquisite girl he had ever encountered and his experience, he had to admit, was extensive. She was very dark, with naturally luxurious curls which she wore gathered on top of her head. She had pale blue eyes fringed with the longest, blackest lashes. Her skin was pale and utterly without blemish, her mouth firm and wide. Her cheeks were faintly tinged with pink.

As they came up she stopped dancing, and gently chivvied the two children in the direction of the nurses, who sat at one end of the ballroom enjoying the rare chance of a comfortable prose whilst their charges cavorted around. Lady Milton introduced them; Aurelia sank into a graceful curtsey. He noticed how unaffectedly she greeted him.

"My lord." She rose; as she did so she peeped up at him from under her lashes; she was utterly ravishing. He found himself almost bowled over by her beauty and that rare, indefinable natural charm which must, he realised, make everyone adore her.

"Will you do me the honour of dancing with me?" he asked.

"If you promise not to whirl me around at double speed as Marcus and Marina have been doing."

"I think I can safely promise you that," he pronounced as he led her onto the dance floor. They were playing a waltz. Aurelia, to add to her other qualities, was an excellent dancer. "We have not met before, I think."

"No, I was to have come out last year but Petty had George and was not considered up to presenting me, so I am to have a ball this summer. Will you come?"

He found her directness enchanting, but as he danced with her he could not help remembering the last person with whom he had danced a waltz. He did not mean to think of Grizelda but she kept creeping into his thoughts, just when he expected it least.

"Of course I shall be delighted to come, if you are good enough to ask me," he replied.

"Oh, I imagine we will ask you. You are, I gather, a most eligible bachelor," she opened her marvellous eyes wide, "even if you are rather dangerous."

He laughed. He did not find her openness offensive but, rather, amusing. "It would be immodest in me to claim that I am eligible," his eyes danced, "or that I am, as you put it, dangerous!"

She bit her lip. "Oh dear, I did not mean to be discourteous. I think it is rather exciting to be just a little wicked. It is so dull to be good all the time."

He laughed again. "I think I can claim to be a little wicked," he agreed, his face solemn, although his eyes were alight with amusement.

She laughed. "Good. Then I think we will be friends."

The dance finished; he looked her in the eyes. "I think so too," he said as he lifted her hand to his lips.

His dance with Miss Milton had not passed entirely unnoticed. Lady Ambrose observed to Lady Morrison who sat next to her, "I see that Jaspar has started another of his famous flirtations, mind you one cannot blame him. Miss Milton is quite exquisite. I do not think I have seen a more beautiful girl."

"No, even the Gunnings' could not have competed with her and she is so unspoilt too; I find it very attractive. I do not like pert, encroaching females."

"Speaking of encroaching females, I see Mrs Darcy is approaching us. How can Julia have invited her?"

"I think Lady Morntarny persuaded her for Clarissa's sake. Really she has been most assiduous in her determination to give the girl a pleasant time."

"I do understand it. The aunt kept her almost as a skivvy. She never presented her at all."

"Do you blame her? She certainly put the shine to Henrietta, and Clarissa is no belle. I shall enjoy seeing Miss Darcy next to Miss Milton." Both ladies giggled in a most unseemly manner.

"It seems that Clarissa has made a most advantageous conquest," Lady Morrison continued in her good-natured fashion.

Lady Ambrose raised an eyebrow.

"Why, Roderick Talkarne." By now Mrs Darcy had borne down on them and had heard the name, her face contorted with dislike, but she said nothing for she knew it only reflected badly on her if she criticised Clarissa too strongly.

Chapter Thirteen

The day after the Maudaunts' party Jaspar walked across St James's Park to pay a visit on Lady Melbourne. The morning was cold and misty. He struck out briskly, pushing his hands deep into the pockets of his greatcoat, determined to keep out the chill, raw weather that swirled about him. The air was heavy with droplets of water which clung to his face and clothes. As he peered ahead of him he could just ascertain the outline of trees, part-concealed in the drizzle, and over the top of their silhouette he watched as the half-hearted rays of sunlight struggled to warm away the dankness. He crossed under the dripping trees, skirting the lake which was shiny with ice, and as he did so he noticed, in some amusement, the tiny birds which skidded across its wetness, in a vain attempt to reach the other side. By the time he reached the edge of the park the sun had won its battle and was breaking through the moistness. He walked down Whitehall, which seemed surprisingly quiet, and up to the Ionic entrance to Melbourne House.

Her Ladyship was downstairs in the suite of rooms that was usually occupied by William Lamb, although he had been out of London for many weeks. His wife, Lady Caroline, had had a desolate and passionate relationship with Lord Byron, which had ended last August.

Lady Caroline was inconsolable, her hysteria causing such disturbance, that in desperation, her mama, Lady Bessborough, and his mother, Lady Melbourne, had arranged for her to be removed first to Ireland and then to the Melbournes' country estate, Brocket. William had accompanied her and had impressed by his unfailing devotion and care of his wife, whose mental state was so unbalanced.

Jaspar liked and admired William very much. They had been at Eton together, and although William Lamb was a few years older, they had been good friends. Jaspar respected his intelligence and the unselfishness of his nature. He felt inordinately sorry for him in his marital trouble and had observed with some distress the protective detached disillusionment that William now displayed to the world.

William's suite of rooms were the ones that had been decorated by Holland for the Duke of York. The walls were adorned by panels painted with flowers and cupids. Lady Melbourne sat facing the terrace which led off the windows overlooking St James's Park and which was bounded by the pillars which supported the balcony above. She was staring at the damp stems which wound their way around the iron work. She was lost in thought.

As the butler announced Jaspar she looked up, stretching out her hand to him, pleasure evident in her face. He went to her and kissed her cheek.

"In a blue study, Elizabeth?" It was most unlike her to allow herself to be affected by anything.

She sighed wistfully. "I was thinking of William. So much lost promise. He could have been a great man. Now he is forced to resign Parliament and all because of that wretched girl." Her face stiffened with dislike.

Jaspar nodded. "It is hard not to deplore the creature, although one must admire William's loyalty and patience."

"Misplaced. If only he could be more hard-hearted." She

shook herself slightly. "But you did not come to be burdened with our troubles."

"Nevertheless, you appreciate that I am much disposed towards you and William," Jaspar stated firmly. "And any help you want from me you know will be forthcoming."

She smiled warmly. "I do know and I am grateful, but before I quite sink, let us talk of more cheerful matters."

"Yes," he agreed, changing the subject. "I had hoped to see you at Staplefield House last night."

"I did not go, for Grizelda does not know the duke and it is so much a family affair."

Jaspar nodded. Secretly he had hoped that Lady Melbourne and her goddaughter would have been there. "I come to arrange to convey Grizelda back to her father's at Vernham Dean, for Christmas."

Lady Melbourne shot him a slightly surprised look. What was Jaspar playing at? It would be great indeed, if she could attach him for Grizelda but no, Jaspar was not the settling-down kind.

As if to answer her unspoken enquiry he went on, "I intend to ask Mr Ludgrove if Laura may come and spend the season with Nillie."

Lady Melbourne looked astonished. Jaspar met her eyes steadily. "It seems that many think, erroneously, as you do, Elizabeth, that I had an affair with Laura. I must do something to redress this misapprehension. Hence my offer."

Lady Melbourne was even more perplexed, Jaspar behaving in a way that must be seen to be quite out of character. "I am sure that Mr Ludgrove will be most gratified. At least with Nillie he may be assured that she will be properly supervised," she remarked tartly.

"Is Miss Ludgrove here?" enquired Jaspar, a mite too mindfully.

His studied carelessness was not lost on Lady Melbourne. No, Elizabeth was certainly most intrigued by Jaspar's involvement with her goddaughter. She did not want to hope that he might be serious about her. One was likely to be disappointed if one entertained those aspirations where one such as Jaspar was concerned. Too many matchmaking mamas had made that mistake. On the other hand he showed such an interest. *I must ask Grizelda back next season too*, she thought to herself. *What a thing if I could marry her to him.*

"I believe she was to have gone to Bond Street to purchase some items for Christmas but she may not have left yet. Please ring for me?"

The footman who arrived in answer to her summons assured my lady that miss had not gone out yet, and two minutes later Grizelda herself came in. She was dressed for walking in a warm mantelet made of blue wool and trimmed with fur. On her head was a trim poke bonnet, and her hair was caught up on the nape of her neck. As usual he was struck by her way of being both different and yet very dashing as well. She curtsied to him.

"Good morning, my lord." Her low husky voice was most enticing.

"Good morning, Miss Ludgrove."

She looked up and met his eyes; there was such a warm look in them that, for a moment, her defenses almost crumbled, but she merely put up her chin and remarked, "I cannot stay for I have arranged to go shopping."

He was amused at the studied insult, aware that she had no intention of being rude, but Lady Melbourne was shocked; it was most unlike her goddaughter, whose manners were singular.

"My dear, here is Lord Heddington come to arrange to convey you back to your papa for Christmas. I believe a shopping trip must wait."

"Oh no, indeed, there is no need for you to do that, I am quite well accounted for, am I not, Lady Melbourne?"

Elizabeth felt quite cross. Her goddaughter was really

behaving most inconsiderately. It was inconvenient for her to have to arrange for Grizelda to be conveyed home.

"Well, Grizelda, I must confess that I would find it a deal easier not to have to take out the coach for you, we must all be carried to Brocket, you know."

Bother, thought Grizelda, *if I refuse I look so ungrateful and yet I do not want to be beholden to Lord Heddington.*

"Really, there is no need, she hurried on. "I can as well take the stage."

"Now, Grizelda, do not be so silly," Lady Melbourne continued sharply. "Please do say thank you to Lord Heddington. He wishes to see your father. He has a most advantageous offer to make regarding Laura."

Grizelda tried to hide her shock; surely he was not offering for Laura; she kept her face calm.

"He wishes Laura to spend the season with Lady Morntarny."

Grizelda looked confounded. "Lady Morntarny! Does she wish to have Laura for the season?"

"Oh yes, she was very fond of her," lied Jaspar; in truth Nillie knew nothing of the project but she would do nothing to disoblige him.

"Oh no, we could not accept such kindness…" started Grizelda in confusion.

"You can and you will." Jaspar's voice was firm and his eyes met hers. She understood the message in them. It said, "I promised to aid Laura, now you must not refuse."

She swallowed. "Well, if Papa agrees."

"If your papa refuses he is a bigger fool than I take him for," asserted Lady Melbourne, "and if he does he will have me to answer to!"

"Yes, of course," Grizelda stammered. "But now, I really must go. I have a deal to do and the morning progresses."

"I will walk with you. I, too, need to buy various articles in Bond Street," agreed Lord Heddington.

"Oh no, there is no need." She met his eyes. They were dancing with amusement at her constant refusals.

"Oh, but I shall be desolate if you will not allow me to accompany you to Bond Street," he teased.

"I am not alone for I take my maid, but alright," she remarked with some asperity. "I suppose it would be churlish to refuse," she chuckled.

Lady Melbourne watched this interchange with interest, and not without some satisfaction. *She is not stupid, my goddaughter,* she mused.

Jaspar and Grizelda walked back through the park. The sun had by this time managed to burn away the mist and the sky was bright blue.

"When do you want to return home?" Jaspar enquired.

"Whenever is convenient to you, my lord," Grizelda responded, feigning mock servility.

He laughed. "Suddenly so docile, Miss Ludgrove?"

"I must be all compliance, my lord," she said, lowering her eyes. Then she giggled and looked up at him. He caught his breath she was so enchanting. "But it goes much against the grain."

"I am glad to see you restored to your combative self. I admit I would have worried if you had become too submissive."

She grinned again. "I am grateful to you for taking me back, but there is no need to arrange for Laura to spend the season with your sister. I am persuaded that Lady Morntarny does not wish for such a responsibility."

"I am sure that Nillie will be delighted to bring out Laura."

"Why? Why are you doing this?"

He was suddenly serious. "You know why I am doing this. I must make amends and I must make you forgive me."

"Oh, I will never do that, you know," she retorted facetiously. "Would you, if it were your sister?"

"No, I suppose I would not," he said sadly.

Grizelda was confused. She did not trust her feelings or his intentions and yet her good sense told her that when he spoke, he spoke the truth. He did wish to redress the ill that he had done Laura.

"But you still have not told me when you need to be at home," he went on.

"Well, I suppose by Thursday."

"Excellent, then I can take you and go straight on to Bardfield."

By now they were in Bond Street. Grizelda fully expected that he would leave her here, but he showed no inclination to do so. Instead he exhibited every intention of accompanying her on her visits to the shops. It pleased her greatly that he should choose to accompany her.

"You will not enjoy shopping for presents for those you hardly know, I am sure, my lord," she stated honestly.

"Allow me to be the judge of that," he teased.

They went into several emporia where Grizelda carefully picked presents for her papa and for Laura; she then counted out the exact money needed to pay for her gifts and Jaspar realised, from her actions, that her funds were clearly strictly limited. He found that he possessed an almost overwhelming and confusing desire to pay for everything she bought, and yet he knew that if he suggested such a thing she would be horrified, although the sums must be considered trifling.

He bought nothing himself, merely content to watch her choose and negotiate. Coming out of the fancy works shop, where they had purchased some flower cases, card racks and hand screens, Jaspar heard his name called by Lady Milton who, accompanied by Miss Milton, was obviously on the same mission as Grizelda.

"Jaspar." Petty smiled at him. "Are you shopping for Christmas presents?"

"Yes." She looked questioningly at his packageless arms and raised an eyebrow slightly.

"In truth, Petty," he went on, kissing her cheek, "I am helping Miss Ludgrove, but I do not think you are acquainted?" Lady Milton shook her head. "Please allow me to present you."

As he did so, he was again struck by Aurelia's astonishing beauty. She curtsied to him, regarding him steadily out of the astounding blue eyes. "My lord, we meet again." She put out her hand. Grizelda observed that she was entirely without guile; the fascination of this startling girl was obvious and a faint flutter of uneasiness swept over her. Of course, Lord Heddington would be attracted to her, how could anyone fail to be? Suddenly, she was conscious that Lady Milton was addressing a remark to her. She flushed slightly at her rudeness.

"I apologise, I was…"

"Amazed by Aurelia," said the down-to-earth Petty. "Oh, please, do not worry, everyone is. She is supremely unaware of it, of course, but that only adds to the allure."

"Yes," responded Grizelda. "But I am sorry, for I did not catch what you asked."

Before Petty could respond to the question, Aurelia broke into the conversation. "Lord Heddington has been kind enough to ask about hunting."

"I was just telling Miss Milton that Gidi comes to hunt for the New Year. Perhaps you, Lord Milton and Miss Milton would care to join us?"

"Oh, I am sure that Edward would be most happy but I do not hunt, I am afraid."

"That will not matter. Nillie does not either and I know that she would be overjoyed to have time with you, you will have much to discuss. I have all my nieces and nephews at Bardfield for Christmas."

"Indeed, I shall love to see Petronilla again and to show her George."

"Then that is settled, but how about Miss Milton?" He smiled at Aurelia.

"Oh, I love riding above all things," said the beauty firmly, "but I do not have a suitable horse."

"Oh, I am sure we can mount you," started Jaspar.

Grizelda was quiet. She suddenly felt discomfited. A sense of isolation swept over her. She wondered whether the ravishing Aurelia would be riding Launcie. The mare was, after all, Lord Heddington's, she had no right to feel proprietorial over her. In any circumstances it must be considered idiotic to let sadness overcome her; she was not part of his life and never could be. Their worlds were different. She was not part of their cheerful family plans. Her own Christmas would be a joyless affair, her papa shrouded in the gloom that had assailed him since Laura had returned in disgrace. The long, boring evenings at Lord Farleigh's. She sighed. Lady Milton glanced at her. She thought how lovely and unusual Miss Ludgrove was and how melancholy she suddenly looked. Being kind and sensitive, she immediately asked, "How we chatter on. Miss Ludgrove, pray tell me, how will your Christmas be?"

Grizelda swallowed. "Oh, ours is very quiet in comparison to the jollity that you describe. My papa is the manager to my Lord Farleigh's estate. We go there for Christmas."

"And does he have family perhaps?" Petty asked concernedly.

"No, he is a bachelor – almost a recluse."

"But you have family?"

"Only one sister. My mama is dead. My papa has no brothers or sisters so we have no aunts or uncles or cousins."

"But did your mama have no sisters either?" asked Aurelia bluntly. Grizelda looked away. Jaspar watched her, concern in his face.

"Aurelia," Lady Milton said gently.

"No," Grizelda responded bravely. "It is a just question. My mama's family will have nothing to do with us. They did not like her marrying Papa." She looked Jaspar in the eyes defiantly. That would do it. He would not want anything to do with her now and probably a good thing. He was assuredly just too appealing. However, my lord just continued to look at her. His eyes held neither pity nor distaste, just faint admiration. Lady Milton patted her on the arm firmly.

"Edward would much sympathy with you, Miss Ludgrove. His papa married to displease Lord Milton, who was his grandfather, and the family would have nothing more to do with them. Would they, Aurelia?"

"No, indeed, I have never met any of my Milton cousins," the girl laughed. "I deduce that they are a pretty horrid bunch. It has never worried me." She looped her arm into Petty's. "But now I have a wonderful sister and I always had Edward and Cuthbert." She looked at Grizelda. "He is my grandfather and he is wonderful, is he not, Petty?"

Lady Milton nodded. "Indeed he is, he is a warm and most loving man. I adore to see him with George, he is quite the proudest great-grandpapa."

Grizelda smiled ruefully. She thought about her father; he loved them but he was essentially an undemonstrative man. Lost in his own world he found it hard to speak to his children of any matters that were not of the most ordinary. She did not think that Aurelia's case was like hers at all.

"Jaspar, I must not delay you any longer." Petty held out her hand to him. "I shall look forward to visiting you. Come, Aurelia."

The girl curtsied gracefully and then rushed off after her sister, leaving a bouncing trail of her exuberance and beauty behind her.

"What a remarkable girl," Grizelda vouchsafed.

"Indeed she is," declared Jaspar as he watched her retreating back. "The most exquisite girl I have ever seen."

Grizelda did not quite know how to reply to his pronouncement. She knew she was surprisingly dejected by the thought that he should admire Aurelia much, and yet it was only to be expected for she really was most unusual. The wind was becoming colder, and in spite of the warmth of her apparel, Grizelda shivered.

"Come, I must return you home, you are looking quite chilly." He grinned at her, taking her arm and tucking it in his.

CHAPTER FOURTEEN

Early on Thursday Jaspar's travelling carriage and a well-matched team arrived in Whitehall to collect Grizelda. It was dark and cold. Harper, who had been instructed to drive, looked up towards the leaden sky and shook his head at his underling, whom he had honoured with the information that he was to accompany them, and pronounced, "I do not like it. Not one bit. Looks very nasty it does. I asks yer, look at that sky."

The sky was grey and lowering, the clouds round and heavy with their burden of snow. A slight pink light suffused them, which, as Harper went on in a voice of doom, "Does not augur well. I jes' hope it holds hoff long enough for us to get down ther and back to Bardfield."

The underling merely nodded agreement to his superior. He was much in awe of Harper and found his master, Lord Heddington, at times far more approachable than the august head of the stables. So Tom, who had not before been appointed to go with my lord on a long journey, and who was determined to do his very best to prove his worth, made no reply, merely hastening to prepare the team.

"I spects we'll be awaiting an age for the young lady. Ladies general do not hurry in their hintentions, in my hexperience," the worldly Harper continued. "My Lady Heddington, very particular in her dress she is and we've awaited an age for her. As for Miss Petronilla, when she was a girl and the toast of the town, she was not one to hurry."

Harper's premonitions were to prove incorrect. Grizelda was ready when they arrived at Melbourne House. Her presents to the Melbournes were bestowed, her bags were bound and all that remained was for her to bid goodbye to her godmother. Hugging Her Ladyship, she repeated her gratitude for her sojourn in London, before laying a hand on Jaspar's arm and allowing him to lead her to the waiting coach.

She climbed aboard and was immediately struck by the opulence of the interior. Grizelda generally travelled post or sometimes on the stage. Her papa's fortune did not run to luxury travel. So Jaspar's carriage was a most pleasant change. Of the latest design, the squabs were tooled leather, the undercarriage excellently sprung. On the seats His Lordship, ever mindful of her comfort, had laid out thick rugs and cushions. She sat back contentedly. Jaspar ordered Harper to be off and sprang in to sit next to her. The team leapt forward, and Grizelda had the considerable satisfaction of driving in a coach with a team that was so expert it felt as if they were moving smoothly through space.

Grizelda wriggled contentedly, then, peering out at the darkening sky, felt obliged to comment, "I do hope that it will not snow."

"So do I, for as I mentioned, I intend to go straight to Bardfield when I leave you and I do not wish to be delayed. There are so many preparations I must attend to before my guests arrive."

"I am sorry that you are plagued with conveying me to Vernham Dean." She smiled wryly.

"It is not a nuisance. If it were I can assure you I would not do it. I am a selfish creature," Jaspar confessed.

Grizelda grinned. "A few months ago I would have agreed with that sentiment, but now I am not at all sure that that is true.

You are so obliging as to drive me home, you are determined to circumnavigate the damage done to Laura. Those are hardly the acts of a selfish man."

"Ah ha! I have fooled you. I am all self-seeking, I can promise you," he teased. His sparkling dark eyes caught her blue ones, which were warm and amused.

"If you are trying to convince me that you have lived entirely for yourself I will not believe you," she responded roundly. "Do not forget you divulged to me your plan to build a hospital for your tenants and that is an act of true generosity."

"No. It is good business. I want my tenants to work harder for me and they cannot do this if they are unwell. Utterly egotistical."

Grizelda raised an eyebrow in disbelief. She did not accept his rebuttal, although she recognised that men who have everything they could covet, as Lord Heddington had, do incline to a lack of consideration for others' feelings or desires, and she must never forget the callousness with which he had left Laura.

"You fail singularly to convince," she asserted. "I am, however, extremely intrigued by the plans for the hospital. Do you yet commence building?"

Jaspar was startled by her obvious interest. Most of the females with whom he was acquainted would have changed the subject quickly, when faced with a conversation about illnesses of the lower classes.

"I am not sure. Although Horace, that is Dr Sugdon, intimated in his last letter that the foundations were about to be laid. But I cannot think that they will be able to achieve much in this weather. So I imagine that it will be spring before we make any real progress."

"Does he intend to live on the premises? Will he have other doctors working with him? How many people can the hospital accommodate?"

"I think he means to remain in his cottage. It is not far away, but he says that he will come and see patients in a room in the hospital. I do not think that any other doctors will work for him, although he says that he has an excellent nurse in mind, and I must admit I am not exactly sure how many beds there will be. Does that answer all your questions?" He smiled.

"I think it is terribly exciting. I would be most interested to see it. I believe that the health and wellbeing of the working people is very important. Now we are in the nineteenth century, we can no longer ignore their right to consideration."

Jaspar looked at her. "You are an odd girl. I cannot think of any other who believes as you do." He grinned. "But of course, you must come and see the hospital, it is very close to Bardfield."

Grizelda flushed slightly. She was genuinely very concerned about advancing the cause of those less advantaged than herself, but her objective had not been to receive an invitation to Bardfield. She suddenly felt as if she had behaved in a presumptuous and uncharacteristic manner. She quickly changed the subject, and as she did so, Jaspar realised that he would, above all, like to extend an invitation to her to come to his home.

"What will you do over Christmas, my lord?" The ordinariness of the question restored her self-possession; she smiled at him.

He regarded her for a moment and then replied, "We will be very busy. The evening before Christmas the servants have a ball and we invite all my tenants on the estate. My sisters generally come to stay, complete with their offspring, although this year, Georgiana, she is my eldest sister, will not be with us. She must go to her parents-in-law."

He went on to enlarge upon the jollity and fun that occurred every Christmas and which made Bardfield such a special place to be. As she listened, a wave of melancholy swept over Grizelda. The contrast between his Christmas and the formal day that she would pass at Farleigh Hall made her unutterably sad.

Fortuitously, the snow kept off and they made good progress, arriving in Yateley for lunch. In spite of the rugs and warm bricks, thoughtfully provided by Jaspar, it was icy in the coach and when, at last, they drew into the Swan Inn, Grizelda was only too grateful to stretch her frozen limbs and have something to eat. As was his wont, Lord Heddington hired a private parlour and Grizelda's spirits lifted when she beheld a huge and welcoming fire burning in the grate. Warming her hands on the abundant flames she discovered memories of another parlour and the events that had occurred there flooding back. She had a half smile on her face as Jaspar entered. "Why are you smiling?" he enquired.

She blushed slightly, meeting his eyes with an honesty he found endearing. "l was thinking of another inn parlour. When we first met."

"Oh!" He turned from her and she was not quite sure whether he was upset or angry. In truth, Jaspar too remembered. The memory tempted him; the desire to sweep her back into his arms and kiss her again was almost overwhelming but he knew that was a quite ineligible activity. Before he could totally regain his composure, there came a slight knock on the door and the landlady entered to lay the covers. She was swiftly followed by a fat chambermaid, bearing a large tureen of soup. He pulled out a chair for Grizelda.

"Will you join me? I am very hungry," was the only remark he made, and as she sat down at the table opposite him, she wondered what he really thought of her actions six months earlier. She peeped at him but he did not return her glance and she found her former dejection returning. She sighed and supped her soup. It, at least, was delicious.

"We must not delay for I think the weather will not hold off much longer," Jaspar mentioned presently. It was with some regret that they left the warm parlour to return to the wintry coach, and worse, as they emerged from the inn, small pearly flakes were beginning to drop from a leaden sky. They settled onto Jaspar's greatcoat and the backs of the horses.

"Drat!" Jaspar commented to Harper. "I hope that it does not snow too much."

His henchman merely grunted. Grizelda clambered back in, and as they sped across the countryside, she amused herself by gazing out of the window. The snow was by now falling fast and the ground was rapidly becoming covered. An eerie silence descended as Grizelda watched, fascinated by the myriad shapes of the snowflakes as they tumbled unremittingly out of the sky.

"Beautiful, isn't it," she enthused, turning to Lord Heddington, who she discovered watching her.

"Yes," he agreed. "In spite of the difficulties it produces, I have to admit that I have never got over my childish fondness for snow. I expect my raggedly nephew will be out with his sisters building snowmen, just as I used to with my sisters when I was a boy."

To Grizelda these references to his childhood were poignant, for she found herself desperate to know all about him. "How many sisters have you?" she enquired.

"Four. I was the last child. My mama died giving birth to me. The longed-for son, I never knew her."

She hoped he would say more but he skilfully turned the question to her. "When did your mama die?"

"Some years ago. I was fourteen, so I knew her, of course. Laura was twelve. My papa found it very hard. It is not easy to be left with two daughters of those ages. He did his best," she responded with some reticence.

"Who looked after you?"

"We had a governess, Miss Hart. She was an efficient but not kindly person. She departed two years ago. Much to Laura's and my delight."

He laughed and all the previous constraints disappeared. By now the snow was cascading down, and although it was not freezing, the horses were forced to slow their pace considerably. It was cold and damp. Grizelda shivered.

"But you are cold, Miss Ludgrove." Jaspar moved closer to her, covering her up in fur rugs. His body felt warm and comforting next to her. She then firmly dispelled those thoughts. He was merely kind to her, as she was cold.

As the snow got deeper and deeper the journey became more and more interminable, and with great relief they eventually reached Vernham Dean. Grizelda directed Harper through the village to the entrance to Farleigh Hall, which was where the Lords Farleigh had resided since the sixteenth century. The gates were thrown open by a grizzled old gatekeeper, who had been there ever since Grizelda could remember. He bowed slightly at the elegant equipage and then peered inquisitively into the coach, exclaiming with astonishment when he beheld her sitting there in unaccustomed luxury. The snow was so deep that they were compelled to move very slowly down the drive until, at last, they finally reached Grizelda's home. It was a pretty square Georgian house surrounded by well-laid-out grounds. Grizelda's mama had been passionate about gardens and had taken it upon herself to create surprising and elegant ones here, emulating the ones she had grown up with at her childhood home, Carnoe Castle. After she had married Mr Ludgrove in a flurry of romance, Jane Ludgrove had never again seen either the castle or, indeed, her parents. This had been a terrible loss and a deprivation from which she never recovered. The marriage, which had seemed to promise so much, had become miserable. It was not that she did not love James Ludgrove. She did, but the difference in their stations and the resulting isolation from their familiar worlds had separated them, placing a strain on their relationship, which could never be resolved.

As soon as they stopped and Jaspar stepped into the swirling flakes, he realised that he would be quite unable to continue his journey tonight. He had not planned to reach Bardfield without spending a night on the road but he had anticipated being able to commence his journey home. The weather now made that utterly impossible.

Tom let down the steps and Grizelda jumped down into the snow. The night was very beautiful, the dark, dark sky studded with delicate white specks twirling and cascading in endless patterns. Grizelda's hair was soon covered in them.

"Come, snow maiden," Jaspar laughed, taking her hand. She grinned back at him, leading him in. The decorations in the hall were very dull and he noticed that the whole place had a gloomy, slightly desolate air. They gave their coats to the elderly butler, who had accompanied Mrs Ludgrove from Carnoe, and Grizelda went ahead of Jaspar into the library. This was a more welcoming room although, again, the order and neatness was rather, to Jaspar's fastidious taste, soulless.

"Please, will you be seated? What can I get you?" he asked.

"Some wine, and please tell Papa that we are here." She nodded to the butler, who withdrew.

"You are surely not planning to continue your journey tonight?" she enquired tentatively. She did not want to appear eager for him to remain, but secretly she hoped that he might, although she was wondering how an evening in the company of her father would entertain a man about town like Jaspar.

"My lord, I must apologise for not being here to meet you." Mr Ludgrove's greeting was reserved and his voice contained no warmth. However, he crossed the room to formally welcome his illustrious guest. In his youth he had obviously been a good-looking man, and the vestiges of this remained, although he now looked worn and dispirited. His thick sandy hair was greying and his blue eyes were ringed with the wrinkles of a man who spent much of his time outside. He was dressed simply in an old-fashioned coat of superfine, breeches and light jackboots.

James Ludgrove was still uneasy in the company of the aristocracy. He came from humble stock, and until he met and married the Hon. Jane Marchant he had never mixed in exalted circles. His wife had believed that when she married him her world would accept and like him, as she loved him, but this was never to be the case. This was as much to do with his inward reserve and belief that he was not good enough, as it was to do with an outward rejection by the polite world. It had never occurred to Jane that she would be ostracised by the friends with whom she had grown up. She was at first desolate and then bitter. The birth of her daughters went some way to mitigating the misery, but the sting was never lost completely. The resulting unhappiness had a stultifying effect on her naturally happy nature, and a regime of conservatism and propriety became established. It was this that gave the house its shadowy feel, as if no one with heart or life lived there.

He shook hands with Jaspar and said uncomfortably, "I must thank you for bringing Grizelda home. I am grateful." His voice was cold and hesitant.

There was an awkward silence. Suddenly, Grizelda was overcome with a rush of protective feelings towards this distant father of hers. He was the one whose solid order had been turned upside down through Laura's misdemeanour, whilst the infuriating Lord Heddington, a slightly sardonic look on his face, stood leaning against the fireplace, as if he had not a care in the world, watching, she believed, the social ineptitude of the older man. Her ready temper flared, and before she could stop herself the words she did not want to say came tumbling out.

"It is the least he could do in view of the wrong he has done to this family, and the damage and hurt he has caused to you, Papa, through his wayward actions." She gulped, gripping her hands together to stop herself. Why had she said that? She had not meant to. She had meant to try to get her father to forgive Jaspar; she had intended to smooth things over and now she had precipitated a quarrel. She flung a defiant glance at Jaspar. He had stiffened but his face betrayed nothing.

"Miss Ludgrove is correct. I have behaved very badly to your daughter. I apologise. I wish to minimise this damage." His voice was indifferent and formal. "I intend to invite Laura to stay with my sister, Lady Morntarny, for the season."

James Ludgrove looked amazed. "I do not think that my younger daughter should return to society."

Jaspar shrugged his shoulders. "As you wish. I thought that if she stayed with my sister it would give the lie to any gossip that there was any connection between us."

"He is right, Papa." Grizelda's temper had dissipated, and with its departure a feeling of desolation swept through her. Jaspar did not seem the man who had been so entertaining a companion on the way down. If she could have only taken back her words and started again she would have done so, but it was too late. "I think that it is a very generous offer on Lady Morntarny's part and I think that Laura should accept it with gratitude."

Her father turned and peered out of the window. The snow was still falling fast. Grizelda looked at his stiff back.

"Papa," she said gently.

Mr Ludgrove turned back. His face was tight with pain. He obviously hated the idea of being beholden to this man and his family but he could not refuse this chance. He nodded. "I agree."

There was another silence. "I had better depart," Lord Heddington started.

"Will you not stay the night? It hardly behoves you to continue your journey in this weather?" Grizelda asked diffidently. Jaspar had intended to stay if asked. He had wanted to spend an evening with her, but her outburst had made him realise that whatever he did, the seduction of Laura hung between them.

He thought an inn would be preferable to this inauspicious beginning. He had wanted to defuse Mr Ludgrove's anger. He had wanted the man to forgive him. He had wanted to do all that he could to help them, but he knew now that that was impossible. Better to leave at once before more damage was done.

 175

Harper thought it a very poor show. He had not been impressed by the Ludgroves' house and was even less impressed by their lack of hospitality. Jaspar found himself treated to a list of complaints from his henchman, which started with a disgust at people who sent others into the night in this weather and then continued with horror at the hurt that might be done to his precious horses. However, they quite quickly reached the inn at Hurstbourne Tarrant, which proved an excellent hostelry, so his worst fears were assuaged.

After Jaspar's departure Grizelda trailed miserably upstairs to her bleak bedchamber. She pulled a shawl around her against the fierce cold and sat at her table staring angrily at herself. *You fool*, she thought, bitterly regretting her outburst. She could find no justification for her stupidity. It could hardly be thought to have improved the situation. Oh no, it had made it far worse and it was not as if she really believed it any longer, for she did not. She sighed deeply. An unwelcome tear slid down her face. She wondered if she would ever see my lord again. Ineffectually she tried to push away thoughts of my Lord Heddington but the memory of his smile, the amused eyes, the swift, sharp exchange of understanding that passed between them when faced with the pompous or absurd would not be suppressed. She was now so cold that she felt constrained to move. She was too exhausted and dispirited to change for dinner, so, risking her papa's displeasure by remaining in her day dress, she went down. However, he hardly appeared to notice. The meal was almost entirely silent. Laura sulked. Mr Ludgrove had informed her that her sister had been brought back by Lord Heddington, and Laura made her chagrin, at what she considered Grizelda's betrayal, all too obvious. Grizelda was distressed at her sister's attitude, although she had to admit with a slight feeling of guilt that it was not entirely unjustified. Perhaps it was a good thing that my lord had not stayed.

Chapter Fifteen

Jaspar awoke the next morning incensed with Grizelda. She had had no right to rake him down in that unpleasant way, particularly in view of all that he was doing to alleviate any repercussions that might transpire towards her sister, through his transgression. It was not, he thought savagely to himself, as if it were all his fault. Laura had been a perfectly willing partner. He had not forced her. Grizelda was really most ungrateful for his efforts. A good breakfast and the realisation that there had been a slight thaw overnight went some little way to improving his temper, and as soon as the horses were put to, he left, delighted to be away from Vernham Dean and its environs. It was dank and wet. The previous day's snow had turned slushy, and dirty water splashed from the horses' hooves as they drove through the countryside. The trees dripped forlornly and the sky was an unrelieved grey. As they crossed the colourless countryside it became gradually colder and colder, and Jaspar was heartily glad that he had not delayed his journey. He suspected that there would be a severe frost tonight, rendering the roads treacherous. It had been a most unpleasant excursion, and Harper and His Lordship were unreservedly grateful when the gates to the long drive to Bardfield were reached. Jaspar ordered Harper to pause at the cottage, so that he could have a word with Williams the gatekeeper. Climbing out to greet him, he plunged his hands into his greatcoat pockets against the biting cold. In the left one his hand came in contact with a small package. It was the jewellery he had bought for Grizelda and Laura which, in his precipitate rush from Vernham Dean, he had forgotten to give them. Touching the carefully wrapped presents made him unexpectedly sad. His face contorted.

"My lord, proper cold." The old gruff voice of Williams brought him back to his surroundings.

He composed himself. "Indeed. I just stopped to make sure that you and Mrs Williams have everything you need?"

"Oh yes, my lord. It looks like we'll be snowed in for Christmas."

Jaspar nodded unhappily, shook the old man's hand and somewhat thankfully made his way to his house.

Netta had been upset when Jaspar had left Bardfield so hastily. She blamed herself for the irritation that had precipitated his departure. Lady Heddington, understanding her dilemma, had tried to encourage the girl to discuss the matter with her but Netta had not been forthcoming.

The dowager had, however, dropped some strong hints as to the inadvisability of treating Jaspar as if he were still in leading strings. Netta, far too intelligent not to comprehend what she meant, had taken the advice to heart. She planned for Christmas, when she knew that my lord must return. Going into Wisborough Green she ordered two new dresses from the excellent dressmaker who had chosen to reside there. One was an evening dress of cream silk and one a pretty morning dress of figured velvet in a rust colour, which suited her admirably. These were not the high fashion that Nillie had made up, from the select and fashionable modiste in Bruton Street who was honoured enough to be the recipient of my Lady Morntarny's custom, but they were very becoming and Netta knew that she looked her best in them. She summoned the best local hairdresser, and between him and her maid they had devised a new and dashing hairstyle. Netta was prepared for Jaspar. She would not repeat the mistakes she had made when he was ill.

She was at Bardfield when he arrived tired and dispirited from his drive. Nillie and his other sister, Emma, had come the previous evening and the house was full of laughter and excited children. Jaspar strode up to his front door, which was flung open by Savage, whose normally urbane face was rosy with the children's demands for Christmas, to a scene of great merriment. His three young nephews and five young nieces were playing tag around the great hall. Netta was helping the baby, Abigail, who, at two, was desperate to join in the antics of her elders. Netta glanced up as Jaspar came in. She had never looked better, he thought. She was wearing the new dress and her face was flushed from the game, her brown eyes were sparkling and Jaspar remembered how good she was. She was excellent with the little ones, too, he observed, and would surely make a most admirable wife.

She curtsied, laughing. "My lord, you catch me playing a most undignified game of tag, I am afraid."

He grinned back. "It is lovely to see them so happy." He started but his nephews and nieces; as soon as they realised who it was flung themselves in a body at him shouting, "Uncle Jaspar! Uncle Jaspar! Hooray!"

"Now, wretches, at least let me take off my coat before you throttle me," he replied, gently removing Frances, Emma's youngest daughter, from around his neck and setting her on the floor.

He stripped off his coat which Savage, his dignity restored, swiftly removed. "Uncle Jaspar! Uncle Jaspar, will you play with us?" demanded Charles.

"It seems I am quite superfluous," laughed Netta.

Jaspar picked up her hand and kissed it gallantly. "You could never be superfluous. It is just that I am a novelty. Wait until I have decreed, 'No noise and no running about in my hall,'" he proclaimed with mock severity. "Then see my popularity slide."

They laughed together, and he was reminded of the many times when as children they giggled inconsequentially. At that moment Nillie, Emma and Margaret emerged from the morning room; they hugged Jaspar. It was exceedingly pleasant to be back in the warmth and bustle of his house. Then suddenly, quite irrationally, he wished that Grizelda were here. His anger against her had evaporated to be replaced with a vague feeling of pity, as he contrasted the ebullient life of Bardfield with the neat soullessness of Mr Ludgrove's establishment.

Christmas at Farleigh Hall was never a cheerful affair. Lord Farleigh was well into his seventies and almost a recluse. He had never married and regarded woman as only a lesser evil to the devil himself. He had one brother with whom he had quarrelled as a young man and whom he had never seen again. It was only his liking and respect for his manager that made him ask Mr Ludgrove and his family over for Christmas, and the occasion was hardly one of festivity. Dinner did consist of the seasonal goose but this was the only concession to the time of year.

The Christmas of 1812 promised to be exactly the same as all previous Christmases, and Grizelda, whose thoughts were utterly and unusually downcast, was dreading it; however, when they reached the big house they discovered that, unlike previous years, they were not to be the only guests.

Farleigh Hall was a beautiful house. Set in 700 acres of park, it had been redesigned by Wyatt in his youth. It was approached by a long and meandering drive which undulated through woods and open acres. Then over the top of a slight hill, gave the first view of the house, nestling in a slight incline. Built of sandy stone, it stood strong and square, pavilions at each corner defined by fluted pilasters and a centre-porticoed entrance, flanked by Ionic columns. It was indubitably one of the most impressive mansions of the age.

The snow which covered the trees and house made Grizelda feel as if they were entering a kind of fairyland. The day was bright and sunny, making the frosty edges of the whiteness glisten, as if the branches were loaded with diamonds. It was breathtaking. Grizelda could not help remembering Jaspar's reminiscences about his childhood and she wondered if he were, even now, playing in the snow with his nephews.

When they arrived they were greeted, much to their surprise, by Lord Farleigh's nephew, the Hon. Jocelyn Farleigh. Jocelyn was well known to be on the worst of terms with Lord Farleigh, which was unfortunate for he was also, much to his uncle's consternation, the heir to all the titles and estates. He was a tall, dark, good-looking, if rather dissolute young man. As he welcomed them, he brushed back the black hair which hung over his eyes, with a white smooth hand heavy with rings. His disgruntled face with its downturned, slightly sullen mouth and fine straight nose was flushed a high colour. He had obviously been imbibing the excellent cellar which would some day, in the not too distant future he hoped, be his. Mr Ludgrove nodded curtly and went straight in to greet his employer.

"Good day," Jocelyn muttered sulkily. The Misses Ludgrove had not been privileged enough to meet the heir before. Indeed, this would have been nearly impossible for he never came near his uncle and had only made an appearance this Christmas under much duress, his gambling debts having reached a pressing need for settlement. The handsome face brightened when his eyes alighted on Laura. He was particularly attracted to blond young girls and Laura was a fine example. She, who since her ignominious return had been suffering from an ill-humoured malaise which infuriated Grizelda, was pleased when she observed the admiration in his dark eyes. He was dressed elegantly, although the negligent and casual way in which he wore his well-cut coat of superfine cloth and the breezy creases in his cravat gave him an aspect of one who cared not for his appearance. This was not true. In everything the Hon. Jocelyn's air of nonchalance was both studied and calculated. He picked up one of Laura's hands.

"An angel. A veritable angel!" he pronounced, cradling the delicate hand gently in his.

Laura giggled coquettishly. "Oh, Mr Farleigh." She peeped up at him from under the dark lashes.

Grizelda loathed him on sight. She thought him both affected and unpleasant; in any case, he ignored her.

"How have I missed such an angel?" Jocelyn rhapsodised. "Come in." He bowed in an exaggerated way and ushered Laura through the double doors. Grizelda trailed behind. Lord Farleigh was seated in a large wing chair in front of a generous fire. He made no attempt to rise, merely waving his hand in his nephew's direction. Grizelda knew that in fact he was hale in brain and body, although he feigned weakness to make everyone wait on him solicitously.

"Forgive my not rising," he said in a voice that was surprisingly strong for one who counterfeited infirmity, "but I am much plagued with illness... I do not think I shall last much longer." Then he wheeled around and fixed a beady eye on his nephew. "But do not think I shall die to oblige you," he contradicted.

Despite her general lowness of spirit, Grizelda's ready sense of the ridiculous overcame her dejection. She was much amused by the unspoken enmity between the two. If anything were to keep Lord Farleigh alive, it would be the hideous notion that his nephew were to step into his shoes. Unbeknownst to Jocelyn, he had left everything that was not entailed, to various obscure acquaintances. One of whom, although he remained in ignorance, was James Ludgrove. His Lordship had also, in so far as he was able, inserted various codicils regarding the property and had beset the inheritance with barriers to stop Jocelyn squandering everything in the gambling halls, of which he was extremely fond. Her father stood next to my lord, and the only other person in the room was a portly, slightly balding man with narrow eyes and a receding chin, who came towards them.

"May I present my friend Colonel Staunton," Jocelyn remarked casually, his eyes on Laura. Grizelda curtsied stiffly to the colonel. She did not much like what she observed of him, although she could not quite work out why she felt as she did. It was clear to her that there was a great disparity between the elegance and air of refinement of Brummell and Heddington and this supercilious gentleman, who regarded her with a contemptuous leer. Under this insolent gaze she found herself colouring. She looked around for help but her father was bending over Lord Farleigh, and Laura and Jocelyn were deep in conversation. She drew herself up and remarked non-committedly, "Do you come from these parts, Colonel?"

"No, from London." The answer was polite but Grizelda was left with her unease unabated.

She was very glad when the butler arrived to announce dinner.

The meal was interminable. Her father devoted himself entirely to conversation with His Lordship. Jocelyn contented himself with flirting outrageously with Laura, and Grizelda was left with her own uncomfortable thoughts. She was seated next to the colonel, whose conversation seemed to consist entirely of boasting of his various exploits, which Grizelda thought both tasteless and boorish. The repast, however, was excellent. Lord Farleigh may have been innately parsimonious but he was inordinately fond of food and possessed a French chef of impeccable credentials. It was sad that Grizelda did not feel more like eating. After dinner they returned to the saloon where Jocelyn led Laura to a darkened corner. Her father sat with Lord Farleigh, and Grizelda was again left to the company of the repellent Staunton, who, having imbibed much of the excellent claret, was halfway to being inebriated.

"Your sister seems to like Mr Farleigh," he remarked with a smirk.

Grizelda, who was aghast at Laura's forward behaviour, did not quite know how to reply, but thought him ill-mannered to remark on it.

"Quite a little goer from what I have heard," he continued.

Grizelda, utterly dismayed, stared at him. "What do you mean?" she answered deceptively quietly. He tried to put his hand over hers but she snatched it away.

"Well, it is a known fact, her and Lord Heddington." He laughed a raucous laugh.

Grizelda was horrified. "What do you mean?" she repeated.

"Everyone knows she went off with Heddington."

"Then everyone is wrong," she said, her temper rising. "How dare you make such an offensive remark to me. As her sister I must tell you, your suppositions are unjust."

"Unjust! Ha, what a fool you must think me. I know what the little slut did. I know and I shall not hesitate to inform the world."

Had Grizelda been of a more rational mien, she would have realised that men in their cups rarely mean their malicious remarks. Staunton would most probably have forgotten them by the morning. However, judicious thought when incensed was not Grizelda's way. She plunged headlong into attack.

"Fool! I do indeed think you are a fool and far worse. You are without doubt the most unpleasant dissembler that it has been my misfortune to encounter. You are a portentous imbecile, lacking in manners or social graces." She paused for breath. Too late she realised her mistake, for he looked at her nastily.

"You will live to regret those words, Miss Ludgrove. You are altogether too complacent!" He rose stiffly and staggered across to Laura and Jocelyn.

Grizelda flushed red. Angry tears sprang to her eyes. She knew she had been unwise but how was anyone expected to put up with opinions of such a nature? It was made worse, for inside she knew that she should have ignored them, or at least informed her papa, who could have dealt with them. She swallowed, a tiny tear escaped from the corner of her eyes; she seemed to quarrel with everyone. She felt wretchedly alone. She would have liked to run to her father, but to do so would occasion more comment, which was just what she wished to avoid. So she remained sitting by herself until it was time to leave.

Christmas at Bardfield could not have been more different. Jaspar's father had believed it to be a time of revelry, for servants and family alike. He had established traditions, which his mother and subsequently, when he attained his majority, his son, followed scrupulously.

The night before Christmas saw a party in the servants' hall, which everyone frequented, from Savage to the lowliest scullery maid and as many of the neighbouring tenants as wished it. It was custom that the family attend for a short time, before retiring upstairs for a cold collation and amusements of their own.

The servants' hall was highly decorated with Christmas greenery: holly and ivy being wound around every conceivable object; there was mistletoe, whose glistening white berries the giggling maids counted firmly, for the tradition went, that for every kiss a berry must be removed and when all had gone, there were to be no more kisses. A Yule log of enormous dimensions burnt in the grate and it was the custom that games of all sorts would be played, from bobbing apples to snapdragon. Jaspar always gave the servants the evening off once the supper had been laid in the dining room and it was a dispensation that was much appreciated.

Upstairs gaiety also reigned. The children who were not babies were permitted to eat with their parents and entered into the fun of serving themselves with all the enthusiasm of overexcited puppies. Two huge wax tapers wreathed with Christmas greens were the sole decoration on the table, which was spread with splendid fare, including hams, pheasant pies, spiced and frilled mince pies; in the centre was placed the decorated head of a pig.

After supper there were games in which children and adults joined. Horace, who had remained in Fittleworth for Christmas, as he could not bear to be parted from the growing walls of his hospital even for a few weeks, proved himself the most admirable playmate for the children. He was adept at blind man's buff and his generous mouth was simply made for fishing out apples. Then a local fiddle player and pianist played for the dancing; Horace again proved himself invaluable, swinging the smallest child around and around until they collapsed in hot, giggling, thrilling piles.

Christmas Day commenced with prayers in Bardfield chapel. The chapel had been built by Jaspar's great-great-grandfather and was one of the most beautiful to be found in a country house. It was customary for the head of the family to take these prayers, attended by family and servants alike, and Jaspar took traditions very seriously. After prayers there was a substantial breakfast before those who wished to, walked across the fields to church.

Lady Heddington and some of the ladies were conveyed in a carriage, but Jaspar always went on foot if he could and today was beautiful. The park was covered in a white blanket and the sun, in a cloudless deep blue sky, had slightly melted the snow on the branches making them sparkle. As he walked he thought about Grizelda. He found she crept, unbidden, into his thoughts frequently. Today, he caught himself wondering if she had any plans to return to London. He had already arranged for Nillie to have Laura. To start with his sister had objected, saying that she had far too much to do to have time to bring out silly girls such as Laura, but when Jaspar pointed out the consequence for him, she, somewhat reluctantly, agreed. He decided that he must write to Lady Melbourne to enquire whether Launcie should be returned to her stables for Miss Ludgrove's pleasure. Jaspar had had Launcie sent to Bardfield, for he did not feel justified in leaving Lady Melbourne to bear the expense of her while Grizelda was not there to ride her. It was, he knew, merely a device, but it would serve.

The New Year at Bardfield saw the arrival of a great many extra guests. Roderick arrived with Gideon and Lord and Lady Milton, accompanied by Aurelia. Brummell came; he was assured that with Jaspar he would not be expected to traipse across icy, muddy fields. He knew his room would be warm and that the company would be exemplary. The day he arrived was cold, windy, with the promise of more snow. Brummell hustled into the saloon, which in the late afternoon was bright with candles and warm from two fires burning in huge grates at either end of the vast room. It seemed filled with people.

Jaspar disengaged himself from a game of spillikins with the children and approached his friend, a broad grin on his face . "George! Just in time for games with the children. Spillikins or snap?"

There were some who might have thought Brummell above these things, but with his friends he was never haughty, and derived great pleasure from playing games with the young. He had even been known to get down upon the floor with them.

"I think that spillikins might be more my line," he teased. "But first let me greet your guests."

"Of course. I think that everyone is known to you, except Miss Milton."

Aurelia rose to her feet. She was warm from her game with Frances and tiny fronds of hair were escaping to curl over her forehead. Her blue eyes glowed. Brummell looked surprised; he, who considered himself something of a connoisseur, had never before seen such beauty. He bent over her hand. "Enchanted."

She smiled back in her unaffected way, pushing away a stray wisp of hair. "Mr Brummell. The famous Beau Brummell." In many people it might have sounded gauche but Aurelia possessed such natural style and dignity that the Beau just laughed.

"Well, I am not sure about famous, perhaps infamous would be better."

"George," a chorus of voices, and Gideon and Roderick swept upon him, "you now have a twelve-mile walk in front of you before dinner. You will not mind the snow and the mud, will you? After that a nice cold evening following hounds," teased Gideon.

"If you think to obtain a rise from me, you are mistaken. I know that hounds do not go out in the dark," observed Brummell, crossing to bid hello to Lady Heddington and Lady Milton seated with Nillie in front of the fire. "I will remain with the ladies. You may indulge in these pursuits, if you so wish."

Nillie hugged him. "Quite right, George, we shall derive much pleasure from your company."

Roderick, who was missing Clarissa in a wholly unexpected way, tried to flirt with Aurelia. This, however, was proving hard. It was not that she was not receptive but it was just that she was entirely without guile.

"Why do you look so sad?" she asked and went on, when she observed his look of dismay, "It is alright, you just look as if something were plaguing you. Is it your arm?"

He shook his head. "No, although I am sad not to be able to fight anymore. There will be more trouble with Napoleon, I am sure of it."

"Is he not safe in Elba?"

"Mmm but I still do not trust the gentleman."

"I'd have thought you would have been glad not to fight. Now you will not be killed."

He hooted with laughter. "A very feminine way of looking at things. We stupid men like to risk our necks in battle. Idiotic, is it not!"

"Well, rather, and of course, we are left behind mourning you. Not a very pleasant prospect for us."

He laughed again. Really this sister of Milton's was a most unusual girl, such directness and yet such incredible charm. "No, I suppose not. Rather frustrating."

"Indeed, yes, being unable to stop men's childish games." He was about to protest but she continued, "If that was not what was troubling you, what was it?"

"I… am…" He suddenly found himself confiding in her. "I am in love. There, I said it. With Clarissa Darcy, do you know her?"

Aurelia looked not the remotest put out by this confession. "No, but I am not out yet. I am to come to London to do the season in February. Petty is to present me. I should have come last year but for George." He raised an eyebrow. "Petty's son."

"Oh yes. Well, Miss Milton, I predict that you will be a resounding success."

She waved an arm to dismiss his flattering comments and persevered. "Now, tell me, have you told Miss Darcy of your feelings? Does she return your sentiments?" There was such a natural, down-to-earth quality in her questions that he could not take exception to her remarks.

He blushed slightly. "No… I… well… you see, she may not be happy to receive my attentions."

"Do you think she likes you?"

He found her directness catching. He responded, somewhat to his surprise, "Yes."

"Then there you are. Simple," she replied triumphantly.

Roderick grinned. "Is it that simple?" Aurelia nodded. He looked relieved and pleased. "Perhaps you are right. I will ask her, I will tell her."

"Good."

"Well, Miss Milton, do you hunt with us tomorrow?" Lord Heddington interrupted her conversation with Roderick. "Or are you one of the Brummell number who must stay in the warm?"

"No. If you can mount me I intend to hunt."

Across the room, Netta observed them; she could not stop herself staring. She realised not only how beautiful Aurelia was, but how utterly enchanting, and she wished and wished that she could only be like her. She did not mind the girl laughing with Roderick but when Jaspar approached her, a warm look on his face, Netta's insides twisted with an entirely unfamiliar emotion. She did not like herself, feeling as she did when watching Jaspar conversing with Aurelia. She knew that jealousy was a most ignoble emotion and yet it seemed that this was what she was experiencing and it was, she discovered to her disgust, uncontrollable. She thought herself hateful when her sole desire was to find fault with Aurelia and thus undermine the girl to Jaspar, for she knew that it was unworthy. However, she found it impossible to keep her invidious thoughts from planning ways to show just what an unpleasant character Aurelia was.

"I have a lovely mare, whom you may try," Jaspar suggested.

"Does she not belong to someone else? Surely one of your sisters has a prior claim to her."

Jaspar paused momentarily. A picture of Grizelda on Launcie flashed across his mind. "I bought her for someone… to lend to someone in London. So please do ride her here, Edward assures me that you have excellent hands."

Of course, as soon as Aurelia saw the mare she could not resist riding her. The little horse was an indomitable, plucky creature who flew over every obstacle. Jaspar had promised his godson that he would take him hunting this year and Charles had been nearly sick with excitement when the projected treat was explained to him. Out to hounds the boy proved to be a natural rider with both courage and tenacity, and somewhat contrary to his expectations Jaspar thoroughly enjoyed taking him. As Charles, his round face flushed with the thrill of it all, jumped and jumped, winning himself much praise from the master, Jaspar was caught by a sudden fierce longing for a son of his own to perform such feats and with whom he could do such things. The feeling was so sharp and so surprising that for a moment he could not believe that he had had such an aspiration, but it was real. He knew it. He wanted a son of his own. He had never previously thought of children. It was all very odd.

All those in the party who wished to hunt went out, whilst the others sat and gossiped. Jaspar was an excellent host and it was, as customary, a relaxing and enjoyable party. As well as hunting, the estate boasted an excellent shoot, and some bracing walks.

One bright January morning, Jaspar announced that he intended to walk across to see how Horace's hospital was progressing.

"May I walk with you?" Roderick asked. "I have heard so much about the good doctor I would much like to meet him."

Jaspar acquiesced readily, happy to have the company of so dear a friend. They set off; the countryside stretched ahead, smoothly white, for although it had stopped snowing, there had been no sign of a thaw, and banks of snow were driven up against the trees and deep in the hollows. Dark hedges criss-crossed the whiteness and in a tiny far-off hamlet, smoke wafted upwards from thin cottage chimneys. Jaspar and Roderick strode on companionably, the frosty snow crunching under their feet. For some time neither of them spoke, enjoying the fresh air and each other's company.

"Jaspar," Roderick started, then he paused, unable quite to broach the subject.

"Yes?"

"Remarkable girl." He paused, striking at the branch of a tree, causing clouds of snow to topple onto the frozen earth. "Remarkable, that Miss Milton."

Jaspar laughed. "Indeed and most beautiful."

"Quite. Possibly the most beautiful I have ever seen."

His friend nodded. "Smitten, Rod?"

Roderick shook his head. "No, but I might have been if it were not for…"

"Clarissa?"

"Mmm…" He kicked a pile of hard snow which broke into pieces under his boots. "What do you think?"

"About what?" teased Jaspar.

"Jaspar! You know!" The Hon. Roderick picked up a pile of snow and threw it at his friend, all as if they were eight years old again. Lord Heddington laughed and did the same, hitting Roderick on the nose, snow breaking up into pieces all over his face. Whereupon both men collapsed into giggles.

"Miss Darcy… Miss Milton seemed to think that I would not be unwelcome as a suitor… at least, she suggested I try."

"Very wise. She is, as you point out, a most remarkable girl. But do you want to marry Clarissa?"

"Oh yes, beyond anything." He kicked the snow once more, then glanced up at Jaspar, an intense look on his sun-lined face. "I cannot describe to you the joy, the wonder. I think of nothing but her. I can be doing anything. Like this, walking through the snow, throwing it at you and I want her to be here." He waved his arm across the vista of the sparkling fields. "This view. I want her to see it. I store things up that I know would amuse her. I see her face. I long for her. I have…" he paused, looking faintly shamefaced, "… I have a handkerchief of hers, it smells of her, I sleep with it. There now you will think I am most silly."

Jaspar shook his head sadly. "No."

"I know we will deal well together. I knew it the first time I set eyes on her. She is not like Aurelia. I do not know if any girl can be like Miss Milton, but I love her sweetness, her ordinariness. Her smile, the way her eyes light up when I see her. I do not think she is aware of that but I notice, and that dragon of an aunt notices."

"Then you must ask for her hand. Why have you not done so?"

"Because I think, maybe, am not worthy of such loveliness. Maybe she will refuse me," he said tentatively. "I am a younger son, and no career now," he said bitterly. "I have no fortune. A mere competence."

"Roderick," Jaspar said mock angrily, "I despair! How could there be a more eligible *parti* ?"

"You?"

"Me ? Why, you idiot," he went on affectionately, "any girl would be lucky indeed to wed you, and the Darcys have not a fortune, you know. John Darcy had only a moderate competence, and I know that Lucy would be only too happy for Clarissa to marry as well as you. She has three more daughters to dispose of and would, I believe, be pleased to get rid of Clarissa, even to such a reprobate as you!" His dancing eyes belied his words.

Roderick wrung his hand. "Then it is settled. I will try my luck. It is strange to be thinking of marriage. I had not thought I would desire the state. A bachelor's life is good. Do you remember our scrapes?"

Jaspar grinned. "That little brown-eyed girl."

"And the one with the yellow hair and that harridan of a mama. How she tried to get you to marry her daughter. Not that she would ever have succeeded. She had ideas much above her station that one."

Jaspar hooted, then was suddenly quiet. He thought over what Roderick had said. His friend was right, his own thoughts were turning to marriage.

"It is odd. I too think," he paused, "since my illness I know I must wed." He went on grimly, "But to whom? I envy you!"

Roderick looked at him discerningly. Jaspar had changed. That much was clear. For Lord Heddington, the most notorious rake, to desire wedlock. Was it possible that Jaspar was in love? He decided to question him further.

"Jaspar, there must be any number of girls only too willing to marry you. You are the most eligible person on the mart."

"Yes, but they want me for my position. For my money. Not for me. At least you know Clarissa wants you for you."

Roderick was truly surprised but hid it quickly. Jaspar had had legions of women in love with him; there were any amount at this moment. He did not understand his friend's problem, although he could see from the wry smile and slight twist of the lips that Jaspar was not happy.

His Lordship shrugged his shoulders. "I am thinking of proposing to Netta." Roderick's eyes opened in surprise, an emotion he quickly suppressed. This was a most peculiar conversation. "My grandmother wishes it. She is all that is admirable."

"And loves you. For yourself, not your fortune."

Jaspar shrugged again. "I suppose so."

"But you do not love her?"

Jaspar sighed. "I guess not. I do not feel what you feel, my dear friend, I never think of her at all, but I find an inexplicable longing for a son and Netta would indubitably make the most excellent mama."

Roderick was even more surprised. It was obvious that Jaspar was not in love. That was not the reason for his sudden change of opinion. He thought over what his friend had just said but did not know how to answer. He was devoted to Netta and would love to have seen her happily wed, and Jaspar was correct, she would be a devoted mother. He also understood the importance of Jaspar marrying, and soon. As Jaspar said it, he could see that Lady Heddington would wish the alliance, but in spite of all these particulars, he was not at all satisfied that it was the right course of action. He would have liked to continue the conversation, for it was not often that Jaspar opened up to him, but he was denied further opportunity by the arrival of Horace who hailed them as they approached his hospital.

"My lord. How honoured I am that you have come." He strode towards them, and Roderick had the impression of a square, solid man with warm eyes and the rough dress of a villager.

Jaspar grinned. "Horace, suddenly so subservient." The doctor's brown eyes twinkled in response. "I must see your building, I have been so deep in visitors that this is the first chance I have had to examine how you go on. This is Mr Talkarne, who much desired the opportunity to meet you."

The two men shook hands and together they approached the site. Horace frisked around like an overenthusiastic child. In truth there was little to see at the moment, just a series of muddy holes and brick foundations; however, it was hard not to be affected by Horace's eagerness as he showed them where the wards would be and rooms for dissection and operations.

Jaspar did not forget his discussion with Roderick. He went over it in his mind that night as he changed for dinner. Roderick was right. Aurelia was the most incredible girl, but he knew that he was not remotely in love with her, and from what he had seen of her astute honesty, she would never compromise and wed someone who did not love her. Netta was different. He knew that she would jump at the chance to be the next Lady Heddington. It would please the dowager so much. Netta had been most charming and sensible over the holiday, and he resolved to do the deed and get this marriage thing over and done with.

Chapter Sixteen

Lady Melbourne received Lord Heddington's letter with some curiosity. She was of the opinion that there was more to it than a disinterested enquiry as to what should be done with a horse. She replied immediately, assuring him of her intention to ask Grizelda to her for the season, and adding that she was sure the girl would be most grateful for Launcie. Then she sat down and wrote to Grizelda.

Grizelda had had a hateful Christmas. It was never her favourite time and this year it had seemed worse than ever. There had been the abominable colonel, who, admittedly, had not stayed very long at Farleigh but long enough to give Grizelda a dislike of him that was as deep seated as it was without real foundation, for after his display on Christmas Day he had been nothing except polite. Then Laura had flirted shockingly with Jocelyn, who, her sister surmised, was probably something of a reprobate. Grizelda could not find it in herself to trust him and she devoutly hoped that Laura would not prove to be foolhardy again. Her sister's forward behaviour with Mr Farleigh gave Grizelda an excellent insight into what had occurred in the summer with Lord Heddington. She tried, gently, to suggest Laura show a little more circumspection but the girl merely flung back her golden curls and laughed. Grizelda grew more uneasy.

She was in the morning room when Lady Melbourne's letter was brought to her. The morning room was the only room that Grizelda liked. It had been the schoolroom, and when the girls grew too old for lessons it had been rechristened the morning room. Her father had, most unexpectedly, allowed her to have the redecoration of it. He had provided her with a small budget and Grizelda, to his surprise, had shown a real flare for making the room warm, light and welcoming.

She was seated in the large shabby wing chair reading *Sense and Sensibility*, her long legs curled up under her. The young maid who brought the letter bobbed a curtsey.

"Letter for you, Miss Grizelda."

"Thank you." Grizelda took the missive, wondering if it were from Jaspar, then reprimanded herself angrily. He would not write to her. It would not be right and why should he, when she had been such a shrew. She sighed and tore open the seal. Lady Melbourne's message was brief and to the point. Grizelda sat for a moment, the note in her hand. Then she made her decision. She got up, went to the writing table, and in her best script wrote a note and accepted. She knew that her father would refuse to let her go. He insisted that his comfort depended on the presence of one or both of his daughters. The reality was he hardly noticed them, all his time being spent at Farleigh Hall. He had been most reluctant to agree that Laura should return to London. So he would most assuredly say no to Grizelda. As she read Lady Melbourne's kind invitation her first thought had been the awful certainty that she would not be allowed to go, and her second was that she wanted to go more than anything. It was so very dull here. She craved the excitement of the metropolis. *What a gadfly I am*, she acknowledged with some amusement, but she refused to admit to herself that her desire to return to London was, in part, because she wished to see Jaspar again. The other reason why she considered it essential that she accept Lady Melbourne's kind offer was her sister. Having had a chance to observe Laura's behaviour at close quarters she was certain she would behave with more propriety if Grizelda were in London to keep an eye on her. This was not a purpose that she felt desirous of confessing to her papa. The smallest whiff of possible misfortune would result in immediate prohibition. Laura would not go and that would be fatal. How could they hope to redeem Laura's reputation unless she were seen to be on the best of terms with the Heddington family?

Once she had sealed and dispatched her letter, she went in search of her papa. He was at his desk surrounded by papers relating to estate matters. He did not look pleased when she entered.

"What do you want? I am busy."

"I have received an invitation from Lady Melbourne to go to her for the season. I have accepted."

Her father looked at her, first in disbelief and then with growing anger. "What? Without even having the grace to consult me! How dare you!"

Grizelda was one of those fortunate people who remain supremely indifferent to the fury of others. She was neither scared nor intimidated by her papa's anger. She merely waited for him to stop raging.

"Nevertheless, Papa, I intend to go. It is important that I am there to watch Laura if…"

"I thought she was going to Lady Morntarny, so that Her Ladyship could perform that office," he roared. "No need for you to do that."

"Yes, Papa," she went on soothingly, "but it will still be preferable that I be there as well. You would not wish Lady Morntarny to have all the accountability."

"Well, I do not agree. You are not going."

Grizelda, whose temper was as sharp and swift as her father's, stiffened; her eyes flashed. "I shall go and you will not stop me. I want to go, it is hateful here and I will not be denied the chance to marry credibly. You should be ashamed of yourself. What would Mama have thought?"

This reference to his late wife and the fact that, as many weak people, he inevitably bowed to the stronger will, made him reluctantly nod acquiescence. "Alright. Alright. You shall go," he rejoindered irritably.

Grizelda smiled her sunniest. "Thank you, Papa." She kissed him on the cheek. "And Mrs Winter will come to make you comfortable." He grunted.

Grizelda rushed excitedly upstairs. Her spirits lifted completely. There was much to be done if she were to spend a summer in London. The two weeks before Christmas had only been the little season and apart from one visit to Almack's and a couple of parties, she had been able to do very little, but a whole season! She hugged herself in anticipation. She must have some clothes and Laura must too. Their mama's modest fortune had provided their portions and the small amount that was left over was to be used for additional items. It was this that Grizelda proposed for refurbishing their wardrobes. Vernham Dean was only a village but it boasted an excellent dressmaker and Grizelda vowed to visit her in the morning. When Laura returned from her walk she was seated surrounded by pieces of paper making lists.

Laura threw off her pelisse and shawl and stripped off her gloves.

"Good walk?" Grizelda enquired absentmindedly, her head deep in the *Ladies' Assembly*, her tone more amiable towards her sister than it had been since Christmas.

"Wonderful! Thank you. You sound more cheerful, thank goodness. Jocelyn says you have looked like a sour cat." She hesitated, for usually the name of her admirer provoked her sister to fury, but today she did not appear to notice. Laura heaved a sigh of relief and swiftly changed the subject. "What are you doing?"

"Oh, Laura, I am to go to London too. Lady Melbourne has today written to me to ask me to stay for the season," Grizelda informed her, clasping her hands together, her eyes sparkling with excitement. Laura, who possessed an uncomplicated nature, was genuinely delighted for her sister, particularly when she observed the transformation in her.

"Oh, Grizzie, how excellent! I am so pleased. I felt that it was most unfair that I should be going and not you but now we shall both be able to enjoy the delights." She paused. "Oh, but will Papa let you? He kicked up enough of a dust about me. He will hate us both to be away."

Grizelda raised an eyebrow and bit her lip. "Well, in truth he was not best pleased," she giggled. "But I gave him no chance. I wrote and accepted before I told him."

Laura's eyes opened wide with admiration. "Grizzie! You are brave. I declare that I could never face Papa's ire."

"No, you could not. I know that but it does not influence me. I let him shout and then told him that I was going. He agreed."

Laura peeked at her, frank admiration in her blue eyes. "Good. How clever you are. I am so pleased for you. I hated the thought that you were to be deprived of the pleasures, although not enough to give them up myself," she replied ingenuously.

Grizelda laughed. "I did not expect that of you, my love, but we shall travel together now which will be excellent, as Papa will not have to send one of the maids with you or pay for her to return. Oh, Laura, we will be able to put quite behind you the events of last summer and you shall not feel crabby because I am in London and I shall not feel envious because you are to go. It is the best of solutions." She hugged her sister.

"You shall deliver me to Lady Morntarny." Laura twirled around.

"Wh… what is she like?" asked Grizelda, a shade too carefully, for she was greatly intrigued by Jaspar's sister.

"Well, you have met Lord Heddington. She is exactly the same. They could be twins. She was most kind to me. Papa met her; she was so sensible to persuade him not to call His Lordship out, although I did not see it like that at the time. For if Papa had challenged him, all the world would have known and I could never have gone back and am so excited by the prospect. It will be more fun than staying with Lady Ambrose for Lady Morntarny goes everywhere, not that Lady Ambrose is not asked, but she was very lazy and did not arrange anything special for me. I am persuaded that it will be very different with Lady Morntarny."

"Does she have any children?" asked Grizelda curiously.

"Oh yes, three I believe. I did not see them for they are at school or perhaps in the schoolroom. But come, let us decide what we must take for we do not have too much time and Mr Farleigh tells me that I will need at least four evening dresses and day dresses and morning gowns and shawls and…"

"Laura, will Mr Farleigh be in London?"

"Oh yes!" her sister remarked unconcernedly.

"You will… take care… l mean there are lots of eligible men. You will make sure that you do not allow one man to dominate…"

"Oh, Grizzie! As if I would. You do not like Mr Farleigh, that is obvious, but he is so much the gentleman. I am very lucky he admires me."

"Perhaps," her sister replied cynically. "But I do not think he is an eligible *parti* or that his intentions are honourable. You would be wise to forget him," she stated bluntly.

Laura pulled a face. "l hate you sometimes, Grizelda. I shall do as I like. I will not be guided by a frosty, strait-laced, prudish stick-in-the-mud!"

Grizelda, whose candidness had merely resulted in increasing her sister's stubbornness, making her more than ever determined to enslave Mr Farleigh, realised her error. She stopped, and laughed. "Oh, I am sorry, it was horrid of me.

Now," she held up a page decorated with an evening dress of delicate silk, with tiny bows all down the back, "how that would suit you, Laura, if we could have it copied."

"Yes. It would. I should like it above all things." Laura, easily diverted, continued, "Can we buy the silk tomorrow?"

Her sister sighed, her misgivings about the summer in London certainly not assuaged.

His mind made up, Jaspar went to visit his grandmother. It was a grey day and voluminous clouds, heavy with snow, scudded across the sky. Lady Heddington was seated, her legs on an embroidered foot stool at the centre window of the library. She was stitching. Jaspar kissed her and sat down next to her.

"Good morning, my dear." She smiled at him, tenderly.

"More snow I fear." Her grandson appeared restive as she watched him, whilst he peered out onto the home park. His premonition was all too quickly realised; the snow started falling in small flecks, growing larger and larger, until, in minutes, the gardens were a whirling mass of whiteness. To Jaspar's eyes it was strangely beautiful. The branches from which the previous snow had melted, leaving them as hard brown stalks, were already heavy with a thick layer of cold fluffiness. The lake and ornamental bridge were hardly visible, so dense was the wall of tumbling flakes.

He turned from the window to his grandmother. "I have been thinking," he started. She observed him. "About marriage." He sighed. "I know I must," he said, suddenly fierce. She felt he did not much want to. "I think you are right, Netta will make an admirable wife," he said hesitantly. Her pleasure and relief was intense. She wanted this deeply. She was so fond of the girl and knew how much she loved Jaspar.

"Oh, Jaspar." The delight in her face was obvious.

"You do believe that I am doing the right thing?" he asked.

"Oh yes, yes. It will be everything that is desirable. I could not be happier."

"Then if it makes you so happy, I will do it."

Lady Heddington had advanced this match for so long that her normal acute and considerable understanding of Jaspar had become entirely suspended. She was so elated by hearing that he had decided to do what she had desired that she failed to hear the miserable and resigned note in his voice.

He kissed her and went up to his own apartments. Sitting at his desk watching the swirling flakes, he reminded himself how kind Netta had been; how good; how successful she was with the children. The house was very quiet. Nillie had left the previous day to visit Morntarny, and Emma and her family had gone to her parents-in-law. The remaining members of the New Year house party had gone, Brummell to London and the Miltons to Yorkshire.

He stared at the delicate rosewood. Absentmindedly he pulled open a drawer and there, nestling among some papers, was the coin bag. Grizelda flashed into his mind, a vivid image of her throwing it at him, her huge pale eyes glinting with anger, her hair tumbling behind her. He pushed away the thought; she would never forgive him. He sighed and went to find Netta.

Lady Heddington sat for a moment after Jaspar had left her, then she rang the bell and asked that Netta be brought to her. She had decided to inform the girl of what His Lordship intended so that she would be quite prepared for the proposal. Netta was first astounded and then overwhelmed with excitement. She rushed to brush her hair and straighten her dress and was ready when she received Lord Heddington's summons. She went down to the morning room, hardly able to contain the bubble of happiness that welled up in her, and scratched at the door. On being bidden to enter she went in. Jaspar was standing at the window, his back to her. Netta, whose disposition was naturally servile, waited a second and then, closing the door behind her, curtseyed low and said, "Lady Heddington said you wanted to see me, my lord." It was a mistake.

Jaspar whipped round. Her servility suddenly irritated him. He looked piercingly at her. It was obvious that his grandmother had told her what he intended. Jaspar felt angry and cross. He shuddered.

"Jaspar, are you quite well? Do you want to sit down?"

He felt smothered. "No, Netta, I do not want to sit down. If I do I am quite able to do so without any prompting from you," he returned irritably.

She swallowed. Sarcasm made her tongue-tied. She did not know how to answer it at all.

She muttered. "I am sorry, so sorry."

Her abject apology infuriated him even more. She should not be apologising, it should be him. He was behaving irrationally. He took a breath and curbed his irritation.

"Netta, yes…" He paused. Grizelda, laughing as she sat on the ground, in Hyde Park, was suddenly with him. He felt hunted and trapped. "I just want to thank you for all you have done this Christmas. You worked so hard to make everything run so smoothly. I really am most grateful."

He watched her face. She looked as if she were about to cry. He felt hateful, but he could not marry her. Even to please his grandmother. He went across to her and kissed her cheek. "I am sorry, Netta." She flung from him and ran out of the room.

Netta ran down the vast curving staircase, her eyes blinded by tears, her face hot with humiliation. Grabbing her cloak, she hurried on through the familiar corridors which led to the back of the house. She let herself out of the door that would bring her closest to the stables. Weeping bitterly she harnessed her old horse to the squire's gig and left Bardfield, promising herself that she would never return. She drove slowly through the steadily swirling snow, the old horse plodding valiantly, his entire body covered with delicate, white, melting flakes. As he struggled onwards his feet left dark holes in the interminable whiteness ahead. Netta cried, the tears melting the snow which fell on her face, her hair, her clothes. Melted snow and salty tears streamed down and dripped off her chin, mixing with the layer of ice on her cloak. The way to her father's house was well known to both her and the horse, so frequent had been their journeys to Bardfield.

Eventually, with great relief, she reached her home. She clambered down, lumps of snow clinging to her clothes. She led the gig into the stables where she ordered the groom to care for her horse. Utterly exhausted by despair and her exertions, soaking wet, her clothes so sodden and heavy each step was hard, she started to shiver, not only from cold but from the growing feeling of misery that threatened to engulf her. Mrs Park the housekeeper bustled out, exclamations of horror on her lips as she beheld her mistress. Netta, stiff with unhappiness, allowed herself to be led upstairs where Mrs Park, accompanied by a litany of reproaches towards those at Bardfield who had encouraged her to travel in that weather, tenderly stripped her of her dripping clothes and installed her in bed. The name Bardfield stung Netta with a pain that she found it hard to contain or comprehend. After the housekeeper had whisked away, she lay propped up on pillows and examined her conviction that she would never be able to return there again. This thought was so unbearable that the ready tears spouted again.

After Netta's abrupt departure, Jaspar shrugged and went back to the window. The swirling snowflakes now obliterated the landscape. He wished he could go out and ride and ride until this unsettled feeling left him, but it was quite impossible. Nor could he yet return to London.

A gentle knock on the door and a footman, the post on a silver tray, bowed to him. "Thank you," Jaspar said curtly. It brought assistance in the shape of two letters, the first from Lady

Melbourne assuring him of her intention to ask her goddaughter to London for the season, and they would be most obliged to Lord Heddington for the continued use of Launcie; the second an invitation from Rutland to hunt. He felt a lifting of his spirits and considerable relief. Thank goodness he had not engaged himself to Netta. As soon as the snow stopped he would go to Belvoir. For the second time that year he left his home without regret.

It was the end of February when he returned to town. London was still thin of company but there were those who were slowly coming back and many of his friends were now in residence. He attended a few parties and found his eyes searching unconsciously for the bright red hair. But it was not to be seen. He was sorely tempted to visit Lady Melbourne to find out when she expected her goddaughter but he desisted, for he realised that Nillie was still at Morntarny and it was probable that the sisters would come to London together. In the meantime he amused himself by flirting with Lady Hestor Caston, a vivacious beauty who was due to be presented this year and who had been brought to town early by her mama, who was no longer able to stand the pressure exerted on her by her determined daughter. Lady Morrison was also back in Park Street with the amiable Sir John and her two high-spirited daughters, the eldest of whom was also to make her come-out that year. She invited Jaspar to attend her rout, which he did with some pleasure, as it was, as usual, splendidly organised, but he found his thoughts straying to the previous occasion and his dance with Grizelda. He was not a naturally introspective man and so he did not examine his feelings, just pushing them away, in a round of friends and gaiety.

When Nillie arrived back in Berkeley Square, however, he went immediately to visit her.

He found her lying resting on a chaise. She looked rather pale.

"Jaspar, how are you? Have you come to find out how your protégée does? For she has arrived, you know. I have sent her shopping with Miss Manners." Miss Manners was the children's governess.

"Yes, I wanted to make sure that she was settled but also to see you." He kissed her gently. "Nillie, what is it? You do not look your best."

"I do not feel my best," she replied with something resembling her previous spirit. "I am with child and I do not get through the first months without feeling very unwell."

"Oh, Nillie, I am delighted about the baby but I am so sorry that you have to care for Laura. Shall I ask her to go?"

Nillie, who had been railing to herself on how inconsiderate Jaspar was to send her a girl to supervise, when she felt so ill, immediately felt contrite.

"No, of course not. I do not intend to spoil Laura's pleasure. I have said that she may stay for the season and stay she will. Yes, I am so happy about the baby, and Greville is ecstatic. It is just that increasing is so uncomfortable I wish it could be over. I wish that babies sprang fully grown without all this." She patted her stomach.

Jaspar laughed. "Nevertheless, I think it must be wonderful to have a child." Nillie's astounded face made him laugh again. "Do not look so surprised. Is it so very odd?"

"N… no," said Nillie quickly, regarding him quizzically. In truth she was much amazed. It was so unlike Jaspar, she wondered what was going on.

He changed the subject. "Did you meet Miss Ludgrove?" he asked casually.

"Yes, a very pleasant girl I thought." Nillie was too surprised by Jaspar's comments about her child to notice the studied nonchalance in his voice. "She is most striking."

"Do you think so? What about the freckles?"

"Well, I know they are not fashionable but on her they are charming."

Jaspar was secretly delighted that his favourite sister was pleased by Grizelda. "Now, I must leave you to rest, my love. Please do not hesitate to ask me if you need assistance. Is there no one we could ask to help you? Surely Miss Manners will return to Morntarny soon?"

"Indeed, for the children must return to their lessons. I have decided that once Charles goes back to school I will keep the girls in London with me so the governess will stay too. She can help with Laura."

"Good, but if necessary we could ask Aunt Maud," he teased.

"What! Jaspar have you gone quite mad? I could not stand her in the house. Oh, you rat. You were just being tormenting. I thought to ask Netta up, if Grandmama can do without her. It is ages since she had any fun and she has been so kind and helpful, I know she will not spare herself here."

He nodded, laughing. "An excellent notion."

Nillie, who had heard of what had occurred at Bardfield, watched him carefully to see how he reacted to her suggestion of Netta, but he seemed unconcerned. He stood, hugged her and made his departure.

So Grizelda had returned, he thought as he wandered back to Grosvenor Square. It was the middle of March and one of those days that seem to herald the end of winter, deceptively beguiling the inexperienced into believing that spring has come. The sun shone and its warmth was enough to make the foolish throw off their thick greatcoats. Tiny snowdrops spread themselves across the lawns in blankets of white and daffodils bobbed their golden heads in a gentle wind.

Jaspar was tempted to visit Melbourne House immediately but he resisted, deciding to wait until Launcie was back in London. Then he could restore the mare to Grizelda without a pretext. However, he did not need any excuses, for she was at the first of Almack's regular Wednesday receptions.

He saw her as soon as he entered. She was talking to Laura at the end of the room. It was the first time he had seen Laura since he left her at the inn in Wimbledon. As he walked deliberately towards them he wondered idly how Laura would react to his presence, but as he reached them she exhibited not the slightest discomfiture, merely curtseying deeply and then turning from him to smile beguilingly at a tall dark young man who was clearly asking her to dance. Grizelda, however, felt acutely disconcerted. She thought that Laura's total lack of embarrassment showed a nature entirely unashamed by what she had done. She was quite mortified on her sister's behalf. She lowered her eyes, flushing slightly. Jaspar took her chin in his hand, lifting it gently. She met his eyes; she wanted to profess how sorry she was for her ill temper before Christmas but the words seemed unnecessary; there was so much understanding and sympathy in their dark depths that she found herself, unaccountably, wanting to burst into tears.

"Will you dance with me, Miss Ludgrove?"

She swallowed and nodded. He led her onto the dance floor, to join the set for the quadrille that was just forming. During the dance they had little time for conversation, but as they finished he took her firmly to a chair. As they sat down he said resolutely, "It is much better that she does not seem moved by my presence."

"Perhaps," she said doubtfully, "but it shows a total lack of sensibility". She bit her lip and looked contrite. "Oh dear, I should not speak of my sister thus."

He laughed. "Maybe not, nevertheless, it is most refreshing to hear someone speak so truthfully."

"I do have an awful tongue," she admitted. "Words just pop out without my meaning them to." She peeped at him appealingly, remembering her acerbity when they had last met.

He smiled with understanding and she felt a load lift from her. Then he continued, "Yes, but at least you do not hide your opinions under a welter of mendacity. Pretending one thing and believing another."

"No, I do not think I do that," she replied seriously. "I would not enjoy being thus. So many hypocritical comments do I hear from people, who then profess quite the opposite once the person has removed."

He agreed. "Exactly. You would not do that. It isn't in you. You are honest." He was quite surprised himself as he made these comments, although he realised they were true. "Laura is honest too, in a way. She does not prevaricate or present dying-away airs, all of which I have to say would make the *ton* convinced in what they believe. Her total lack of any abashment will have the gossips wondering if their suppositions are correct. It is the best rebuttal, I promise you."

She thought for a moment on his words and then nodded. "You are right, my lord." He wanted to stay talking to her but at that moment Lord Mannock appeared.

"Miss Ludgrove, you have returned. May I have the pleasure of your hand for this dance?" he asked pompously. Grizelda shot a glance at Jaspar, who raised an eyebrow by the merest whisker but whose expression remained inscrutable.

"I must leave you, Miss Ludgrove." He bowed over her hand and then lifted it to his lips. He kissed it and she felt an unnerving quiver inside her. She lifted her eyes and smiled. Then he was gone and she turned regretfully to Lord Mannock.

CHAPTER SEVENTEEN

For some little time it seemed that Netta's resolution would remain exact. It was only after His Lordship had left for Belvoir that a summons from the dowager made her reconsider her position. Lady Heddington's letter did not refer to the meeting between Jaspar and herself; it merely asked that Netta visit. Her Ladyship was missing her. Netta sat, the letter on her lap, thinking. She was desperate to go back. Bardfield meant Jaspar to her. Her spirits had been so downcast since their last meeting that she was finding it impossible to do anything except sit and mope. She had no one to talk to. Her father, a well-meaning squire, was only interested in his hunting, his shooting, local events, such as were relevant to his comfort. He loved his daughter but he was an inherently selfish man and certainly hardly noticed her distress. Netta missed Bardfield. She missed Her Ladyship and Margaret and the wide beauty of the house. The decision did not take her long. *How ungrateful I am*, she convinced herself. *I have had so much from them, it is both rude and discourteous of me not to visit.*

She ran upstairs, changed into her new dress and set out to drive the short distance across Lord Heddington's estates to his house. It was still freezing but the sun shone determinedly from a cloudless sky that was so blue it could have been summer but for the snow which clung to every part of the mansion, and the stark black outlines of the trees behind the house. The familiar ugly caw of the rooks who inhabited these sounded to her starved ears like the greatest of music. As she was alone Netta allowed herself to whoop with a certain swift pleasure, then she giggled at her own silliness, but she felt a release from the misery that had bound her for so long in its insidious folds. Bardfield. How could she have ever thought of never returning here? Soon it must be spring. She remembered the bluebells in the woods, the lawns, the trees unfurling their greenness. It was inconceivable never to be here again.

On reaching the house she was shown into the library, where the dowager sat, in her customary position in front of the central windows, watching the strategically placed statues sparkle as if they were made of ice and might melt at any moment. She turned as Netta came in, her face alight when she saw who it was.

"Oh, my dear, I am so pleased that you have come."

Netta ran across and kissed her, her cheeks glowing with the cold and her happiness. She sat at her feet and the dowager smoothed her hair.

"How are you, my love? I hope that you have recovered?"

Netta blushed. "I… I…" she started.

"The fault was mine, I should not have discussed with you Jaspar's confidences. I was quite wrong."

Netta looked at her. The unwelcome tears started in her eyes and ran down her face, destroying her mood of joy. "It was so awful… l thought I was… I thought… he…"Her voice entirely suspended with tears, she was unable to continue.

Lady Heddington patted her head. "Mmm, shhh, Netta. All is not lost. It is in his mind but we must tread carefully. I am sure that all will be well."

Netta sniffed. "Oh, do you truly? I have been so unhappy. I did not think that anything could pain me like this." She paused half embarrassed by the strength of her feelings. As she looked up to Lady Heddington's face, she could read intense sympathy.

"Go on. I do understand, my dear. l, although it may seem strange to you, did love once."

Netta would have liked to have asked her about it but somehow she could not quite find the courage. She choked, "It was the dashing of every hope. I thought that I had done something wrong."

"No, the fault was not yours but mine." Lady Heddington paused, caught in thought for a moment, then she looked up and smiled. "Fetch me the letter on that desk."

She pointed to the corner. Netta, a slight questioning look upon her face, nevertheless did as she was bid. Her Ladyship spread the page on her lap. "Now, I have had this from Nillie. She is with child and is not at all well. She writes to ask you to come to help her, if I can spare you. Would you like to go?" She peered at the girl piercingly. "It is an age since you were in London. It will do you nothing but good." When she saw the doubtful look on Netta's face she said firmly, "Nillie really needs you."

"Oh, of course, if she needs my help," Netta, instantly contrite, replied. Her naturally submissive nature made her immediately desire to help, and London meant Jaspar.

As March progressed more people returned to town. London grew fuller of company. The number of parties increased, until the season was well underway. Laura was enjoying herself hugely. She was far too beautiful not to be feted by all the bucks and her faint notoriety certainly did not go against her. She was taken everywhere by Lady Morntarny or if not by her, then in a party emanating from her house. Slowly the *ton* came to accept that the rumours that had been circulating in July must have been false. Laura showed not the slightest degree of embarrassment or interest in Lord Heddington, and by the end of April everyone was completely convinced that it had all been an unpleasant calumny.

Netta arrived in Berkeley Square. She was excited to be back in London and when she saw Nillie's wan face, only too pleased to be of assistance. When it was explained to her that her duties were to help escort Miss Laura Ludgrove, she was rather pleased. It was ages since she had attended any *ton* parties and her expectation was that she would enjoy it. Then she was introduced to Laura. The girl was so enchanting and talked so glibly of His Lordship, that Netta felt a return of a twinge of that disagreeable feeling which had settled on her stomach when she viewed Aurelia. Perhaps Laura was enamoured of Jaspar? She panicked. However, by the time she had been back in London for two weeks, she realised how foolish she was being, for apart from the indubitable fact that Laura was not remotely interested in Jaspar, he would never form an attachment to her. She was beautiful but not very intelligent and much too self-absorbed, thought Netta, to provide His Lordship with the devotion that she knew must be his due. She heaved a sigh of relief and set about getting on with her fair charge. She was not to be so sanguine when she met Laura's sister and observed her with Lord Heddington.

Laura was much in demand and far more so than she had been before. She now knew her way around socially, she was exquisitely beautiful, with a way of pleasing men that endeared her to all of that sex. Grizelda did not find herself so popular. She was not in the general way. Red hair was most unfashionable and the sprinkling of freckles was definitely not the vogue. In addition, her forthright personality and total rack of duplicity made her disliked by some. Lord Mannock remained a devoted suitor, but as he was very much under the thumb of his mama it was most unlikely that he would offer for a penniless female of doubtful parentage. For Grizelda had also discovered, much to her chagrin, that in spite of being escorted by Lady Melbourne, whose position in society was unassailable, the polite world, while tolerating her for her godmother, kept a slight distance.

Laura, who was not by nature perceptive, noticed nothing, but Grizelda became gradually aware that her lineage was not impeccable enough for them to be accepted without reservation. She hated it. It made her feel apart and uneasy.

Her other problem was Jaspar, who remained attentive whilst she remained confused. Having observed the *ton*'s reaction to Laura and herself, it became even more imperative that she did not allow herself to become embroiled with him. He, who could have any girl he wished, would certainly not marry a girl with no background. Keeping Jaspar at arm's length was easier to strive for than to achieve. Whenever they met, he asked her to dance with him, ride with him, which was impossible to refuse, seeing that she was riding his mare and Launcie was too wonderful for Grizelda to relinquish her with equanimity; and never seemed the slightest bit bored with her. On the contrary, he laughed at her comments and seemed genuinely to enjoy being with her. At night, sometimes, in her comfortable bed she wondered how it was going to end. For, however careful she was, she knew that a step and she would no longer be paddling in the shallows but be tumbling down the rivers of love.

Netta met her first at Lady Bessborough's. Nillie having been forced to retire to bed, she was escorting Laura. They arrived at Cavendish Square where they were greeted by Her Ladyship. Netta observed that, although she welcomed them warmly, Lady Bessborough seemed worn, her eyes most abstracted; she imagined that it must be due to worry about her daughter. It was well known that Lady Caroline was very unbalanced at the moment; Netta found a ready sympathy for Lady Bessborough. She was such an amiable and tender-hearted woman, who wished everyone well and hardly deserved the distress caused by her daughter's affair with Byron and the scandal that it had occasioned.

Netta followed the butler and Laura up the curving staircase and as they reached the top Laura squealed, "Grizzie! Grizzie!"

She bounded up the last two steps towards a striking girl who stood, with great poise, in front of the long ornamental mirrors which decorated the delicately painted walls. Netta observed a reflection which revealed tumultuous red hair tumbling down the girl's back and over her smooth slim shoulders. She was dressed all in white, with waves of lace around her neck and skirt. She was dazzling.

"Netta, this is my sister, Grizelda." Laura introduced them conscientiously.

Grizelda curtsied, smiling. Her smile was, Netta reflected, charming and her extraordinary pale blue eyes danced. Netta felt plain and most commonplace beside her. As they spoke, she knew swiftly that this girl was very different from her charge. Grizelda, too, was curious; Netta, she had been informed by Laura, was an old friend of Lord Heddington and Lady Morntarny; she saw a modest and unassuming person whom she quickly dismissed.

"Delighted, Miss Ludgrove." Netta curtsied.

"Miss Egremont. I must thank you for taking care of Laura. I do hope she is not a burden to you?"

"Of course I am not! Am I, Netta? You like looking after me, do you not?"

"Yes, Laura, I do," Netta laughed.

"Well, do not let her plague you," Grizelda pronounced. "She can be very trying."

"Thank you so much! My own sister!" Laura stuck out her lower lip sulkily.

"I know you," Grizelda said in her direct way, "and you can be…"

"What beautiful hair," Netta interrupted. It was clear to her that Grizelda would provoke Laura and she did not want any quarrels.

Grizelda flung her head sideways and the cloud of gold curls fell over her shoulder.

"Thank you. I am afraid a temper accompanies this colour," she pronounced ruefully, grinning. "But I endeavour to contain it."

It was at this moment that Lord Heddington appeared at the top of the staircase; he had not seen Grizelda for some days, as she had been visiting with Lady Melbourne.

"Miss Ludgrove, your servant, Netta. How delightful to see you in London." He kissed her on the cheek. In spite of his formality to Grizelda, Netta could not help observing the light in his eyes as he greeted her. Her insides twisted with the, now familiar, irksome feeling.

"Can I escort you?" He held out an arm to each of them; by this time Laura had been whirled away to dance by Lord Alvanley. Netta pushed away her suspicions, for Jaspar led her to the dance floor and was as friendly and chatty as she could remember. Grizelda joined them in the set, standing up with Lord Ponsonby. It was only when Netta saw Jaspar's unconscious glance in Grizelda's direction that her heart plummeted. He was unaware of the warmth in his eyes but Netta, acutely perceptive to his every action, could not miss it. Later as he danced with Grizelda she watched with a sense of foreboding, and however hard she tried to dismiss her fears, she could not fail to remember Jaspar's dreams.

"What are you gazing at, Netta?" demanded a voice by her elbow. It was Laura; she was on the arm of a young man whom Netta did not know. She flushed and jerked her eyes away from Grizelda and Jaspar. Then she looked enquiringly at Laura's escort.

"Oh, sorry, this is Mr Farleigh. Miss Egremont, who has charge of me." Netta curtsied shyly.

"Miss Egremont. Then I must make sure that I am all conciliation to you if it is indeed the case that you have charge of the fair Laura," he laughed, kissing her hand politely.

His manners were impeccable but she could not rid herself of a slight feeling of unease. Grizelda, returning on the arm of

Lord Heddington, froze when she saw her sister cavorting with Jocelyn. Jaspar noticed the look of dislike that flitted across her transparent face with some amusement. Then he saw Jocelyn; the look on the spoilt dandy's visage was one of opprobrious intent. Jaspar glanced from one to another.

"Mr Farleigh." Grizelda spoke in a tone of loathing, inclining her head. "Laura, a word."

She drew her sister aside and said ferociously in a loud whisper that Jaspar suspected Jocelyn could hear, "I have warned you to have a care, Laura, he is most unsuitable."

Jaspar, concerned by the malevolent glance that Jocelyn threw in Grizelda's direction, tried to divert his attention; before he could do so they were joined by a man whom Jaspar regarded as even more undesirable.

"Lord Heddington." Colonel Staunton's voice was supercilious and evil. "Oh, and the Misses Ludgrove, how charming! All together, quite like old times."

The audacity and effrontery of the remark was beyond bearing to Grizelda who, overhearing it, flared up immediately.

"Colonel Staunton, I find your remarks off…" She got no further before Jaspar interrupted her and quite literally dragged her towards the dance floor.

"Stop it!" she cried. "He is the most utterly contemptible, rude, boorish…"

"Definitely! But not a sensible adversary. He has the most malicious and spiteful tongue. You would be well advised to exercise caution. We do not want him spreading disagreeable calumnies. I would suggest you reserve your temper where he is concerned." He looked down into Grizelda's penitent eyes. "Oh, my dear. Have you engaged yourself with him already?"

She nodded. "Yes. I am afraid he accompanied Mr Farleigh to Lord Farleigh's at Christmas and he made suggestive remarks about you and Laura. I gave him a regular setdown," she went on contritely.

Jaspar hooted with laughter. "I see that it behoves upon me to haul you out of trouble. Do you never curb your tongue?"

"Not very often. I do try but it is very hard when one encounters imbeciles like that," she continued, repentant.

Jaspar laughed again. "Well, I think you should try harder. Seriously, if he ever causes you any trouble, let me fight your battles. Promise you will come to me?" He smiled. She had little problem agreeing to such a generous offer.

It was a gloriously warm spring and the beginning of May was positively hot. The trees in Hyde Park were well advanced, as were the flowers which bloomed in abundance everywhere. Jaspar got into the habit of rising early so that he could ride in the park before the rest of the *ton* was up. However late he went to bed he asked Pickering to bring his chocolate so that he could be out on Valiant and cantering through the translucent bright green before breakfast. On a particular morning he had left very early and returned to his house ravenously hungry.

"I will breakfast before I change, York," he commanded as he strode across the hall, picking up a pile of letters from the side table. Entering the breakfast room, the liveried footman pulled back a chair and as Jaspar seated himself, he hurried to present a series of dishes for his delectation. Jaspar tore open a letter and, as he did so, he heard a loud knocking on the front door. He was curious; it was rather early for callers. He heard York open the door and, interested, he went silently into the hall.

To his surprise Grizelda stood at the door. She appeared to be arguing with York.

"I am sorry, miss, but His Lordship is not available at present." York drew himself up grandly. "I cannot undertake to advise him of your presence."

Jaspar stood quietly at the door.

"But I must see him! Go and tell him I am here."

Jaspar watched, amused, as York, uncommonly unsure, paused. "I am afraid that His Lordship is not here, miss."

Grizelda moved forward and as she did so Jaspar observed a small boy clinging to her skirts. He was most intrigued. He drew back slightly so that she would not see him and, fascinated, watched the battle between his immutable henchman and the indomitable Miss Ludgrove.

"I do not believe you!" She looked York straight in the eye and Jaspar watched his butler flinch. He was unused to such directness. "Of course His Lordship is in town. I need his help. Go and wake him up and tell him I am here," she commanded.

The butler appeared uneasy. "I cannot do that," he said unhappily.

"Yes you can." Grizelda's eyes had started to flash. Jaspar smiled to himself; he did not envy York being on the receiving end of her anger.

He went to the rescue. "What is it, Miss Ludgrove?" He moved forward.

"You see, he is in town. You lied." She turned to York accusingly.

"Your Lordship. I was just…"

"Quite. York was doing his job, Miss Ludgrove. Do not get angry with him."

Grizelda smiled. "I apologise. It is not your fault if your master orders you to deny him." She faced Jaspar and raised an eyebrow slightly. He burst out laughing.

"Now that you have ascertained that I am indeed here, although I am afraid not fit to receive you," he motioned his grimy breeches and coat covered with horse hairs, "what can I do to help you?"

She shook her head impatiently. "That is irrelevant. I need…" She stopped.

"Who is this?" He indicated the child who was hidden behind her.

"Oh, this is Tarn." Pulling him out from behind her skirts, she addressed the boy gently. "No need to be afraid." He clung to her convulsively. He was, Jaspar judged, about ten. He was filthy and looked terrified.

"That will be all, York." Jaspar started to dismiss the interested servants.

"No, wait," Grizelda interrupted him. "Please, take Tarn and give him something to eat, he is starving." York, surprised, glanced at Jaspar for guidance.

"Yes, take him. Feed him. Oh, and you had better clean him up."

The butler started towards Tarn, who cowered in fear. Grizelda knelt down next to him. Jaspar noticed that her dress and face were smudged with dirt as well. "Go with York. He will not hurt you, I promise. I must arrange how we can get you home." With a scared look the boy obeyed her, and after a moment Jaspar led the way into his library.

Grizelda had never been to His Lordship's house before and she regarded it curiously. She liked it.

Jaspar closed the door behind them. "Well?" he enquired.

"I want you to give me fifty pounds. Please." She raised her eyes to his.

Jaspar's eyebrows shot up. "Fifty pounds? Why?"

"I want to take Tarn home. It seems he lives in Newcastle. He was sold by his parents to a man down here, a saddler. He was supposed to have been cared for but he was beaten and terribly treated. I found him. The poor child. I am afraid I completely lost my temper but it was to no avail. I could only get him away by giving his master all the money I possessed. It was only then that he allowed me to take him. He was a fierce brute."

Jaspar regarded her quizzically. "And you were not afraid?"

"No, why should I be?" she giggled. "Shouting does not scare me. I think the man was more frightened of me. I threatened all kinds of terrible things."

Jaspar, his admiration for her increasing, merely smiled. "You did not fight him?" he teased.

"Good heavens, no. Oh…" She looked down at her grubby dress. "Well, I did have to chase them through a particularly dirty passage."

"Miss Ludgrove, you are remarkable."

She blushed. "No. Anyone would have done the same. One cannot stand by and watch children being mistreated, you know."

Jaspar, who could name any amount of people who would do just that, did not reply.

"So you see, now I must have the money to return him to his parents."

"Suppose they sell him again?"

"From Tarn's description I do not think they will," she replied pensively. "It appears that they were desperate. I will have to make sure that they are not forced to act in such a way again." Jaspar looked doubtful.

"Now you see why I need the money. I think it will cost at least fifty pounds for us to travel stage to Newcastle."

"Do you propose to take him yourself?" asked Jaspar curiously.

"Why not?" Grizelda's chin went up. She met Jaspar's laughing eyes defiantly. "I cannot tolerate that kind of cruelty. He is only a child. So will you give me the money?"

"Do you intend to give it back? Is this a loan?" His Lordship asked. Grizelda turned away angrily, without noticing the dancing amusement in his eyes.

"No," Grizelda, incurably honest, replied. "Well, I will try. Will you give it to me?" she said impatiently.

"No."

Grizelda turned, a look of amazement in her pale eyes. *At least she is surprised I have denied her*, thought Jaspar.

"What!" she cried. "You will not do…"

"Well, do you think you can just breeze in and ask for all that money?" Jaspar, laughing, asked her.

Her fine eyes flashed and then, as she observed his amusement, she stopped.

"l will not give you the money for I do not think it is suitable for you to be traipsing all over England by yourself, returning small boys to their parents."

"But I…"

"Wait," Jaspar interrupted, "I do not think it is right for you to take him. So I intend to deliver him myself."

"You?"

He laughed again. "Yes. Me! Your face tells me that you have little faith in my ability to do so."

"N… no, I mean…" Grizelda sat down on the chaise, "… l have every faith in your ability, but do you want to take him home?"

"No. Not particularly. But I do not want you to have to do it."

Grizelda digested this statement. She found it made her heart beat in a peculiar fashion.

She looked up at Jaspar, meeting his eyes steadily.

"I will take the greatest care of him. I promise. I will drive my own cattle. He will travel in my chaise, not on the stage. I will undertake to return him to his parents and I will make sure that he is provided for. Will that do?"

Grizelda swallowed. "Yes. It… it is…"

"Now you must go. You must not stay in my house unchaperoned. I do not want your reputation sullied in any way."

"l did not think you cared about anyone's reputation or the proprieties," Grizelda commented, the words no sooner out of her mouth than she regretted then. She saw Jaspar stiffen.

"You will never forgive me," he murmured under his breath.

 223

Grizelda, who had by now forgiven him wholeheartedly, did not hear his muttered comment, or she might have refuted it.

"You are fair in your accusation," he remarked bitterly. "Now go." He pulled her up and as he did so she caught his eyes again. The hurt look in them surprised her. Their eyes met. Her body trembled.

"Grizelda." Jaspar held her arm; his eyes locked deeply with hers. She found that all she wanted to do was to fling herself into his arms. She wanted to say, "Take me with you?"

A gentle knock at the door. Jaspar released her arm, turning from her. York appeared with Tarn. The boy had been bathed and was wearing a shirt that was far too big and some worn breeches turned up at the bottoms. Jaspar noticed that his hair was very fair and that his eyes were blue. He looked petrified.

"Lord Heddington is to take you back to your parents." Grizelda spoke with difficulty, her head in a whirl. "You will travel with him. He will not hurt you."

"No," the boy pleaded in a small tearful voice. "Please let me stay with you?" He clung to her hand.

Jaspar found himself curiously moved. He knelt down beside the child and took the hand that was not desperately clinging to Grizelda in his very gently. He smiled, and said almost tenderly, "Tarn, I will not hurt you. I will take you in my carriage. It would not be right for Miss Ludgrove to convey you. Do you understand?" The boy bit his lip and hung his head. Unable to speak, he nodded.

Grizelda knelt beside him. She kissed the blonde curls. "I promise that as soon as I can I will come to visit you. You will be a great deal more comfortable with Lord Heddington, you know."

Tarn flung his arms around her neck. Disentangling him gently, she stood up.

Jaspar escorted Grizelda to the carriage that was to take her home. "He will be safe with me," he told her.

"I know. I trust you. Thank you," Grizelda said shyly. She raised her eyes to his for a second and then climbed into the carriage.

"Go now," Jaspar muttered, closing the door.

Chapter Eighteen

Jaspar walked thoughtfully back into the library. Tarn was standing, without moving, just as Grizelda had left him. His small face was puckered up and he looked as if he were about to cry. Jaspar was overwhelmed with pity for him. He was hardly older than Charles, and when he thought of what the child had had to endure, it made his blood boil with surprising anger.

He went across to him. "Tarn." The boy raised his huge eyes to his; they were brimming with unshed tears. Jaspar put out his arm to touch him but he shrunk away as if expecting to be hit. Very gently Jaspar picked up the small rough hand which was hardly one of a child, so scarred and torn it was, and led him to the chaise where he sat the boy next to him. He touched the huge shirt which he expected was one of Pickering's.

"I think before we leave for Newcastle we had best obtain some clothes for you. You cannot wear these."

Tarn looked at him. "Please, sir, I like them. They're canny. Dinna take them away, please," he begged.

Jaspar smiled, patting his hand. "I was suggesting that we get you some new breeches and shirts. Ones that fit you."

Tarn's eyes opened wide. "New?"

"Yes." Jaspar stood up and rang the bell. When York answered he asked him to send Pickering to him. The valet bustled in to obey the summons immediately.

"Pickering, I wish that you take Tarn out and buy him something to wear. You will know what is suitable."

"Yes, my lord."

"No, sir, I do not wish to go with anyone but you." Tarn now clung to Jaspar's leg. "Please, y' take me."

"Now, young man, do not you go bothering His Lordship," Pickering ordered in a firm voice. Tarn shrank back against Jaspar in terror. Pickering's tones would not have disconcerted Charles, Jaspar thought, but Charles was brought up with love. He made a decision. "I will take him."

"But, my lord, it is hardly what Your Lordship would want to do with your morning. Do not let him get above himself, my lord. You come here, boy, and don't you be naughty."

"No, Pickering, I have said that I shall take him." Then to mollify his aggrieved valet, he smiled. "But you shall tell me where to go, for I have no experience in these matters."

Pickering sniffed. "I think, my lord, a bazaar."

"A bazaar?"

"May I suggest the one in Soho Square. It has all kinds of stalls and I am sure that you will discover everything you will need there."

"Excellent. What a good fellow you are. Ask Harper to bring around my curricle. We are going to Soho bazaar!" He grinned at Tarn, who unexpectedly managed a small smile back.

Grizelda sat in Jaspar's comfortable town coach. She felt strangely elated. Her nature was too honest not to face her unequivocal feelings towards His Lordship. The battle was lost but she did not feel sorry. No, she hugged herself with inexplicable hopefulness. Deep down inside part of her recognised that His Lordship was not indifferent to her. His eyes had given him away. She had no idea whether Jaspar had admitted this to himself but she just knew that it must be the truth. This insight made her tremble. She felt alive and in touch with the world outside. The leaves on the trees seemed greener, the sky bluer, the flowers smelt sweeter.

When she arrived back at Melbourne House, ran quickly to find her godmama. Lady Melbourne was at her writing desk composing a letter to William. These missives cost her dear. She knew that she must sublimate her desire to criticise her daughter-in-law, for her stubborn son would not tolerate any attempts to reprove the brazen behaviour of his wife. As she threw away another useless page Grizelda entered. Lady Melbourne immediately noticed her heightened colour, glowing eyes and filthy dress. She smiled and raised an eyebrow.

"Where have you been? You appear remarkably dirty, my love."

"Yes, I rescued a small boy from a brutal and cruel master. I had to almost fight him."

Lady Melbourne stared at her in amazement. "But why do such a thing, my dear? You could have placed yourself in danger."

"Oh, I care nothing for that. This poor child! I am persuaded, Lady Melbourne, that you would have done the same." Her godmother looked doubtful. "Oh, you would. You could not have passed him by without aiding him. No one could."

Lady Melbourne, who could have named any number of her acquaintances who would have done just that, made no further comment.

"So what did you do with this child?"

"Oh, I took him to Lord Heddington."

Lady Melbourne looked horrified. "What, to Jaspar! What a quite unsuitable thing to do." Privately, she thought that any warmness that Jaspar might have entertained for Grizelda before, would most certainly have disappeared when he was faced with this peculiar behaviour.

She sighed.

"Not at all. He was not in the slightest put out. He offered to return the child to his parents."

"What?" Lady Melbourne was utterly astonished. "Jaspar! You mean that Jaspar has taken your protégé? No, I do not believe it!"

"Nevertheless it is true," Grizelda remarked. Lady Melbourne digested the implications of Jaspar's strange behaviour.

Then she peered at Grizelda shrewdly. "You seem very exhilarated, my dear. Has anything else occurred with Lord Heddington?"

Grizelda blushed. "N… no." She looked straight at her godmother. "Lady Melbourne, were you ever in love?"

Lady Melbourne hooted at her forthrightness. "Yes, many times."

"Many times?"

"But once, once very deeply." She paused, remembering the feelings that her goddaughter was so obviously experiencing. "It is both very wonderful, very all-engrossing, and at times tormenting. You feel an increased sensitivity to the world." As she remembered, an odd yearning flitted across the proud features. Grizelda watched her. "There is no human emotion so inspiring or, if lost, so desolating." She smiled.

"I know," Grizelda answered, too unreserved to hide what had happened to her. "I had a mind to be prudent but I have ignored my own cautious advice."

Lady Melbourne put her hand over Grizelda's. She chose her words carefully. She knew the girl was no dissembler. She hoped that Jaspar would see how excellent a wife she would make for him, but with Jaspar one could never be sure. It would be judicious to offer a recommendation of wariness. "Jaspar, my dear, is a very attractive man. There have been many women. I would not wish you to be hurt. Have a care, my sweet."

Grizelda stood up and paced the room. "I know what you are saying and believe me, you cannot give me stricter warnings than I gave myself. But my strictures have been to no avail." She turned to her godmother and said simply, "It is too late. I cannot go back now."

"Mmm. I understand, Grizelda. No one better. It will, I think, be alright but you must have the greatest care not to exhibit your love."

Grizelda nodded. "I know that your advice is sage." She kissed her godmama. "He will be away for some days, I think, for her has to take Tarn to Newcastle."

"Newcastle?" Lady Melbourne was amused. "All that way at your behest." She pursed her lips and cocked an eyebrow. "Well, I am confounded, I must admit."

When Tarn viewed the glories of equipage in which he was to travel he was rendered speechless. He stared at Jaspar's elegant curricle and the dashing team which drove it with reverence. Then he went to the dappled head of the grey and buried his head in the horse's neck.

"Oh, you lovely animal," he murmured into the sleek mane. Harper, caught between amusement and astonishment, enquired, "Do you ride, young man?"

Tarn looked up at him and shook his head. "No."

"But you like horses, Tarn?" Lord Heddington remarked.

The boy nodded vigorously. "Oh yes. I have wanted to ride."

"You cannot ride?"

"No, sir. We never 'ad no money for hosses."

"I see. Well, we will see what we can do about that. Jump up now."

The rest of the afternoon passed in a haze of glory for Tarn, who had to pinch himself to make sure that he was not dreaming.

Soho Square bazaar was quickly reached. Jaspar, who had imagined that an outing with a boy would be very dull, was pleasantly surprised. He enjoyed pointing out places of interest to Tarn, whose enrapt expression was most gratifying. He explained that the statue in the middle of the square was Charles the Second and that the square had originally been called King Square. When they entered Mr Trotter's bazaar, Tarn became almost intoxicated with joy as he beheld the treasures that were displayed on the long mahogany benches. They went from counter to counter, exulting in the variety of goods available to purchase. Jaspar found that he had to drag Tarn away from the toy shop, where they had bought a drum and some toy soldiers. The boy was looking wistfully at a slate and chalks.

"Do you want some, Tarn?" asked Jaspar, who was by now enjoying himself hugely.

"Oh, sir, you have bought me so much but I do so want to read and write and..."

"You cannot read?" Jaspar was surprised and then the sight of Nillie teaching the housemaid flashed into his mind. He nodded. "We will buy these and on our journey we will start to write." They also purchased some simple books.

The pastry cook and music shop took up Tarn's attention and it was only after much coercion that Jaspar could get him to the clothier. Here they bought a complete wardrobe for a small boy, and the pile of parcels that Jack, the footman, carried grew larger. Eventually, after some persuasion, Jaspar managed to get Tarn to leave fairyland and return home.

Grosvenor Square was soon attained and as they drew up Tarn catapulted down the steps and into the house; by now all the fears and reservations that he had experienced had melted into nothing. He knew that they meant him well and his adoration of Lord Heddington was complete. He pranced in, determined to show his new belongings to anyone who would be interested. Pickering, who had been quite put out when his company had been rejected so forcefully was determined to find favour with this young boy who had taken his master's fancy, was crossing the hall when Tarn bounced in.

"Well, and what have you got?" He grinned at the boy.

"Such a time have I had! Such a time you would not credit it." Tarn jumped around excitedly.

"Indeed!" Jaspar who was following him pronounced.

"My lord, Mr Talkarne is in the library."

"Tarn, run along with Pickering and show him everything. York, we will partake of nuncheon before we leave." He spoke as the footman threw open the library door. Tarn watched him disappear with apprehension, but the warm smile on the valet's face reassured him and he was only too pleased to have an attentive audience while he extolled the glories of their purchases.

Roderick was standing gazing out of the window; he had a look of such happiness on his face that Jaspar strode across to him.

"I see that congratulations are in order," he asserted, grinning, grabbing his friend's hand.

Roderick appeared bemused. "She accepted! She accepted. Her mama pleased, nay delighted." He wheeled around next to Jaspar. "She accepted! She is going to marry me!" His face broke into creases of joy.

"Roderick, oh, I am so pleased. It is the best news."

"Jaspar, I cannot tell you how I feel."

"I have some inkling. Your face tells much," Jaspar laughed.

"It cannot reflect the true rapture, the real joy. I am part of another now, I have her concerns, her happiness. She is the most wonderful, beautiful, enchanting person and I have never felt such bliss, it is beyond…" He shrugged. "No. I have not the words to describe it."

"I think you have described it well," Jaspar replied wryly.

"Will you come? We will celebrate?"

"No, I would like to, above anything, but I cannot, I have to take… to take a child back to its parents."

Roderick looked astonished; he raised an eyebrow.

"l know that it sounds irregular," Jaspar continued, "but I am charged with returning Tarn, that is his name, and I must fulfil my obligations."

"Jaspar, of course, if you have other plans, I understand," Roderick replied hesitantly, "but what child? Who is this Tarn?"

"You will meet him." Jaspar crossed and rang the bell. When York arrived he requested that Tarn be brought to them; the boy bounded in but stopped when he beheld Roderick; he looked at Jaspar intently.

"This is Mr Talkarne, Tarn. Roderick, this is the boy and we leave for Newcastle immediately." Tarn looked uncertainly at Roderick.

"Mr Talkarne was injured in battle, he lost his arm," explained Jaspar; the boy's eyes opened wide. He regarded Roderick with a mixture of admiration and alarm.

"Oh," he breathed. Roderick laughed.

"One day he shall tell you about it but not now. We must eat before we leave. Do you care to join us, Rod?"

His friend nodded and the three went to partake of nuncheon. By the time they were ready to go, Tarn and Roderick were firm friends, but Roderick was left with an unanswered question as to whom the boy was. Jaspar did not choose to enlighten him.

It was a beautiful day as they left the grime and dust of London behind them. The sky was bright blue and not a single cloud sullied its purity. The trees had by now completely unfurled their summer greenness; abundant foliage covering their bleak winter stems, a gentle breeze stirred their brimming branches. As they bowled along, Tarn, staring entranced from the window, could observe rabbits and other wildlife hopping across the fields. Jaspar had not relished the thought of the long journey but Tarn proved to be far better company than he had anticipated. The child was enchanted by all that they saw, and as he had quite lost his inhibitions, he questioned Jaspar endlessly, a prospect that His Lordship might have anticipated as exhausting but which, in reality, proved highly entertaining.

"Now, my turn for a question." The boy nodded, willing to help if he could. "I would like you to relay to me exactly how Miss Ludgrove rescued you. How did it come about?"

Tarn thought for a moment and then he started. "Me father had to sell me, to a saddler... Me master... he was hard. He beat me. I had nothing to eat. I lived in a stable. It was damp and there were rats and... and, I was very sad." He looked at Jaspar, his blue eyes worried. Then went on, "I thought I would run away. I was helping to deliver harnesses to a big house near the park and when me master went to receive his money, I gave him the slip. I ran down a narrow passage next to the house but he ran after me. He caught me and he started to beat me with his belt. I heard someone else running down the alley. It was Griz... Miss Ludgrove. She grabbed me master and pulled him off me an' all. He swerved round and I thought he was going to hit her, but she got cross. She is very fiery. 'How dare you,' she told him. He was so surprised he stopped and she grabbed me. I clung to her. Then she got very angry with me master. I do not remember what she said but lots of words. Then me master whined and said he wanted money and she pulled out her purse and gave him all that she had. She took my hand and we ran away. She said that she would take me home, then I told her it was in Newcastle and she said, 'Oh,' she did not have enough money to get to Newcastle and I cried and she said not to cry, she knew someone who would help us and we came to you, and you did." He beamed at Jaspar.

"Miss Ludgrove was very courageous. Was she not scared of your master?" he asked.

"No, I do not think she was. She was very angry."

Jaspar laughed. "I think I can believe that. She was brave though," he repeated, admiration in his throat.

"I was very happy," Tarn vouchsafed. Then he peered out of the window again and became entranced by a small dog that was chasing a flock of sheep across a field. Jaspar sat back thoughtfully. It had to be admitted, Grizelda was extraordinary; he could not think of another girl of his acquaintance who would behave as she had done.

Jaspar had decided that it would be efficacious to take their journey in easy stages and had chosen the Wheatsheaf Inn, outside Hitchin, as their first stop. The Wheatsheaf prided itself as being a hostelry for the nobility. It never received the stage nor post-chaises, unless the occupants were well known to the proprietor. As they drove through lanes narrow with overhanging branches the evening sun was throwing pink tendrils across the blue sky, suffusing the fields in pale pink light. The Wheatsheaf was set back from the main thoroughfare; it was a solid red brick building built around a substantial courtyard where stables and postillions and horses resided in luxurious quarters. Around the door the wisteria wound its sturdy branches, heavy with purple flowers, exuding their sweet fragrance. Their carriage stopped. The landlord hurried out to greet them; he was a tall, spare man with thinning hair.

"My Lord Heddington, how gracious to have the pleasure of your company again." He bowed low.

Jaspar climbed down. "A room, a private parlour and dinner," he commanded. Tarn hurled himself down the steps and ran about like an excited puppy.

"I like this place," he commented.

"So I should think," Jaspar, amused, told him. "Now come in and choose your dinner!" The prospect of being allowed such munificence quietened his excitement. He grinned at Jaspar and the landlord and bounded in through the front door. The beamed and polished interior of the inn was dark and cool after the warmth of the day. The landlord walked quickly down the spotless corridors and flung open the door of the private parlour, which he hastened to inform Lord Heddington was the best the Wheatsheaf could boast. Low oak beams criss-crossed the ceiling, and the window, which overlooked the rear, was framed in huge pieces of oak, which formed an attractive window seat. Tarn immediately climbed onto it, to gaze out longingly at the expanse of green, verdant grass which led into a small wood.

"Can we go in the woods?" he asked, turning glowing eyes towards Jaspar, who smiled and said non-commitedly, "Perhaps."

Whereas this answer would have prompted his nephews and nieces into more pleading, Tarn did not. He accepted Jaspar's authority and merely climbed down, going to his bag, which Harper had deposited on the floor, and pulling out the slate and chalks that they had bought in Soho bazaar; these he carried to the table. His blue eyes anxious, he ventured, "Then may we read and write?"

"Yes," Jaspar laughed, sitting next to him. He was, His Lordship realised, a quick pupil, and by the time the dinner arrived he had mastered the idea of his name and was carefully trying to copy out the letters which Jaspar had written.

"Come, eat now." Lord Heddington picked up the slate and put it away; they went to the table. The food was, as Jaspar had known, delicious, and Tarn polished off a substantial quantity. As soon as the covers had been removed and His Lordship settled over a brandy, he fetched the slate and started again. Jaspar watched as he sat in the gathering gloom, his small tongue between his teeth and a determined look on his face. Then, just as suddenly, his head sank and he flopped down over the slate, fast asleep. Jaspar smiled; he picked up the bundle of boy tenderly and carried him upstairs. Tarn's blond hair tickled his; he was very light and Jaspar could feel all his bones through the smart new shirt. He put him gently on the truckle bed, that he had had set up in his bedchamber, and stripped off his clothes. The child's back was covered with livid blue and red bruises, and the marks of the belt could be seen clearly along his thin shoulders, bright and violent against the white skin. Jaspar gently traced one of the larger marks with his finger as he did so. He was overcome with a ferocious possessive anger. "No one will ever do this to you again," he swore under his breath. Fury coursed through him; if Tarn's master had been present, Jaspar was quite sure he would have taken pleasure in slowly squeezing the very life out of him. Gently he pulled the brand new nightshirt over the child's head and as he did so a discreet knock revealed Harper.

"Can I help you, my lord?"

Jaspar shook his head; the old groom joined him by the bedside. Harper looked at Tarn and his bruises; he muttered angrily, "Jes' look you at that, me lord, right it ain't, poor little beggar."

"Indeed it is not right. We must make sure that nothing ever happens to him again."

Jaspar then went back down to the private parlour where he drank his brandy sitting at the open window and watching the moon come up and the stars slowly twinkle into light. He thought about Grizelda. He found her obtruding into his thoughts all the time. Jaspar had not yet confronted his feelings towards her. For one of such experience he was totally untried when it came to love. Jaspar had never been in love, except once as a green young man, an affair that was more infatuation than love. He knew that he admired her. He knew that he enjoyed her company more than any other girl but he was not sure. He was not sure about anything. Eventually he went up to bed. Tarn was asleep with one arm flung out sideways; his small face was flushed with childhood. As he looked at him Jaspar was again overcome with an unpredictable fierce longing for a son of his own.

Grizelda changed her grubby dress and decided that a visit to Laura was imperative, for she had not seen her for several days.

She was not complaisant enough to leave her unsupervised for long. Netta, she gauged, was alright but would be no match for her flighty sister. When she reached Berkeley Square she discovered that her misgivings were not unfounded.

Parker informed her that, "My lady is most unwell, so bad that Nurse is sitting with her."

"Oh, I am so sorry to hear that Her Ladyship is still indisposed. I did not come to disturb her but to see my sister. I hope that Laura is not being a charge to Miss Egremont?"

"Miss Netta has responsibility for the children, with Miss Manners having taken Lord Steeple to Morntarny. Miss Laura went to the park with a young gentleman."

Grizelda went cold with apprehension. Just as she had feared. It was not Lady Morntarny's fault but rather that her silly sister had no idea of how to behave. Grizelda sighed. Parker observed her quietly; he had formed his own opinion of Miss Laura Ludgrove.

"l had better go and search for her. Do you perhaps know where she went?"

"l believe Hyde Park, miss. It is the time for the promenade."

Grizelda set off to walk the short distance to Hyde Park. Lady Melbourne had insisted that if she went out, she be accompanied by her maid, and Grizelda was glad that if she were to confront the fashionable in the park she would not be unchaperoned.

CHAPTER NINETEEN

Laura was pleased with herself. She had become quite satisfactorily fashionable, and had managed to collect quite a coterie of young gallants, all ready to write paeans to her beauty. Amongst these was Jocelyn, who was not as devoted as she would have wished but who certainly seemed full of admiration. She was of the opinion that she managed her admirers with the skill of one far more experienced in society than herself, although she would never have admitted it to anyone, for Laura was keen at all times to present an image that was most sympathetic; she was, secretly, rather pleased that Her Ladyship was not able to supervise her properly. Not that she wished Her Ladyship ill. No, she was very fond of her but her indisposition meant that Laura could do much as she wished, for Netta did not have the strength to restrain her. Laura found the freedom exhilarating. Her newfound liberty went straight to her head. She was in some awe of Grizelda and knew her sister would prohibit the worst excesses, but then Grizelda was not around on a day-to-day basis and could not watch over her. So Laura was glad that Lady Morntarny was pregnant. It would have been disagreeable if she were really ill but that was not the case, for at the end there would be a dear baby.

Carefully, Laura encouraged Jocelyn, determined not to make the same mistake as she had made with Lord Heddington.

She was complaisant enough to believe she could deal very well with Mr Farleigh. He would not slip through her fingers. She was not the green girl she had been last summer. Oh no, no, she knew a thing or two. She was not particularly fond of Colonel Staunton, he tended to the sardonic and Laura did not know how to deal with irony, but Mr Farleigh was often accompanied by his friend, so she had no choice but to put up with him. She had contrived to make several friends, who were also doing the season with her, and was generally well pleased with her lot.

She awoke late and sat in bed sipping her chocolate and going over, in her mind, the events of the previous evening. She had been taken to a ball given in honour of Lady Hestor Caston, who had become her particular friend. Lady Hestor was the daughter of an impecunious Irish peer, the Earl of Gallagher. Her mama had brought her to London with the express object of contracting an advantageous match. She was a vivacious and very pretty girl, and Lady Gallagher was hopeful that she would succeed. Unfortunately, within weeks of arriving in London she had set her cap at Lord Heddington. This was not entirely her fault for she had been thrust in His Lordship's way and he had indulged her liveliness with a mild flirtation, which had been thoroughly misinterpreted by her mama. As Laura thought over Hestor's problem, she remembered being enamoured of Lord Heddington and how ineligible and uncomfortable that emotion had been. *I am glad I am not Hestor*, she reasoned. Then she wriggled down in her bed and, Hestor's predicament forgotten, gave her thoughts over entirely to Jocelyn. Last night, she had arranged to walk in the park with him this morning, and she faced the dilemma of what to wear. Should it be her sprigged muslin or the pale silk dress which exactly matched her eyes? In the end of her deliberations she came down in favour of the sprigged dress. It was delicate and deliciously pretty, and she knew that the tiny yellow flowers complemented her golden hair perfectly. Her next obstacle was how to lose Netta whom, she had to agree with Mr Farleigh, was becoming a frightful bore. She was still ruminating on what she could do about her chaperone, when, attired in the muslin dress, she reached the breakfast parlour. Netta was there with Abigail on her knee; she appeared preoccupied.

"Laura, my dear," Netta started, "I hope that you can manage to amuse yourself today for poor Nillie is most unwell and Nurse is to sit with her. Miss Manners has taken Charles to Morntarny, so I must take care of the girls."

Laura's spirits brightened, her problem solved. "Oh, I am so sorry. Please do not worry about me for I will be fine. Perhaps I will go and visit my sister." She let the suggestion hang in the air.

And Netta, too absorbed in how best to amuse the children, did not notice.

Laura waited impatiently for Jocelyn to collect her. She sat in the small morning room off the hall. She wanted to be available instantly that she heard Mr Farleigh arrive; she was not going to give any meddlesome butler such as Parker a chance to question what she was doing. She heard the knock and sprang up, smoothing down the muslin dress. She took a quick glance at herself in the glass and was pleased with what she saw. Her curls shone; the poke bonnet that sat so charmingly on them was garlanded with tiny flowers; her dress was, as she knew, undeniably the most fetching. She smiled captivatingly and went to meet Mr Farleigh.

He stood in the hall. His nonchalant good looks made her heart tremble. He certainly was the best looking of men, far better than Lord Heddington. Now that she had beheld Jocelyn, she could not understand how she could ever have regarded His Lordship as the epitome of male beauty. Mr Farleigh was dressed with studied casualness in a blue coat of superfine, cut tight over his excellent shoulders. His hessians shone like a mirror and his black locks were brushed à la Brutus. Laura was determined to marry him, but she realised that to do so she was going to have to be very clever. He must never know of her brief affair with Lord Heddington; mind you, she could hardly credit it herself now, and with Jaspar's steadfast denials and her own, it was as if it had never been.

Jocelyn regarded her as she came to greet him. He was particularly fond of blonde girls and Laura's apricot blonde curls and clear blue eyes were bewitching. He had quickly discovered that she was unlikely to languish and sigh over him, as others were, when faced with his looks and his expectations. He found this most refreshing. He had not the smallest intention of marrying her; men with his future did not waste themselves on trumpery girls with no fortune and a dubious father. After all, one did not wed the daughter of one's manager, however enchanting her eyes.

"Mr Farleigh." She curtsied. Laura's voice was very pretty; it was not low and husky as Grizelda's but neither was it shrill and hard as those of many of her friends.

"Miss Ludgrove." He bowed over her hand, bringing her gently to her feet; her laughing blue eyes met his in exactly the way to make his heart beat faster. "Are you quite ready to accompany me to the park?"

"Quite ready." He was pleased. He hated to be kept waiting, as Laura had discovered quite soon in their relationship. She made sure that she was always prepared. She smiled and gave him her arm. She was pleased to discover that the colonel was not with Mr Farleigh. The pleasure in his absence, however, was short-lived, for as they came into the park he sauntered across to join them.

"Evening, Jocelyn. Your servant, Miss Ludgrove." He picked up her hand and kissed it; his eyes were mocking. Laura felt her customary discomfort but determined not to let it show; she merely smiled sweetly and said, "Thank you, Colonel Staunton. How well you look."

"Thank you, and may I walk with you?"

"Of course." She smiled.

"And where is Miss Egremont today?"

Colonel Staunton enjoyed taunting Netta. He had understood almost without knowing of her feelings for Lord Heddington, and as he had suffered at the hands of Brummell, Morntarny and Heddington, he was more than happy to be able to effect mild reprisals on someone who did not have the astringency to answer him with his own.

Laura put up her chin and responded, "She must care for the children, as Lady Morntarny is so unwell."

"Ah, so you are alone and unchaperoned." His small eyes were spiteful. "Not scared, Miss Laura?"

"Indeed no," she responded sharply. Whatever Laura lacked it was not character. "You are both gentlemen. I know that I am quite safe with you." She smiled bewitching at Jocelyn, taking his arm.

The colonel laughed mockingly.

"Laura! Miss Laura!"

Laura turned as she heard her name called in a reedy voice; she saw, hurrying towards her, a thin wispy woman. As the creature drew closer Laura observed that her breath came in short bursts as she struggled to catch up with them. It was Miss Clarges. Laura's heart sank.

Life had not been kind to Miss Clarges since she had been summarily dismissed from Lady Ambrose's employ. She had lost what she now fondly remembered as a gentle sinecure, a secure and easy job with a kind and considerate employer. She had been, in her own words, "thrown out onto the street at a moment's notice after years of devoted service". She had been forced to go to an elderly cousin who lived in Clapham. As Euphemia had always looked down upon this cousin it was doubly galling, not only to be thrown out, but to be forced to grovel to Cousin Mildred. Mildred Clarges was as fat as her cousin was thin. She was an ill-tempered, and to Euphemia's fastidious nose, evil-smelling old woman. She lived in a small cottage near Clapham Common which had belonged to her mother. The Clarges brothers had been tradespeople who had both married above themselves. The brothers had remained close but their wives had cordially disliked each other and their only daughters had carried on the enmity.

Euphemia had gone to Mildred on the morning after Lady Morntarny's visit to Curzon Street. She considered she had been most unfairly treated and her bubbling resentment had become an obsession. Mildred was bored with hearing about her trouble, but as Euphemia, in gratitude for a home, acted, rather unwillingly, it must be admitted, as unpaid skivvy, laundry maid, cook and everything else, she was prepared to tolerate her. Revenge festered in Miss Clarges's breast, revenge against Lady Ambrose and more particularly Laura, whom she thought had misled her most dreadfully. Why, the girl had told her that Lord Heddington had proposed. She had only been trying to help and now look what had happened.

Jaspar and Tarn were heartily pleased when at last Newcastle was spread before them. The journey, for one that was such a distance, had been accomplished very smoothly, but both were tired of the confines of the carriage by the time they reached the city. The weather had remained beautiful and it had seemed even worse to Jaspar to be cooped up when he could have been out on these wonderful days. Tarn had been charming; he had never once complained. He had been unfailingly studious, trying to master the rudiments of reading, and was becoming fairly accomplished.

As they drew into his native city, he was only too happy to point out St Nicholas's and the sturdy facade of the keep. It was a calm, sunny evening as they approached the gates, and Tarn efficiently directed Jaspar through the narrow passages that would lead eventually to the Bigg Market. Just before the market was reached, in a narrow, dirty street, Tarn pointed to a crumbling two- story cottage, which was where he lived. Before the carriage had had a chance to come to a standstill he flung himself out of the door and jumped to the ground. He ran into the house.

Jaspar climbed down rather more slowly as Tarn emerged from the small peeling door dragging a heavily pregnant woman behind him. Mrs Grant was as blonde as Tarn and so nearly resembled him, that Jaspar knew her to be his mother. She was dressed in clean but heavily darned clothes and her hair was pulled back from her head. Three small children were clinging to her skirts and a smaller female version of Tarn followed them. The small girl stared open-mouthed at the carriage.

Tarn pulled his mother to Jaspar. "This is Jaspar! My friend. He brought me back. He is teaching me to read. This is Harper and these," he dropped his mother's hand and laid his small head on the steaming horses' necks, "are Sparkle and Apple. Aren't they canny?"

Jaspar held his hand out to Tarn's mother. He met her questioning grey eyes with a slight smile. "As Tarn says, I have brought him back to you."

She looked worried. "We 'ad to sell him. It goes against the grain, sir." Her fine eyes filled with tears. She reached for her son and held him tightly against the hump of her stomach. She was crying wordlessly, and Jaspar watched quietly until she looked up and sniffed. "I'm glad he's back hyem but what of the saddler?" She looked scared.

"Oh, Grizelda dealt with him," Tarn answered blithely.

"Grizelda?" his mother repeated.

"Miss Ludgrove. It is she whom you must thank for rescuing Tarn," Jaspar started.

"Oh, where are me manners? Please you to come in, sir, if it's not beneath y,. a fine gentleman like you."

"I shall be only too pleased to come in, but I would like to find an inn where I can spend the night. I would like to send Harper there to bespeak rooms and rest my horses."

She bobbed a curtsey. "Well, sir, close by there's nowt but the Unicorn, only it's not for the likes of you," she said doubtfully. "Or opposite the theatre, there's the Turk's Head."

"Is the landlord of the Unicorn honest?"

"Oh, aye, sir, most honest and the beds are clean. Mrs Mudd runs a spotless hoose."

"Then it shall do for me. Tarn, go with Harper and show him the way. See him bestowed and then come back."

"Yes, Jaspar." The boy bounced up onto the seat next to Harper and directed him down the street.

Jaspar followed Tarn's mother into the tiny cottage. He had to stoop to get under the doorframe, but once inside he noticed that although there was hardly any furniture, everything was very clean.

Mrs Grant whisked a pile of mending off the small settle and motioned Jaspar to a seat. "Would you like some tea, sir?" she enquired, removing a small child from her skirts and depositing it on the floor.

"That would be most agreeable." Jaspar smiled his most charming smile. She put the kettle on the range and busied herself making the tea. When she had handed Jaspar a mug, she sat herself on the three-legged stool and regarded him steadily as if awaiting his explanation. A slight silence settled in the room, broken only by the children who played on the floor.

Jaspar drank his tea and pondered how to explain the decision he had arrived at during the journey.

"I have been teaching…" He paused. "No. I think I had better start at the beginning of the story."

She nodded. "That'd be the best, sir."

"Miss Ludgrove, whom I mentioned before, arrived at my house with Tarn. She had managed to wrench him from the saddler. Tarn tells me that she got very angry with the man when she saw him beating Tarn."

Mrs Grant took a sharp intake of breath, but she said nothing. She watched Jaspar carefully.

Jaspar grinned to himself. "Which does not surprise me for she has the devil of a temper. Apparently she had to pay him for Tarn. She then promised the boy to return him to you but it had cost her all her money to release him from the saddler, so she brought him to me. She was intending to borrow from me. No, that is not quite right. She expected me to give her the money," he remembered fondly. Mrs Grant smiled; she understood. "I refused," he raised an eyebrow, "to give her the money. I did not want her running all over the countryside on the stage. It is not acceptable!" Mrs Grant observed the warm look in his eyes when he talked of Grizelda. "So I undertook to return him to you myself."

"Naturally, y' wouldn't want someone you love to be exposed to the danger of travelling all that way," she remarked.

Jaspar continued, as if he had not heard her remark. "I was only going to bring him back, but I have grown fond of the boy. He wants to read and write. I want to help him to go to school. Is there a school around here that he could go to?"

"Don't rightly know, sir. W' couldn't afford t' send him t' school. Why, none of them can go."

As she spoke the latch on the door lifted and Mr Grant came in. He was a man of medium height, shabbily dressed but with warm intelligent eyes. He looked astounded when he observed the elegant stranger seated in his room.

He crossed and kissed his wife's cheek.

"Zephaniah, this is…" She stopped. "Oh, sir, I don't know your name. Tarn didn't say it."

"Tarn?" Zephaniah Grant exclaimed.

"Tarn. I have brought your son back," Jaspar explained; he turned to Mrs Grant, "and Jaspar will do."

"You have brought Tarn back?" Zephaniah Grant struggled between anger and joy. "But, sir, y' hev no right to remove him from his master."

"Oh, he did not. His lady did that."

Jaspar smiled. "His lady." The idea gave him a not unpleasant jolt.

"She was ganna bring him but Jaspar…" she balked slightly at his name, "would not allow it, quite right too. Zephaniah, it seems he was being clouted." She looked to Jaspar for confirmation; he nodded slightly.

Her husband seemed perplexed. "Am sure it were kind of y', sir, but the truth is," his voice went bitter, "I cannit keep him." He inhaled a deep breath. His frank eyes met Jaspar's. "And that is the truth. I cannit have him back…" he gestured the other children, "… cannit feed those I have". He turned his face harsh. "Aa can get nee work. Just the odd bit o' casual labour."

"Jaspar here said he wants to help Tarn go to school," his wife went on hopefully.

A wonderful chance for her first born swam before her eyes.

"School?" Her husband savoured the word. "Why, w' couldn't accept, sir."

Jaspar realised that he would have to completely rethink the issue. He had become determined that Tarn would never suffer any deprivations again, but now he realised that to do this he must help the whole family. Tarn's father was proud; he would not accept charitable handouts. What kind of a world was it, Jaspar wondered, when a man who was clearly hardworking and clever could not support his family. He thought quickly.

"l have made a promise that Tarn will receive an education." He drew himself up and said in a detached voice, "l am not in the habit of breaking my word." He surveyed the two people. Tarn's father stood next to his wife, his arm around her shoulders. "I intend to open a school. It will be a very special establishment. I cannot do this, however, unless I have someone who is prepared to assist me." He paused to let his words sink in. "This school will be free. It will be for children whose parents cannot afford to give them a chance of education." Mr Grant stiffened. "I want to ask you to help me, by running the school for me."

"I cannot take…"

"So," Jaspar's eyes went cold, "so, you will refuse to help me and to help children like your son, who is very discerning and who wants to read so badly that he falls asleep over his slate." He let his words hang in the air then he caught Mrs Grant's eyes; a slight smile passed between them.

How clever he is, she thought. *He handles my proud Zephaniah, as a master.*

"I will have to look for someone else who cares more, and employ him." He started to stand.

"Please wait." Zephaniah stopped him. "Naturally I want to help but a divent want charity."

Jaspar waved an arm to stop him and smiled a smile of enormous charm.

"It is not charity. At least, except that my school will be free." He looked into Zephaniah's steady eyes. "I need someone I can trust. I want a school where children learn. I will not permit children to be beaten. I insist they have good food, and they learn all manner of skills. I do not intend to remain up here. I must have a man to run my school, who is totally honest. I want you to do the job. If you do not want it perhaps you can recommend someone else?"

Zephaniah Grant smiled; he knew when he was defeated. He wanted to run this school. He was not an educated man, but he knew he could organise such an enterprise. "Aa accept w' pleasure."

His wife exhaled with relief.

"The job will be hard but you will be paid good wages." Jaspar extended his hand to Zephaniah and they shook hands formally.

Mrs Grant hugged her husband. "Oh, sir, oh, sir. How can w' thank you?"

"Do not thank me," said Jaspar. "I want you to be part of the school as well. You must love and care for the children in your keeping. I can see that you will."

At that moment Tarn erupted back into the small space. His father caught his son to him, tears in his eyes. "Tarn, oh, my Tarn." His voice choked with joy.

"Father! Do you like Jaspar? Is he not the best an' all?"

"The best," his father repeated, smiling.

"Jaspar! Jaspar! Bartram Mudd tells me Billy Purvis is at the Golden Lion. Bartram says he has hydraulics! Water hydraulics. Will you take me, please! Please." He tugged impatiently on Jaspar's sleeve.

"Yes, brat, if it will give you pleasure and if you stop ruining a perfectly good coat, but we must first find premises for…"

"Premises, what is premises?" demanded the incorrigible Tarn.

"We are to run a school, Tarn," interrupted his father.

Tarn, immediately diverted, turned to Jaspar. "A school? Here?"

Jaspar laughed. "No, Tarn. Not here." He looked at Zephaniah. "I think that that is our first task tomorrow, we must find a building."

"Now, baggage," he said affectionately, "did you see my horses bestowed? I think you should take me to the Unicorn Inn."

"The horses are fine and Harper says he has bespoken dinner. Mrs Mudd's quite overcome when she found she was entertaining a real lord," he went on ingenuously, unaware of the amazement on his parents' faces.

"L… l… lord," Mrs Grant ventured, curtseying as low as her condition would allow.

"Afraid so," Jaspar replied apologetically, helping her to her feet.

Tarn looked at his parents. "He is not grand, honestly. Are you?" He put his arms around Jaspar. "He is so kind."

Jaspar tickled him affectionately. "You wait until I do not get taken to my dinner."

"Maybe I will. Maybe I won't," teased Tarn.

"Tarn!" his father expostulated. "Sir, I apologise."

"Unnecessary," responded Jaspar, turning his recalcitrant son upside down. "Come, brat."

Chapter Twenty

Euphemia Clarges haunted Hyde Park, wistfully watching the society in which she fondly remembered she used to play so prominent a part. She now recollected her life with Lady Ambrose with nostalgia. "It had been so perfect," she told herself, with a sublime disregard for the reality of her emotions, which is so often the case after removal from a situation that had been much bemoaned. She was both surprised and elated to behold Laura in the park. For she had wanted to contact the girl since discovering that she had returned, through her perusal of the society columns, an essential part of her everyday reading. Indeed, she had succeeded in thoroughly infuriating her cousin with her constant, cherished references to members of the *ton*, whose doings were documented in these pages.

Laura, she observed, was walking with two gentlemen to whom she could not immediately put a name. Removed for so short a time from the polite world and already her knowledge was deficient. She sighed to herself morosely. Pulling her shawl around her, she hurried towards them as fast as she could, with the expectation of being welcomed with nothing but kindness by Laura. After all, had she not assisted her in her pursuit of Lord Heddington? She conveniently forgot the monstrous fantasy that she had promulgated, and the problems which might have resulted from her artifice.

"Laura! Miss Laura!" She struggled for the words.

"Miss Clarges," Laura said in a most unencouraging voice. "What do you want?" she continued sullenly.

"Why, Laura, are you not pleased to see me, my dear?" Euphemia managed, recovering her breath.

Laura bit her lip and stared at her. "Y... yes," she lied.

The colonel watched with interest. He had no idea who this strange woman was but he had no doubt that Laura was very discomforted by her presence.

Laura was not particularly wise. If she had been, she would have made sure that she was uncommonly agreeable to Miss Clarges, for she could not afford her as an enemy. Instead, she decided that the best method of ridding herself of this woman, who knew her secret, was to be as dismissive as possible. If she were horrid to Euphemia, with luck she would accept the message and never encroach upon her again. So she stared at her in a most unfriendly manner.

"We really cannot waste time talking to you," she uttered coldly, turning to Mr Farleigh with a radiant smile. "Let us be on our way."

Miss Clarges gave the appearance of one who had been stung. A look of evident dislike flitted across her face.

"Are you not going to introduce me to your friends, my dear Laura?" she voiced, with a boldness born of desperation.

"No!" answered Laura abruptly. "We must be off." She tucked her arm into Jocelyn's and made to ignore Miss Clarges.

She had, however, reckoned without the colonel, who came swiftly to Miss Clarges's rescue.

He picked up her fluttery hand and held it tenderly.

"I am Colonel Staunton. This is Mr Farleigh, and you?" He raised an eyebrow questioningly.

"I am Euphemia Clarges," she sighed, "late of Curzon Street." He smiled encouragingly. "I was the governess to Lady Ambrose," the colonel pricked up his ears, "for so many harmonious years, only to have it end in," she gave a small sob, "unfair and miserable dismissal." She stopped and raised her eyes to Colonel Staunton, who tutted sympathetically.

This old bat has something to tell, he thought, *no wonder the little stuck-up madam is so nervous of her*. "I am so sorry to hear of your reversal in fortune. Where do you abide now?"

"With my cousin." Euphemia's tones left the colonel in little doubt about the enmity between the two. "Thrown out without a character after twenty-two years. It is too shocking."

"And quite undeserved," he agreed.

"Come on, James," Jocelyn said impatiently, starting to walk off.

The colonel offered his arm to Euphemia. She clearly had things to divulge and he certainly was not going to relinquish the chance to exploit such a heaven-sent opportunity. His outraged sensibilities still smarting from the affronts that he imagined he had sustained from Grizelda, Lord Heddington and his cronies saw a possible means to avenge these insults whilst protecting his friend from the claws of a fortune hunter. He regarded his windfall and smiled in a thin curve, commencing by discreetly enquiring about her circumstances. "Have you managed to find alternative employment, Miss Clarges?"

"No," she confessed, "I had hoped never to have to start again. It is so depressing at my age. I have a little saved but I might be forced to seek another post."

"Perhaps I can help you?" He smiled again.

"Really! Oh, you are too kind, Colonel."

"I cannot promise, of course, but rest assured that I will spare no effort on your behalf. First, tell me what occurred to precipitate your abrupt removal from Lady Ambrose's protection."

Miss Clarges, however, was not willing to disclose her precious secrets so easily. She nodded vaguely. "Matters. Matters. That were not my fault."

Before the colonel was able to probe further, an interruption occurred. Grizelda was hurrying across the grass towards her sister, calling to her. In the intervening moment the colonel took the opportunity to give his card to Miss Clarges, charging her to be sure to visit him within the next few days.

Laura stopped when she heard Grizelda's voice. This trip to the park, which had promised so well, was rapidly turning into a nightmare. First Miss Clarges, who seemed to be unprisable, and now Grizelda; she smiled weakly.

"Hello, Grizelda." Her sister kissed her on the cheek. "You know Mr Farleigh and Colonel Staunton." Grizelda curtsied to these gentlemen with obvious distaste, which immediately exacerbated the colonel's determination to bring down these arrogant sisters. "And this is Miss Clarges," continued Laura.

"Good afternoon," Grizelda returned with studied politeness, her mind racing. Miss Clarges? Now where had she heard that name? Then suddenly remembered. Her heart sank. The awful governess who engineered Laura's downfall. The one person who knew the truth. It did not auger well. Grizelda was not stupid. She realised that to antagonise the governess would hardly be beneficial to Laura, and she was too acute neither to miss the look of hatred that Laura flashed towards Miss Clarges, nor the fact that Miss Clarges also noticed it. This business was not going to end well, she could see that; whilst forcing herself to be polite to Mr Farleigh, inwardly she groaned, for she was aghast at the company her sister was keeping and horrified that she should be in the park unchaperoned. It was not easy to go on blaming Jaspar, when Laura was so patently silly.

Although the Unicorn Inn was not quite to Jaspar's taste, he found the countryside around Newcastle very much to it. He had never visited Northumberland before and the wild freeness touched a chord in him. The coast, with its pounding seas, was unlike anything Jaspar had ever seen, and he found himself watching, fascinated, the exuberant waves and the luminous light ever-changing over the water, and then trying to recall it so that he could describe it to Grizelda.

Despite running a modest establishment, Mrs Mudd proved an excellent housekeeper, and once she had recovered from the shock of discovering that she was to house a lord on her premises, she looked after him extremely well. The bed was comfortable and if the boots did not make his hessians shine in the way of Pickering, that was hardly the boy's fault, but rather Jaspar's for leaving his valet at home.

He rose early on a bright morning, ready to start his search for a suitable location for the school. As he drove himself slowly down the narrow, dirty lanes towards the market, the clear warmth of the sun and the deep blue of the sky provided an almost unbearable contrast to the stench and squalor of the criss-crossing alleys that led him to the dilapidated cottage; filthy urchins with bare feet and torn clothes ran desperately after him, their skinny hands pleading for alms. The sight of these pitiable scraps of humanity, with their hollow eyes, sunken faces and ragged apparel, made Jaspar suddenly ferociously angry: for their loss of childhood; for their pathetic destiny. This trip, he owned, was making him completely re-examine all that he had previously so light-heartedly believed. He understood with a devastating swiftness that the changes which seemed so inappropriate and which horrified so many of the world in which he moved so blithely, had to take place, and none too soon, he recognised resolutely. Grizelda must be right this could never be acceptable any longer. His face was serious as he approached the cottage. Zephaniah Grant was outside. A shaft of sun that had managed to escape the dingy surroundings alighted on the crumbling bricks and rotten woodwork, underlining the decay and hopelessness that pervaded the neighbourhood and which was entirely unfamiliar to Jaspar. Mr Grant glanced at His Lordship, observing his grave mien. Tarn, who had apparently been watching for them, noticed nothing but simply flew out of the front door.

"Jaspar! Jaspar! Mr Harper." The boy bounced around as Jaspar, in leisurely fashion, climbed down, grinning at the informality with which the child greeted him and the formality applied to his groom.

"Good morning, brat! How do you like being home?"

"Oh, very well, sir, but I miss you. The hosses and my reading lessons." He put his arms around Sparkle's neck; Jaspar smiled inwardly. He wished that his sister could hear this child, who was so desperate to learn. He certainly could not remember feeling like that himself, nor, in his recollection, had Nillie. In fact they spent much time as small children trying to escape their governess and avoid their tutoring. It had been too easy for them, he thought ruefully.

"Well, we are going to look for a school for you, this morning." Tarn looked puzzled. "A building, I am going to buy a building for a school," His Lordship went on.

Tarn's blue eyes opened with amazement. "Can I come?"

Jaspar pondered. "Yes, I think you may." He glanced at Zephaniah for confirmation, then asked, "Are we ready?"

"Certainly." He hesitated, took a breath and asked, "My lord, is there anything wrong? Do y' wish, the day, to change your mind?"

"No!" Jaspar snapped. "Most certainly not. I am appalled by the conditions..." He stopped, turning away from the questioning eyes of Zephaniah. "And ashamed," he added harshly under his breath. There was an awkward pause and then Tarn, perplexed, pulled Jaspar's sleeve. "Jaspar? Me dad's got a list an all..."

Mr Grant pulled out a piece of closely written paper. "I've got here a list of possible places."

Jaspar was impressed. It would appear that he was correct in his judgement. Tarn's father was most capable. He smiled.

"Thank you. You are thorough." And taking the piece of paper that Zephaniah handed to him he cast his eye down it.

Zephaniah, much gratified, made to climb up next to Harper, but as he did so Jaspar put an arm on his to stop him. "Please will you not join me inside, where we may discuss this?" He held up the paper. "Tarn may occupy the front seat."

Zephaniah bowed. "Whatever Y' Lordship wishes," he responded.

They started off. The first three or four houses that they visited all had something which did not recommend them to Jaspar. In one the rooms were too poky; one was much too small; and they all had too little ground.

"Is there anywhere bigger?" he enquired. "I visualise woods and gardens."

Zephaniah thought for a moment. "I know that Hasbro estate is for sale," he said doubtfully, "but it's very expensive, my lord."

"You let me be the judge of that. I would like to see it. Let us go there."

"Well, it's beyond Monkseaton," Zephaniah remarked, directing Harper out on the Monkseaton road.

It was not long before they reached Monkseaton itself. Zephaniah, who was gradually relaxing under the benevolent eye of His Lordship, took pleasure in telling them about the village.

"See ther', me lord, that cottage with two cannon on the parapets. It were owned by one Robert Ramsey, who ordered the village blacksmith to turn the cannon to, 'freeten away the French'." He laughed. "And that's the famous Ship Inn, once owned by one John Mills and then sold to the Duxfields."

Further down the road they came to Monkseaton brewery with its whitewashed walls, and then right into Pykerty Lane. Jaspar liked Monkseaton and hoped that the house they were about to see would be suitable. A few yards up the lane

Zephaniah pointed to some broken gates, which led along an overgrown drive.

"There's much to do here, to put it straight, my lord," Zephaniah remarked, looking around at the disordered hedges.

"We will see."

At that moment the drive turned and they came in sight of a pretty house. It was built with two wings, one of which had obviously sustained a fire, for it stood open to the elements; plants scrambled through the gaping windows and all over the walls. The rest of the house seemed sound enough. They pushed open the creaking front door. Rays of sun struggled through the dusty windows, allowing them to see the well-proportioned hall, with various doors off it. The house had obviously been well cared for in the past, for these doors were made of mahogany, and the cornicing and wood carving on the stairway were noble.

"This is it!" Jaspar pronounced in a satisfied tone as they wandered around.

"My lord, is it possible?" Zephaniah, the vision of being in charge of such an establishment dancing before his eyes, enquired.

"Of course," Jaspar answered impatiently. "Do you not think you can manage such an estate? There must be 200 acres."

"Oh, I can manage it, my lord, no question of that, but I was worried it'll take a great deal of…"

Jaspar turned on him. He drew himself up and Zephaniah saw that in spite of his easy manners, the man was very much an aristocrat.

"Will you please banish these thoughts from your mind? The financing of the venture is outside your sphere. You must merely occupy yourself with the expenses of the day-to-day running of the place. I will expect accurate accounts."

Zephaniah looked suitably chastened. "Yes, my lord," he muttered.

This air of grandness did not appeal to his son. "Oh, Jaspar, come off y' high ropes, an' all," Tarn stated without ceremony.

Jaspar laughed. "Quite right, Tarn. Does the idea of living here appeal to you, brat?"

"Live here?" Tarn's eyes opened wide. "Live here!" He executed an excited cartwheel. "Jaspar, it's reet marvellous!"

"Then that is settled. You do think that there is enough space, Zephaniah?"

Zephaniah nodded. "Oh aye, my lord, and there are several cottages attached to the estate. We could live in those."

"No, I think it will be necessary for you to be in the house, but the teacher could live in the cottages and you will need tenants to help farm, there must be accommodation for them."

The deal to buy the estate was swiftly executed and to celebrate, Jaspar took Tarn and his sister Lizzie to see the great Billy Purvis and his displays. The next few days were spent in a whirl of activity concerned with obtaining architects, builders and making plans. Jaspar was, therefore, gone from London for far longer than he had originally anticipated. He knew that it was imperative that he complete these arrangements for the school, but he found himself impatient to get back to town, for he was longing to tell Grizelda about his enterprise. He was sure she would be both excited and approving of such a step. Education for the underprivileged, she would like that, he knew. He had also discovered, somewhat to his surprise, that he missed her in an entirely unexpected way. Jaspar could not remember ever missing anyone, at least not with the restless ache that he suffered for Grizelda. The Unicorn Inn was quiet and as he spent every evening there alone, he had time to examine his feelings, which for the first time in his life, he did in some depth. In his mind he went over all he had known about her, from their first shocking meeting nearly a year ago, to the quiver he felt when he gazed into her eyes on the day she brought Tarn to him. The enforced solitude also made him reflect on all that he had seen in Newcastle and the anger such sights raised in him. Contemplating the conditions that prevailed here, he understood that they would hardly be an isolated example; they must be thus all over the country. That they must change he knew also and he supposed that this could only take place through government but not, sadly, through the ideas of the party that had been so much an integral part of his upbringing.

Grizelda. His thoughts returned to her; without her none of this would have occurred. Then he knew he was glad that it had. Glad that she had opened his eyes.

Meanwhile the object of these thoughts was in his sister's house, addressing her sister. "Really, Laura, you are too silly! You must not go walking with two gentlemen alone."

"Netta could not go with me, for she was pledged to care for the little girls," Laura replied sulkily, her eyes on the floor, where she dragged one foot desultorily across the Aubusson rug. Grizelda observed her.

"Nevertheless you should take a maid. I am sure that Mr Farleigh means…" she paused; she had been going to stress the lack of trustworthiness that she was sure existed in Jocelyn but being a sensible girl, she knew that the surest way to make Laura like him more was to forbid him to her, so she swiftly changed her words, "… means well, but I cannot be persuaded that the colonel is totally honest. Although, I must admit that I am at a loss to know why he should be so against us. I suppose I was a little forthright at Christmas but you have always been all cordiality to him. He is definitely most antagonistic though." She frowned slightly in thought.

"Miss Ludgrove." Netta closed the door behind her; Grizelda discomforted her, she could never see the red hair without remembering Jaspar's delirious ramblings or the warm look in his eyes when they alighted on her. A wave of impotent anger swept over her. Why did Lord Heddington like her? She was not beautiful, all those ugly freckles, and not in the least conciliatory. She closed her eyes momentarily to shut out the ire and then composed her face into a polite expression. "Parker told me you came to look for your sister. I am glad that you found her."

Grizelda found herself in a quandary. She wanted to berate Netta for not supervising Laura properly but she knew that to do so would be most ungrateful. Also it was imperative that Laura remain in Jaspar's sister's house if the rumours of Laura's transgression were to be laid to rest.

"I was just suggesting that it was a little unwise to walk without the company of a maid," Grizelda implied mildly.

Netta looked shocked. "Indeed, yes, I must apologise," she said uncomfortably. "You must think I am most remiss in my duties to Laura."

"Oh… not at all," Grizelda replied quickly. "I did not mean… I know that you have your hands full. It is Laura who must be more sensible." She fixed her sister with a firm stare.

"Oh, alright," Laura replied grudgingly; she did not want to appear at a disadvantage in Netta's eyes.

Grizelda curtsied and then took her leave; she was curious as to why Netta seemed so stiff with her but attributed it to shyness and thought no more about it, her mind too full of Laura and the unfortunate meeting with Miss Clarges. She had wanted to tell her sister how stupid it was to be unfriendly to her but had been interrupted before she had the chance.

Miss Clarges paid her visit to the colonel at the first possible opportunity early the next day. She indulged herself by taking a hackney to the elegant house in Hay Hill. As she paid the garvey, she felt her heart fluttering. She took a breath and mounted the steps.

What could he want? she surmised. Well, she would know soon.

The imperturbable butler who opened the door was perfectly polite, but Miss Clarges felt he was regarding her dress with a disparaging air. He led her into a pleasant morning room which overlooked the gardens of Berkeley Square. She peeped out of the windows and sighed.

Ah me, she thought. *If only I was still in Curzon Street.* A small tear escaped from the corner of her eye; she fished into her reticule and found her handkerchief, dabbing at the stray spot of water.

"Miss Clarges, I hope that I do not distress you?" Euphemia turned to view the rotund person of the colonel, standing smiling at the door.

"Oh, Colonel, so silly," she blinked. "I was just thinking of dear Lady Ambrose and my happiness, so irretrievably smashed and all…" Miss Clarges stopped.

"Yes," he said encouragingly.

"Oh, how I miss the joys of Curzon Street, such a genteel household. So high, so grand, so perfect," she sighed again.

The colonel watched her astutely. Then remarked sympathetically, "Such a pity that you were forced to leave so precipitously. But please won't you sit down. Let me offer you some refreshment, then you can tell me all about it."

He rang the bell. Miss Clarges sat down. She had a suspicion that the colonel was interested in Laura and her relationship with Lord Heddington. Miss Clarges was not naturally malicious; all she wished for was a restitution of her original place in society. She was apprehensive of saying anything which might make her position worse.

"Please, understand that I only wish to help you. I may be able to help you to another position." Miss Clarges jumped. "I sense a reservation in you; you have no need to be thus. I do not want to cause trouble but merely to aid you." As this was said with a warm smile Miss Clarges relaxed, too innocent to understand the gentle manipulation that was taking place.

"What a beautiful room," she remarked.

"It is, isn't it. I particularly admire the view and on a day like today it is…" he went on reassuringly.

Miss Clarges nodded happily, any doubts she had thoroughly assuaged. "I miss this part of London terribly," she interrupted.

He smiled sympathetically again. "I would too if I were forced to live elsewhere. Your cousin's house is…?" He raised an eyebrow enquiringly.

"Clapham. Not a very salubrious place, I am afraid. Oh, Curzon Street! How I pine for your delicate walls!" Miss Clarges clasped her hands together in a gesture of desperation.

What a tedious woman, the colonel thought to himself. "So very distressing for you," was all he said.

Miss Clarges sniffed. "And all because of that trumped-up, foolish girl." The colonel waited; he was far too wise to interfere.

"That Laura, you see, so ungrateful." She sniffed again. "After all I did for her."

"What was that," he asked very gently, "that you did for her?"

"Put her in the way of a wonderful marriage. Helped her to… to…"

"To?" he probed smoothly.

"To Lord Heddington. He was wild for her, you know. He adored the ground she walked on." Her eyes glistened as she enlarged upon the romance so dear to her heart. "Worshipped her. He would have swept her away; carried her on his white charger."

The colonel gave a stifled grunt for he was hard pressed not to laugh.

"It was all my doing! She was the great love of his life."

"Lord Heddington?" he blurted in utter surprise.

"Oh yes." Miss Clarges was too caught in her fantasy to notice his incredulous voice. "Lord Heddington, one of the oldest families in the land, and Laura Ludgrove, a common servant girl!"

Colonel Staunton omitted a suppressed gasp.

"A girl of such beauty, it was no wonder he was so enrapt with her, such exquisite temperament, such forbearance. They eloped together…"

Suddenly the colonel was very interested. So it was true. At least, true if one could trust this mad old bat.

"Eloped?" he questioned.

"Yes. They eloped to Gretna together."

"If that was the case why are they not married?"

Miss Clarges came back to a sense of her surroundings. "Because her sister interfered," she improvised.

"That I can believe. A very unpleasant girl."

"Oh yes," agreed Miss Clarges readily.

"Did Laura spend a night in His Lordship's company?"

Miss Clarges stared. "Y… y… yes," she vouchsafed, although in truth she was no longer quite sure. She had been sure that that was what Lady Ambrose and Lady Morntarny had told her on the dreadful day of her dismissal, but it had been so faithfully denied by everyone, that she was now doubting her own memory. She had been so terribly upset that she could not now recollect any of the conversation before her hateful sentence.

"Ah, good, that is what I want to know."

Miss Clarges would have liked to voice her doubts but she did not possess the confidence to retreat from the colonel's assumptions. She swallowed. "I think."

"It is obvious to me that we, that is society, have been hoodwinked. The girl is little more than a fallen woman. It is what I need."

"Why?" Miss Clarges said in a small voice; really this was getting out of hand.

He smiled but the smile did not reach his eyes. "Because I do not want my friend Mr Farleigh to become embroiled with such a fraudster. She has treated society with contempt and such people must be ostracised."

"But we cannot be absolutely sure…"

"You have just told me. Oh, your evidence is what I need, believe me."

"But suppose they deny it?"

"Mmm… We will have to make sure that they cannot. I must prove it to Mr Farleigh. You understand."

"Yes, I do see the importance," Miss Clarges agreed readily. "How will you prove it?"

"With your help."

"My help. I cannot say anything."

"No, you do not have to. I promise you that if you assist me, then you will be amply rewarded."

CHAPTER TWENTY-ONE

The refurbishing work commenced and the Grants took up residence in a small cottage at the foot of the drive. Zephaniah proved admirable. He had thrown himself into the scheme with enormous energy and a certain deep joy. Eventually, everything that he could usefully do having been achieved, it became evident that Jaspar could now return to London. As he drove he found a strange exhilaration sweeping over him, in part produced by the gratifying sensations occasioned by being able to help, and in part, Grizelda. It was strange that he could not rid himself of his desire to please her. He would never, indeed, have started on this journey with Tarn had it not been for her, but now he would not have missed the experience for the world. In his mind, he retraced the last year. It was hard to equate the life that he and his friends had led in London, a life of reckless hedonistic pleasure, with the one he wished to live now. The desire for a life of seduction and, he realised with some remorse, gratuitous pain, had become, inexplicably, impossible to condone. Trying to fathom what had produced such fundamental change in him, his mind returned to the shooting and the hopelessness he had experienced in the forest. Was it the impotence he had felt as he was forced to beg for help? Was it the brush with death? His own mortality? These had certainly played some part in it but did not account for everything. Then it came to him in a flash. Grizelda. He wanted her but not in the way that he had coveted his many conquests of the past. No. He wanted her with him always. He knew with a fierce suddenness that he had to marry her.

The weather had continued fine. They sped across the fields and woods, the evening throwing long shadows of trees over their path; the setting sun throwing fronds of deep pink across the soft leather of the squabs. The whole countryside was luminous with the light of the falling sun, which could be glorified as a deep red sphere on the horizon. Jaspar stared at its splendour without really seeing it.

"Grizelda!" The word was half murmured to himself. "You must marry me. I must have you for my wife." He was abruptly overcome with delicious happiness. Then a faint unease. Would she have him? Would she forgive him for Laura? The episode with Laura seemed so long ago. It was as if it had never happened. He could not even recollect the night with her, only the uncomfortable aftermath. Surely such a transient experience could not mar their future happiness. Then he knew that it could. Grizelda's clear pale eyes as she had looked into his had held an enigmatic expression which he hoped was affection but perhaps he had misunderstood. Jaspar had never experienced any feelings of doubt; never had the slightest hesitation where women were concerned. He had accepted their adoration without thinking about it but Grizelda was different. He was unsure of her, unsure whether she loved him, unsure whether she forgave him, unsure whether she would marry him. He must have her. He knew now that his existence would be stark without her.

"My lord." His reverie was interrupted by Harper. "My lord, we should stop for the night." Jaspar jumped; it had grown quite dark and tiny stars twinkled at him from out of a navy blue sky.

"Yes, certainly we should," he declared. "The Goat Inn… we will make for that."

Miss Clarges left the colonel's full of thought. He had promised her considerable remuneration in exchange for her help and the prospect was certainly an attractive one. She was a little troubled, for she was not naturally a devious person and she slightly feared possible repercussions from what the colonel intended to do. He, however, had reassured her that nothing would happen to her and he had also assured her that he would protect her from anyone who implicated her in the conspiracy. Euphemia was of a naturally nervous disposition, but predominant over her dread was a strong sense of fantasy. So, although she was fearful of the consequences of the colonel's plot, she was also excited by it. Revenge and retribution figured largely in Miss Clarges's dreams and the idea of abductions appealed to her sense of the dramatic.

She trotted home, pleased with her morning's discoveries and ready to play her part in the ensuing drama. Mildred was at home when she arrived at the poky, and not very clean, cottage.

She could not help contrasting it with the lofty rooms of my Lady Ambrose and the understated elegance of the colonel's abode. She removed her shawl and picked up a dirty plate and cup which reposed in the middle of the sofas.

"Really, Mildred, you are most untidy! You should not eat in here and then leave it to be cleared up," she remarked sharply.

"If you do not like it you can just find yourself another place, Miss Snooty," Mildred replied nastily.

"I might just do that," Euphemia, flushed with the triumphs of the morning, responded.

Mildred regarded her with astonishment. She knew that her cousin was entirely dependent on her for succour. "Oh, has Lady Ambrose relented and reinstated you?" she went on disagreeably.

"No, but she is not my only friend," Miss Clarges said airily.

Mildred laughed. It was an unpleasant sound. "Oh yes, lots of friends you have. Come visiting every morning, they do." She hauled herself out of the chair. She smelt, to Euphemia's fastidious nose, stale and dirty. The entire room was thoroughly malodorous. Euphemia sniffed and then wished she had not.

"I shall go for a short walk, before it gets too hot to be bearable. Do you care to accompany me?" her cousin demanded.

"No," responded Euphemia with relief. "I have a couple of letters that I must write. I will attend to those." She picked up her shawl and left the room. Her cousin stared after her. Euphemia was up to something, No question about that. She heaved her not inconsiderable bulk towards the door and out into the sunlight.

Miss Clarges hurried up to her room where she sat at the small table which passed as a desk. She took out a sheet of paper and a pen and prepared to write. When she had finished, she sanded it off and tucked it into her pocket and thought a little. Then she got up and went to deliver her letter.

Laura had been unnerved by meeting Miss Clarges. She did not like the fact that she possessed the knowledge that could certainly destroy the carefully constructed lies that Jaspar had endorsed. In bed that night she tossed and turned, unable to get comfortable. The next morning she arose not the slightest bit refreshed and went down to breakfast. Here an agreeable surprise awaited her, for sitting at the head of the table looking much more herself was Nillie. She greeted Laura warmly.

"Laura, my dear, you see I am quite recovered." She smiled at Laura, who observed that Her Ladyship looked blooming: her skin gleamed, her face glowed, her hair shone, and apart from a slight thickening of the waist, she seemed completely returned to normal. The pasty, green, pale creature that she had been only last week had quite disappeared, to be replaced by this radiant example of incipient motherhood.

"Come, sit down, I am so sorry that I have been such an awful hostess. I do hope that you have been well cared for."

"Oh yes," Laura stammered. Her Ladyship's generosity to her made her feel such a heedless guest.

"But you look pale, my dear, did you sleep quite well?"

"No," Laura bit her lip, "I just could not rest." Lady Morntarny regarded her shrewdly; the girl had something on her mind, of that she was sure.

"What do you plan to do today? I thought perhaps you would care to come with me, I am going shopping. I must needs order some new clothes, for my condition makes those I have ineligible."

Laura nodded vigorously. She looked less worried. "Oh, I should like that above anything," she replied. Her desire for rebellion and walking out unchaperoned had quite disappeared. She could think of nothing she would prefer to do than to seem to belong to the respectability occasioned by Her Ladyship. So they went to Bond Street. Laura thoroughly enjoyed herself; Lady Morntarny took it gently but they went to the fashionable modiste who enjoyed Her Ladyship's custom and ordered a great many new frocks.

It was late when they returned to Berkeley Square. "I shall just go to my room and then perhaps we can have nuncheon together?" Nillie asked.

Laura agreed happily. She went into the small dining room where nuncheon had been laid out and sat to await her hostess. A footman knocked at the door. "Come in!"

"Miss Laura Ludgrove." The footman had a silver tray on which reposed a letter. "This is for you." He bowed.

Laura took the letter from the tray. Probably from Grizelda, she thought. "Thank you." She dismissed the servant and broke the seal.

Miss Clarges's letter was short and to the point. Laura stared at the few lines in horror. She was still gazing at them when Nillie joined her. She looked up guiltily as Her Ladyship came in. She stuffed the letter in her reticule and smiled weakly at Nillie.

"Bad news, Laura? You look as if you had seen a ghost."

Laura swallowed. "N... no," she stammered. "I am alright, it is just a little hot."

"Yes," agreed Nillie; she had not missed the fact that instead of flushed with heat, her guest was ashen.

"I think I might have a rest after nuncheon, Your Ladyship. If that is alright?"

"Of course, my dear. I too shall lie down."

Laura picked at her food. As soon as Her Ladyship had finished, the footman drew back their chairs and Laura escaped to her room; here she pulled out the note and peered at it. Then she rang the bell.

"I have to go out for about an hour," she informed the young maid who answered it. "Please being me my yellow muslin."

The maid hurried to obey her and Laura sat at her dressing table and tried to make herself look less strained. She read the note again and then she threw it angrily into the wastepaper basket. She pinched her cheeks, put on the dress and her prettiest bonnet, then she slipped downstairs and out of the side door.

It was a beautiful afternoon. The sun was high in the sky and the flowers in all their bright colours bobbed and dipped in the gentle breeze. She was far too pretty to go unnoticed, so as she hurried along, she found herself the recipient of many curious glances. In normal circumstances Laura would have relished these looks, but she was in no mood for either the appreciative ones or, more particularly, the disapproving ones,

She reached the deserted corner of the park which was where Miss Clarges's note had suggested they meet. She had information for Laura, Miss Clarges had written, information that Miss Ludgrove could not afford to ignore. No one was present. Laura sat down on a deserted bench in the shade and waited for Euphemia. She wondered what the old idiot wanted. Perhaps it was money; Laura had no money. She tried to consider whether Miss Clarges had any proof of her night with Jaspar. Having reflected carefully, she decided that she did not and this made her feel much better. All she had to do was to continue to utterly deny the matter; nothing could be proved.

She was standing up to leave when she was grabbed from behind. Laura squealed and a strong hand clamped her mouth shut, whilst a scarf was wound around her eyes. She struggled and managed to dig her teeth into the hand which gripped her. Her captor yelped with pain. "Bitch!" he uttered, and she felt a handkerchief being thrust into her mouth and tied very tightly. She was dragged along the ground and then lifted roughly and thrown into what, she surmised, was some kind of carriage. She landed with a bump on the floor. Her arms were pulled behind her and bound. The cords cut into her wrists. The conveyance started to move. Laura felt herself go icy with fear. She was utterly petrified. Tears welled up into her eyes, soaking the scarf that bound them. Who had taken her? she wondered. Too late she realised the idiocy of not confiding in Nillie. *If only I had told someone*, she regretted. By now the coach was bowling along but to where?

Laura was not missed until much later in the day. Nillie had rested for quite some time and when she arose, refreshed, she had sent for Laura. Quarmby, who had little respect for the girl, informed Her Ladyship that Laura appeared to have gone for a walk by herself. "Is she in the habit of going out alone?" Nillie demanded.

Quarmby sniffed. "Silly hussy," she pronounced.

"Quarmby, I will not permit such comments of my guests!" Nillie reprimanded. Quarmby gave another of her sniffs. "Please make sure that she is sent to me as soon as she returns. She should not have left here without her maid."

But Laura did not return. By early evening Nillie was most concerned. They were promised to Lady Eglinton's rout and she knew that Laura was much looking forward to it. Why then had she not come back?

The Lady Lucy and baby Abigail, who was beginning to regard herself as very much not the baby, but who was still denigrated thus by all the members of the family, had been to the park with Netta and the nursemaid. As soon as they discovered that Nillie was up, they rushed straight to their mama and were delighted to discover that their parent had recovered her previous spirits. "Mama, Mama!" Abigail's little hands, still with their baby roundness, pulled energetically at her mother's skirt. "Look what I got!" her clear voice was demanding.

"What is it, darling?" Nillie bent down to the little girl who unclenched the fist and showed her some scrumpled-up flowers. The small face looked horrified and then it crumpled. "What, Mama! Look they are all broken."

A large round tear started in her eyes. Nillie laughed gently and hugged the child to her. "Oh, sweetheart, you must take the greatest care of the flowers, they are very delicate."

"But I bring them for you to make you better," Abigail sobbed.

"They have made me better, see I am quite myself." Abigail brightened; her face beamed in a wide smile.

"I have made you well!" She jumped up and down with delight.

"Abigail, you had nothing to do with Mama's recovery," started Lucy scornfully, to be stopped by a warning look from her mama.

At that moment there was a knock at the front door. Nillie heard it. She went to the door and listened; she appeared concerned. Netta watched her. "What is the matter? You look disturbed," she queried.

"It is Laura. She has not come back. It appears that she went out sometime this afternoon, telling the maid that she would be gone for an hour, but no one has seen her since. I am naturally worried."

"She is rather a foolish girl," Netta remarked carefully. "You do not think she has decided to go off?"

"No! I do not!" retorted Nillie sharply.

"I apologise. It is just that I am afraid that both those sisters are rather flighty," Netta went on in a sweet voice that belied the malice behind her remarks. As soon as the words were out of her mouth she wondered why she had said them. She was not naturally spiteful but the Ludgroves made her feel angry and unlike herself.

Nillie, who might have renounced those opinions, remembered that awful day with Mr Ludgrove. She shuddered. "I do not agree," she responded but without much conviction, and then as she saw Netta observing her, she ameliorated her words. It would not do for Netta to discover Laura's transgressions with Jaspar, particularly in view of her preference for His Lordship.

"She might not be the wisest but she has been well brought up by her sister," she said quickly and stopped. "Of course, her sister…" She sighed with relief. "How stupid I am. I am sure that she has gone there. I will send to Lady Melbourne immediately. I am convinced that that must be the answer."

Netta, who, in fact, did not believe that Laura had gone to Grizelda, for if she was going to do that why had she not told anyone, merely agreed. "Oh yes, I am sure that is the case." If Nillie wished to think that, then it was not up to Netta to disagree. The Ludgroves were not at all acceptable, Netta told herself firmly, and the sooner they were out of the way the better. So she said nothing. Part of her hated the worm that seemed to be eating at her inside but she seemed incapable of stopping it.

Petronilla went to the writing table and composed a short note for Grizelda, in which, she said that she imagined that Laura would attend the party with them. She was so sure that this must be the explanation, that an alternative never occurred to her. Her footman was quickly dispatched to Melbourne House and she went upstairs to her room to change. She was sitting at her dressing table, lost in thought, when Greville joined her.

"My love, you look blooming." He kissed his wife on the back of the neck and ruffled the dark curls.

"Take care of my hair," Nillie laughed at him. "It has just been arranged."

"In a most becoming style." He kissed her again. "I am so delighted that you have revived."

"Not as pleased as I am." Nillie grinned. "It is not at all agreeable to feel as unwell as I have over the last few months."

Greville turned her round to him. "My darling, I do understand and you know how ecstatic I am about this baby but I hate you to feel so miserable." He kissed her tenderly. "This baby means so much to me."

"I know and the worst is over now. I look forward to being able to enjoy the rest of the season. I feel I have neglected Laura and I must make it up to her now. Oh, and talking of Laura, I think she must have gone to her sister's. I do wish she had informed someone."

"You mean she went to Lady Melbourne without telling you? That is the height of bad form. You must give her a dressing-down when you see her tonight. You do feel well enough to come, don't you?" he asked anxiously.

"Oh yes," she grinned. "But I do not think I will be able to dance the night away!"

"Certainly not." He bent over her again and Laura was quite forgotten. She did not think of her again until she did not appear at Lady Eglinton's.

Lady Morntarny's note reached Melbourne House shortly after Her Ladyship, accompanied by Miss Ludgrove, had departed for dinner in Park Street with Lady Hamel before attending the rout. The butler who received it laid it on the hall table, to await Grizelda's return.

Lady Hamel was all boastful conciliation that she had managed to secure Lady Melbourne for dinner before the Eglintons' party. Her joy was, however, not long lived; Lady Melbourne was not at her best A nasty summer cold had laid her low for several days and although she had risen from her sick bed to chaperone Grizelda, it was clear to that sensible maiden that her godmother was not well. They sat twenty-four to dine. Lady Hamel's French chef had prepared a splendid six-course meal and Grizelda watched with some alarm her patroness grow paler by the course. Lady Melbourne, who usually enjoyed her food hugely, hardly touched a morsel. When the ladies withdrew, leaving the men to their port, Grizelda hurried over to her. "My dear Lady Melbourne, I am persuaded that you are not well. Please let us go home."

"Grizelda, I must admit to not feeling quite the thing but do not want to spoil your pleasure. I think I shall be forced to return to bed but that need not deter you from enjoying yourself. You can go to the ball with Lady Hamel and Miss Hamel."

"As if I would," Grizelda replied indignantly. "I am not so caught up by my pleasure that I would neglect you, who had been so very good to me."

"But I shall be alright. You go, my love."

"I have been to lots of balls. It will not hurt me to miss one."

Nillie was not unduly perturbed when she got to Lady Eglinton's ball and found that Laura was not present. The absence of Lady Melbourne and Grizelda reassured her, and particularly when she learned that Lady Melbourne had been taken ill. She did not stay long herself, for Greville considered that she needed her rest and whisked her home quite early.

Grizelda sat in the carriage with Lady Melbourne. She was increasingly worried about her, for she was alternatively burning hot and then shivery cold.

"Oh, my lady, you should have stayed at home," she ventured solicitously. "I had no need of going."

Her Ladyship lay back on the squabs, her eyes closed. Grizelda watched anxiously but the comparatively short journey seemed to take an age. Eventually, they reached Melbourne House, and during the ensuing consternation about Her Ladyship's health, no one thought to show Grizelda Lady Morntarny's note.

Laura lay on the floor of the carriage weeping, until the crying threatened to overwhelm her. Then, exhausted, the scarf around her eyes uncomfortably sodden, no more tears would come. In spite of her apparent silliness Laura was not a girl without resource. She swallowed hard and decided to examine her predicament. She still had no idea who had taken her or where she was going, or for what purpose. Her legs were so stiff that she was unable to feel them and it was impossible to think. Gingerly, she summoned her courage and stretched, then with her foot she felt the edge of the seat. She managed to swivel her body around and pulled herself until, with some difficulty, she heaved herself onto the squabs. She was quite pleased with her efforts. The carriage was bowling along at quite a speed. Laura wondered where she was being taken, and almost as if to echo her thoughts, she realised the horses were shortening their pace; they were definitely slowing down. She heard the blowing sounds from the leaders as they slowly came to a halt. People were talking but she could not hear what they said. The noise of a hand on the door made her heart beat so fast, she was sure that whoever was out there must be able to hear it. A breeze assailed her as the door was wrenched open. Someone reached in and she was dragged, none too gently, down the steps. Her captor did not speak to her as they made their way across what Laura deduced was a yard. She found that being unable to see made her want to move slowly, but her impropriator would not allow this; he pushed and shoved at her until her legs gave way under her and she collapsed on the ground. A stream of coarse expletives issued from his lips as he yanked her to her feet again. Laura felt tears prick her eyes but she was determined not to let this uncouth man, whomsoever it was, have the satisfaction of hearing her weep. He pushed her through a door and she could smell the odours of an inn; the faint aroma of roasting fowl came from somewhere to the left and the smell of ale issued from the right.

"Up!" ordered the man, pushing her forward.

She caught her heel and found herself falling onto the staircase. She banged both her knees but her howl of pain was muffled by the gag around her mouth. She crawled up the stairs, feeling her way with her knees until she reached the top. Here the man pulled her to her feet and shoved her forward; she felt herself toppling again. As she landed she realised that it was soft. She was in a room with a carpet. The door closed behind her with a bang, swiftly followed by the sound of the key turning in the lock.

CHAPTER TWENTY-TWO

Grizelda did not enjoy her customary repose that night. It seemed that she was awoken every few minutes by a dream in which someone tumbled off a cliff, whilst she desperately tried to prevent them. Finally, she rose exhausted and, scrambling out of bed, pulled on her clothes, tugged a brush roughly through her myriad curls and hurried to her godmother's rooms. Here she was much mollified to discover that Her Ladyship, although still hot, was not burning as she had been the previous night and was certainly not causing her iron-faced dresser the concern that she had when she had been brought home. This redoubtable lady shooed Grizelda away, reassuring her that there was nothing she could do to aid the nursing.

"May I suggest, miss, that you get yourself something to eat. You look proper wan-faced yourself and we don't want you going down with anything, do we?" she went on.

Grizelda, happy to comply, thanked her and proceeded to breakfast. As she descended the curved staircase, she admired, as she always did, the round hall, with its smooth marble pillars, which stood like sentinels around the vestibule.

"Miss Ludgrove," John, the young footman who had been detailed to wait on Grizelda, stopped her.

"Yes, John?"

"This came for you last night after you and Her Ladyship had left. I am afraid what with Her Ladyship's illness and what, we did not give it to you last night." He grinned apologetically.

"Oh, that is alright." Grizelda smiled. "I am sure it is not at all important."

John bowed, opening the door to the breakfast room to allow Grizelda to enter. He drew back a chair for her and she sat down, placing the letter beside her plate. John handed her a selection of dishes and Grizelda helped herself.

"Will there be anything else, Miss Ludgrove?" he enquired.

"No, thank you, John." She smiled. After he had left she picked up the note and examined it; the writing was unfamiliar. She turned it over and broke the seal. As she read the few words the colour drained from her face. Then she sprang to her feet.

"John! John!"

The footman answered her summons with all swiftness. Seeing her pale face, he queried, "What is it, miss?"

"My sister... please... order the carriage with all haste. I must go!"

"Yes, immediately." He hurried to obey her demands and Grizelda ran upstairs to Lady Melbourne's rooms, where the dresser informed her that Her Ladyship was asleep.

"Please, tell her that I must go out."

"Is there something amiss?" She looked at Grizelda with concern in her face, for despite her formidable appearance, she was the kindest of creatures and had conceived of a considerable fondness for Grizelda. "Will you be gone long?"

"I hope not but I cannot tell."

"You take care and do not worry. Lady Melbourne will be fine with me."

"I know that. I... Tell Her Ladyship... no, it does not matter." Lady Melbourne's dresser watched as, distractedly, Grizelda whirled out of the room.

She ran downstairs as fast as she could and waited impatiently for the carriage. The progress to Berkeley Square seemed incredibly slow. She found herself peering out of the window, willing the horses to move faster. In her mind, she hoped that when she reached Lady Morntarny's she would discover that Laura was there and safe. Perhaps they had merely failed to let her know.

Hard as she tried to reassure herself, however, in the pit of her stomach there lurked a ready sense of foreboding. She did not believe for a minute that Laura would repeat the mistake she had made with Jaspar. She knew that the girl wished to marry Jocelyn, a desire that Grizelda found to be as curious as it was unlikely. If that were the case, and Grizelda was sure it was, why should she run off with anyone? No, there must be another explanation for her absence and maybe, indeed, she would find that Laura was safely ensconced in Berkeley Square. Grizelda tried to make herself sanguine but disagreeable dreads kept intruding into mind. Quite irrationally, she wished that Lord Heddington was back in town, for she was confident that he would aid her, but she had no means of knowing when they might expect His Lordship's return.

At last the carriage drew up outside the Morntarnys' house. Grizelda was out of the door and up the steps almost before the coachman had reached the horses' heads. Breathlessly she banged on the door. Parker opened it.

"Miss Ludgrove?"

Grizelda rushed in. "My sister! I must see my sister!"

"But she is not here. I understood that she was with you, miss," Parker replied, his face impassive.

Grizelda gulped; she was about to say, "Then where is Laura?" but she managed to swallow the words. Instead, she demanded, "Please may I see Lady Morntarny?"

Parker, who would, in normal circumstances, have denied his mistress, realised the urgency of the situation. He merely nodded, leading Grizelda into the morning room.

"I will inform Her Ladyship that you are here," he said.

The morning room was a very pretty room. It was octagonal, with a curved and decorated plaster ceiling. The pale green walls were covered with paintings of rural landscapes, set in delicate gold frames. Each painting represented another scene of life in the country. They were beautifully painted and carefully detailed. If Grizelda had not been so preoccupied, she would have been fascinated, but she was too restless to observe them correctly. The morning room faced south and sunlight poured in through its long windows. On the trees in the square gardens, birds sang and a mother duck with ten ducklings waddled majestically across the grass. Grizelda sighed; she stared out of the window unseeingly and wondered where Laura was.

"Miss Ludgrove." Nillie, elegant in a flowing negligee of pale lemon silk edged with mechlin face, unbelted and loosely tied at the side in satin ribbon, held out her hand to Grizelda. Behind her Grizelda noticed Netta, sensibly attired as usual in a plain poplin dress, in a rather unbecoming shade of brown.

"Lady Morntarny, where is my sister?" Grizelda, too distressed for any social niceties, demanded.

"Won't you sit down?" Nillie said gently, arranging herself on the chaise longue. Reluctantly Grizelda obeyed her, her eyes fixed on Her Ladyship's face.

"I thought that Laura was with you," Nillie continued.

"Why?" Grizelda was direct and urgent. When she received no answer, she looked between Netta and Petronilla, sensing their unease. "Why did you think that? Did she say she was coming to me?"

"Not in so many words, " Netta said defensively. "But we assumed..."

"Assumed! I do not understand. How could you assume?"

"The fault was mine," Nillie said. "I thought Laura was with you."

"The fault was Laura's. She should not have gone out alone," Netta replied aggressively. "Anyway, Miss Ludgrove, you are complacent enough. After all, Lady Morntarny wrote a note to you yesterday and you only seem vexed today."

Grizelda stared at her in horror. "I did not get the note until an hour ago. It was delivered after we had left and Lady Melbourne was taken ill so we did not go to Lady Eglinton's."

"I noticed that you were not there. I should have realised. I should have done something. I am so sorry." Her Ladyship's worried tone grated on Netta's envious sensibilities.

"Please, Nillie, it can hardly be your fault," she went on, overcome by a desire to discredit these Ludgrove girls in Nillie's eyes, to make Nillie dislike them.

"It is my fault but arguing about that is not going to find Laura. Netta, perhaps could you ask the servants if they know anything, but be discreet."

Netta did not enjoy being sent away but she could hardly disobey. When she had gone Nillie turned to Grizelda. "I am most reluctant to say this and I did not want to remark on anything in front of Miss Egremont. She is a kind girl but it would not help Laura if she knew of her and my brother. Do you think your sister could have gone off, as she did with Jaspar?"

Grizelda shook her head. "No! No, I do not. Laura can be silly." She smiled a rueful smile at Nillie, who, somewhat to her surprise, found herself warming to her. She had not expected to like Grizelda but, oddly, she discovered she did. "But she is also shrewd and she learnt a lesson; she would not be taken in again. She knows that thanks to your good offices she was lucky in that case."

"Oh." Nillie bit her lip guiltily. "Oh dear, I have just remembered something. When we came back from shopping yesterday, I went to my room and when I came to join Laura for nuncheon, she was reading a letter, which she pushed into her reticule. She appeared rather discomforted. I asked her if it was bad news."

"What did she answer?"

"Nothing really, she merely coloured a little but I did not particularly remark her behaviour. I had no reason to," she responded pleadingly.

"If only we could know what was in that letter," agonised Grizelda. "I am convinced it is material in some way."

At that moment Netta returned with the abigail in tow.

"She has something to show you," Netta remarked in a hostile manner.

"Yes?" The countess's voice was gentle. "What is it?"

The abigail held out a crumpled bit of paper. "This, my lady."

Grizelda took it impatiently from her and put it on the table to smooth it out so that she could decipher it.

"Thank you." Nillie dismissed the abigail, who curtsied and left.

"Miss Ludgrove," Netta reproved, "I think Lady Morntarny should read the letter..." She got no further before a flash of anger from those extraordinary pale blue eyes silenced her.

"She is my sister, Miss Egremont."

"She is Miss Ludgrove's sister, Netta," placated the countess; both she and Grizelda were by now too concerned about Laura to be curious as to why Netta should exhibit such unwarranted antagonism towards Grizelda, so her animosity went unnoticed. Netta flushed slightly and dropped her eyes, moving to the back of the room, where, ignored by the other two, she could observe what was happening.

Grizelda read the words quickly and then handed the note over to Nillie. "She obviously went to meet Miss Clarges but why?" Nillie mused.

"I must immediately go and see her." Grizelda stood and prepared to leave.

"Wait! Do you know where Miss Clarges lives? She is no

longer with Lady Ambrose." Nillie's sensible tones halted her.

She turned back. "Oh no. You are quite correct." She thought a moment. "I will have to visit Lady Ambrose I suppose."

"Then I will accompany you." Before Nillie could finish, the door opened. Jaspar strode into the room. He had returned to London late on the previous night and made his sister his first visit of the morning. His eyes swept the room; when they alighted on Grizelda, a warm look leapt into them, a look which was observed with a stab of pain by Netta.

"Jaspar!" Nillie's voice was eloquent with relief that her brother was here. "Thank God."

Jaspar, glancing quickly between these two, who were more to him than anything in the world, realised that both were frantic with consternation. Without pausing, he crossed to Grizelda and picked up her hand; her eyes met his and as they did, she felt a large lump in her throat and thought she was going to cry.

It was left to Nillie to explain. "It is Laura. She has gone missing."

Jaspar frowned. "Missing?"

Grizelda nodded speechlessly. She held out the note. Netta shrank further back into the curtains but nobody noticed her.

"Missing!" he repeated. "From where and how?" He took the note from Grizelda's outstretched hand.

"This is a note from Miss Clarges. Did Laura meet her?"

"We assume so," Nillie rejoindered. "We have not seen her since."

"Not seen her since." Jaspar looked perplexed. "You did not miss her last night, Nillie?"

"It is all my fault."

Netta opened her mouth to protest and then thought better of it.

"I assumed that she was with Miss Ludgrove and I sent her a note but unfortunately she did not receive it until this morning," she explained. "We were all to attend the Eglintons' rout. I thought Laura would be there with her sister but they did not come, due to Lady Melbourne being taken ill…" She stopped. "Oh, what a mess."

"l see." Jaspar was suddenly businesslike. "You must not worry. I will find her. First an interview with Miss Clarges."

"Let me come with you?" Grizelda pleaded. "Please."

He thought a moment. "No, I think it will be preferable that I visit her alone."

"But I cannot just wait," she gulped. "I cannot bear it."

The catch in her voice touched him more than he could say. He smiled at her, a smile of such warmth that it made her insides tremble and Netta's squirm with misery.

"You can come but when I interview her you must wait in the carriage." He raised an eyebrow. "You agree?"

She nodded wordlessly, for the tears that pricked her eyes made her know that to speak would result in a flood of weeping. "Let us waste no time." He kissed Nillie's hand. "You are not to worry. That is an order."

Laura crawled across the room, bumping into various pieces of furniture; finally, she came to what she realised must be a bed. Her arms were still tied her but, using her legs, she managed to pull herself up onto it. Thankfully, breathing heavily she lay back; the bed was hard, the rough cover smelt stale and dirty but at least it was more comfortable than the dusty floor. She wondered what the time was. She thought it must be considerably advanced for she was very hungry. Lying back she sniffed. She must not cry again, she told herself vehemently. She sensed that she was in real danger but, think as she could, there seemed no reason why Miss Clarges should wish to damage her in this way, after all she had done to the hateful old bat. Then a thought so horrendous overtook her, that for a moment she was utterly terrified. Suppose they had brought her here to kill her? Then she realised that if that had been their intention, surely they would have done it immediately, for why waste money on coaches and inns, when they could have just disposed of her? She shuddered.

Suddenly she heard the key turn again and someone came in. Laura sat up, her mouth dry with fear. She heard heavy boots cross towards her and the gag was removed from her mouth with the injunction, "Jes' you don't make any noise or this here food will be thrown to the pigs."

Laura bit her lip and swallowed. "Please..." Laura had not been a reigning belle for the past few months for nothing and she had decided that it would be better to have her captor on her side rather than against her, so she smiled her most beguiling smile and continued in the sweetest of tones, "Please, would you be so kind as to remove the binding around my eyes, for it is so uncomfortable."

There was a pause and then the man said, "Well, put like that I cannot see the harm in it. Jes' while you eats, mind."

"Oh yes, I understand," said Laura breathlessly with another beaming smile. She felt the man stoop down to her and untie the binds. The pink light of evening streamed in, making Laura blink, its brightness making her eyes stream.

"Oh dear," she said, covering them slightly.

"Ye'll get used to it," the man remarked sagely.

Laura wiped her face and looked about her. She was in a shabby room, which contained the bed she was sitting on, a small rickety table, one chair with moth-eaten covers and nothing else. Her abductor was holding a tray on which reposed a bowl of something, which was probably soup, and a plate with a chicken leg. There was also, she remarked thankfully, a large glass of water, for all the crying had made her terribly thirsty. He was much younger than she had imagined, hardly older than eighteen, she gauged. Thickset but not very tall with sandy hair and blue eyes. His freckled face was streaked with dirt and his clothes were also none too clean. Laura smiled again and had the satisfaction of seeing him flush a dull red. *Not averse to my charms*, she thought, *that is a good sign.*

She patted the bed invitingly. "Is that for me?" she enquired, nodding towards the tray. "Umm... y... yes." He put it down next to her. "Best eat up."

"But how? My hands..." She grinned again.

"Oh."

He pulled at the cords that bound her wrists. "If I take these hoff you got to promise to behave.

"Yes, I will."

The bindings came off and Laura rubbed her arms. Her wrists were red and painful. "Oh, what a relief. My poor wrists, the ropes hurt so much."

"Mebbe I'd best go now." He scuttled off, locking the door behind him.

Laura examined the food. It did not look very appetising but she thought she might need her strength for whatever was ahead, so she drank the soup and tried to swallow the chicken, which was tough and dry. She gulped down the water. When she had finished she stood up and peered out of the window. She thought she must be in a rural inn, for from the window all that she could see were fields and to the left a small copse of woods. The sun was a fiery ball on the horizon and as she watched, it slowly sank from sight, throwing wild pink tendrils of fire behind it, which were slowly overtaken by the darkness which crept across the countryside. Laura left the window; her room was dark now. Just as she was wondering what would happen next, the key turned again.

The young boy returned holding a candle. He was followed by a man who was shielded by the darkness of the passage and the brightness of the small flame.

"Gentleman to see you, miss," the boy remarked, setting the candle on the wobbly table. The stranger came in and moved into the shadows so that Laura was unable to see his face. The boy backed away, locking the door behind him. Laura stared at the man in the shadows.

"Who are you?" she remarked uncertainly.

He moved forward slowly. Laura gasped as she saw his face.

As no one knew where Miss Clarges reposed, it was necessary to visit Lady Ambrose first. Jaspar discovered Her Ladyship at breakfast when he called. The young butler had tried to deny him but had been swept aside, in what, he reported to the housekeeper later, was a most imperious manner.

"Jaspar!" Her Ladyship put down her cup and held out her hand. She was becomingly attired in a dressing gown of layers of chiffon edged with lace, her hair dressed in curls tucked under a lace cap.

Jaspar picked up the outstretched hand and kissed it tenderly. "Marjery, how beautiful you look."

"Flatterer!" Her Ladyship pronounced, pleased nevertheless. "You have returned. Nillie told me you were out of town on business." She raised an eyebrow questioningly.

Jaspar smiled a half smile to himself. "Yes, I have started a school!"

"What!" Her Ladyship's eyes opened wide. "What possessed you to want a school?"

Jaspar, a ruminative look in his eyes, merely replied, "It's a long story and too long to tell you now."

"Oh, Jaspar, come sit, have some coffee and tell," Marjery, intrigued, implored.

But the infuriating Lord Heddington just laughed. "I do have a favour to ask. I need your help, Marjery."

"My help. Why?"

"I need that old governess of yours, Miss Clarges's, address. I assume you know where she went?"

"Yes, but why do you need it?"

Jaspar had thought of this, he smiled his most enchanting smile. "I cannot tell you at this moment but if the situation changes, I promise that you will be my first confidant." He kissed her hand again. Lady Ambrose was never impervious to Jaspar; indeed she would have given him anything he required.

"Well, she went to her cousin's. I could not keep her after that unfortunate incident with L…" She stopped unsure of whether to continue.

"Quite." His Lordship waved a hand to show her that she need say nothing more.

"I think I have the address." Marjery rose and gestured to Jaspar to follow her. She crossed the hall and went into the pretty morning room. Rummaging in her desk she found the piece of paper she wanted and held it out to Jaspar. "Rose Cottage, Clapham."

"Sounds pretty enough," was his only comment. "Bless you, Marjery, I am truly grateful," and with a quick bow he was gone.

Lady Ambrose returned to her breakfast perplexed. Why should Jaspar want to see Euphemia? It must be to do with the dilemma over Laura but what did Euphemia know? What information did she have that Jaspar could need?

Jaspar leapt back into the coach where Grizelda waited restlessly. "Well?" she demanded. "Do you have it?"

He grinned at her impatience. "Yes, I have it. Harper, Clapham Common, please."

"Clapham! Does Miss Clarges live in Clapham?"

"It would appear so."

The journey seemed to take an age. Grizelda gazed out of the window, fretting anxiously, whilst Jaspar sat back, quite content to watch her. Although she had dressed in a hurry and was certainly, according to her own fastidious standards, looking a mess, he found her enchanting. The stray curls which escaped from her bonnet were charming, the slight disarray of her garments was touching; the only thing he disliked was the worried furrow between her brows and the dark shadows that outlined her eyes. He watched, slightly amused that in her distress she had quite forgotten why he had been out of town in the first place, but the stories of Tarn and the school would have to wait until they had retrieved Laura. Just as she twisted back to him for the hundredth time to ask when they would arrive, Rose Cottage was reached.

It was, Jaspar decided, an inaptly named place, for the cottage was ill-kempt and not a rose bloomed in any proximity. He was about to point this out to Grizelda, who would, normally, have much enjoyed the irony of the ill-named house, but a glance at her face made him desist. She was grey with fear and all he longed to do was to take her into his arms and kiss away the furrows. However, that would have to wait. He got down, bidding Grizelda to stay where she was. She watched agitatedly from the window as Jaspar knocked on the peeling door. Finally, it was opened, she observed, by a huge woman with grimy clothes and a sour face. Jaspar spoke to her but Grizelda could not hear what they said, and reluctantly the women stepped back to allow Jaspar to enter. He found himself in a dingy hall.

"This way." Mildred spoke grudgingly. "I will call Euphemia."

She opened the door on the right and Jaspar went into a small sitting room. This was a great deal cleaner than the rest of the house and he deduced that Miss Clarges cared for this room. A small settle reposed in front of the fireplace and fresh flowers stood on a scratched occasional table whose surface someone, Miss Clarges he assumed, had tried to improve with polish.

"L... Lord H... Heddington." Miss Clarges, a terrified expression on her face, closed the door behind her. She swallowed.

Jaspar raised his glass and looked at her. Miss Clarges trembled. Jaspar swiftly decided that as she was clearly so fearful of him, the best way to proceed would be to use her apprehension. He did not mince words.

"Where is Laura?"

Miss Clarges blanched. "I d… d… d… do not know," she stammered, quailing from his fierce look.

"Do not underrate my intelligence by lying to me," he said unpleasantly. Miss Clarges decided that all she had heard about Lord Heddington being so charming was a mistake.

"Truly, I do not know," she repeated in a squeaky voice. "Honestly."

"I repeat, do not lie to me." Jaspar came closer. "You had better tell me the truth otherwise you will find the consequences for assisting in a kidnapping grave. I know that you summoned Laura." Miss Clarges, who might have been able to resist Grizelda, was no match for His Lordship; she started to sob noisily.

"It was not me, I never wanted to… all I wanted was to be appreciated for what I had done for her. It was him."

"Him? Who?"

"C… C… Colonel St… Staunton. It was his idea."

"Colonel Staunton?" Jaspar was astounded. "But why would Colonel Staunton want to kidnap Laura?"

"I… I think…" she swallowed, "I… He seemed to want to… find out so that his friend would not marry her."

"Friend! Who?"

"M… M… Mr F… Farleigh."

"Oh." Light began to dawn. "Find out what?"

She blushed and quivered with embarrassment. "About y… you and…"

"Yes, me and who?"

"Laura!"

"But there is nothing to find out. What rumours have you been spreading, you evil old woman?"

Euphemia quaked. "But Lady Ambrose said…" Lord Heddington fixed her with a brutal stare. She quailed before the most disagreeable look she had ever seen. "N… noth…ing," she managed to stutter out.

"Then, who gave him the idea that he could discredit Laura in this way?" he demanded.

"I do not know."

"Where has he taken her?"

But here Miss Clarges could not help, she only knew that she had to write to Laura and arrange to meet her in the park. With this Jaspar had to be content.

CHAPTER TWENTY-THREE

Laura stared in utter amazement at the man who stood in front of her, silhouetted against the light in the door. Whomsoever she had expected, it had not been him. Slowly, in case the dark betrayed her, she moved closer to him. No, she had not been deceived. It was Colonel Staunton. For a moment, she thought that he had come to rescue her but then she swiftly realised that he was, indeed, the instrument of her misery.

"You! What do you want with me?" On receiving no answer, she demanded again, "Why have you kidnapped me?"

The colonel regarded her steadily. "Slut," he remarked maliciously.

The fear that had been so much a part of Laura's day receded abruptly. Now that she was faced with a known quantity, she was no longer alarmed but utterly furious. She drew herself up. Ill-advised as it may have been to quarrel with Staunton, she could not contain her temper.

"How dare you call me that!"

"Because it is true." He grabbed an arm.

"Let me go!" She wrenched away from him. It did not occur to Laura to be scared of this man, as she had been when her kidnappers had been unknown to her. She repeated, "Let me go."

"Ha!" the colonel sneered. "Why should I?"

"Because you do not want to be disgraced by being part of a kidnap plot like this. You value your position in the world too much."

She had touched a nerve. Colonel Staunton went a dull red; he moved closer to her and slapped her hard. Laura's hand went to her flaming cheek. Without retreating she continued, "That's right, hit me. See how the *ton* approve of hitting defenseless girls," she brazened.

Colonel Staunton stiffened angrily. He would have liked to have beaten her but he knew that she had a point, so, clenching his hands, he turned away from her. This was not going quite as he had planned. He grimaced and tried a different approach.

"I will let you go but before I do so you must tell me the truth about your relationship with Lord Heddington. I bear you no ill will but I need to avenge myself on him, as I am sure you, too, will wish to do," he wheedled.

But here he erred. Laura had not the slightest streak of retribution in her. She was a straightforward girl, who bore Jaspar no malice; in fact she was most grateful to him for protecting her from her own silliness. She had long ago decided that being married to him would have been hateful, so she was inordinately glad to have escaped from her exploit with so few scars.

"The truth is that I had no 'relationship' as you call it with Lord Heddington," she responded defiantly.

"Oh, come now, you must not regard me as naive. You are a fallen woman and as such are not suitable for Jocelyn." These words succeeded in truly enraging Laura, who had a high regard for herself.

"I am not!" she stated firmly.

He turned nastily. "Until you sign a written confession you will remain here. Sleep well!" He went out, locking the door behind him.

Laura lay on the bed, her mind in a whirl. She was no longer fearful, she could defeat the colonel, she was sure of it. What she could not understand was why he should be bothered with her. It was surely a matter of indifference to him should Jocelyn be induced to marry her. No, she was convinced that her abduction must have a deeper significance. Laura was growing up. She was not the foolish creature that she had been last summer and she was blessed with a down-to-earth native wit that she had inherited from her papa's family. In her dealings with Lord Heddington all her natural sense had been totally suspended. Her infatuation, coupled with Miss Clarges's romanticism, had made her ignore signs which she now came to acknowledge had been present. Laura was not a particularly clever girl, in fact in matters of Latin and Greek she had been the despair of her governess, but she did possess this inherent intuition and it was that which made her doubt the colonel's expressed reason for her kidnapping. She had noted the wild look in his eyes when he spoke of Jaspar, although she had no understanding of why he should feel such hostility towards His Lordship. For the colonel was rich and seemed to her untutored eyes to occupy a perfectly satisfactory position in society. It was a puzzle. She fell asleep pondering on the vagaries of the case.

Jaspar returned to the carriage slowly, thinking hard what to do next. As he climbed in, an impetuous Grizelda pounced on him.

He paused before answering her. Then, having made a decision, he turned to her. "We know now who abducted her. What is not clear to me is why."

"Who? Who took her?" Grizelda, chafing to find out what Miss Clarges had said, hardly heard the second part of his question. "Who took her?"

Grizelda's wonderful red hair had now entirely escaped its clips and was tumbling down her back. She pushed it back impatiently, but as soon as she moved her head, it swung in front of Jaspar again. He had an irrational desire to catch it to him and bury his head in its goldness. He desisted and laughed at her beauty.

"Do not laugh. It is not a laughing matter," she asserted.

He was suddenly serious. "I know, Miss Ludgrove, but I am hopeful that it will all be resolved. You will have to trust me."

Grizelda's pale blue eyes opened wide. "You mean you are not going to tell me anything."

"I am formulating a plan. As soon as I know that I am ready, I will inform you. With that you must be content."

"At least tell me who took Laura."

"The colonel."

Grizelda's brows shot up. "Colonel?"

"Staunton."

"Oh!" she exhaled quickly. "Colonel Staunton?" She spoke in incredulous tones. "But why?"

"That, I confess, I do not know."

She bit her lip, pondering. "Do you know where she is?"

He shook his head and then, as he saw a wave of apprehension cross her face, he took her hand. "But do not fret. I will know very soon, I promise."

Grizelda gazed into his dark eyes. She trusted him. She felt comforted by his presence; she was pleased that he was here. If anyone could find Laura it would be him.

Jaspar thought. He was much more concerned than he would show Grizelda, not least because he knew that Laura's already fragile reputation would never stand another scandal. She had already spent one night from home. It was essential that she now marry. He would have moved the world for the girl who sat next to him and if necessary he would arrange for Laura to be wed.

"Where are we going now?" Grizelda's husky voice touched him.

In answer, he patted her hand gently. She sighed a deep miserable sigh but said nothing more. She was not as unaware of the proprieties as Jaspar hoped. She understood all too well that her sister had been missing for a whole night, and she knew that her reputation would be in ruins. How to solve the problem? She felt desperate and suddenly exhausted. She left her hand in Jaspar's; it felt so strong and warm and comforting, she laid her head back against the squabs, her eyes closed. Her head ached.

Presently, the horses stopped outside a lodging in Grosvenor Street. Grizelda did not know who lived there. Jaspar bid her wait and much as it irked her, she obeyed him. Then he strode in. Luck was with him for he found Mr Farleigh with a late breakfast laid out in front of him. His dissolute face was pale and his eyes heavy with the excesses of the previous evening. He staggered to his feet as Jaspar came in.

"Lord Heddington?" His words were slightly slurred. "To what do I owe the pleasure…" He got no further.

"Where is Laura Ludgrove?" Jaspar did not mince words; there was, in any case, no point. If what he deduced was true and if what he had planned was to occur, then Jocelyn would have to know the truth.

Farleigh stared back at him through red-rimmed eyes in what Jaspar perceived was genuine bewilderment. He brought his brows together and with some little difficulty repeated, "Miss Ludgrove? What are you talking about? At home in bed, I should imagine." He laughed drunkenly. "Walking in the park with an admirer. How should I know where she is? Silly question, Heddington. Now if you don't much mind I'll go on with my breakfast. Care for coffee?" He flopped back on the chair and Jaspar sat down opposite him, accepting a cup from the footman, who Jocelyn then dismissed with a careless wave of his hand.

"I do much mind. Laura has been abducted by your friend," Jaspar replied.

There was no mistaking the genuine shock on Jocelyn's face. He sat up and said in an altogether different voice, "Abducted!

Poor little thing." The concern was unquestionable; Jaspar began to feel more hopeful. "But no friend of mine. No, old man. No one I know would do such a thing."

"Oh?" Jaspar remarked wryly. "Really! Well, perhaps he is not a friend of yours, that shall be for you to judge, but Laura has been taken by Colonel Staunton."

"Colonel Staunton?" Jocelyn nearly fell off his chair with surprise. "Colonel Staunton! James! Why should he take Laura?" He suddenly got angry. "The blackguard. If he has done her a mischief, I tell you, Heddington, I will call him out."

"If I do not first," Jaspar could not resist slipping in. He felt much better. It was clear that Jocelyn had some warm feelings for Laura and that must be beneficial. The next proposition had to be proffered with subtlety, for he did not want to put Jocelyn off. He looked at Farleigh consuming his food. He took a breath.

"Jocelyn, this is not easy but I do not think there is any alternative. You realise that Laura is completely compromised. She must marry. I believe that she is not indifferent to you. So I think you must marry her."

Jocelyn looked up without surprise. "Can't do. Oh, I admit she is a taking little thing but must marry money. Pockets all to let." He attacked his ham with vigour.

"But you are Lord Farleigh's heir, you have great expectations."

"Yes, but pressing debts. Can't wait for the old man to pop his clogs. I thought he might settle the creditors but the old miser refused; only went to see him at Christmas because I need some of the ready." He thought a moment. "Pity, I like Laura. Better than most females. Doesn't bleat like the rest of them. She keeps me amused. Not many girls do that." He grinned at Jaspar.

"Then the debts will be paid. Marry Laura and they will be paid."

"By you? No, I cannot accept that."

"Call it a wedding gift. You will be doing me a favour and getting someone I care about out of a hole."

"Alright." Slowly he nodded agreement. "Answer me one thing. Is it Laura you care about? Did Laura go with you?"

Jaspar shook his head. "No, I just took her to her father." He was not sure just how far Jocelyn's fondness towards Laura would go. He was clearly not opposed to the idea of marrying her. The truth might change that. The two shook hands.

"Now that we have agreed, we can waste no time. You go to get a special licence and I will go to see if I can find out where the colonel has taken Laura," suggested Jaspar.

"With due respect, old man, think we should reverse those tasks. I can get a deal more out of James's servants than you could. For they know me."

Jaspar could immediately see the efficacy of this suggestion. "I have Laura's sister outside in the carriage."

Jocelyn pulled a slight face. "Don't like me, opposed to me."

"I think in these circumstances she will bless you," grinned Jaspar. "We will go for the license, and return as soon as possible."

Having ordered Harper to drive to the registrar, Jaspar climbed in with Grizelda. She was bouncing with suppressed curiosity and apprehension.

"You must not worry. It is all working out very well," was all that he intended to say to her.

Grizelda, however, was not content with such sparse fare.

"Why are we going to the Temple?" she demanded. "You must tell me."

He grinned; he was not proof against her pleadings. "We are going to purchase a special licence for a marriage."

For a moment her heart leapt; she wondered whether it would be for them. She swallowed. "A marriage?"

He paused. "Miss Ludgrove... Laura... you will appreciate that after this absence it will be imperative that your sister weds."

Grizelda nodded unhappily. "If we find her... yes."

"We will find her. I have just left Mr Farleigh. He agrees to marry her."

 301

"Mr Farleigh!" she said in shocked tones; then she went on miserably, "It is good of him. I appreciate that, it is just that it is not what I have wished for her."

"Do we ever get what we wish for?" he repeated, conscious of her disappointment, but unconscious of its reason.

"No... I suppose not."

"It is a good marriage."

"I cannot approve of his unprincipled behaviour but I do see that it will be the saving of her."

"It is good of him. You know he clearly has a kindness for her. I must own that I was agreeably surprised that he consented so readily."

Grizelda nodded slowly. "Yes, I see that it will do." She sat back and her thoughts were not comfortable. She told herself that to have expected a proposal from Lord Heddington was mere spin-weaving. To have been so inanely optimistic because he went to buy a license was stupidity of the highest degree. She sighed. Jaspar, watching her carefully, was convinced that she worried over her sister.

The sandy-haired young boy brought her breakfast. Laura smiled at him sweetly and had the satisfaction of seeing him blush bright red. She wondered whether he could be induced to help her escape.

"It is another lovely day," she remarked conversationally. He grunted agreement and fled, firmly locking the door behind him.

"Bother." Laura peered at the tray. She ate some bread and ham and drank the coffee. Then she occupied herself by watching from the window. It was very boring for there was nothing to see. She wondered if anyone came to the front of the inn. She had heard some noises but no sounds that could possibly be a coach's wheels.

It was very hot in her room for the sun flooded the windows which were firmly barred and impossible to open. Laura's muslin dress was crumpled and dirty; no one had brought her water to wash and she felt uncomfortable and sticky. She wanted to cry, but told herself firmly that the colonel was beating her down. He wanted her so uncomfortable that she would acquiesce to his demands. She decided that it was imperative that she did not give in. She lay back on the bed and dosed. When she awoke, the relentless sun was further around in the sky and was no longer streaming through the windows. She was terribly thirsty. The lock turned; it was the boy again. He had some more food on a tray; obviously the colonel was not going to starve her.

"Please, it is so hot, may I have some more water?" She smiled as sweetly as she could. "And do you have anything to do? A book perhaps?"

Laura was no reader but even her Latin primer would have been welcome at this point to relieve the boredom.

"I's sees what I can find," he muttered and left, returning a few minutes later with a pile of dilapidated books and a flask of water.

"Oh, thank you, thank you!" Laura was genuinely grateful for such relief, and when he had gone she drank a quantity of water, saving some for the future, and set herself to look at the books which were, it turned out, quite agreeable. Someone obviously had a taste for novels and she set into one describing the adventures in a gothic castle of a young girl and a philandering count.

Jocelyn arrived at the colonel's house in Hay Hill, still looking faintly the worse for wear. This proved to be an asset.

"Good morning, Mr Farleigh." The colonel's elderly butler deplored of his master's more incorrigible friends. "Colonel Staunton is away from home, sir." He started to close the door.

"Oh, Mansell, I know…"

"Thank you, sir." He closed the door a little more.

"Now, Mansell, just a minute, I find myself in a spot of bother."

The butler looked him over disapprovingly. "Yes, sir."

"Just let me in a minute. It is to do with the colonel and I am sure he would not wish his business discussed on the doorstep."

Reluctantly Mansell let him into the hall. Jocelyn, whose brain was beginning to clear, thought quickly. "Fact is, I was supposed to meet up with the colonel today, he gave me his destination, but well, you know how it is." He smiled. Jocelyn had a disarming smile. "I had a bit too much last night, in me cups, you see…"

"I can observe that, sir," Mansell returned frostily.

"Fact is, I forget where I am to meet him." The butler regarded him disparagingly. "Thought you might be able to help a chap out of trouble…" Mansell stared at him. "Think how James is going to feel when I do not turn up."

"For the fight?" Mansell suggested.

Jocelyn thought quickly; so he had told Mansell it was a prize fight. "Yes, for the fight. I wondered if you knew where it was, damned important that I get there."

"Wouldn't know, sir, I'm sure."

Bother, thought Jocelyn, then he had another notion. "Perhaps the groom would know? Could he be sent for?"

Hesitantly Mansell showed him into the morning room and impatiently he waited. The undergroom, who eventually arrived, was an inspired idea. He was a loquacious man, recently employed by the colonel and eager to help any friend who might advance his cause. He was quick to divulge that the colonel had ordered the coach to take him to Aveley on the Chelmsford road. This was far more than Jocelyn could have hoped for. Excited, he hurried back to Grosvenor Street to discover that Jaspar had not yet returned. He ordered his valet to put up what he would need for the next few days and set to await Jaspar. He did not have to wait long. Jaspar came soon after him. Jocelyn greeted him triumphantly.

"I have it! He has taken her to Aveley," he crowed.

His Lordship grinned with relief. "Well done, Farleigh, we must make haste, there is no time to be lost."

"I am ready. I have asked my valet to pack what I will need."

"More than I have done. I will, I fear, be impinging on you, for I do not think that there is time to delay for collecting even essentials. May I ask another favour that your coachman drive Miss Ludgrove to Lady Melbourne?"

"Of course, and I will order some extra shirts. We are much of a size and can share if necessary," Jocelyn laughed. This was soon accomplished and they went out to the carriage.

Grizelda was heartily fed up with being in its comfortable interior. She wanted to be off to search for Laura and the enforced wait was making her increasingly restless, so she was pleased to see the two men emerge from the house. Jaspar crossed to the carriage and opened the door.

"Miss Ludgrove, I have arranged with Mr Farleigh that his coachman convey you to Lady Melbourne."

Grizelda stared at him. "No," she stated firmly. "Have you discovered where the colonel took Laura?"

"Yes, I have."

"Good morning, Miss Ludgrove," said Jocelyn.

Grizelda looked at him in her direct way. She immediately said, "Mr Farleigh, I must express my gratitude to you. I do not know how to thank you for what you have agreed to do."

Whatever reception Jocelyn had thought he would get from Grizelda, her unstinted and unequivocal approbation pleased him greatly and made him believe that they would, most unexpectedly, get on.

He smiled at her. "Thank you, Miss Ludgrove. I am horrified to think what Miss Laura will have suffered and I am keen to make it up to her if I can."

Jaspar watched, well satisfied with the burgeoning friendship between these two. "Now, come, Miss Ludgrove, we must be off. Mr Farleigh's groom awaits you."

"No, my lord, if you search for Laura, I must and will come with you." She put up her chin challengingly.

Lord Heddington laughed. "If you must and will, then you shall, but we must away as fast as possible. However, I make one condition: you must write a note to Lady Melbourne to reassure her. I do not want any more worried scandals."

Grizelda laughed. "You are, of course, correct but I think that you must also inform Lady Morntarny how the matter progresses, for I am sure that she too will be much concerned."

The notes were soon written and equally soon dispatched and the three departed for Essex.

Chapter Twenty-Four

It was Netta who received Lord Heddington's note from Farleigh's footman. She recognised the writing immediately and turned it over to gaze at his seal. Mesmerised, she leant her cheek against it gently, as if by touching it, she could touch him. She sighed and, smoothing the paper tenderly, she made her way upstairs to Lady Morntarny's dressing room, for she knew that the countess would be found resting. On being bidden to enter, she passed the note to Nillie.

"Do sit down, Netta." Her Ladyship smiled encouragingly at her, patting the end of the chaise.

"Thank you." Netta perched next to her and watched somewhat anxiously as Petronilla tore open her brother's letter.

"Oh!" she exhaled. "It seems that Laura has been kidnapped! However, Jaspar has found out who has taken her and where they are. He has gone in search of her."

Netta felt a twinge of guilt. She had not believed that anything untoward had occurred. She just thought that Laura, whom she regarded as spoilt and inconsiderate, was behaving in a flighty fashion. But it seemed that the girl had been taken, by whom and why? Then another pang assailed her; she wondered if Miss Ludgrove were still with Jaspar.

"Has Miss Ludgrove gone with him?" she found herself

constrained to ask. She would have preferred to be indifferent but she was incapable of stopping herself.

"Jaspar does not say but I imagine she will have returned to Lady Melbourne. It would hardly be seemly for her to accompany him, I would have thought."

"No," agreed Netta, her heart lifting. "Indeed, it would not."

"We will send to Lady Melbourne and ask Miss Ludgrove to call, to tell us more," Nillie decreed. "Please, Netta, bring me paper and pen." The note quickly written and dispatched, the two sat anxiously to await Grizelda and perhaps news.

The afternoon drew on. Miss Ludgrove did not appear, the only diversion being the arrival of Nillie's two daughters, who had been to the park with Miss Manners and were full of their adventures.

"I wonder why Miss Ludgrove did not come," Netta observed, "when you expressly requested it. It seems she could not be discommoded."

"Maybe Lady Melbourne needed her," Nillie remarked kindly. "I wonder how Jaspar is and whether he has reached his destination."

"Did he say where Laura was or where he was going?"

Nillie shook her head. It was at this moment that they were joined by Greville who, on being informed of what had occurred that day, was aghast, for he fully realised that they had been in charge of Laura and that their dereliction of duty was dear.

"Netta, how could you take your obligations so lightly?" he admonished severely.

Netta, stung, replied, "But it can hardly be termed my mistake if the girl is frivolous and capricious."

"It is most certainly your responsibility. You were brought here with the express order to take care of Laura whilst Nillie was unwell. I hold you accountable," Greville stormed.

Nillie regarded her husband, usually a most mild man, with surprise. "Greville, I do not think there is anything much to be gained from that now, some of the fault must be mine. I saw Laura yesterday. I should have…"

"Have what?"

"Well, I am not sure… I just feel I could have prevented this."

"Probably not," Greville, his temper assuaged, said. "Nillie, you must not blame yourself."

Netta, tears pricking her eyes, her lips trembling from the unwarranted attack, mumbled an excuse and left the room. Once outside she allowed a tear to run down her face. She felt most hardly used. It was those hateful Ludgroves. If only they did not exist. If only they had never come into Jaspar's life. She gave a stifled sob and ran to her chamber. *I shall go home*, she thought. *No one appreciates me here*. She would have been mollified had she heard the conversation taking place between the earl and his lady.

"Greville, you were hard on Netta. She did try and truly I do not see how she could have prevented Laura going out, any more than I could have done."

"You are probably right, my love, but she does not like Laura, I have observed that."

"Umm. I have too. Do you think she knows of Jaspar?"

Greville shook his head. "No, I do not. There is something else. It is as clear as the nose on my face that Laura is not remotely interested in Jaspar, so why does Netta dislike her? She is a most unexceptional girl and damned pretty."

Petronilla laughed. "Perhaps that's why. Netta can hardly be termed a beauty."

"But not as beautiful as you." The earl bent and kissed his wife.

It was early evening before Aveley was reached. Lord Heddington had driven his horses hard and every time they had changed,

Harper had hired the best possible cattle. Thus they had made excellent progress. Aveley itself was a small market town with, as they were informed, only one inn, the Pear Tree, set by the village pond. Eagerly they hurried to it but it was found to be rather a disappointment. It was very small with almost no stables and certainly did not promise well. Jaspar went in, leaving a despondent Jocelyn and Grizelda in the carriage. The entrance was empty. He called for assistance, and a huge and not, to Jaspar's fastidious eyes, terribly clean lady came to answer his call.

"Yes, can I help you?" she asked in a surly tone.

Jaspar put up his glass and surveyed her. He was quite unused to being addressed in precisely that way. "Are you the landlady?" he returned imposingly. Without thinking, the lady dropped an ungainly curtsey.

"Yes, sir." She peered at him from under thick eyebrows.

"l am looking for..." here Jaspar paused, "... a gentleman, who may be accompanied by an exceptionally pretty girl with golden hair and blue eyes."

She shook her head. "No one 'ere."

"No one answering that description? The man is six foot tall with thinning brown hair and rather plump."

"Nooo... no one 'ere. No one stayin'. Ain't got anyone in my rooms and that's the truth."

"Umm. Is there another inn hereabouts? We need to find the gentleman for his sister is ill," he improvised.

"Nowhere else."

At that moment they were joined by a stringy elderly man who was obviously my lady's consort. His blue red-rimmed eyes glistened when he saw the equipage that was drawn up outside his inn and he hurried in to find out who was inside. As he arrived he heard his wife's unhelpful comment.

"Can I help, yer worship?" he grovelled.

"It seems not." Jaspar picked up his driving gloves and prepared to depart.

"Oh, they must be some hinformation that yer worship would like."

"Give over, Jo." His disgruntled wife shuffled off.

"Well," Jaspar considered, "I am searching for a friend, whose sister has most unexpectedly been taken ill. It would appear that they are not here." He took out a guinea. "I need to find another inn thereabouts; your wife says you run the only one but I find that hard to credit."

The old man's avaricious eyes gleamed. "Well, sir, thes a few. The Freckled Horse, that's up Orsett way. Then, the Swan on the Rainham road… oh, and the Cartwright, but a gentleman like you would not want to go there."

"Nevertheless, where is it?"

"Oh, jes' down the road here. You go out…" He pointed. "When it becomes country then you'll see it."

"Thank you." Jaspar tossed the coin at him and watched as the old man's eyes lit up with the splendour of the gold.

He rejoined the others in the carriage. Grizelda was by now quite frantic. Her hopelessness was so touching that both Jaspar and Jocelyn could not fail to be moved by it.

"Well?" she demanded.

"Not there, but I have hopes of another inn some way down the road." He climbed back in.

Grizelda twisted her hands desperately. "Do you think we will find her? Maybe he has ki…" She swallowed. "K…"

"No, he has not." Jocelyn put his hand over hers. "I know Staunton. He is no murderer."

"Yes," she turned her brimming eyes to his, "but she must be so despairing, so alone and…" She choked.

"Do not think like this," Jocelyn said comfortingly.

"But she is so forlorn, so without help." A tear brimmed over and ran down her pale cheek.

Laura had decided she must escape. She was a girl of some resource and had decided that if only she had some kind of weapon she could attack the colonel and be gone. Throughout the boiling day, she pondered on what she could use. She tried the table but despite its rackety appearance it proved to be surprisingly solid. The chair, however, had one leg that she thought might well, with a bit of work, come out. She set to with a will but it proved a hot and thankless task. She was on the point of abandoning the prospect as hopeless when, finally, the leg seemed to be loosing its glue bonds. Then suddenly it broke free. Laura pushed back her hair with a grubby hand and jumped up with glee. She had done it. She whirled around, feeling very proud of herself. She had managed a weapon. She tried the leg. It was hard and would make a formidable stick. She decided that for the moment she had better reinsert the leg in the chair and bide her time. She flopped down exhausted on the bed and thought about her situation. That the colonel would return she was sure, for had he not said that he would come back today to receive her answer? The problem was that she would not know when the door next opened whether it would be the boy or the colonel. She was mulling over this quandary when she heard sounds of the door being opened. Drawing in her breath quickly, for stupidly she had placed the chair between herself and the door, impossible to reach before the person entered, she prayed it would not be the colonel. She was in luck for it was the boy, holding a tray of food and some more water. Now she was certain that her next visitor must be her kidnapper. Having eaten as much of the mouldy food as she could stomach and drunk all the water, she did not repeat her mistake; she took the leg back out of the chair and sat, clutching it, on the bed, gazing at the world outside from what she had now come to regard as her prison.

It was nearly dark before she heard any more sounds. The inn was quiet and through the window the sun had set, leaving a faint pink haze in the dusky sky. She watched the thin trails of grey clouds, delineated by luminous orange, gradually darken to black. A few scattered stars came out. A dog barked in the distance. The bright moon rose slowly in the sky. Laura shivered. It was not cold but she found she was very frightened. She tightened her grasp on the wooden shank and prayed that she was strong enough.

Finally it came. Sounds of a man walking along the passage. Laura's heart beat so fast she thought the world must hear it and her body trembled violently. Quaking, she stood behind the door. The key was being inserted into the lock. She hoped it would not be the boy again, but even if it were, she had decided she must escape. She could not stand another day in this room. The key turned and slowly the door opened. Laura felt weak with desperation. She raised the wooden leg. The man entered the room; he was holding a candle and its light cast his shadow backwards. He moved forward from the door. Laura struck as hard as she could on the top of his head.

"Yaa." He dropped the candle, whose light was extinguished, and yelped with pain. He turned and advanced towards her. Laura struck blindly at him and he retreated, his hands in front of his face.

"Bitch!" he yelled. Laura kept hitting him but try as she might she could not knock him down. Her breath came in short bursts from the effort and her strength was failing fast. One last hit and he sprawled across the floor. Unfortunately, although he was down, he was not unconscious. He pulled himself to his feet and in her unguarded moment, he grabbed the leg, wrenching it from her hand.

Laura screamed and the colonel seized her and pinioned her hands behind her back. Laura was petrified. She knew that now she was lost.

"Bitch! Slut! Unnatural trollop!" he panted, twisting her arms until she cried out with pain.

"Let me go, let me go, please!" she howled.

"No! Not now! You have had it now!" he screamed. He was holding her facing the window with his back to the door. Through her tears Laura could see the tranquil night sky, the deep darkness decorated with tiny twinkling stars. She sobbed, wailing so loudly that all other sounds were obliterated. His grip on her tightened.

"Be quiet!" he commanded. But even if she had wanted to Laura was quite unable to stop the sound which emerged unbidden from her.

"Stop it!" He shook her hard. Her head flopped from side to side and then, just as suddenly, his hold slackened and she felt him pulled off her. She slid to the floor. Laura gulped. In her confusion there seemed to be candles and people. Still shuddering violently she felt herself pulled to her feet and held against a welcoming chest. She groaned.

"Shh, shh. It is alright now," murmured a familiar voice. She peeped upwards and there, holding her tightly, was Mr Farleigh.

"Oh," Laura, recovering slightly, exclaimed. She had no desire to move from the comfort of the firm arms which held her. She peered around. There holding Staunton was Lord Heddington and next to him, pale with worry, was her sister. Laura swallowed. Her throat felt like sandpaper; she tried to speak but no words would come out. She swallowed again.

"Laura, are you alright?" Grizelda asked. Laura nodded wordlessly. Farleigh released her reluctantly and led her back to the bed. She sat and Grizelda hurried to her. She smoothed her curls and Laura felt her senses returning.

"How did you find me?" she managed in a hoarse voice.

"Shh... do not speak yet," her sister said. "Through Miss Clarges and Colonel Staunton's servant," she answered Laura's question.

"My servant. Oh no," the colonel groaned weakly. "Let me go, Heddington." He was covered with blood and one eye was nearly closed and a huge bruise was appearing across his cheek. "I am not going to run away."

Jaspar regarded him sagely. "No, you are not."

"Why? James?" Farleigh demanded. "What possessed you?"

Staunton shrugged. "l was trying to save you from making a mistake. I thought I would just discredit Laura. I wanted the truth about her and Heddington."

"But you hurt her. How could you?" Farleigh spoke in disbelief.

"That was not part of my plan. You must believe me." He gazed around pleadingly at the blank faces. "l just wanted to find out the truth for you," the colonel went on imploringly. "Then she hit me over the head, I lost my temper." He sat on the bed, his head in his hands. "It has all gone horribly wrong... Jocelyn, you must believe me," he begged.

"Oh, and what would have happened if we had not arrived?" Jocelyn said coldly.

"I w... I would have let her go. l would not have kept her prisoner. Truly."

"You would not," Laura rejoindered. "You wanted me to sign a piece of paper. All lies. He said he would not let me go unless I signed it." Her voice broke.

"Well, all I wanted was an admission that you had been Heddington's mistre..."

He got no further. Lord Heddington drew himself up. "I have told you Laura was never my mistress. Why do you continue in your calumny?" he said in a tone so icy, that even Grizelda felt unnerved.

"Miss Clarges says..." the colonel stuttered.

"Why do you assume that Miss Clarges is anything but an old woman of an idiotic romantic turn? Who would imagine fairies where there are none? She is certainly a most unreliable source," the glacial voice continued.

Grizelda watched. She said nothing. Jaspar was going so far

for her and Laura. Far more than they deserved. How would she ever be able to repay his kindness?

"What do we do with him, Jaspar?" Jocelyn enquired.

His Lordship thought a moment before replying. "He is going away for a very long time," he pronounced. "You have a choice, Staunton, either you go to jail or you may go abroad tonight and stay there. If I see your face in England again, I promise you will regret it."

"You leave me no choice. I will go abroad. May I have permission to go back to London to set my affairs in order?"

Jaspar went white with fury. "Do you not listen? You leave tonight. Your affairs, as you call them, will be settled from… wherever. You leave on the first packet."

"l agree. Now, let me leave… I will go." He pulled himself up and started for the door.

"Not so fast, Staunton." His Lordship's words cut across the room like a gunshot. "Do you think I trust you? You will be accompanied by my groom. Miss Ludgrove, perhaps would you be so good as to fetch Cope up here. I will lay information about you with Bow Street along with the fact that you have fled. Do not think you can sneak back into England, for you will not be able to."

A look of acute dislike flashed across the colonel's face. He sat down again. Grizelda returned with Heddington's groom. Cope was a giant of a man, possessed of broad shoulders and strong arms. It was impossible to imagine that anyone would escape from him.

"Cope, I wish you to accompany Colonel Staunton to, let me see, Greece. If you have any trouble with him, you have my permission to break whichever part of his anatomy seems appropriate to you."

The giant grinned. "Very good, me lord. Come on, you." He pulled the colonel to his feet roughly and marched him out of the room.

"Well, that seems very satisfactory," Jaspar exclaimed. "I do hope that you have not suffered too much, Miss Laura?"

She shook her head. "It was very scary. I did not know what would happen."

"My poor sweet." Jocelyn took her hand tenderly.

"It is important that no one knows about this. You do realise, Laura?" said Grizelda pointedly.

"I hope that Laura will do me the honour of becoming my wife?" asked Jocelyn.

"Oh! Yes, please!" Laura, her eyes aglow, answered brightly.

"Then all that will be known was that I took my wife out of town. I will send a notice to *The Post* accordingly."

"Excellent, Farleigh. The wedding shall take place tomorrow."

"Tomorrow! But what about my clothes?" objected the vain Laura. "I cannot get married tomorrow."

"Yes, you can and you will" Grizelda answered firmly " We shall find you a pretty dress to wear in the morning and then you can purchase anything else you need" She caught His Lordship's eye. He gave an imperceptible nod. Laura might have been tempted to argue or sulk but she had no desire for her bridegroom to see her less attractive qualities, so she merely inclined her head.

"Now that is settled I think we must now repair to one of these other inns. I certainly do not wish to spend a night under this roof or under that of The Pear Tree," laughed Jasper

Chapter Twenty-Five

Grizelda had the satisfaction of seeing her sister married the next morning. They passed the night in the Freckled Horse, which seemed a tolerable house. Not the kind that generally enjoyed Jaspar's custom but a deal cleaner and up to snuff than The Pear Tree or the dreadful place where they had discovered Laura.

After they had bespoken rooms, Jaspar went off with Farleigh to find a willing cleric who might be prevailed upon to perform the ceremony in the morning, leaving Grizelda to enjoy her first private converse with her sister, who had changed from frightened captive to ebullient bride in only the minute it took for her to realise that she was to marry the man of her dreams. Laura could speak of little but the wonders of Mr Farleigh and the beauty of their future life together. Grizelda, far more sceptical by nature, was well aware that Jocelyn, who seemed fond enough of Laura, would by choice probably not have married her. She was also aware that Jaspar had probably exerted some pressure on Farleigh to make him agree so readily to what she suspected would not be his natural inclination. What she did not know, and could not ask, was what that pressure had been. Sufficient that her sister would, after all her misadventures, be so respectably wed. It would suit her papa too, for Laura would eventually live adjacent to him and all Mr Ludgrove's careful husbanding of the

Lord Farleigh's estate would now benefit his own offspring. It was an outcome that was all she could have wished. The only tiny flaw was Mr Farleigh's personality. She was sure that he would not make a particularly exemplary husband. However, he was more than Laura could hope for after her indiscretions. So Grizelda was content. She put her doubts aside and entered into listening to all Laura's fantasies.

The chambermaid took Laura's dress to sponge and press it, having been quite taken in by Jaspar's story of 'the overturning coach and the luggage which had descended into a ravine'.

Whilst the girl dealt with the dress and Laura washed away the ravages of the previous two days, Grizelda brushed her own hair and wondered how long His Lordship would be. She had had no thought as to her own predicament, too caught up by the necessity of saving Laura's reputation to give a thought to her own. It was true Lady Melbourne knew that she had gone with Jaspar to find Laura, but she was no gossip and after all, Grizelda had her sister for chaperone and soon Laura would be a married woman. Grizelda grinned to herself; the idea that Laura could lend her respectability was very funny.

Although she had not thought about her position, Jaspar had. He intended to ask her to marry him as soon as was feasible, and now that he had so satisfactorily resolved Laura's problems, there was nothing to stand in his way except his own insecurity. For he felt most unsure of Grizelda's reactions. He hoped that by redeeming Laura, Grizelda would find it in herself to forgive him but he was not confident that she would. If she still felt his transgressions to be inexcusable, she might not be prevailed upon to marry him. The idea of life without her was unendurable. It made an almost unbearable wave of despair course through his heart. He shuddered.

Jaspar had always got what he wanted. No one crossed him. In such a particular, he was spoilt. Although it would never have occurred to him, if indeed he thought about it, that he had been so indulged. It was an entirely new condition and he swiftly discovered a not very pleasant one, to be uncertain about anyone. The doubts ate into his being. He could not conceive of being without Grizelda, and the very possibility made him feel utterly wretched.

The wedding took place in the tiny village church of Aveley. The vicar, an old, plump man with almost no hair and rather evil-smelling breath, performed the ceremony as if it bored him stiff. Laura, her looks restored, wore the only dress she possessed and a lace shawl that she and Grizelda had discovered in the lone shop in the village. Happiness, however, made her apricot curls shine and her blue eyes gleam. There had been a hiccup about a ring, for the shop certainly did not sell wedding rings. In the end the dilemma was resolved by Grizelda offering to lend the delighted couple the tiny amethyst ring which had been her mother's and which had never left her hand since her mama's untimely demise. After the ceremony they all repaired to the inn for a glass of wine.

"Dearest Grizzie, I am so blissfully happy," pronounced the new Mrs Farleigh as she hugged her sister.

"Congratulations, Farleigh." Jaspar shook his hand. "I wish you joy."

"Thank you. A word."

"Of course." They removed a little way from the two sisters.

"Two things. Firstly, well, Heddington, I hesitate to mention but you did say…" he paused; Jaspar raised an eyebrow, "… that if I did the decent thing…"

"My dear chap. Send all the accounts to me. In addition, I think, it would be only proper for you to take Laura on a bridal trip. If you have not the means, I would be only too happy to oblige. Think of it as a wedding gift," His Lordship stated firmly. As he saw Mr Farleigh starting to demur: "I think you should also occupy yourself with a note to Mr Ludgrove. I know that Miss Ludgrove writes as well, so I do not anticipate any opposition."

"Opposition?" Jocelyn laughed.

"No, I did not mean to you but merely to the indecent haste of the marriage."

Jocelyn grinned again. "Yes, I think your advice is sage. We will away to Italy, to allow the *ton* and Mr Ludgrove to have time to accept us."

"Good, then that is settled, and the second thing?" Jaspar enquired.

"We are obliged, I fear, to bear you company to London, for we have no other means of transport."

"Naturally, I would have expected nothing else. I will drop you at Grosvenor Street."

Jocelyn looked slightly shocked, as the idea of a wife in his bachelor lodgings bore in upon him. "Would it not be easier for Laura to return to Lady Morntarny to explain and get ready to leave?"

Jaspar understood his fears. "I think you had better leave the explanations to me. I believe she has an abigail at my sister's who can bring her things and wait upon you."

"Oh, er… yes, I expect that will be for the best," he responded doubtfully.

Jaspar grinned. "It will take a little getting used to," he commented sympathetically.

Grizelda came up to Jocelyn; she kissed him on the cheek. "Thank you, Mr Farleigh." Her eyes met his. He understood the look in them and gave her hand a little squeeze. "I am delighted that you are my brother."

"And I, that you are my sister."

Grizelda, somewhat surprisingly, blushed. "Oh," she responded in a pleased voice.

Jocelyn caught Jaspar's amused eyes on her, the expression in them so loving. *Ah, so that is the way the land lies*, he thought to himself. *Well, they will suit very well.*

As soon as they had finished nuncheon, they departed for London. When they were seated Grizelda turned to Lord

Heddington. "Now, my lord, you have not told me how you got on with Tarn. I am all impatience to know."

Jaspar laughed. "l did not observe much impatience over the last two days," he teased.

Grizelda giggled. "I admit I did have other things on my mind but now I must know."

"Where to start? Tarn is a remarkable child. I was astounded by his resolve. Do you know he was determined to learn to read? I took him to the Soho bazaar and all that he wanted was books. Well, nearly all he wanted; he was also enchanted by the toys, the pastries, the musical instruments, particularly the drums, the hatter, the optician, the work trunk maker, the bird seller, the gunsmith, the grocer, the brushmaker and nearly every other stall," he laughed.

"Who is Tarn?" interjected Mr Farleigh.

"Grizelda's protégé. She found him and rescued him from his preceptor…"

"You took him from his master?" continued Farleigh. "Surely that was not wise, you had no right to intercede between apprentice and…"

"I had every right." Grizelda fired up, much to the amusement of Jaspar. "He was being beaten. It cannot be right to mistreat children."

"Oh, Grizzie is always like that," asserted Laura. "She spent all the time at home trying to bring justice to those who were underprivileged." She shrugged.

"Things are changing, Laura, and they must alter, must they not, my lord?" She turned to Jaspar for support.

He grinned at her. "I rather think they must. I did not think so before my illness but now my attitude has changed." He met Grizelda's eyes, amused by the sudden guilt in them. "I am glad that I was attacked, for it has made me understand issues which previously I had not addressed."

"Good, but proceed. Where did you take Tarn?"

"To his parents'. They lived in a filthy street in quite the worst part of Newcastle. There are five children and his mother expects another one. At the inn on the journey, I saw the abrasions and weals on his body, and I was resolved that never again should he be subjected to such cruelty, but the family has no money. His father, although he is a good man, has no job. It is altogether shocking that a man such as Mr Grant can find no work."

Grizelda looked at him curiously. "Then we must find him employment," she interrupted, her eyes burning.

"Wait until the end of my story. I had promised Tarn that he should go to school. It was my intention that I should pay for him but when I saw the parlous state of the family's finances, this became ineligible. So I undertook to start a school."

"You, a school!" Grizelda's amazement made him smile ruefully.

"I do undertake some worthy tasks, you know," he muttered without rancour.

"Oh... y... y... yes, I..." she said in some confusion.

"I bought an estate! Mr Grant, Tarn's father, is to run it and they are all to live there." He laughed. "I am now awash with good works, I own a hospital and a school. How astonished my friends would be," he remarked, gazing at Farleigh whose look of wonder was clear.

Grizelda clapped her hands together. "I am so pleased. It is just as it should be."

Laura squeezed her husband's hand. "Did I not tell you, Jocelyn, she is determined to alleviate misery."

Her statement had the effect of making them all laugh. Then there came a distant peal of thunder, for during Jaspar's tale the weather, which had been so balmy, suddenly in an hour had changed. Dark, lowering, scudding clouds covered the sun and the wind came up. Just before they reached the heath there was a flash followed swiftly by a loud crack of thunder. Grizelda shivered. It started to pour, huge drops which tumbled out of the sky in abundance.

"How hateful!" Laura spoke fearfully. She stared out of the window at the slanting water. Another flash and more thunder. "It is a good thing that we are not scared," she giggled. Her comments broke the slight feeling of melancholy that had descended on the other three. It rained solidly over the last few miles into London, slowing their progress as the horses slipped on the muddy roads.

When, eventually, they reached the metropolis, they made their way to Grosvenor Street where they dropped Mr and Mrs Farleigh at their lodgings. Laura clung to her sister in an affecting manner. Her earlier exhilaration had evaporated as the reality of married life sunk in upon her. Grizelda looked concerned. She opened her mouth to suggest that Laura accompany them but she was stopped by Jaspar who said firmly, "We will send Laura's abigail to her with her things and Jocelyn intends to take her to Italy on a wedding trip." He took Grizelda's arm and shepherded her towards the carriage. As her sister waved a tentative goodbye, Grizelda tried to wriggle free but Lord Heddington restrained her.

Once they were back in the carriage, she turned to him and remarked with some asperity, "Surely I am allowed to bid my sister farewell. Perhaps she should have come with us to collect her belongings and explain to Lady Morntarny."

"No, Miss Ludgrove, it is better this way, believe me."

Grizelda fumed. Really my Lord Heddington could be too overbearing. Incensed as she was, his next words, therefore, completely stunned her. He sat in the corner staring out of the window, feigning unconcern, and said, without glancing at her, "Now that we have satisfactorily salvaged Laura's reputation, I suppose we must do the same for yours. You had better marry me."

Grizelda, who wanted nothing so much in the world, stared at him enraged; the offhand proposal made her stiff with fury.

"I do not want to marry you!" she rejoindered angrily. No sooner were the words out of her mouth than she regretted them.

Jaspar, in the hurt of her refusal, withdrew directly. She felt the care and protection that had surrounded her throughout the last two days disappear as a rainbow did. Too fraught and downcast by the recent events to begin to try to understand why he had asked her in that indifferent fashion, she instantly imagined that it must be because he had not the slightest fondness for her and was merely making reparation for her journey with him. If she had been able to think rationally or apply her considerable understanding to her situation she might have remembered the look in his eyes, the warmth of his smile, and she might have realised that here was a man who, whilst usually possessed of all the polish, was at a complete loss when trying to express what mattered most to him. As it was, all she saw was a sullen, withdrawn man, who raised not the slightest objection when she said she could not marry him. He did not even try, she thought, with an inward sob; if he had wanted to marry me he would have protested a little.

Jaspar sat in his anguish, totally unaware of hers. She cast a quick glance at his face. His stern, forbidding profile, which did not remotely resemble the charming companion of an hour ago, stared out at the rain. She wanted to say something to him to break the mood but of no words could she think. They reached Berkeley Square in silence, both sitting in abject misery in opposite corners of the coach. Jaspar handed Grizelda down and followed her into the house. As they mounted the steps, Nillie rushed out.

"Jaspar! What has happened? Is Laura safe?"

His Lordship nodded. Fast behind her came Netta, who realised with horror that Grizelda had arrived with Jaspar. Had she been with him all the time? The implications of what she saw made her shiver with apprehension.

"My sister is safe. She has married Mr Farleigh. They have gone to Italy," Grizelda said in flat voice, hardly trusting herself to speak.

The countess looked amazed. "M... m... married? To Italy? Jaspar, can this be true?"

"Yes," he responded stiff-lipped. He kissed his sister's hand. "I have an urgent appointment, I must to Bardfield directly."

He turned and abruptly departed. Nillie stared after her brother in astonishment. This rudeness was so unlike Jaspar. What could have occurred? She turned to Grizelda, standing like a stick next to her.

"Miss Ludgrove?" she questioned.

Grizelda bit her lip. "It is the truth. Perhaps I could see Laura's abigail and explain where to send her things."

She lowered her head. Netta, attuned as she was to Jaspar, had with some joy sensed the estrangement between him and Miss Ludgrove. Now she heaved a hidden sigh of relief. Maybe she could find out what had happened.

"May I help, Miss Ludgrove?" She smiled a subservient smile. "If I could assist you in any way, I would be only too happy."

Nillie smiled gratefully. "Oh, Netta, would you really? I am sure that Miss Ludgrove would be most appreciative."

Grizelda was forced to acquiesce to her offer, although there was nothing she wanted less.

All she desired was to be left alone to examine her feelings.

"Let me show you the way." Netta smiled ingratiatingly and Grizelda, whose heart felt as if it were shredded to bits, wanly nodded back. She followed Netta out of the room, leaving a bemused Nillie wondering what on earth had happened.

Laura had occupied a pretty room on the south side of the mansion. Netta opened the door and ushered Grizelda in.

"Why don't you sit down, Miss Ludgrove," she said solicitously. "You look completely distraught. This kidnapping must have been so troubling."

Grizelda, who responded to the kindness in her voice, gave a slight sob. "Indeed, I did not quite appreciate how worried I must have been." She dropped her head into her hands, unable to stop herself from trembling.

Netta sat beside her; she put an arm around her shoulders. Netta was a kind girl and she would have felt much for Grizelda's distress, except that she guessed that it was not just to do with Laura's problems. It had to do with Jaspar, she was sure of it.

"Shhh…" she murmured. "You rest whilst I attend to Laura's things."

"Thank you."

"Where did you go with Lord Heddington to find Laura?" she asked carelessly. Her inner soul desperately needed to know if Grizelda had accompanied His Lordship. She dreaded the knowledge but had to possess the information.

"We found her in a village called Aveley. She was incarcerated in this awful inn," she shuddered. "Colonel Staunton had kidnapped her, although I still do not understand why; what he hoped to gain from it. Lord Heddington was wonderful. I do not know how I would have managed without him." She sniffed.

Netta grimaced. A wave of anger swept over her. How could she accompany him? She battened down her ire and said in the sweetest tone, "You were with him. Oh, do you think that was quite right? I mean… oh… I know that Jaspar, Lord Heddington, would always behave with decorum, he would always do what was right. He would not allow your reputation to suffer."

She stopped and sounded confused. Grizelda looked up at her quickly, but all she could see in the other girl's eyes was sympathy and concern.

"Oh, he is indubitably a gentleman," she continued, biting her lip to prevent the unwelcome tears.

"Most certainly. He would never allow anyone to be compromised by his behaviour. Oh no. He would have made an offer out of a desire for reparation, even if he had not the slightest wish to marry the person," Netta lied firmly.

If Grizelda had been less bewildered, she might have questioned this statement, remembering what had happened to her sister, but in her dazed state she simply accepted Netta's words, in their seeming innocence, from a girl who had known Jaspar all her life, although these words struck ice in her heart, but then she had always known that His Lordship's offer had not been meant. It had been a thing he thought he should do. She inhaled quickly and shivered.

None of the thoughts that flitted across her expressive eyes were missed by the percipient Netta; so he had offered for her. Then why had she not accepted? Netta was curious. She did not repeat her allegation for she could see by Grizelda's face that she had no need to. Grizelda had clearly understood the implications, just as Netta had intended.

"Now rest, Miss Ludgrove, I will see to everything." She patted her shoulder gently and crossed to ring for the abigail.

Jaspar drove back to Grosvenor Square but stayed only to order Harper to remain there and a new team to be put to. He wanted to drive himself, as if the action of controlling the horses would assuage the pain in his heart, comfort the affliction. He found an overpowering need to be alone and wished that Valiant was not at Bardfield. As he drove out of London the rain had slowed to a thin drizzle. The unremitting greyness of the sky in front of him was alleviated by strips of white light thrown across the horizon. Dark silhouettes of trees stood in front, illuminated by the watery sun behind them.

He discovered an atavistic desire to see Bardfield. Just to go home. The journey was a slow one. The weather was inclement, but it was not the wet that delayed him. He plodded, unable to find any desire in his heart to travel at his usual breakneck speed. Slowly the clouds cleared, tiny stars twinkled, the moon was almost full and by its bright light he saw the Angel and Harp ahead of him. As he came upon the inn, an overwhelming, deep need to stop there, where it had all begun, swept over him. He pulled into the yard. Melow hurried out to greet him.

"My lord! 'ow late it is. 'ow is you?" He beamed.

"I am well, thank you," Jaspar replied in a desolate voice. "Can I have a parlour and perhaps some lemonade?"

Melow could not hide his astonishment. "His Lordship ordering lemonade, fair took me breath away," he confided to his good lady. "Y... y... yes, me lord. Will you be a'stopping?"

Jaspar thought for a moment and then he nodded bleakly; better to stay here and leave in the morning.

"You 'avn't Mr Harper with you?" Jaspar shook his head. "Then I'll jes' rustle up the ostler."

He took the horses and led them into the yard. Jaspar stepped into the inn. Noise of merrymaking came from the taproom; a song pealed forth and gales of laughter greeted its perpetrator. Jaspar sighed. He walked across the hall and down the passage. He stopped outside the door of the private parlour where Grizelda had come that July day. There was no sound from inside so he opened the door slowly. The parlour was empty. Moonlight streamed in through the window, alighting on the polished furniture. He remembered her coming in, the golden-red hair, the huge blue eyes, her laughter, the feel of his lips on hers, the touch of her skin. He grimaced with the pain. Yet he wanted to think about her. Wanted to remember. He wanted to remember kissing her and the softness of her small breast as he cradled it in his hand. Their moment together in this room had been so short. A few minutes to see her, and, he realised with a sharpness that took his breath away, to fall in love with her. He thought about his search for her, of seeing her at Almack's and then the unendurable. To have lost her. He felt tears prick at the back of his eyes. He had not cried since his father had died. He pushed back the feeling and then he heard footsteps in the corridor. He brushed an arm across his eyes.

"Lord! Yer Lordship in the dark. Have you dined?" Mrs Melow's plump figure was framed in the open doorway; her anxious tones stopped his recollections.

"No, I have not dined but it is late; just a cold collation and some bread and some lemonade, please."

"Yes, Yer Lordship," she said curiously. Really Lord Heddington did not sound quite himself.

She hurried away to obtain his supper.

His Lordship turned away back to the window. The sky was sooty black and sprinkled with stars. The moon high in the sky shed a light so bright it was almost as if it were day. For a moment he considered continuing his journey, it was after all only ten miles to Bardfield, but he was so weary and so much in need of this time alone to mourn his loss. It never occurred to him that perhaps Grizelda had not meant her precipitate words. She had been so definite, so clear. He sighed. A faint knock on the door brought a small, sleepy scullery boy who laid up a cover. He was followed by Mrs Melow, bearing a tray on which reposed some cold meats and bread and a jug. After she had left he drank the lemonade, for he found he was very thirsty although he was quite unable to eat anything. In respect for Mrs Melow he tried to struggle down a few crumbs but they stuck in his throat.

He passed a restless and sleepless night and woke early and unrefreshed. His first thought was to wonder where Grizelda was. Had she stayed with his sister or with Lady Melbourne? He had to stop himself writing to her, so strong was the desire. He crept downstairs and out to the stables, remembering that other time he had left, injured, early one morning nearly a year ago.

The morning was beautiful, clear and sunny with no trace of the previous day's thunderstorms. He drove the few miles to Bardfield and paused at the top of the drive to gaze on the clear lines of his mansion. The sky was blue and tiny white wisps of cloud floated across the clear morning light; the sun shed a faint yellow light on the stone giving it a warm and inviting appearance. He urged his horses forward and proceeded down the drive. The trees were green and fresh; wild flowers bloomed in the parks. The peace and tranquillity soothed him.

CHAPTER TWENTY-SIX

As soon as they had finished ordering Laura's belongings and Grizelda had departed for Whitehall, Netta proceeded decisively to her room. Here she packed a small bag.

Then she went in search of Lady Morntarny, whom she discovered resting in the library, her head buried in a book. She looked up as she heard Netta come in.

"Oh, Netta, this Jane Austen is wonderful, I have rarely enjoyed a book so much. Have you read her?" she started impulsively and then went on without pause, "Has Miss Ludgrove gone?"

Netta grinned. "The answer is yes, to both those questions." She took a breath and said bluntly, "Nillie, I find that it is essential for me to go home for a few days."

Her Ladyship looked surprised. "Isn't this rather sudden?"

"I suppose so but I think I ought to visit my papa and now that you are so much recovered and the problem of Laura has been so excellently resolved, I thought perhaps you could spare me for a day or two."

"Oh, my dear, please do not think that you are a prisoner here. It is not a case of my sparing you, you are not my servant. Of course you may go. You hardly need my permission. When do you intend to travel?"

"l thought that I would catch the early stage…"

"The stage! You must not think of it," interrupted Nile. "You have been of invaluable assistance here. Please accept my travelling carriage."

"Nillie, this is kindness indeed but it is essential that I depart early. I hope that that does not inconvenience you?"

"No, I shall not need the carriage tomorrow but you better arrange with the coachman tonight."

"l shall do so immediately, and thank you, Nillie."

Lady Morntarny kissed her goodnight and first thing in the morning Netta left for home.

She was grateful for the comfort afforded by the travelling carriage. Its unaccustomed luxury made her feel relaxed and important. Netta had suffered all her life from feelings of inadequacy. She had always felt lesser than the Heddington children. It was not so much that they treated her as if she were negligible, so much as that that was the role she assumed. Lady Heddington, it was true, had always valued her qualities; her organisational abilities; her way of happily undertaking even the most dreary of tasks with such willingness; her helpfulness; for she could be relied upon to shoulder anything that could ease the burden on others. Through the dowager's gentle tutelage, she had begun to value herself, and Her Ladyship's firm conviction that she would make Jaspar the most admirable wife had encouraged her to believe that that was, indeed, the truth. In this, Lady Heddington, usually so perceptive, had erred. Netta might seem the ideal consort for any man, so blessed was she with all the useful attributes for this role, but these were not in themselves enough. Lady Heddington had loved her husband wildly, but in her old age she had forgotten the miraculous raptures of loving and could only see the disadvantages. She was sensible to Bardfield's need for an heir, and Netta would make the most commendable and conscientious mother. She would love and nurture her offspring, and as she seemed to have no real inclination for a dashing life in London, Jaspar would be able to indulge his romantic affairs with no expectation of returning to reproaches from his wife. Here again her assumptions were misplaced, for Jaspar did not wish this kind of marriage and Netta had discovered a deep jealous streak, which would make her quite unable to tolerate a husband's intrigues, in the way that Her Ladyship anticipated.

The day was clear and sunny. Netta had plenty of time to compose her thoughts and deliberate on her plans. By the time she reached her home it was early evening but the sun was still shining brightly. She thanked Nillie's coachman politely and, having sent him around to the stable for food and rest before he returned, she went into the house to change. She called for the maid who attended her, and bade her help her dress. In London, Netta, guided by Quarmby, had purchased several new and very pretty dresses. Now she changed into a delicious silk evening dress and combed her hair in the latest and prettiest fashion. Then she sent for her papa's coach.

She arrived at Bardfield just as dinner was finished. Her Ladyship had retired to her rooms and Jaspar was in the library. Netta enquired for him, and Savage, who was slightly surprised by her calling at this late hour, but could see no way to deny her, merely bowed his head slightly and led the way to Lord Heddington. He opened the door and through its portals Netta could see Jaspar standing at the centre windows. These were wide open, allowing the soft evening air to drift in, bearing the delicate scent of summer blooms. He had his back to her and she could see from the tense cut of his shoulders that all was not well. She nodded dismissal to Savage before he could announce her and firmly closed the door behind the butler. Then she crossed to Jaspar and very gently put her hand on his arm.

He started, staring at her with an odd look in his dark eyes, then he remembered his manners. He bowed. For a moment he thought perhaps she had come from Grizelda with a message; his heart jumped.

"Netta, I thought you were in London?" The question hung in the air. She moved away from him and perched on the chair overlooking the terrace. The room was quite dark, for the only light came from the few candles on the wall brackets which burned at the far end and the moonlight, which slanted in through the open doors and alighted on Jaspar's face. He seemed austere and removed; she felt her heart beating wildly but she knew that it was now or it would never be. Deep lines of unhappiness were etched around his unsmiling mouth.

"Jaspar…" She spoke very gently.

"Netta, I thought you were in London?" he repeated.

"I was but came to see you."

"Me?" He shrugged.

"I wanted to make sure that you were…" She paused. Inside she trembled so hard that she was sure he must see it. "That after what Miss Ludgrove…"

"Miss Ludgrove?" The words whipped across the room. "Miss Ludgrove! What did Miss Ludgrove say to you?"

Netta swallowed, her hands at her side and her nails dug into her palms, but she made her voice warm and sympathetic. "Just that you had asked her to marry you and that she could never contemplate such a match."

Jaspar's face contorted. How could Grizelda discuss him in this way? How could she disclose to a comparative stranger such intimate details? He was first desolate at her words and then furious with her that she had imparted such matters to Netta.

Netta stood. She said nothing more, for she knew she did not have to; she watched Jaspar's face intently. Eventually he looked at her. Her gentle eyes held a look of such care and concern. If Grizelda had to confide in anyone, rather such a girl as Netta, who was so honourable and virtuous.

"I am sorry, Jaspar." Her voice was low and sweet. She touched his arm again, in almost a caress.

Lord Heddington gripped his hands together. Then he swung round and started to leave the room. At the door he stopped, his handsome face rigid with misery.

"I see. Will you do me the honour of becoming my wife?"

He did not look at her. A feeling of exultation swept over her. It was true. She had done it.

He would marry her. She would make him happy. She would. She would. She knew it.

She smiled slightly and inclined her head. "Oh yes, Jaspar. I would like it above all things."

He flung himself out of the room, allowing her to enjoy her victory alone. She whirled around for a moment in glorious triumph and then rang the bell. When Savage answered she demanded to know whether Her Ladyship had retired for the night. On being informed that she had not, she ran up to Lady Heddington's rooms.

She knocked gently on the door. The dowager was sitting in a chair at the window; she turned as Netta entered.

"Netta, my dear, how lovely." She extended her hand and Netta ran to her, her face aglow. "What is it?"

"The best of news. Jaspar has just asked me to be his wife. I have, of course, accepted."

"Oh, my dears, I am so pleased, my dearest wish was that you should be united. It will be the most happy of unions but why did he not come to tell me?"

"I think he wanted to let me have the pleasure of telling you," Netta improvised.

Lady Heddington laughed. "Well, wait until I see him. I will… No, I am glad that you came to tell me. You have done so much for us, Netta. Nursing him to health. Helping me, helping Nillie. You deserve all this." She waved an arm in the direction of the house and smiled.

Grizelda arrived back at her godmother's house into an atmosphere of disapproval. Her Ladyship was still indisposed and Emily, who had come to care for her mama, had opened Grizelda's note. She sat stitching in Lady Melbourne's dressing room when Grizelda, white-faced with misery and exhaustion, entered. Lady Cowper could not be termed as strait-laced but after the scandals occasioned by Lady Caroline, she was careful of her family's reputation.

"Miss Ludgrove," Emily emanated disapproval, "where have you been? My mama was most concerned about you. She is not well. It was most inconsiderate of you to add to her worries."

Grizelda, afflicted by such intense suffering that had no resources to answer this unwarranted attack, bit her lips and looked at Emily.

"I… I am sorry," she gasped, "I am truly sorry, I had no choice."

Unable to speak anymore, her eyes blinded by tears, she ran from the room. Emily watched her, unsure of what she should do; she had not meant to distress the girl and she was at pains to understand how her mild rebuke could have had such a dramatic effect. Eventually, she decided to do nothing; perhaps Grizelda was exhausted. A good night's sleep would assuredly renew her equilibrium. Once in the safety of own chamber, Grizelda crawled into bed where she cried and cried. She much regretted her hasty words, her impetuous tongue. If she had just said yes, how happy she would be. Then she checked herself. It would never be fair to trick His Lordship into marrying her, which must surely have been the case if he had proposed to her because of her compromising position. She could never start a marriage based on that deceit. Slightly mollified, she decided that the next day she would go and see Lady Morntarny and see what she could recommend. On that thought she fell into an uneasy asleep. A few hours later she was jolted awake. As she struggled into consciousness she became aware of the portentous feeling which clung in her heart. Vainly she tried to push it away but this proved impossible. Tears seeped from the corner of her eyes, running unchecked onto the fine lace pillow. It was very early and the birds were singing with a sweetness and joyfulness which only served to increase her misery. Desperately, she climbed out of bed and pulled back her curtains. Her chamber overlooked St James's Park and as she watched the morning sun brighten the trees she could not help but remember the winter rides with Jaspar. She screwed up her eyes and climbed back into bed; perhaps sleep would bring its respite from her pain, but as so many others before her, insensibility would not come; instead her mind went over and over her idiocy. At last, it was time to rise. She dragged herself down to breakfast. She drank some coffee and tried to force some bread and ham down, but the food made her shudder. When she had finished she went up to Lady Melbourne's suite. Her Ladyship's dresser was there and she greeted Grizelda warmly.

"Miss Ludgrove, how lovely that you are back. I am sure it will do Lady Melbourne no end of good to find you returned."

Grizelda felt tears prick her eyes, so grateful was she for her kindness. "Indeed, I am pleased to be home. Is Her Ladyship recovered?"

At that moment Her Ladyship's voice called, "Is that Grizelda? Come, my dear."

On going in she was pleased to see Her Ladyship looking so much more the thing. She leant over and kissed her god-mama. Lady Melbourne patted the bed. "Come, tell me what happened?"

Grizelda told her, for she knew that Lady Melbourne was no gossip; too many important secrets had been confided in her and never once had she betrayed them. She was aghast by the tale of Staunton's perfidy but pleased by the outcome for Laura. Grizelda did not, however, tell her about Lord Heddington's proposal and her refusal, for she knew that her godmother would consider it madness in her that she had rejected so admirable a suitor. For this, she was later in the day to be heartily grateful. When Her Ladyship appeared, Grizelda left her, declaring her intention of visiting Lady Morntarny.

It was such a lovely day she decided to walk across the park. She thought that perhaps the fresh air would quiet her disturbed thoughts and take away some of the exhaustion that assailed her. This was, indeed, the case and she arrived in Berkeley Square feeling altogether more refreshed. She enquired for Nillie and was led through the well-proportioned hall and up the winding wood staircase, with its delicate iron balustrade and curving mahogany handrail, and along the corridor to my lady's boudoir. Nillie was resting on a chaise longue; she looked up with pleasure when she beheld Grizelda.

"Miss Ludgrove! How charming. You find me resting again! It is my hateful condition. Everyone insists that I rest. It is famously boring!"

Grizelda laughed. "Do you hate it?" she remarked.

"Well, not the baby but the condition, yes, I do. I am afraid it is very tedious, uncomfortable and dull. Shall I tell you a secret… but I forget my manners please, sit down. What can I offer you?"

Grizelda felt cheered by her friendliness and for the first time since her hasty words in the coach, she felt that maybe there was some hope for the future. She sat down opposite the countess and declined any refreshment. She grinned companionably and enquired about 'the secret'. Nillie grinned back. "I know it is frivolous but I long to dance."

Grizelda hooted with laughter; it felt good to laugh again. She was comforted by Nillie, by her frank confidences, by her uncanny resemblance to Jaspar, by sitting in this commodious room.

Her solace was not to last long.

"I am delighted," Nillie went on. "It is the best of arrangements for your sister. You must be most gratified."

"Oh, indeed I am gratified and, I must admit to you, much relieved," she blushed slightly, "after the incident with your brother. I thought, perhaps, her expectations were totally ruined but thanks to you and to Lord Heddington she has been rescued. I am really most obliged to you both. There is nothing I can do to repay your kindness but I want you to know how much I feel my accountableness..." She paused.

Nillie grasped her hand. "Please, you must not think that the indebtedness lies only on your side, my brother has a disposition... for... being something of a rake. It is a reputation that has long distressed my grandmother. It would not have done him any credit had it been known that he seduced a young and innocent girl."

Grizelda smiled wryly; she knew her beloved had been of that inclination. He had, she knew, loved and discarded many; she felt a wave of despondency creep over her again. Given his propensity, what stupid right did she have to make her think he cared for her? After all, his offhand proposal showed that he did not. She sighed. Her sigh was misinterpreted by Nillie.

"Oh, please, you must not worry, I have this morning the best of news regarding my brother." Grizelda watched her; she nodded slightly. "My grandmother writes that he has, this day, become affianced to Netta Egremont; it is an outcome for which we have all devoutly wished."

Grizelda felt the blood drain from her head. She felt icy cold. Jaspar engaged to Netta. She clenched her hands and by an act of stoical will managed not to betray herself. She swallowed. "Miss Egremont! I had no idea that his... f... feelings were engaged?"

"Well, they have been friends for an age and she has adored him ever since I can remember. It was quite a family joke," the countess went on airily, unaware of the devastation her words were wreaking in her visitor. "My grandmother wished it very much and Jaspar adores her. We all thought Netta was destined to a life of unrequited love," she laughed. *And that would have been the case if I had not been so stupid*, Grizelda thought bitterly.

She stood up. Her legs felt as though they would collapse at any minute. She wanted to run from the room screaming; instead, she stiffened her muscles and forced her face into a smile. "I must not tire you any longer, Lady Morntarny," was all she could manage.

As she went downstairs, it was as much as she could do not to fling herself on the ground in a fit of sobbing; however, she managed to hold back the ready tears that threatened, until she reached St James's Park; here she could no longer contain herself and her brimming eyes escaped and flowed unchecked down her face. To hide she put her head down and hoped that no one would notice her. Eventually, she reached Melbourne House. She rushed to the solace of her chamber where she collapsed onto the bed. Sobs surged over her in convulsive waves. Finally, she could cry no more; her head ached, her nose was blocked, her eyes were swollen and red. She sat up. She could not stay here, of that she was sure. She quickly packed her clothes and sat and wrote a note to Lady Melbourne. Then she rang for the maid. In a blank voice she told the girl that she must go to her father and instructed her to find a hackney to convey her to the Swan with Two Necks in Lad Lane; for it was here that she knew she could catch the evening stage to Vernham Dean. She gave the girl express instructions to put the note into Lady Melbourne's hands. Then she left Whitehall and London for ever.

Jaspar did not visit his grandmother that evening. She was perplexed by his absence but so pleased by Netta's news and the success of all her plans that she gave it very little consideration.

The next morning she sent for him. It was another gorgeous summer day, with an endless blue sky and warm sun with a soft breeze. Her grandson, who had slept fitfully, arrived looking drawn and forbidding. Lady Heddington was so jubilant that she hardly noticed his unusual taciturnity.

"Jaspar, my dear, such wonderful news, I am so happy."

Jaspar appeared faintly surprised. "News?"

"Of you and Netta."

Jaspar felt a wave of rage sweep over him. So Netta had rushed straight to his grandmother with the news. Could she not have waited? He turned away to hide his anger.

"Do you think so?"

"Oh yes, I do. You know how long I have aspired to this. It is the best of tidings. Oh, my dear, I could not be more contented. As soon as I heard, I wrote to Nillie for she has your interests so much at heart."

Jaspar froze. He had spent most of the night with his thoughts tumbling over each other. It had not taken him long to grasp the mistake he had made. He had been so dispirited when he had returned and Netta's words about Grizelda had made him think that nothing mattered anymore. However, a few minutes' quiet reflection made him realise that it could not be. He simply could not marry Netta. Before he eventually fell asleep he had determined to go to her this morning before it became common knowledge and beg her to repudiate his offer, but now, he sighed heavily, now she had told his grand-mama, who was in ecstasies about his impending nuptials. He still intended to ask Netta to declare that she could not wed him, but it made it much more complicated now that the dowager and Nillie knew.

It was to get worse during the course of the day, for he found that his grandmother was not the only person whom Netta had told. She had imparted her glorious news to everyone, including her papa. Jaspar, who felt himself sliding further and further into the mire from which it would be hard to extricate himself, became harsher and harsher. He regretted his rash words spoken in haste and distress. He could not withdraw from his engagement. It would be a most terrible breach of manners. In desperation he took Valiant out for a ride.

He rode the horse hard and long, galloping furiously over the fields, jumping hedges in a wild and unruly fashion. It was years since he had ridden so recklessly. He came to the outskirts of his land and was puzzled as he glimpsed a building ahead of him. What was it? Then he chuckled wryly. Of course, Horace's hospital. How the building had grown. He reined in and, tethering Valiant to the post outside, he entered the portals of his hospital. The hall was cool and wide; it was tiled in shiny blue and white tiles. A nurse, who was dressed in a dress which resembled a habit, came out through a door.

"Is Dr Sugdon here?" he enquired.

"Who shall I say wants him?" Her reply was calm.

"Lord Heddington."

Her face changed. She dropped a small curtsey. "Immediately, my lord." She bustled away to fetch Horace. Jaspar glanced around; he was pleased with what he saw. The hospital was built on surprisingly graceful lines and was spacious and very clean. Two wide corridors led off the central hall and it was down the right-hand one that Horace hurried out to greet him, a broad smile on his freckled face.

"Jaspar! When did you arrive?" His discerning eyes examined Jaspar's face carefully. They observed the strain and the unhappiness etched around his mouth. What had happened to His Lordship to make him look so severe?

"Horace, this... this place. It looks good enough to treat everyone, not just the poor," Jaspar observed.

His friend grinned and bristled humorously. "Of course, we shall have everyone queuing up to be admitted here. I have so much going on. It is so thrilling. Let me show you."

He led Jaspar down the left-hand corridor talking excitedly. "I have heard of a man called Henry Hickman from Ludlow. He believes that nitrous oxide gas might help pain in operations. This would be truly wonderful."

He showed Jaspar the wards, which were light and spacious. "I am sure that we can control fever here by my hygiene rules and…" He paused and stared at Jaspar. "What is it, my lord?" The suddenness of his question and the gentleness of his tone disconcerted Jaspar, used to hiding his feelings. He stared blankly at his friend. Horace, perturbed, led him into his rooms.

These served as office and consulting room and were large, light and, Jaspar noticed, spotlessly clean.

"Come now. You can tell me." The words were simple and very kind.

"It is nothing." Jaspar turned away. "The hospital is excellent. I am proud of it."

Horace watched him carefully. He was too wise to enquire further, so he merely asked if Jaspar would dine with him that night. His Lordship nodded, made his excuses and went, leaving his friend to conjecture on what had gone wrong.

Jaspar rode around to the stable where he encountered Harper, who also regarded him curiously. Valiant was hot, flecked with foam and blowing loudly. It was most unlike His Lordshlp to neglect his beloved horse. Something was very wrong. Harper was not only devoted to Jaspar but was also very observant. He knew far more about Jaspar's feelings than His Lordship would have deemed possible or would have appreciated. Therefore, he understood just how much in love with Miss Ludgrove his master was. Harper thoroughly approved of Lord Heddington's choice. He had watched many of the females who had drifted through Jaspar's life and had never thought any of them suited his master, but Miss Ludgrove, now she was different. Harper had sensed the tense atmosphere between the two of them on the way back from Aveley but had not understood what had gone wrong. When Pickering informed him of Netta's news, Harper was at first disbelieving, and when he realised that it was true, very perplexed. It would not do, of that he was sure.

"Harper, I want to ride to Miss Egremont. Rub Valiant down and bring him around in five minutes."

"You ain't going to take him out again like that, are you, my lord? Jes' look at him," Harper returned in tones of disbelief.

Jaspar looked at his horse and reddened slightly. "No," he replied. Which was how Harper came to drive His Lordship to his affianced's house and how he came to overhear their conversation.

Chapter Twenty-Seven

Jaspar changed from his riding attire into a coat of blue superfine and pantaloons. He put one diamond ring on his finger and, attired with his usual quiet elegance, he was ready for his interview with Netta.

She was in the still room when the butler came in search of her, to inform her that her fiancé awaited her in the gardens. She had been supervising the making of preserves, and was hot,sticky, her arms covered in fruit and sugar. Jaspar's unexpected arrival put her somewhat in a fluster, but she rushed away to change out of the dull day dress that she wore for tending to the housekeeping duties in her papa's house, into something altogether more fitting to greet her future husband.

The day was sunny and clear and as Jaspar walked along the terraces, his thoughts kept returning to Grizelda. It appeared that however much he wished it, and in truth, he was not sure whether he wanted to banish her, he was unable to stop her obtruding into every minute of every day. Jaspar gazed unseeing across the flat countryside. Mr Egremont's house was not well aspected and this view was unexceptional. The squire had never exhibited any particular interest in his gardens and they suffered the fruits of this neglect. The stones of the terraces were covered with lichen, and small plants pushed their triumphant heads through the pebbles.

"Jaspar!" He heard the call of his old childhood friend and sighed. He hated himself for what, in a moment of weakness, he had contracted to do. He was not unaware of the hurt that Netta would suffer and he was disgusted with himself that he should have allowed her feelings to be jeopardised in this way. She came along the walk towards him, her skirts catching the unclipped bushes which bordered the path.

"Good morning, my lord." She curtsied. Jaspar's face was unforthcoming. He appeared stern and unapproachable.

"Good morning, Miss Egremont." The formality of his greeting was not lost on Netta, who felt a wave of apprehension sweep over her. "Would you care to take a turn around the garden with me?"

The squire's home was a small manor house built in the sprawling fashion of previous centuries. As they walked towards the rose garden they passed the back of the stable block, where Harper and his crony were enjoying a gossip in the sun.

"I have something to request, Netta."

She felt suddenly very nervous. "Yes, Jaspar."

"I have come to ask you to release me from our engagement." Jaspar did not waste time on niceties, he came straight to the point. "I know that it is the most enormous favour but please discharge me." On receiving no reaction, he persisted. "Netta, I cannot marry you. It would not be fair." He glanced at her face as she stared straight ahead but still she gave no answer. In response to her silence he felt obliged to persevere. "I do not love you." The words were bald and unadorned and pierced her like arrows. This girl who had seen her coveted dreams become reality and which were even now being snatched away from her.

"No!" she shrieked. "No!"

"I do not love you," Jaspar continued inexorably. "I do not! Oh, Netta, I was wrong, oh so wrong. I cannot tell you of the remorse I feel for the distress I have caused you."

"No! You will be happy with me. You will, I will make you happy. You cannot go back on your word. I will not permit it," she shouted.

He stared at her in disbelief. "Netta, do you not hear me?" He raised his voice to hers. "I love someone else."

"I know!" she screamed. "I know that, but Grizelda hates you. She does," she went on desperately. "She told me she hates you. She despises you. You bore her. She thinks…" She searched desperately for anything else she could think of and Jaspar knew. He knew now that Grizelda would never have said such things and he knew, through her contrivance, Netta had trapped him. He groaned at his stupidity.

"I will not let you go. I will not release you," she bawled. "I will never let you go. Your grandmama would never let you treat me like this. You will be happy with me. I will make you happy." She collapsed sobbing.

"Hardly!" he said bitterly, but too much the gentleman to renege on his word, to her and to Lady Heddington, he turned in despair and left.

Horace was caught up at the hospital; he found his work there so absorbing that he often forgot the hour, and his guest had already arrived by the time he drove his trap into his tiny stable at the back of his cottage. Slightly to his surprise he found Harper standing, anxiously waiting for him.

"Sorry I am late, Harper." He climbed down, grinning apologetically. Automatically, Harper took the reins.

"Dr Sugdon, I need your help."

"Are you ill?"

Harper shook his head. "Oh no, nothing like that, but His Lordship…"

"Ill?"

"N... no. It's... well, I'd better get straight to the point. He's in love, see."

"With Miss Egremont?" Horace had heard of the engagement.

"No, it's Miss Grizelda, Miss Ludgrove. I ain't never seen His Lordship like he is over her."

"Forgive me if I am stupid, then why is he marrying Miss Egremont?"

"She... oh, well... I suppose he quarrelled or somethink with Miss Ludgrove." He appeared puzzled. "And you see, Her Ladyship kept pressing him to marry Netta," he sniffed. "In a moment of weakness... misery... he asked her, then today he went there and begged her to release him but she won't. I couldn't help overhearing them, so loud as they were shouting." He looked worried. "Oh, I know I shouldn't talk. I wouldn't but you care about His Lordship and someone has to do somethink."

Horace nodded. "I see." He paused; a frown appeared between his brown twinkly eyes. "I had thought that there was something amiss," he shrugged, "for he looks so disheartened."

"Proper miserable 'e is. Miss Egremont kept a'yelling that Miss Grizelda hates him but that's balderdash. Miss Ludgrove, she's as keen on His Lordship as he is on her. I jes' don't understand what's gone wrong. But I knows something, I's not sitting by and letting that Netta get away with it." He paused, wondering whether he had gone too far but the doctor nodded agreement.

"Yes. Poor girl." Harper was unsure whether he meant Miss Ludgrove or Miss Netta. "I am glad you told me. Try not to worry," the doctor went on in his calm voice.

During the course of dinner, Horace did not discuss Jaspar's forthcoming marriage. The conversation centred around his aspirations for the hospital and Jaspar slightly disjointedly told him of Tarn and the school.

First thing the next morning, however, found Horace at Bardfield seeking an audience with Her Ladyship. She was seated in the library in her favourite spot in front of the open doors overlooking the Italian statues of the park.

"Good morning, Horace, such a lovely day." She extended her hand. He kissed it formally and, following her summons to sit and tell her about his hospital, he perched on the chair opposite her. Horace was a direct young man. He did not mince matters.

"Lady Heddington, I come…"

Before he could get any further she interrupted him. "Such wonderful news, Horace, I am so pleased. Netta will make Jaspar such an admirable wife." Her Ladyship's eyes twinkled with pleasure.

Horace took a breath. "That is what I have come to see you about, Your Ladyship."

"Oh, to join me in my happiness, what a dear man you are."

"Lady Heddington! Please bear with me a moment."

She paused in her enthusing and regarded him; she inclined her head. "Yes?" she remarked.

He sighed. "There is no easy way to say this but I think you must stop encouraging this alliance. It will not do."

"What! If I may say so this is nothing to do with you, Dr Sugdon. I find it very offensive that you should meddle in this way. I would be obliged to you if you would absent yourself." She drew herself up and faced him with her dark eyes cold and angry.

Horace, however, was so not easily deflected. "It is to do with anyone who cares about your grandson. Can you not see how unhappy this marriage is making him?"

"Allow me to say that I know my grandson a great deal better than you. Netta will suit him admirably. She will be the most exemplary wife and will allow him to… to… live…"

"To have a marriage of convenience and have affairs, you mean?"

She blushed slightly. "How my grandson chooses to live is no concern of yours," she replied furiously.

Horace was, fortuitously, a man whom it was impossible to ruffle. He did not readily lose his temper so he continued, patiently. "It must be the concern of everyone who cares for His Lordship. Lady Heddington, you must stop this notion of yours. This is *your* idea of what will suit Jaspar but he does not want to marry Netta."

"Nonsense! Then why would he ask her?"

"A moment of desolation. Jaspar is very much in love with someone else. Miss Egremont told him, I believe, that Grizelda cared not for him. It was not true."

Lady Heddington opened her mouth to protest but something on Horace's calm face told her that he was speaking the truth. She raised an eyebrow. "How do you know all this, pray?"

"From all sorts of sources. Sufficient for the moment to say that, this morning, Jaspar begged Miss Egremont to release him but she refused, saying that you wanted this marriage. Your grandson would do much for you."

Lady Heddington's face twisted slightly. "I... do want this alliance... but not at the expense of Jaspar's happiness. Do you think that it is at stake?"

"Indubitably. He will be desperately miserable if Netta forces this to go ahead and so, incidentally, will she. He is not a tolerant individual." She smiled wryly. "But he is also too much the gentleman to break off the engagement himself."

She was thoughtful. Images of Jaspar's stiff face, which she had chosen to ignore, intruded into her mind. "I see. I just wanted them..."

"I had to tell you."

She nodded. "But who is the girl who makes him so unhappy?"

"Miss Ludgrove."

She started, "Miss Ludgrove? But my daughter tells me that he cares not for her and she has married."

"No, that is Laura. This is her elder sister, Grizelda."

"l see. Well, if the fault is mine…" Horace made to demur. "No, I see that it is. I must sort things out. Do we know where this Grizelda resides?"

"I do not but I think you might find that Harper will be able to help you."

"Harper?"

"Yes." There was a moment's silence between them as both were preoccupied with their own thoughts, then Lady Heddington looked up.

"Thank you, Horace. There is no time to waste, please ring for Harper."

Grizelda's journey was the worst she had ever undertaken. She was lucky to obtain a place on the coach for the waybills were quite made up when she arrived and it was only by dint of giving the coachman a handsome gratuity that he squeezed her in, and squeeze it was. The inside passengers were so many, that Grizelda was squashed between a huge perspiring woman who clutched a vast bag on her knee, which constantly buffeted her neighbour, and a man who seemed to have imbibed solidly since he mounted the stage. Grizelda was afeared that he might be ill over her at any moment. However, when they started to move he fell loudly asleep and snored raucously for the whole journey. It was a warm night and the fullness inside the coach made it boiling. She thought sorrowfully of the comfort in Lord Heddington's carriage. After a night of jolting and bumping, arriving at Vernham Dean seemed a blessed relief, but another problem assailed her, for her departure had been so precipitate that, naturally, no one knew she was coming; this in itself would not have been a problem but there was no one to meet her, no comforting Paul with his pony and trap. The coachman extricated her case and dumped it in the entrance to the inn and Grizelda made her way inside. Luckily for her, she and her papa and Lord Farleigh were well known in this hostelry and she was quickly provided with the means to convey her to her home. By the time she crossed the threshold, she was hot, dirty and thoroughly exhausted.

A footman showed her into the dining room where her papa was breakfasting. His astonishment at seeing his eldest daughter was manifest.

"Grizelda! What on earth…? Why are you here?"

"I… Lady Melbourne is most unwell, Papa, so I thought I would pay you a visit." Her carefully chosen words did not ring true, even to her, but luckily the news of Laura's wedding had pleased Mr Ludgrove inordinately and Grizelda, who had expected the opposite, found to her relief that he was almost excited. He was, therefore, quite benign about her precipitate arrival home.

"It is excellent news of Laura," her papa continued, pride in his voice. "Lord Farleigh is much pleased too."

Grizelda stared at him; that Lord Farleigh had also greeted the news that his heir had married the daughter of his manager with equanimity had not occurred to her. It was quite beyond anything she had expected but she knew that it would make her sojourn at home far more agreeable than it would otherwise have been, had her papa and Lord Farleigh been downcast by the match.

She gulped. "Oh, Papa, I am so pleased, it must bring such pleasure to you."

Her father grunted. He had never at any time since her mama's untimely death shown any direct response of any kind. "Umm, well, I must be about my business." He stood up. "Have you breakfasted?"

That she had clearly come on the stage and had obviously been up all night seemed as nothing to Mr Ludgrove, who, without giving her another glance, left the room.

Grizelda sat down sadly. She poured herself a cup of coffee and swiftly drank it before proceeding up to her chamber and lying on her bed. She was thoroughly fatigued but sleep alluded her; only tears would not leave her alone.

The day passed without incident. No visitors came to relieve the monotony and she discovered how hateful it was to be back in this neat, orderly and soulless place. Her spirits, which were despondent anyway, were hardly improved by the dullness and solitary nature of her tasks.

Her papa did not return for dinner so she had it alone, sitting in the dining room at the head of the table, unable to eat a morsel of the ordinary fare that was presented to her. The next day promised more of the same, and Grizelda found herself frantic with misery and boredom. She was beginning to wish that she had stayed at Melbourne House, for at least there were things going on there and the lack of activity here, was, she knew, quite the worst thing for anyone suffering from deep dejection. In the afternoon she went out into the gardens. It was a beautiful day and the sun warmed her melancholy spirits. She made her way through the paths, listening to the joyous song of the birds who swooped, feeding on seeds or worms, wherever she looked. She wandered along until, without realising it, she was in the rose garden that her mama had made. It had been Mrs Ludgrove's favourite spot and while she had been so ill she had often been brought to sit on the bench, in the arbour under the entwining roses. Here her eldest daughter, who was only fourteen at the time, had sat and discussed everything with her.

Grizelda sat on the bench, her head in her hands, and cried out to her mama. All this would have been so much easier to bear if her mama had still been alive. She tried to remember her mother's words: "All life is loss, my dearest," she had told her daughter when Grizelda had raged against her mama's illness. "All loss is life. We must live, my love, we must take what happens and use it to make ourselves stronger, only then can we truly say that we thrust ourselves into life. It is all we have here on Earth. It is what we must enjoy, for we do not know what will happen in the hereafter."

When Grizelda had made to demur against her mama's thoughts, which contradicted the teaching that had so often been instilled in her by her governess, her mama merely proceeded in her calm way, "We have an obligation to life, my dear. There are things that happen, from which we never recover." She paused a moment and sighed. Grizelda noticed a flash of pain across her fine eyes, which she thought meant her mama was thinking of the separation from her own family, who even now in her acute illness would never forgive her. "But we must live. You know the love that I have for you. It will always be with you. I will be with you. You must be strong and you must grasp the things that transpire, whether good or bad, and you must use them. Do not sink, my sweet, do not waste your life. You must make the things you want come to pass." Her mother had nodded vigorously at her at this point and Grizelda had understood.

Now, in the depths of the worst misery she had ever experienced, she remembered her mother's words, particularly the notion that she had an answerability to life itself. Grizelda sat for a long time, close to the tiny pink roses, so perfect in their delicacy, which wound themselves around the posts, and the large single pink and yellow and white roses which shed their sweet-smelling petals into her lap, until at last, the sun started to slip away in the west. Then she stood up stiffly and, filled with a resolve given her, not so much by her mother's thoughts as by the scent and beauty of the roses, she picked a bunch of the fullest, most voluptuous blooms and then slowly she made her way back to the house.

Fletcher greeted her as she came in. "Visitor for you, Miss Ludgrove." Grizelda raised an eyebrow. Who would visit at such a time?

"I have put her in the morning room, miss," he went on. She nodded, her arms full of the soft, redolent flowers. "Lady Heddington, miss."

Grizelda felt herself go icy. A cold tremble started in her stomach and spread over her entire body. She swallowed desperately. Netta had wasted no time, she thought bitterly; she had made him marry her with all haste. A desire to scream was quickly rebuffed. The new Lady Heddington must not see that she cared. She took a deep breath and nodded to Fletcher to open the door to the morning room.

Chapter Twenty-Eight

Grizelda took another deep breath and steeled herself. Then, her arms still full of flowers, she marched determinedly into the room. Inside the doorway she stopped, amazed. Instead of the triumphant Netta, whom she expected, a stiff-backed old lady, with perfect features, was seated in a chair next to the fireplace. She was dressed in a rustling pale blue silk gown, with wide skirts. Her grey hair was perfectly groomed. Grizelda noticed that she had very dark, intelligent eyes under thick brows. Grizelda stared at her open-mouthed. The old lady smiled slightly at Grizelda's startled expression.

"No, he has not married her yet," she said in distinct tones.

Grizelda felt the blood drain from her head and her legs buckle under her. She dropped the roses; which tumbled prodigiously in bright colours over the subtle shades of the tapestry and clutched at the chair near her.

"I am Jaspar's grandmother and you, I assume, are Grizelda, Miss Ludgrove?"

Grizelda, still clinging to the chair for support, nodded wildly. Lady Heddington smiled again as she examined this girl whom Jaspar loved so desperately. Under the freckles which covered her face, the girl was white with trepidation. Her hair hung down in wind-blown tangles; the sun which slanted through the window caught its myriad colours, making her appear as if she were framed in gold; tiny rose petals clung in the curls. Her features, Lady Heddington noted, were fine and her mouth pretty, but determined. Her eyes were an exquisite pale blue but with an inner glow and spirit. Then she smiled, and Lady Heddington understood why her grandson loved this girl so much.

"Please, come and sit where I can see you," she demanded.

Grizelda bent and picked up a rose, then she smoothed down her skirts and crossed and sat shakily on the stool at Lady Heddington's feet.

"I apologise. I thought you were Jaspar's wife," she remarked with her customary directness; her voice choked slightly on the last word but she felt she did not give herself away.

Lady Heddington smiled again. Did this delightful creature not realise that in every movement she betrayed herself?

"You love my grandson?" Lady Heddington did not mince words.

Many young ladies faced with such a question would have blushed, prevaricated and denied. Grizelda looked straight into my lady's eyes and said simply, "Yes."

Lady Heddington admired her honesty. "Good, for I am told that he is very much in love with you." She saw happiness leap into the girl's eyes. "Did you not know?"

"I had thought perhaps, but when he asked me to marry him, he was so brusque, he said I had better marry him."

Lady Heddington laughed. "Not the most romantic of offers."

"No and then Miss Egremont told me that he would ask me merely to save my reputation."

"And you believed her?"

"Yes, at that moment but later I thought about Laura." She glanced at Her Ladyship to see if she knew of Jaspar's dealings with her sister. "He did not ask her to marry him to save her reputation."

"Did you not think that maybe he was unsure of you?"

"Jaspar?" she gasped. "It seemed rather unlikely."

She laughed. "Nevertheless, I think that that was the case. It would account for his diffidence."

"Yes," Grizelda mused. "But not for him offering for someone else within hours of my refusing him."

"I think Netta has been rather remiss. It would appear that not only did she tell you that Jaspar was proposing merely to fulfil the proprieties, but she also told Jaspar that you had advised her that you hated him and would never marry him." She watched as anger flashed into Grizelda's eyes.

"And he was prepared to believe such a calumny!"

"Remember, he thought you did not care."

Grizelda paused and thought about her remark. "But why should Miss Egremont lie?"

Lady Heddington appeared a little disconcerted. "I am afraid that the blame must be laid at my door. It is my fault and I must apologise to you both. I encouraged Netta. I wanted Jaspar to settle down so much and I am very fond of the girl. It seemed an ideal match. Jaspar made the offer to please me, after you had refused him. Apparently he was so unhappy that he just asked Netta. The next day he went back to ask her to release him. She refused."

Grizelda's eyes opened in horror. "Does she have no pride?"

"She is desperately in love with him and I see now, deeply jealous of you. Sometimes pride dissolves in those circumstances."

"But how can she want to hold a man who does not want her?" Grizelda spoke in tones of disbelief.

"Quite. I agree with you. I came to ask you to come back with me so that you can help me remedy the bungle that I have made of things. Will you?"

Grizelda regarded her steadily. "Before I agree, I must ask you one thing." Her Ladyship nodded. "Are you content that

Jaspar should marry me? My father is factor on Lord Farleigh's estate and although my mother's lineage is impeccable, his can hardly be said to match hers."

Lady Heddington took her hand, her eyes moist. "Miss Ludgrove, how much I admire your honesty. There is much to be said for probity, even if it is not accompanied by unimpeachable lineage."

Grizelda stared; she was surprised that Her Ladyship, who was born into the highest echelons of the *ton*, could take so liberal a view. She took a breath and made a full admission of her disadvantages. "You must also know that I believe in the proposed shifts that I think will occur in politics and society in the next years."

Her Ladyship smiled wryly. "At my age it is hard to see the order that one has grown up with change. My family are all Whigs. We have governed England for the last hundred years. Our traditions are glorious, our society infectious in its refinement; our civilisation, which once possessed such strength and careless grace, is one that I think will not be seen again but I am not unaware of the pressures for change that are starting among the manufacturing classes." She sighed. "It makes an old woman sad, my dear, that all that beauty and spirit should be extinguished." There was a slight silence, then she patted Grizelda's hand. "So you will come?"

"Yes." Grizelda's answer was simple, her thoughts tumultuous.

"Good. I do not think we must waste time. Please go and make ready, we should leave as soon as the horses are rested."

"Lady Heddington, do you think that you can undertake another journey so readily? Would you not prefer to spend a night?"

"No. I think we should be underway. Do not worry about me. I shall enjoy the journey. But now what about your papa?"

No sooner than the question out of her mouth, than the gentleman in question appeared in the room. Grizelda thought that her father might not approve of Lady Heddington but she had reckoned without Her Ladyship. Within five minutes her papa was eating out of Lady Heddington's hands and had happily relinquished his daughter to her care.

In the end they were forced to spend one night on the road, at Medstead, and it was late morning when Grizelda had her first sight of Bardfield. The sun was high in the sky and a faint breeze ruffled the tops of the trees as Harper drove them through to where Jaspar had been set upon. When Lady Heddington told Grizelda about the footpads, Miss Ludgrove, incurably truthful, made a clean breast of her part in Jaspar's indisposition. Lady Heddington laughed a great deal and informed Grizelda that in the circumstances she would have behaved in exactly the same fashion.

Bardfield sat, mellow in the sunshine, at the end of its long drive and Grizelda thought she had never seen such a beautiful house. As they reached it, Lady Heddington turned to her.

"Miss Ludgrove, it is not the most hospitable of suggestions but I think you should go in through the stables entrance. Harper will take you to my rooms. It would not do for Jaspar to see you before we are ready."

Grizelda nodded happily. "I agree. I will remain concealed for as long as it is necessary."

Quickly Lady Heddington gave instructions to Harper who drove around to the stable block. He helped her down and led her into the house whilst his undergroom conveyed Her Ladyship to the front.

Savage threw open the front doors. "Welcome back, my lady."

"Thank you, Savage. I would like to see Miss Egremont immediately. Perhaps you could send a footman to her house to ask her to come and see me at her earliest convenience."

"Oh, that will not be necessary. Lord Heddington is to carry her to London within the hour. She is inside, I believe."

Lady Heddington heaved a quick sigh of relief. *Just in time*, she thought. Thank goodness she had not stayed her departure. For if Jaspar had transported Netta to London and she had spent such time in her company, how much harder it would be for her to untangle the muddle she had so inadvertently created.

"Please ask her to come to my rooms as soon as possible, Savage. It is imperative that I see her before she departs."

"Very good, my lady." He beckoned to a footman who scurried off to do Her Ladyship's bidding.

Lady Heddington trod the stairs to her room. She sent away her dresser and peeped into her bedroom, where Grizelda sat awaiting her. "I have asked Netta to come and see me, my dear. She was about to go to London with Jaspar. I have a plan. I think you should take her place."

Grizelda stood up and went across and kissed the old lady, her eyes luminescent with exhilaration.

"It will be my pleasure," she giggled. "Perhaps I can pretend that I am Netta and unmask myself," she said wickedly.

"An excellent notion, my dear, but I hear a knock."

Both ladies proceeded to the drawing room. Netta was standing uncomfortably in front of the sofa table, clutching a large hooded cape. Lady Heddington and Grizelda exchanged glances. *Exactly what we need*, they thought in unison.

"Please sit down, Netta," suggested Lady Heddington.

"I prefer to stand. Jaspar will be waiting for me. We leave for London directly."

"I believe that you know Miss Ludgrove." She indicated Grizelda, who had slipped into the room behind her and who now stood quietly at the side.

Netta blushed uncomfortably. She mumbled something. "Why do you look thus?" Her Ladyship continued inexorably.

Again Netta mumbled an answer, adding uneasily, "I really must go. Jaspar will be wanting to know what has delayed me. You know he does not like his horses to be kept waiting."

"No. I have something to say to you before you go." Netta swallowed but she said nothing. "Did my grandson come to you and ask that you release him from your engagement?"

The question hung in the air. Netta looked even more discomforted. It was clear to Grizelda that she could not decide what answer to give.

"Well, not exactly," she answered vaguely.

"What do you mean by that?" Lady Heddington's eyes were hard and her mouth firm.

Netta twisted the cape desperately. "He said... I told him that you would not let him jilt me. It would not look good with the world." The words tumbled out defiantly. Grizelda could see tears in her eyes. She felt very sorry for the girl.

"You used my name to hold Jaspar to an alliance which was distasteful to him?"

"But you wished it," Netta said on a little sob.

"Yes," Lady Heddington sighed, "I did but not if he was to be so unhappy." She was suddenly gentler. "You knew of his feelings for Miss Ludgrove, I did not."

Tears flowed unchecked down Netta's face. "You encouraged me. You helped me," she blurted out. "You thought it would be good for Jaspar. He would have been happy with me but for her."

"No. I was wrong, Netta. I am sorry. He would not have been happy with you. I see that now. The mistake is mine." She went to the weeping girl. "I am so sorry," she repeated. "I want you to write Jaspar a letter withdrawing from the engagement."

"No! No!" Netta fell to her knees on the floor, sobbing.

Grizelda moved across to her and put her arm around her shoulder. "You cannot want to marry a man who does not want to marry you. It will only make you miserable."

"He will be happy with me. He will! I will make him happy!" Netta repeated hysterically.

"No," Grizelda said very gently. "You will not."

She glanced up at Her Ladyship, who was looking at Netta

with such distress on her face. "Oh, what have I done?" she entreated. "How foolish I have been."

Grizelda left Netta's side and put her arm around the old lady's shoulders, then she led her to a chair.

"You must write the letter, Netta, I will dictate it," Lady Heddington said, her own voice suspended with tears.

Grizelda helped Netta to the desk, where she put a pen in her hand and Netta wrote:

Dear Jaspar,

I was quite wrong to hold you to our alliance yesterday. I no longer wish to marry you and I am withdrawing from our engagement forthwith.

Netta Egremont

As she sanded the note, there was a knock on the door and a footman asked, "Is Miss Egremont ready? My lord is most impatient."

"Tell Lord Heddington that she is now ready," said Her Ladyship with a watery smile to Grizelda, who kissed her cheek and, picking up Netta's cloak, put it around her, covering her head completely.

Jaspar was waiting impatiently in the hall; he did not glance at her.

"At last!" he said icily. Grizelda could not imagine how Netta wanted to persist with a marriage to anyone who spoke to her in that glacial tone. He handed her into the carriage coldly. She settled down in one corner and he sat in the other. Jaspar stared out of the window, his face rigid and forbidding. Grizelda watched, amused. She wondered how long it would be before her deception was discovered. In the meantime she was content to observe him. There was not an inch of softness in the austere profile that was all she could see and he made no attempt at conversation. The carriage bowled along. No one could doubt the efficacy of His Lordship's horses, thought Grizelda. Still Lord Heddington volunteered not a word. Grizelda was hard pressed to suppress her giggles. Would he discover nothing until it became time to change horses? Even then His Lordship addressed no words to her and merely jumped down and spoke in sepulchral tones to Harper.

"Change as quickly as we can," he commanded. "I will not stay for refreshment."

Grizelda, with His Lordship out of the carriage, gave way to a fit of chuckles. Harper peeped in; he met her eyes and she read the surprise in them. She put her finger over her mouth and the old groom nodded sagely and went on his way, humming tunelessly. Grizelda thought to herself, if this cavalier treatment did not put Netta off, nothing would. Lord Heddington climbed back in. Grizelda stole a look at his stony face, black with fury. They might have remained this way until London was reached but for the reckless driving of an inebriated young blade, who swept his team around a corner on their side of the road and but for the exemplary driving of Harper, would have collided with them.

Grizelda was thrown forward out of her seat. His Lordship, whose manners appeared to have deserted him, made no attempt to pick her up, but as she struggled to regain her balance, her hair escaped, cascading down the cloak; before she could tuck it back in she found her arm grabbed and His Lordship's dark eyes bored into hers.

"You!" he exclaimed. "What are you doing here?"

"What a pleasant greeting, my lord," rejoindered Grizelda, her eyes alight with amusement. She shook off the hand that held her so steadily.

Lord Heddington stared at her in bewilderment, pain and confusion apparent in his face. Grizelda smoothed off her dress. She flung back the hood of the cape and grinned at His Lordship.

"It is you," he said sadly. "I do not understand why you are here." His eyes held hers and there was so much hunger in them, that Grizelda wanted to fling her arms around his neck and comfort him, but not yet.

"I am having a lift to London, my lord. Do you object?"

He turned from her and clenched his hands; his voice was hard. "No, of course I do not. I will do anything to oblige you."

"Except stop for refreshment when you change horses," Grizelda teased. "I admit I was passing hungry."

"But I did not know it was you. I thought…" His bafflement was manna to her battered sensibilities.

He put his head in his hands. Grizelda leant towards him; he could feel the soft curls against his cheek and the warm smell of her. His heart felt as if it would break. He did not understand why she was here instead of Netta but her presence was unendurable. He gripped his hands together to stop himself from pulling her into his arms.

Grizelda put her hand underneath his chin; she lifted his face. "Jaspar, look at me." Her husky voice pierced his insides. "Please, I have one question. Will you answer it truthfully?"

He gazed into her beautiful pale eyes, which were warm and unbelievably loving. His throat caught; he nodded. He did not trust himself to speak.

"Jaspar, do you…" she swallowed, "… love me?"

His eyes contorted, his face winced with pain. "Grizelda, you know I cannot answer that question. I cannot." He ran his hand through his hair and turned from her.

"You must. You must, my lord."

"I… I cannot…"

"Jaspar, do you love me?" she repeated, demanding the answer that she knew already.

"Don't. Please, please," he begged.

"Jaspar, answer me. Do you love me?" She ran her finger

very gently along his face and across his lips. Her action broke his reserve. His eyes bright with moisture, he responded.

"Yes! Damn you! Yes, I love you. I love you as the only person I have ever loved. As the only person I will ever love, now and for the rest of my life. I love you, Grizelda, I love you." The words were wrung from him; he clenched his hands together frantically. Grizelda pulled them apart. Very gently she slid her body into his, feeling the hardness of his muscles, the belonging of his arms. Desperately he gave way and clung to her, holding her so tightly she thought she might not be able to breathe. She lifted her lips to his; tenderly she kissed him. He battled with his conscience and then, overcome, he kissed her firmly. Grizelda felt she had come home. Then wildly he pushed her away.

"I must… Netta…" He spat the word out viciously.

Grizelda took two pieces of paper from her reticule and threw them into his lap. He raised his eyes to hers questioningly. She laughed, leaning across to him and kissing him boldly. He exhaled with pleasure. She pulled back.

"Read your letters, Jaspar."

He shook his head as if in a dream and picked up the first piece of paper. He tore it open and read the few lines written on it. Grizelda watched as his face broke into a broad grin. "Wretch," he muttered happily under his breath as he kissed her as if he had never kissed anyone in the world before. He ran his hands over her responsive body, feeling its smooth contours, cupping the delicate breast in his hand. Then, very carefully, he pushed her away. "Not until we are married," he murmured.

"Oh, are we getting married? I do not remember being asked," she teased.

"I have taken enough from you this morning, young lady," he chuckled, grabbing her hands and covering them with kisses. "You are going to marry me if I have to carry you to the altar screaming."

"Oh, my lord!" she giggled. "How Miss Clarges would approve. I have one condition."

He went suddenly serious. "Anything."

"You are to marry me in the next village!" She laughed. "Look at your other present."

He picked up the second piece of paper. It was a special license. My Lord Heddington laughed. "I hate managing females!" he pronounced, drawing her resolutely back into his arms.

 **Matador**

For exclusive discounts on Matador titles,
sign up to our occasional newsletter at
troubador.co.uk/bookshop